WAR SONGS

A NOVEL

LOOKING GOOD PRESS
Portland, OR

Leonard Harris
Copyright 2014 Looking Good Press
All Rights Reserved

This is a work of historical fiction. Accounts of historical figures in this work are fictionalized. All other characters are fictional and resemblance to any persons living or dead is purely coincidental.

Interior design by Heidi Whitcomb

Printed in the United States of America

ISBN: 978-0-9914438-0-2

For Mary

CHAPTER 1

"Against *Jews*? I've nothing against Jews, Mary."

Mary Wheatley looked upset. Her eyes darted around, taking in the scene at the Gotham: 200 of New York's most carefully chosen WASPs buzzing decorously in the club's dignified old Founders' Room, celebrating the rites of the annual spring cocktail party.

Dede had to smile at Mary. Trying to be daring, yet so frightened. "It's all right," she assured her. "No one heard." Then she repeated herself in an elaborate whisper. "I have nothing against Jews."

"Then why would it be so dreadful to have one in the Gotham?" Mary formed the words with her lips; there was hardly any voice behind them.

"It wouldn't be dreadful. But do you have any idea what kind of dollar volume I do through members of the Gotham? Let's just say it comes to millions a year. Do I want to jeopardize that to get a Jew into the club? Do I want to antagonize my Stone Age husband? Speaking of which, how is Roger taking your . . . crusade?"

Still trying to be brave, Mary couldn't keep her eyes from flicking over to where Roger Wheatley IV, his lank hair slicked back, his face flushed, was sipping his martini and chatting in a circle of men that included Dede's husband, Tru Martindale.

"He said it was grounds for divorce. He was joking . . . I think." She managed a small smile. This attempt to get a Jew into the Gotham was as close to a statement of independence as she had ever made. And Dede was the first Gotham wife she'd approached for help. Diana Penrose Miller—Dede to her friends—was not only married to the great-grandson of one of the club's founders, she was the kind of strong, outspoken woman you wanted on your side.

"I honestly don't understand why you'd want to take this on," Dede said. "I'm not the least bit prejudiced—For heaven's sake, nearly half my brokers are Jewish! I work with them all day, get along with them just fine! But . . . they are different. In many ways. Is it any crime to suggest we might prefer our own clubs? And they might prefer theirs?"

"I thought we'd gotten beyond that . . . "

"Of course we haven't. It's just fashionable to pretend to. All men are not created equal. Look around this room. Wheatley. Martindale. Brewster. Schuyler. Farnsworth. The names, the faces, the families. They're all comfortable with each other. Why put a . . . Goldberg . . . in here, and make them, and him, uncomfortable? Besides . . . I should think that if you want to crusade, you'd push for *women* in the Gotham before you started worrying about Jews, who most noticeably do *not* need worrying about."

"Are you against women in the club, too?"

"What I am against is making waves. I just don't think people should be *forced* upon people who don't want them."

"Actually, you'd be ideal for the first woman in the club."

"The Jews and I. Fellow pioneers. No thanks, Mary."

Roger Wheatley came over to claim his wife, put an arm around her and fixed his eyes on Dede. Roger seemed to think his stares turned women on, and Dede didn't disabuse him of that idea; she saw no point hurting his feelings. Only last week a Wall Street colleague of his had bought a three million dollar apartment from her.

Besides, Dede was used to being stared at. At 44 she was a striking woman and she knew it. Tall, strong, with riveting blue eyes, strong jaw, chiseled nose, great smile . . . and great legs—an athlete's legs. She knew her looks had helped her career substantially and she was not about to joust with the world's sexists.

"And what are you two gals cooking up?"

The frightened look returned to Mary's eyes; she was speechless. Dede jumped in.

"Oh, Mary and I were just saying haw lucky we felt that you boys let us into your club a couple of times a year."

"It's four times a year now, beautiful, and you know it. Just don't get greedy."

"We would not presume, sire. We know our place, sire. We genuflect."

"A great position for a woman to be in."

"Roger!" Mary pretended to be scandalized by her husband's pretended flirting. Behind both pretenses there was the reality: he fooled around; she knew it, and didn't like it.

Dede was honestly surprised Mary would dare to take on her husband on an issue so important to him. Both he and Tru would go to their deaths guarding the thinning ranks of Upper East Side WASPs, manning the battlements around their private schools, their Episcopal churches, their clubs, their unofficially restricted co-op buildings, their tranquil summer enclaves; fighting off the hordes trying to breach the walls and ravage the tradition, the order, and the purity of their domain.

"Tru made a dinner reservation for eight at 8:30 at the Walker House, and you get to sit next to me, so we can continue our discussion of positions." Roger said it with a wink that Dede could take as a joke, if she wanted to.

"Oh, I wanted to try that new place, Salle à Manger," said Mary.

"Impossible to get a table unless you're a Jew billionaire," Roger answered.

"And who are the lucky couples my husband has deigned to invite?" Dede asked.

"The Cantwells and the Armstrongs." Roger put his arm around her, his face close to hers. "The Cantwells' younger son is getting married. Soon be looking for an apartment. Diana Penrose Miller strikes again! Can't say I don't look after you."

"How can I thank you enough?" Dede replied, setting up the big wink that he threw at her. If playing the game brought in the business, she'd play it, as long as men like Roger knew the rules. She led Roger toward Tru to get their dinner group together.

It was not until next morning, on the brisk one-mile walk from the apartment to the office, that Dede realized how annoyed she was with Mary for being a do-gooder. What was she trying to prove? Of course Dede knew the reason: Mary had no career, two children away at school and nothing to do with her time. She'd tried tutoring in Harlem; she'd tried the board of a modern dance company; she'd tried ceramics. Now this. For her own sake, not for the Jews'. God knows Jews didn't need her help, or anyone's.

As she walked, she saw a man she knew vaguely as a Central Park jogger. "Beautiful morning!" he said.

"Good morning! Yes, it is," she replied automatically. Was it? She looked up; in the shadowed canyons of New York, you had to find the sky. It was a splendid April morning indeed: bright blue sky enveloping a puffy cloud or two, the air clear, the temperature around 60. When did I last look up at the sky? she asked herself. She had no time for beautiful mornings.

By eight, when she pushed through the glass doors that said PENROSE MILLER ASSOCIATES, she was focusing on the work ahead, not the beautiful morning, not Mary or the Gotham.

Penrose Miller Associates occupied three full floors of a building at Madison Avenue and 56th street, one of the dozens of Manhattan buildings the firm managed. Built on spec, it was ugly, boxy, a tired copy of glass curtain wall architecture, but it had what Dede needed: good location, lots of space, and reasonable rent. Elegance she confined to her own corner office, and even there she chose an understatement that put some people off. Her desk was teak, lean and spare on simple tapered legs. On it stood IN and OUT baskets; an 8-by-10 portrait photo of her, Tru, and Jimmy; a phone console; and a silver medallion mounted on a pedestal, awarded to her as Real Estate Person of the Year. Until she won it, it had been Man of the Year.

Her friendly competitor Fred Rudolph had once looked around her office and said, "Diana, you're so feminine. Yet your office . . . "

"Hold on," she'd replied lightly. "I'll run out for some puff pillows and a few yards of chintz."

Her relationship with Rudolph was emblematic of the way she got along with Jews. She liked him, respected him, yet never invited him into the inner circle of friends who called her Dede, not Diana. Of course she knew he was right; she had deliberately kept her office from looking too feminine, just as she'd dropped her first name from her company title. She liked men to admire her as a woman, yet treat her as an equal. If she could have it both ways, why not?

Outside the big corner office her secretary was at her desk. Rita Lopez, a Puerto Rican New Yorker, was as quick and efficient as anyone who'd ever worked for her. Get an English secretary, friends told her, they sound better. Get a male secretary; make a statement. Rita had a sharp New York accent and was decidedly a woman, but no one could do the job the way she could.

"Morning, Rita. Any calls?" It came out as one long word.

"Morning, Ms. Miller. Seven."

"Just the headlines."

Rita consulted her pad. "Mr. Martindale." She always used just the last name, never said "your husband."

"Later. Next."

"Your son."

"Get me Jimmy."

"He said not till after school. Around 6:30."

"What did he want? Any problems?"

"Didn't say. He didn't sound worried."

"We call him at 6:30. We don't forget." Rita looked slightly hurt. It was the kind of thing she never forgot.

"Anyone else? Important?"

"Fred Rudolph."

She just nodded. She knew what Fred wanted. Let him wait, she couldn't seem too eager. She started for her inner office.

"The reporter from the *Times* is here, you know," Rita said. "He's using a phone in the conference room."

Dede stopped short. "Reporter from the *Times*?"

As if on cue, a tall man came around the corner. "Kenneth Glass, Ms. Miller. It is Miller? You don't use your married name?"

She took his outstretched hand. It was big and warm and dry, the kind of hand she liked. He was 6-2 or 3, almost as tall as Tru. Broad-shouldered, perhaps a bit heavy, in a comfortable way. His curly hair was sandy, going gray around the ears and a little scruffy. He had a snubby nose, brown eyes that crinkled at the corners when he smiled. Except for the nose, he reminded her of the actor Jeff Chandler whom she'd seen in 50s movies on cable. Just about my age, Dede thought, then reluctantly amended that: perhaps a bit younger.

"My maiden name is right. But . . . "

"The editor said any morning if I got here by eight."

"I told whoever it was who called, any morning by eight . . . *just let me know.*"

"Ahh . . . people in the communications business! They're so bad at communicating. Is this a bad time then?"

"Can't say no to the *Times*. Come on in. Rita, would you get us some coffee?"

She gestured for him to sit on the spare modern sofa in a corner of the office, while she took a chair that was separated from it by a low glass coffee table. He glanced at her legs as she sat; she smoothed down her skirt. When his eyes came up, hers met them. She let him know she'd seen him; he let her know he was not embarrassed to have looked. If you wear skirts above the knee, she reminded herself, you have to expect men to check out your legs. From his breast picket he took a steno notebook and a pen—a real pen, not a ballpoint.

"No tape recorder?" she asked.

"I'm an old-fashioned guy." He had the kind of easy relaxed smile she seldom encountered in her business day. As he sat there in a rumpled blue work shirt, woolen tie, tan canvas jacket and chinos, he was not at all her image of a *New York Times* reporter.

"You work for the real estate section?"

"No. I'm a free-lance writer. This is an assignment for the Sunday magazine."

"The magazine. Oh my!"

"They have bigger things in mind for you than the real estate section. Successful. Powerful. Political. Young and beautiful. Is that sexist?"

She did not smile back at him. "Isn't it?"

"Was it sexist to call John Kennedy young and handsome? And sexy? Would any writer worth his salt omit it? It was part of the package that makes a President. Or a Senator."

"I'm not a candidate for the Senate, or anything."

"Really?"

"Really. I'm just interested in Democratic politics. And a contributor. That's all."

"I'll have to double check my sources." His smile said, relax, this isn't life and death.

"Do you know anything about real estate?"

"Not a thing. I have started doing some homework."

"Then why would they assign you to me . . . to this story?"

"I told you: this is not a real estate story, it's a human story. And I asked to do it. When I saw your name on a list of story ideas, I jumped at it. I'd seen you on TV, talking about the future of New York City, and said to myself: There is one interesting . . . story."

"How much time will you need? This is a hectic day for me."

"Today we'll just get some basic stuff. Then I'll have to meet with you a couple more times. Maybe even follow you around for a day or so. That do-able?"

She hesitated.

"Look," he said, those amused eyes inviting her into a kind of intimacy. "You know how many people read the *Sunday Times*, and who they are. Can't hurt, even if you don't run for the Senate."

"All right," she said briskly. "Shoot."

"All right," he answered, as if he might be gently mimicking her briskness. "What kind of music do you listen to?"

"Music?" She looked puzzled.

"The kind of music someone listens to tells me a lot about him, or her."

"Well, my dad always had big band music on . . . and Sinatra. I loved it." She smiled thinking about it. "I used to sing along with Frank." Be careful, she warned herself; don't get too cozy. Journalists love demolishing business types. But she kept on going. "There was one Sinatra, with a big band. I still remember the words, 'I never knew the technique of kissing. I never knew the thrill I could get from your touch. Never knew much. Oh, look at me now.' I thought they were so . . . daring. A young girl's fevered imagination." She shrugged, forced herself to stop.

"Were you any good at it? Singing?"

"My dad thought so. He told me I had a great ear. 'I don't know where you got it,' he'd say, 'Sure as heck not from me!'"

"And now?"

"I've given up my singing aspirations," she said lightly.

He laughed. "I meant what kind of music do you listen to now."

"I hear my son's rock music in the apartment. It's hard not to."

"But you? What do you listen to?"

"We have season tickets to the opera. Most of the time I'm too busy to use them."

"OK. I know what you *used* to listen to and what you *don't* listen to. What *do* you listen to?" He was relentless.

She had to think. "Honestly," she said after a couple of moments, "I don't have time to listen to music. Sorry."

"There are no right . . . or wrong . . . answers." She had the feeling she'd disappointed him. "Now, tell me a little about the wife and mother."

"Not much to tell. One husband for a little more than 19 years; he's a stockbroker. One son, 18, going off to college in the fall. Quite ordinary, I'm afraid."

"Lot of women, men, too, for that matter, will wonder how you manage to run a big business and be a wife and mother at the same time."

Be careful, she warned herself. Don't sound smug. Don't sound arrogant. Don't put down the housewife. The press is lurking, waiting to pounce. "We are three independent people with busy lives. We try to spend quality time together." Not a lot of time. She didn't say it, but she knew the implication was clear; he was too sharp not to catch it.

"Sounds like you're carefully scheduled."

"When there's a lot to be done, one has to be."

"No time for frivolity? No, let's drop everything for a week and run off to Bermuda, just to hold hands?"

"I can tell you haven't been married for 19 years." Almost at once she wished she hadn't said it.

"No. Didn't make it that far," he offered, and offered no more, just smiled and went on to something else. She liked his smile, and she liked his big warm handshake when, 30 minutes later, she had to break off the interview and they said goodbye. She would have to be careful of this man.

CHAPTER 2

As Herb Ellinson drove in from Malibu toward West Hollywood, the freeway traffic light early on this hazy Saturday morning, he could not get last night's dream out of his mind. Jake was in his dreams a lot, but this one was different.

The two of them were in their schoolyard in the Bronx, just hanging around with a bunch of kids. Oddly, though they were only 13 or 14, he and Jake were in their army uniforms. A group of girls stood near by. Jake started looking them over, whistling the hit tune "Bei Mir Bist Du Schön." The title meant "I Think You're Lovely," and Jake was using it to flirt with them. Herb stared at only one of them. Again, oddly, she was Marian, although this was many years before he was to meet her.

"Go on and talk to her, kid," Jake urged. "She's got her eye on you."

Herb was too shy. He was back then; he was to this day.

"You can do it, kid!"

But Herb couldn't, even though he could see that Marian was staring back at him.

Finally, Jake said, "I'll show you," and he started toward her. With fascination and dread, Herb kept watching Marian, hoping she would respond to his brother and dreading it. He wanted to speak, yet couldn't, until at last he managed to shout, "No, Jake, no! Come back!" But Jake kept getting farther and farther away, until Marian rolled over in bed, nudged Herb to awaken him.

"You were talking in your sleep," she murmured. "To your brother."

Jake had looked so real, so vivid, Herb thought as he pulled his car into the parking lot and turned off the ignition. Walking to meet Chris Ecker, Herb forced himself back to the matter at hand. He took a long look at the expanse of low buildings, then up at the big letters silhouetted against the Los Angeles sky: EPS. And just under them the words ELLINSON PRODUCTION SERVICES. He sighed.

The younger man coming toward him must have seen the expression on his face, because his first words were, "You're not leaving this place, Mr. Ellinson."

"Call me Herb, Chris. Don't make me feel any older than I do already."

"Of course . . . Herb. Don't forget, we're counting on you to be in here regularly. After all, we are paying you handsomely."

Herb liked Chris Ecker. Though he could hardly be more than 35, he said things like handsomely, expressions Herb rarely heard from anyone under 50. And he dressed like an Easterner, today in a tastefully muted tan plaid sports coat, blue button-down shirt, and print tie in earth tones. The dark baggy jackets and dark shirts, buttoned to the neck, no tie, that young California types wore these days offended Herb.

"Handsomely," Herb echoed.

The younger man chuckled. "Not that you need the money."

Herb shook his head no. The money. Beyond the wildest dreams of a young World War II vet from the Bronx when he and Vinnie Buono scotch-taped their first sign, hand lettered, to the door of a shabby office in a rundown building on West 21st Street in Manhattan: BUONO-ELLINSON SOUND STUDIOS.

That was 42 years ago. It remained Buono-Ellinson for only two years, until Vinnie was offered a good network job and Herb bought him out. From then on it was all Ellinson. Herb held onto it fiercely, through the move to L.A., through the expansion when they were dangerously under-capitalized. Held on, kept it all his, made it grow and prosper until Global made him the offer that, at 67, he couldn't refuse.

Forty-seven five. Forty-seven million, five hundred thousand dollars, cash, plus a five-year consultancy at $250,000 per, plus stock in Global to be paid out over five years according to a complicated formula keyed to the profitability of EPS. Herb had relied on his lawyer to work that out and he would rely on his accountant to monitor it. He didn't really care. It was more money than the boy from the Bronx had ever dreamed of; more than he would ever need or spend.

"Not as if I need the money." He said it almost as much to himself as to Ecker. Again, he stared at the sign. Again, Ecker got it . . . a quick young man.

"We'll leave it as it is, maybe put a smaller sign under it, 'A Division of Global Films.' After all, it's a name that's worth a lot; that's one of the things we bought. Sound all right?"

"Sounds fine."

Ecker was being courteous. Global had paid for the right to call it anything they wanted. He was also quite right; the name was worth a lot. Herb liked to believe it was the best facility of its kind in Los Angeles, which meant in America, probably the world. Where Buono-Ellinson had been a tiny outer office, an even tinier control room, and a cramped sound studio, the buildings under the EPS sign in West Hollywood housed a formidable array of audio studios, tape and film editing bays, storerooms filled with video, film, audio and lighting equipment, a garage with three huge production trailers, even two small sound stages. Herb had pulled off what no one else in the business had been able to: combined post-production services with rental, hardware, studio facilities—everything an independent television or film producer needed. To people surprised at the money he was getting, Herb pointed out that each of those 18 editing bays held a million dollars worth of equipment and each of the remote trailers represented three million dollars on wheels. And all state of the art.

It was Herb's life's work. And now?

Ecker was reading him brilliantly. "Hey, this is not like you're turning over the keys or anything. We're counting on your input. It's your talent, your know-how, we're buying, as much as anything else."

"And paying handsomely for."

Ecker smiled at him. He had the feeling the younger man wanted to pat him on the shoulder to comfort him. Herb liked Ecker more and more. From the moment he'd met him, he'd thought that if he'd had children, this was how old they'd be.

"Well . . ." said Ecker. He stuck his hand out.

There was no real reason he and Ecker should be standing here, except that today was the official day of the transfer and Ecker wanted a bit of ceremony—another reason Herb liked him. Herb grasped his hand and shook it. He could see that Ecker was as touched as he was. Not letting go of his hand, Ecker said, "Mazel tov."

"Mazel tov," Herb replied. Good luck. He hadn't even realized Chris Ecker was Jewish. When Herb was a boy no one named Jewish kids Christopher. Then the trim older man and the tall, dapper younger one walked through the parking lot. When they got to Herb's car, Ecker stopped to look it over.

"Like the Jag?" he asked. Dressed like an Easterner but a Californian after all, Herb said to himself. For Herb's part, he never thought about cars at all. He bought them and drove them without ever developing affection for one. In fact questions like Ecker's startled him.

"It gets me where I want to go."

"I hear they're in the shop a lot."

Herb smiled. "Gives me something to do."

Ecker waited for Herb to comment on his 450SL. When nothing came, he pointed to it. "To me the Mercedes is still a great car. I'm not talking about the new cheap stuff. For the top of the line . . . " He nodded in the direction of his car. "Mercedes is still the best. I guess I'm old fashioned." He shrugged.

No, you're not old fashioned, thought Herb. Old fashioned is when you won't buy a Mercedes because it's German. He got into his Jaguar and drove off. He wanted to be home before Marian left for wherever she was always going on Saturday mornings these days. As he turned out of the parking lot, he got a last glimpse of the big EPS sign. Not really a last glimpse, he tried to tell himself. But he knew. He felt unattached, as if he were floating free of the ground, and he wondered, is this supposed to feel good?

When he got home he could see the station wagon still in the garage. He walked around to the beach and entered the house by way of the deck. Marian was not in the huge picture-windowed room that served as living and dining room, so he walked through to look for her. When he got to the den, he stopped and entered. In it were books he hadn't yet read, CDs and tapes he hadn't yet listened to. Lots to do, but would it be enough? He went straight to the table beside his easy chair. There in a thin silver frame was the smiling young soldier in World War II dress uniform, the khaki jacket and tie, the tan shirt, all shades of gray in the black and white photo. The face was thin almost to gauntness, the nose strong, the neck muscular, the eyes filled with a self-assurance just short of arrogance.

Herb stared at the picture as he had so many hundreds of times over the years, and he asked it, "Jake, what do I do now?" He waited for a moment or two as if expecting an answer. Then he went off looking for Marian and a cup of coffee. Once she'd have come out to meet him.

She heard the Jaguar pull into its space next to the station wagon, started to walk out to him, caught a glimpse of herself in the big bedroom mirror, stopped. There facing her was a sturdy woman, the body strong, almost muscular, very fit for a woman over 50, yet displeasing to her, as always, for being too short, too stocky, the limbs not long enough, not slender enough. And the hair. Once he'd said he liked the gray, that it provided a natural streaking in the dark brown. Now it was vestiges of brown in a head of gray.

No, she told the woman in the mirror, she would not run to him, not show herself so vulnerable, such an easy mark for hurt, rejection. She'd done that once, the first time out, and she'd found herself alone in an uncaring world, a woman of 40 with a loving heart, a fair sense of humor, no money, no profession, just a pitiful smattering of secretarial skills between her and indigence.

Herb had been the answer to her prayers then; she had thanked God for him. It would be right the second time around; she would be willing to share him with his brother and his swing music. But they seemed unwilling to share him with her. Now she faced the dismal prospect of being alone again, only this time 11 years older. She had to get ready for it.

No, she would not run out to meet him.

Herb spotted her in their bedroom, waved to let her know he was back before heading to the kitchen to pour himself a cup of coffee. He carried it with him as he put an audiotape into his player, walked onto the deck and sat looking out at the Pacific, listening to the Buddy Benson Big Band playing "All The Things You Are."

No matter how many times he heard it, and he'd heard it many, many times, it always took him back to Times Square, the Paramount Theatre, the fall of 1941 . . . God, nearly 50 years! . . . Jake standing up in the horn section to play his solo, the lights bouncing and shattering off his trumpet, Herb in the audience, sitting next to their parents, all so proud, even their mother, though she had other things in mind for Jake entirely than playing in a band.

He heard the mail truck come and leave; then Marian walked out on the deck bringing him a second cup of coffee and the mail. Along with the junk there were three magazines and two letters, one of them from Joe Wiggins. Wiggins' letter he knew about before he opened it. Joe and he went way back. Joe had played in the band with Jake, before that in pickup groups with their father. He'd retired a few years ago as head of the Jazz Studies Department at Long Valley State and now he was raising money for it.

Marian wore a lime-colored linen dress, sleeveless to show off her tanned arms. Dressed to go somewhere, he could see that, and she could see he saw.

"My aerobics class," she said.

He looked at her for just a moment, hesitated. Then all he said was, "You can't improve on perfection."

To him, she did have a wonderful body, for a woman of 51—for any age, for that matter—beautifully shaped, the kind he'd admired on the nightclub dancers when he was a young musician. Ponies, they were called, and God help you if you called one a showgirl, who had no talent whatever, unless you considered long legs and big boobs a talent.

"Thank you, dear. It's an unending fight to keep what you've got, even if it's a lot less than perfection."

He wondered if it was the fight she was going to fight on this particular Saturday morning, and if not . . . he didn't even want to think of the alternatives. "Be back for lunch?" He made it sound as casual as he could.

"I may have lunch with some of the girls in the class. Count calories." Again, they just looked at each other. He thought she was about to relent, hoped she would. She didn't.

The tape had gone from "All The Things You Are" to "Begin The Beguine." She listened for a moment.

"You've got Benny Goodman for company," she said.

"Artie Shaw," he answered.

"Oh, I thought it was a clarinet." In the nine years they'd been married, she'd managed to keep his music at arm's length.

"Artie Shaw is a clarinetist too, some people think better than Goodman."

"I'll take the station wagon," she said.

"Take the Jag. Even though you got it wrong."

She managed a quick smile. "The station wagon will be fine." And she left.

He heard the wagon start up and drive off. Like Ecker and most of the world, he supposed, she would have preferred a Mercedes; she didn't think the Jaguar was a good car. He bought one anyway. The difference was she was two when the U.S. got into the war; he was 18.

The sun was fighting through the haze, the temperature still low, a breeze blowing from the ocean. It would be a lovely day, but then days at Malibu usually were. Through the open glass doors the Shaw band was playing "Any Old Time," vocal by Billie Holiday. If ever in the history of popular music there was anything greater than the stuff they played in the late 30s, he didn't know what it was.

Usually on Saturday mornings Herb would go in to work a half day, then come home and sit out and listen to a public radio station that played jazz, unless it was too modern—which to him meant anything to the left of Charlie Parker—in which case he played one of his CDs, tapes, or old records. Once one of the kids who ran Global asked him if he still listened to LPs. "Hell," Herb told him, "I still listen to 78s!" In truth, Herb had transferred most of his 78s to tape, yet he kept the old disks packed in cartons, not because he put them on a turntable anymore, but because he couldn't bear to part with them. He liked the traditional stuff, always had. He'd read somewhere that younger brothers were usually followers. He agreed with that absolutely. Jake was the leader, the trail-blazer; he would probably have loved Charlie Parker. Herb had found the music he adored, late 30s, early 40s. He was happy with it.

He held the two letters, moving them so his head shadowed them from the sun, opened the one from Joe Wiggins first. It said just what he knew it would.

". . . follow-up to our chat . . . wonderful talent kids have today . . . don't want our kind of music to die . . ."

Joe was right . . . and dead wrong. Their kind of music *was* the best. But it had lived in the glory of its time, and that time was gone. Born in the 30s and died after the War. Well not quite dead, but not a living thing either: a museum piece, a fossil. He and Wiggins and their generation had outlived their music. Jake hadn't. Jake and a lot of others. We were the lucky ones, Herb reminded himself. We lived to hear rock and roll.

He picked up the other letter and looked at it: an ordinary business envelope, with a return address sticker that said Allen Breecher, 14 Ash Street, Dubuque, Iowa 52001. Herb's address was written out in a careful penmanship they hadn't taught in years. As he started to open the letter, Herb saw it had been sealed with scotch tape as well as its own glue. Carefully, he pulled at the tape to open the envelope. In it were a note from Breecher and an old V-Mail letter, the kind that had been used during the War.

He started reading the note, and when he got to the part about the 101st, his hands began to tremble. Then something about the name struck him . . . Allen Breecher . . . Al Breecher. Of course! Until a year ago, maybe less, this was the kind of moment he'd so much wanted Marian to share. Now, it was just as well she was gone. She never said so, but Marian had a belly full of Jake. That could be the reason, as much as any other, for what was happening to them, whatever that was.

"Dear Mr. Ellinson,

"Perhaps you remember me. We met once long ago. 1943, I think it was, in a jazz club on 52nd Street. Your brother and I were in the Army together . . ."

Beecher's wife had died recently, and going through the attic, through things she'd stored away, he found the letter. Way back in December of '44 Jake had given it to him to mail, but things had gotten pretty hectic right about then, and he had tucked it away, forgotten it.

The letter had been with some old army stuff, and when Al found it, he mailed it to the address on the envelope, but it came back, addressee unknown. So he wrote to the Veterans Administration, which finally supplied him with the names and addresses of Mr. and Mrs. Martin Ellinson and Herbert Ellinson as next of kin. He'd sent the letter to Jake's parents, only to have it come back again. Someone had marked "Deceased" on it. Finally, he'd mailed it to Herb.

He ended the letter with: "Jake Ellinson was a fine man and a great trooper. I was proud to be his friend and to be a Screaming Eagle with him."

Herb wiped his eyes, waited for them to clear before confronting the V-Mail letter. It was addressed to June Hopkins, 1410 Broadway, Hicksville, Long Island, New York. The name meant nothing to him. He turned the letter over, started to open it, then stopped. Jake had written this letter, held it in his hands. Now Herb was going to read the words Jake had written 45 years ago, words no one had ever read before. He stared at the envelope. Then, carefully, trying to control the trembling of his fingers, he started to open it.

CHAPTER 3

Spring-Summer, 1940

Hitler plans Operation Sea Lion, the invasion of Britain. In the U.S. the deal to give Britain 50 old destroyers is ratified. President Roosevelt signs the Burke-Wadsworth Bill, establishing the first peacetime draft in American history.

The War Department, noting the effectiveness of German airborne troops in the invasion of Holland, orders the formation of a test parachute platoon at Fort Benning, Georgia.

Hit records: "Tuxedo Junction" and "Fools Rush In," Glenn Miller; "I'll Never Smile Again," Tommy Dorsey, vocal by Frank Sinatra; "The Breeze and I," Jimmy Dorsey, vocal by Bob Eberly.

Jake is whistling the Artie Shaw arrangement of "Frenesi" as he opens the door to the Ellinson apartment. He stops as soon as he hears the sounds of bad trumpet playing coming from the living room; his father is giving a lesson. He moves quietly along the small hallway into the bedroom he shares with his brother Herb, quickly puts the trumpet case on his bed. Somehow, in the brief silences between the cracking and braying of the horn, his mother has heard the whistling. In no time at all, she is out of the kitchen and in his room.

"Jacob the music man," she says, standing in the entrance to the boys' room, pushing her hair from her face, taking in the trumpet case at a glance.

"Ma, we know each other well enough. Call me Jake."

She will not be deflected. From the trumpet case, her eyes move to something she likes even less, a purplish bruise on his left cheekbone.

"So what is that?"

"Nothing, ma." He turns away. She moves to him, puts a damp hand on his bony, handsome face and turns it to her for a better look.

"That's nothing? That's some nothing!" She strokes back the silky brown hair.

"It's OK, ma. Just give it a little kiss, and it'll be fine." He leans over. She kisses.

"Ahh! All gone!" He beams down at her. He is a charmer, her son, but right now she is not to be charmed.

"You were in a fight again."

"I didn't start it."

"You never start. How come people are always starting with you? How come they never start with your brother?"

"They start, what can I say?" He balls his hand into a fist. "I finish."

"Joe Louis. You want me to be proud? My son goes to college so he can play the trumpet and get into fights. What mother wouldn't be proud?"

"I've been studying, ma."

"A trumpet case I see. Books I don't see. I'll bet the trumpet's still warm. Should I touch it? Show me the warm books."

She moves toward the trumpet case; he doesn't try to stop her.

"Go ahead. Check for fresh spit while you're there."

She pretends to be stopped by that. "Don't be disgusting," she says.

"Sherlock Ellinson, the great detective. You should be head of the FBI. I'll call President Roosevelt."

"Don't bother. I have a harder job already, looking after my sons."

"Bronx woman turns down top FBI job! J. Edgar Hoover breathes sigh of relief! It was on the radio today, ma, honest."

She gives him a worried look. "I'll tell you what was on the radio today. They're going to draft boys into the army. You know what that means? I'll tell you. *My* boys. You. Herbie."

"How come it's Herbie, not Herbert, mom? But it's always Jacob? 'cause you love him better, right?" Neither of them takes that remark seriously. Jake is her favorite and everybody knows it.

"I love both my sons exactly the same and I don't want to see either of them go into the army and get killed."

"We're not in the war, ma! It's a question of training people. Just in case. A year and they're out."

"Not even in yet, and already they're out. Only there are a lot of boys who go in and never come out. I remember the war in 1918. Your father was in the army. Thank God he was in a band, and nothing happened to him."

"Ma, somebody's got to stop the Nazis!" He is very serious now.

"Not my boys."

"It's got to be somebody's boys. They hate the Jews, ma. We talked about it in my history class. About how Hitler blames everything on the Jews, and what he wants to do to them. That's how I got into the fight."

She looks at him with disbelief. "You got into a fight in your history class?"

Jake laughs, then fidgets, looks down at the trumpet case. "No, on 48th Street." West 48th Street in Manhattan is where the music shops are and where the musicians hang out. Going from the City College of New York to the East Bronx by way of West 48th Street is like going from New York to Philadelphia by way of Chicago.

"I . . . just wanted to look at some mouthpieces. I didn't buy anything."

"Who had time to buy? You were too busy fighting."

"Ma, there was nothing I could do. This guy from one of the oom-pah bands in Yorkville . . . he was looking at a horn, and he thought the price was too high. So he started talking about how the Jews were robbing him. And, you know, the goddamn Jews. And how Hitler had the right idea. So I told him to shut up."

Mildred Ellinson shakes her head. "Sticks and stones can break your bones . . ."

"He said something; I said something. I would have left it at that. Then he asked me how come I was sticking up for the Jews. I said I was one, so he said in that case I was a goddamned coward. Then I had to invite him outside to say that to me again."

"You could have gotten badly hurt."

"Even if I had, ma . . . I couldn't back down. But I didn't get hurt."

"What do you call that?" She reaches up to touch the bruise on his face, and then softly strokes his cheek.

"This? This is nothing. You should see him! He was big, but slow. He managed to graze me on the cheek then I broke his nose. There was blood all over him."

None of this impresses his mother. "A street fighter. Who's going to respect a boy who gets into fights on the street?"

"I'll tell you one guy who's gonna respect me, ma. Not only me, but the Jews."

CHAPTER 4

Dede Miller strode into the marble lobby of 951 Fifth a little after nine, got a cheerful good evening from the doorman and the elevator man. The building staff always gave her special attention; she was a friendly person and a good tipper. And her company managed the building.

She changed into jeans and a t-shirt, took the *Wall Street Journal* and a diet Coke into the library and had just begun reading when Tru came home. He stood there in a gray pinstripe suit, tall, slim, a wisp of faded blond hair falling onto his forehead; he was handsome, aristocratic and faintly condescending in a way that Ralph Lauren could only approximate in his Polo ads. Only the redness in the eyes showed he'd had a few martinis. Or more than a few.

"Entrepreneuse finds a quiet moment in the den."

Entrepreneuse; den. His little jokes. "Entrepreneuse" to remind her of his distaste for successful women. "Den" to remind her that the girl from Garden City, Long Island, had once used a déclassé word that a Park Avenue boy would never utter except as it pertained to lions or iniquity.

"Hi," she said, smiling, pretending, once again, to share his amusement. "Have you had dinner?"

"I'm drinking my dinner, as they might say in Garden City." He headed for the bar to mix himself a martini that was little more than straight gin. "Do they?"

"The people I knew there ate their dinners." He sipped from his glass, folded himself into an easy chair with that lanky grace she used to think so elegant. "Where's Jimmy? He called me at the office. Didn't have a chance to get back to him. Do you know what he wanted?"

"He's in his room working on his senior thesis. He wanted to tell us he was going up to Massachusetts for a road race this weekend."

"Honestly, Dede, what does he see in that sport? Why not tennis? Squash? Golf?"

"Don't forget polo. Croquet."

"Long distance running is for skinny Africans and micks from . . ." He smiled, "I will *not* say Garden City."

"I guess he likes it. Busy day?"

They both knew he didn't have busy days. Tru was a broker at a Wall Street firm in which the Martindales owned a lot of stock. He usually got to the office at nine, went to a long lunch at noon and returned for an hour or so before heading uptown for his squash game at the Gotham or "appointments."

"Just another day in the rat race. Met Roger at the Goth." Insiders called it the Goth, not the Gotham, never the club. "We're on Jew patrol."

"I hope he's not going to be too tough on Mary."

"Roger is not a happy man. He told me she was trying to enlist you in her dreadful campaign. I told him: not bloody likely!"

She was not pleased to be so predictable. "Why were you so sure?"

He leaned forward in his chair. "It's called pulling up the ladder after you, darling. Garden City girl, having married her way up to the Goth stratum, is not about to help some Jew waltz in. Do I read you right, you lovely arriviste, you?"

"As always, Tru." He was more right than she wanted to admit. "And how do *you* feel about Jews in the club, Tru? Or women?"

"Need you ask? It was my great-grandfather who co-founded the Goth. Adam Augustus Martindale wanted a place where a few like-minded men of a certain . . . class . . . could spend time together. If he'd wanted Jews and women in it, he would have invited Jews and women into it. Do you read me, beautiful?" He threw her a mock-earnest stare.

"I read you, handsome," she replied as he got up to refill his glass. She managed to look amused.

CHAPTER 5

Herb Ellinson's life read like an inspirational American success story, one of many lived by the young men who got back into civvies after World War II and started the nation on the road to unparalleled expansion.

At 22, he returned to a civilian routine very much like the one he'd left three years earlier: classes, studying, and on weekends, playing the jobs that helped support him and his parents. Though Herb lacked Jake's improvisational spark, he was a first-rate reeds man who could play anything from swing to waltzes and polkas. And he had strong credentials: three years in a top army band led by Matt Gerard.

When, upon induction, he listed himself as a professional musician, his army buddies told him that would guarantee he'd not be assigned to a band. This time they were wrong. Two weeks into basic training, Herb was called to audition for Gerard, who in civilian life had a well-known dance band, although strictly what musicians called "mickey-mouse," square and full of show-business gimmicks. Using a horn supplied by a sergeant, Herb sight-read some standard arrangements flawlessly.

He spent the war with Gerard, playing for GIs in the U.S., Europe, and Africa. When he was discharged in December of 1945, he plugged into a network of young musicians returning to civilian life, and he had more jobs than he could take.

To his father, the return of all the young musicians meant tough times; there was not much work left for a 50-year-old trumpet player, not many students either. As the father struggled, more and more the support of the family fell to the son. For the two years until Herb got his degree, his life followed a routine of classes, study, and work, from early morning when he awoke in a room dominated by the smiling picture of Jake in dress uniform, to evening when he came home from a job or finished studying and took one last look at the picture before switching off the light. In those two years, Herb did not have a single date.

With a degree in electrical engineering, he had no trouble getting a job in a recording studio; an engineer who was also a musician was a rare find. There he met Vinnie Buono, who'd been in the Army Signal Corps, and the two opened their sound studio. But still he played weekend jobs, until rock arrived in the early 50s. For Herb, the end came in the late fall of 1954. He was playing a dance where the kids were clamoring for "Shake, Rattle and Roll." The band obliged, and at the end of the evening, when the men were packing their instruments and getting ready to leave, a sax player in his 40s shook his head. "That's all they want to do every night. Shake, rattle and roll." Sitting on the subway on his way home, Herb made the decision to quit. In his room he turned on the light and spoke to Jake's picture, something he'd come to do more and more.

"You wouldn't like it, Jake. It's junk. I give you Charlie Parker, Dizzy Gillespie. Not this."

Ironically, the music that made him quit playing also made him rich, as kids began buying rock LPs in quantities the music business had never dreamed of. Meanwhile, as a businessman, he was keeping an eye on the growth of TV and he got into full production services: equipment rental, editing facilities, post-production, sound stages.

In the mid-50s, he moved his parents out of the Bronx, which was deteriorating fast, to a house on Long Island. His father, who was then nearly 60, found a few trumpet students and even played a job once in awhile, mostly thanks to Herb's friends. His mother joined organizations, learned to drive a car and seemed to thrive on her new turf, as well as she ever thrived after the death of her Jacob.

Herb was now sole owner of his business, and a wealthy young man. One day he looked around and he was in his 30s, still single and, as his mother put it directly, with "no life." She'd usually precede the judgment by saying, "Sure, you have plenty of money, but what kind of life do you have?" Then she'd answer her own question: "No life."

Herb's problem was that in the years between 17 and 25, when young men were establishing the patterns of what his mother called "a life," he'd either been in the army or doing double duty working and going to school. He had no real idea what "a life" was. So even when he finished school and gave up playing, he continued the only habit he knew: unending work.

Unlike his brother, he was very shy with women, an embarrassment he never could conquer or outgrow. When finally, at 35, he told his parents he was getting married, they were delighted. But their delight was short-lived. Soon after he moved his business to California, the marriage broke up. Maybe, he thought later, if Emily hadn't had the miscarriage . . . but he didn't dwell on that. Emily was a New York girl, a schoolteacher, who hated Los Angeles. Even with a child, it probably would have happened anyway, and been a lot more complicated.

For a time, he didn't tell his parents about the divorce, and on every trip east, he heard the same question from his mother: "When are you going to give us a grandchild?" Finally he told then. The question stopped. They seemed to accept the probability that their only living child would not be a father and they'd never be grandparents.

CHAPTER 6

Fall-Winter, 1940

Simultaneously the battles of Britain and the North Atlantic rage. The Germans try to subdue the British by bombing their cities and cutting their supply lines at sea. British troops fight a lethargic Italian foe in North Africa.

In the United States, the first men are called up by lottery for the draft. The monthly pay for a buck private is $21, which will inspire a popular song: "$21 A Day Once A Month."

Hit records: "Only Forever," Bing Crosby; "Blueberry Hill," Glenn Miller; "Ferryboat Serenade," the Andrews Sisters; "Frenesi," Artie Shaw.

One night Joe Wiggins is sitting at the bar of the Unicorn on 52nd street, sipping a scotch, when he hears Jake play a hot solo on "Taking A Chance On Love" with a pick-up group. Joe knows Marty Ellinson; he helped Jake get his first jobs when he was only 16. They played together at weddings and dances, until Joe was hired as a tenor man by the Buddy Benson band nearly three years ago. At 23, Joe has been a full-time pro for five years, since high school. He knows Jake has talent, but being on the road so much, he loses track of him. Now he is bowled over by what he hears. As soon as Jake is off the bandstand, Joe goes over to tell him how great he is and that he ought to be with Buddy Benson. Jake is thrilled but doesn't take it as a serious suggestion until he sees Joe again at the Etemore, a cafeteria on Seventh Avenue and 51st Street, where, starting at about noon, musicians gather for coffee and talk.

Arriving at the cafeteria on his regular Saturday pilgrimage, Jake sees Joe poking at a piece of gelatinous cherry pie and glancing at a copy of the Daily News while half joining in a conversation with a couple of other musicians. As soon as he spots Jake, Joe waves him over.

"You're something else, man!" he shouts as Jake pulls up a chair. "I didn't know you could blow that way. Jeez!" Joe turns to the others. "This kid can play!"

The others wave to Jake and smile and go on talking. Joe pulls Jake off to the side and begins to whisper. "I don't want *him* to hear." He nods in the direction of a trumpet player across the table. "We're losing our second trumpet. He's getting married to get out of the draft and his wife doesn't want him on the road." He leans closer until Jake can smell the cherry pie and the residue of last night's scotch. "You interested? We do a lot of those humpty dumpty ballads, but we work steady, we work all the time. And once in a while we really swing. Once in a while."

"Gee, Joe . . . I . . ." Jake is hardly ever at a loss for words. But this is too close to what he's dreamed of. He has recently turned 20, eight days after the draft was signed in fact, which gives him one year before being called up. He doesn't want to spend it sitting in classes and playing junk music on weekends. He wants to be in a real band, a band like Goodman or Shaw or Dorsey or Miller. The Buddy Benson Big Band, the 4Bs, as it's called, is a notch below them; it plays a lot of commercial music, some good stuff too. It works major rooms all over the country, and plays on coast-to-coast radio.

"When do you need . . . him?" Jake can't bring himself to say "me."

"Casella's going on this trip with us, then he's getting married right after Christmas. So it'll be after New Year's."

Jake doesn't think it's possible for Joe to lean any closer, but he does. "Listen, I haven't even mentioned the idea to Buddy, and he'd have to hear you first; he might even have someone lined up. I just want to know if you're interested."

Jake takes a deep breath and lets it out quietly. "You bet."

Benson arranges for him to sit in for a set at the Unicorn on a Friday night. On the subway down to the club, Jake is nervous as hell, but that disappears the moment he climbs onto the tiny bandstand. Playing with a small improvisational group is not the same as a big band, with all its written arrangements, but as soon as Benson hears Jake's first solo, he turns to Joe, who's sitting with him in back of the club, and says, "The kid's got a job."

CHAPTER 7

As she was leaving for work, Dede asked Tru, who was sitting in his pajamas sipping orange juice, if he wanted to go with her to the Rudolphs' cocktail party that evening. She knew the answer even before it came.

Tru allowed his face to show theatrical distaste. "With the Temple Emanu-El crowd?"

"It's business for me, Tru. You know that. Besides, the Rudolphs are not so bad. They invite a lot of people in the arts."

"Fags, too? So sorry, I mean gays." He turned on a sibilant "s." "Say, how do those queens manage to hold onto their drinks with their limp wrists?"

"So few people meet your standards, Tru."

"Just think of yourself as one of the lucky ones. And while you're at the Rubins . . ."

"The Rudolphs."

"Vottever." This with a Yiddish accent. "Please, *don't* do any recruiting for the Goth."

That evening as she walked into the Rudolphs' immense Park Avenue duplex, she could feel the difference between "them" and "us," feel it in a restless energy, a competitive edginess, an animation she didn't feel at WASP cocktail parties. But she wouldn't miss this chance to keep her channels open to her industry and to Rudolph. Especially to Rudolph, because she knew what he wanted to discuss with her: a merger that would create New York's biggest real estate sales and management firm, bigger even than Douglas Elliman or Brown Harris Stevens. Though she was playing hard to get, she was interested. In her business, you couldn't stand still; at any rate, she didn't want to.

Now Fred Rudolph was walking across the huge entrance hall, past his Picasso, his Chagall, his Degas, to offer her his soft hand. He was a small man, mostly bald, unprepossessing except for the responsiveness in his dark eyes, which always seemed to know and understand, and which made him very appealing.

"Welcome, welcome! Do you know people here, Diana, or shall I introduce you around?"

"I'll be fine," she answered. "Don't worry about me." Just as she spoke, she saw, over his shoulder, at the other end of the room, a tall curly-haired man she recognized.

"Fred," she said. "That big fellow. Isn't he the newspaper reporter, Kenneth Glass?"

Fred turned. "Ken Glass? *Newspaper* reporter? He's *the* Ken Glass. The novelist. Nominated for a National Book Award last year. Don't tell me you never heard of *Lonesome Tonight?*"

"Did he write that?"

"And a half dozen others. Want to meet him?"

"We've met. Look, Fred, I can't monopolize you. You see to your other guests. I'll find myself a glass of wine."

"We really should find time to talk . . ."

"And we will. Quiet time. In a quiet place."

"That a promise?"

She nodded brightly, waved a hand at him, and he went off. She asked a waiter for a glass of white wine, and while waiting, examined a bookcase lined with rich leather-bound classics she doubted had ever been cracked open. She was staring at *The Collected Works of Charles Dickens* when a voice said, "White wine, Ms. Miller?" She turned, expecting the waiter.

"Glass with the glass. I intercepted the waiter," he said, giving her the wine and that crinkly smile. He wore a gray tweed jacket, corduroy pants, and again a dark blue denim shirt, with a maroon knit tie. He'd almost managed to tame his hair. His eyes were bright; he was glad to see her and showing it. It made her feel warm.

"Thank you, Mr. Glass," she said, smiling back as she took the drink.

"I spotted you . . . across a crowded room, as they say in the song."

"Oh my, what song is that?"

"Forgot you don't listen to music. 'Some Enchanted Evening.' 'South Pacific.' Probably came out before you were born, so you're excused."

"What year was that?"

"1949. In fact, the year I was born."

"Thank you kind sir. The sad truth is, I was born in '45."

"I would have said '55.'"

"I'll take a moment to blush." She was very pleased. "Why didn't you tell me you wrote *Lonesome Tonight?*"

"Strong silent type."

"And why is a National Book Award nominee doing interviews for the New York Times Magazine?"

"In a word? Money."

"I thought famous novelists were rolling in money."

"Alas, I'm not a famous novelist. I'm what's called a respected novelist. Know what that means? 5,000 copies in hard cover, 10 if you're lucky."

"Everybody talked about your book!"

"It was much talked-about, little read, and even less purchased. Did you buy one?"

"Oh dear. I'm going to now."

"I have a stack of them in my apartment. I'll give you one."

"No you won't. I'll buy one, if you'll sign it."

"With an inscription that encompasses gratitude, esteem . . . and admiration." He hesitated for an instant. "Look. A little later, I'm going to have a hamburger at a place nearby. We could get some more interviewing done."

"Sure." She said it straight out, then had to remind herself not to be too charmed by this man.

On Madison Avenue just above 79th street, the Madison Pub was a dark, almost shabby bar and restaurant that had been around for years. She'd never been in it before, immediately liked its homey, self-assured modesty. It reminded her of Glass. She had spinach salad, he a hamburger; she admired the way he chomped at it un-self-consciously.

"How do you know the Rudolphs?" she asked him.

"Irene Rudolph asked me to read at some benefit. Now they invite me to their parties."

"They like to collect literary types. Why are you willing to be collected?"

"Maybe I like to collect real estate types."

"I should know better than to cross words with a writer."

"Why were you there?"

"Business."

"Not really your crowd, eh?"

She shrugged. "Not really."

"Bit of a snob?"

"Aren't we all? Why were you there?"

"For a touch of human contact. A writer spends his days in solitary."

"No significant other?"

"Not even an insignificant other."

"Eligible bachelor? Gay?"

"A wife who decided to put an ex- in front of her title, went home to Scarsdale with our two daughters, subsequently remarried. Very well, as they say. Hey, remember who's doing the interviewing here. My turn. When you were a kid did you ever dream about really being a singer?"

"Singer?"

"You know. 'I never knew the technique of kissing . . . ' Sinatra."

"Oh, that! When you grow up you move into the real world."

"So whatever happens to youthful dreams?"

"You mean, how do they turn into the banal world of real estate?"

"Well, let's face it. Real estate is not the stuff of dreams," He saw the expression on her face. "Oh oh. I've offended you."

"Diana Miller the—ugh—snob. Diana Miller the—ugh—real estate person. Let's put it this way: you're sure not trying to seduce me with flattery."

"I'm not trying to seduce you at all."

She felt her face flush. "I didn't mean it that way."

"I know, I'm sorry. You can tell me to buzz off any time. I hope you won't."

She did not tell him to buzz off. You don't do that to the *New York Times Magazine*, even though this man was dangerous, seemed to see right inside her. She was careful for the rest of the evening. But he did have a wonderful handshake.

CHAPTER 8

Carefully wrapped and boxed in Herb's bedroom closet were more than three years of letters written by Jake while he was in the army, to Herb and to their parents. From time to time, he would unwrap them, remove one or two from their envelopes, re-read them, and run his fingers over the angled scrawl that was so distinctively his brother's.

Now, more than 45 years later, sitting in the midday sun on his patio, looking out at the blue Pacific, Herb held in his hand another letter from Jake, this one to a woman named June Hopkins. When he opened it and saw that familiar scrawl, he had to look away, stare at the ocean for a few moments. He blinked a couple of times, slowly sipped his coffee, and began to read.

It was dated December 24, 1944. The numbers swam before his eyes. He daubed at his cheeks with his napkin, blinked some more to bring the letter back into focus.

> *Dear Junebug,*
>
> *Sorry about that last letter. Wanted to say that right after I mailed it, but things have been pretty rough. We . . .*

Here several lines were censored.

> *I've been thinking about your news. I still don't agree with you. Please think about it, carefully. However, if you decide to go ahead, I'll stand by you, whatever your decision. After all, I'm a little involved, too!*
>
> *Whatever happens, don't worry. One day, this war will be over and then, as you like to say, everything will work out. Meanwhile, do what you think is right. You can count on me.*

I actually miss you! Can you believe that? I'll write as soon as I can.

Love, Jake.

Herb looked away from the letter, and wondered what the news was. Whatever it was, it was 45 years old now.

CHAPTER 9

It's at Sunday dinner in December of 1940 that Jake decides to break the news. They sit at their table in the kitchen, eating pot roast, which Jake loves. This time he sits there picking at it, waiting. He knows that once he makes his announcement, there'll be no more eating, so he holds off until the dessert, which is one of his mother's specialties: lemon jello with pieces of canned fruit cocktail suspended in it.

Millie gives him an opening. "Why is my Jacob so quiet today?"

"I'm thinking about . . . the future."

"Yes?" He can almost see his mother's antenna go up.

"You know, I could be drafted in just a few months, and . . ."

"Ten, eleven months. That's not such a few months."

"It's not a long time," Jake continues. "If I go back to school next month . . ."

"What do you mean, if?"

"Millie!" Marty defends his son's right to speak. Jake forces his way through her interruption.

"I mean, it looks like the army is going to interrupt college for me anyway, and you know I'm not all that crazy about school."

"Crazy about school? What is it, a chocolate malted, you should be crazy about it?"

"Ma! Let me finish!"

"Let him finish, Millie."

She clamps her lips shut, but the flush on her face signals she is making no long-term promises about silence. This time Jake stares straight at his father, "I have a chance to do something I really want to do. I've always wanted to do."

Marty knows his son is looking for help. "What is it, Jake?"

"Go on the road. With Buddy Benson."

Millie knows who Buddy Benson is. She knows even better what the road is. "Are you crazy? Marty tell him he's crazy! Tell him!"

Marty speaks from a combination of spousal duty and feeling. "It's no fun, Jake. It may sound like it, but believe me, you never get a decent night's sleep . . . the travel, the crummy hotels, the food . . . it's terrible."

"Why do you think your father stopped? It will be the biggest mistake, you'll be . . ."

"Ma, I'm not talking about a lifetime! I'm just talking about from the end of the semester in January, to when I go into the army."

"Why are you so sure you'll go in the army? Maybe you'll have flat feet or . . ." Even in her anguish, Millie is not about to conjure up anything serious, ". . . a perforated ear drum."

"But I don't, ma!" He turns to his father. "I know it's not easy, that's why I want to try it now, while I'm young, and single. When I have a family, I won't want to do it either. But it's a chance to play with a really first-rate band and I . . . I've got to try it."

"Got to" are strong words, and Millie knows her son. But she isn't ready to give up. "Just wait, they'll probably put you in an army band. Then you can do all the horn playing you want!"

"I'll have a much better chance in the army if I've played with a top civilian band. So this will really help me."

Marty looks at his son and asks, "When do you have to decide?"

No one moves. Jake looks at his mother, who is staring at him, transfixed, and he almost doesn't have the heart to go ahead. He stares down at his jello, then knows he's got to look right at his mother when he says this. It isn't easy. His bright blue eyes meet her tired ones.

"I leave the second week in January."

"That's all? No discussion? You make up your mind and that's it? What your family has to say doesn't count at all?" There is still fight in her eyes. "You can just tell them you're not sure yet. Maybe you'll do it when you get out of the army instead!"

"Ma! They need somebody in three weeks."

"And we don't count?"

"Sure you count, ma. But I'm 20 years old. And I've got to decide that for myself. I told them I'd go."

The fight is giving way to tears. "So what's the use of talking. You raise a son, and . . ." The tears begin to come, and she gets up. Jake leaps to his feet to intercept her, puts his arms around her. She tries to push him off, but he does not budge.

"And I suppose when I'm at the Paramount you won't come to see me?"

"Your college graduation, that's what I want to come to."

"Ma, I've got time. Time for everything." She shakes her head no, and tries to free herself, but he has her pinned. Finally, she gives in, puts her arms around him and hugs him. But he can feel her sobbing.

"Let me go, your father needs his coffee."

He releases her; she walks to the stove, he goes back to the table, sits and for the first time stares at Herb, who is looking back, his face both adoring and stricken. "There are three, four guys in the band who played with Goodman," says Jake, not knowing what else to say.

Marty puts his hand on Jake's. "I'm not kidding, son. It's no picnic. It's harder than you think."

"I've got to try it, pop."

"What does it pay?"

"A hundred a week, pop."

"That's good money." Marty squeezes his eldest son's hand. He hasn't realized how big and strong the hand has become.

CHAPTER 10

Jimmy Miller walked into the guest bedroom at 6:30 in the morning while Dede was working out on her Nordic track machine, which she preferred to an exercise bike because it made demands on the upper body as well as the legs. She alternated days between it and a jog in the park.

"Lookin' good, mom!"

"Then why does it hurt so much?" Sweat dripping into her eyes, she looked up at him. She loved to look at her son. He had a runner's build, broad shouldered, lean to the point of gauntness. With his silky dark hair, light blue eyes, strong jaw and nose, he seemed to her very fine looking, not as conventionally handsome as his father, yet with a gentleness she preferred to Tru's hauteur.

"No pain, no gain, mom! Dad said you were out late last night."

"Went to a party. Business. Then I was doing an interview for the *New York Times Magazine*."

"The magazine? No kidding!"

"Didn't know your mom was such a big deal."

"Yes, I did."

"I was only kidding."

"So was I."

They both laughed. Her son was not only handsome; he was clever, too. She was so proud of him!

"You're almost off at college. That's hard to believe."

"My big question right now: Should I ask for a roommate or a single?"

"What did your father say?"

"He told me to ask for a Yale man."

"Ha ha."

Jimmy was headed for Dartmouth in the fall, despite Tru's hope that the boy go to his alma mater. Without wanting to undercut Tru, Dede told Jimmy the choice should be his, and that she would support him. When he chose Dartmouth over Yale, Tru was miffed; he suggested that Dede had sabotaged old Eli.

"What do you think, mom?"

"I think a roommate. Making friends is an important part of college."

"Networking?"

"You're too young to be cynical. I'd call it socializing."

"I like my privacy, mom. You know that."

She knew. He had a streak of stubborn, unorthodox independence. Sometimes she wondered which conventional parent he got it from.

"Well then, which are you going to choose?"

"I think I'll ask for a single, more chance to study."

"If you've already made up your mind . . ."

"I always value your input, mom!" He grinned that grin that made his mother wonder how anyone could refuse him anything.

"Anytime you need advice, son, you know where I'll be."

"Where, mom?"

"Not on this torture device!" she said, getting off the Nordic machine.

Thirty minutes later, showered and dressed, she walked into the kitchen, where Tru, in his pajamas, was sitting at the breakfast table, sipping a cup of coffee.

"Must have been ah vondaful pahty," he said.

"It was all right. I'm glad I went." She poured herself a large glass of orange juice, drank it without sitting down.

"And stayed late."

"No. Went out for a hamburger."

"With?"

Whether because of the question itself or its imperious tone, she disliked telling him. "With a writer who's interviewing me for the *New York Times Magazine*."

His eyes opened wide, his face took on the pseudo-earnestness she liked so little. "Tell me, Ms. Penrose Miller, how do you manage to be so powerful and so sexy at the same time?"

Although she didn't like the game she went along with it. "Power is sexy. Haven't you heard?"

"In a man, Ms. Miller. In a woman it's a turn-off. How does your husband handle it?"

"You'll have to ask him that." She wanted to end this game.

"He is not available for interviews." His eyes darkened for a moment; then he ended it. "And where did you go for this interview, Elaine's? Isn't that where all you media celebrities hang out?"

She sighed. "The Madison Pub."

"Never heard of it."

"It's comfortable. Sort of feels like a club, for those of us who can't get into the Gotham." She gulped down the rest of the orange juice and turned to go.

"Speaking of which," he said, "do you think you might find a moment to phone Roger and reassure him that you are not supporting this radical assault on the Goth?"

"You want to show him that though he can't control his wife, you can control yours."

"I certainly hope so. Be a good girl, Dede."

On the way to the office she tried to put Tru and the club and everything else out of her mind and concentrate on one thing: the 7:30 meeting with Fred Rudolph. She wanted things to move along, yet she didn't want to seem eager. Merger, yes. Money, negotiable. Command, not. Dede would have to run the new outfit, or no deal.

Rudolph, early as usual, was already in her conference room, sitting in one of the sleek leather swivel chairs, when she arrived. He got to his feet stiffly, one hand on the table for support. Dede knew the signs of a bad back when she saw them.

"Morning, Diana. Glad you could make it last night!" He had the typical New York accent of an earlier day, one of the last people to pronounce "first" and "third" so that they would be spelled "foist" and "thoid," but don't actually sound quite like that.

"Morning, Fred! Marvelous party. Please sit. How's the back?"

"That obvious, huh?" Gingerly, Rudolph took his seat. Dede sat next to him, rolled her chair back and pivoted it to face him.

"To anyone who's had back problems, and who hasn't?"

"So what's the answer?"

"Tried stretching exercises?"

"And massage. And acupuncture. And chiropractors. Ice. Heat. Ultra sound. You name it, I've tried it."

And there, suddenly, was an unplanned opening for her. "There's a doctor at New York Hospital who says the problem is tension and the cure is learning to relax. Take it easy. Don't work so hard. Don't worry. He'd charge you hundreds for that; I give it to you for nothing."

Fred looked at her quizzically. "You taking it easy, Diana?"

"If I had your money I would."

"Money a problem for you? Poor Diana."

She shook her head. "Getting off the treadmill is the problem. Isn't it for all of us?"

"What would I do with myself if I didn't go down into the salt mines each day?"

"Is this Fred Rudolph, America's great collector of minimal art, talking? Is this Fred Rudolph, board member of the Israel Museum, talking?"

"Vice-chairman. Since last month."

"Vice-chairman? Well, congratulations! Is that going to leave you any time for landmarks preservation? And how about that boat down in Florida? Doesn't sound much like a guy who doesn't know what to do with himself."

"Hobbies. Love 'em. But it's not the same as work."

So it went, she telling him to smell the flowers, he warning her he had no intention of slowing down to smell anything. Until Fred pulled a surprise of his own.

"Frankly," he began, "I thought you might not want to meet with me at all."

"Really? And why is that."

"I just couldn't imagine your wanting to get into any new business thing while your mind was on politics."

"Hobbies. Love 'em. But it's not the same as work." She smiled at him. He didn't smile back.

"As you know, Diana, I'm involved in politics a bit myself, but I stick to the money end. One thing I've learned: if you think of politics as a hobby, you're best out of it."

"Who said I was in it?"

"Aha! So I was wrong." Now, Fred, bad back and all, scrunched forward on the chair. "After you agreed to meet, I said to myself, I wonder if maybe Diana is not thinking real estate at all? Suppose, I asked myself, she has another agenda in mind: a run for, let's say, the Senate! And she wants me to back her, in a big way, a serious way. And I began wondering what Diana might offer if I agreed to back her . . . in a big way, a serious way. Which could pretty much assure her the nomination . . ."

Sitting in her office later, Dede had to acknowledge that indeed it was Fred who'd come up with the surprise. His offer was simple: She gets the Democratic nomination for Senate; he gets to run the merged companies. The idea of being a Senator suddenly began to take on a tangible reality. She felt herself liking it.

Interrupting her thought came a call from Aunt May down in Palm Beach. Aunt May was her stepmother, the second wife of her dad, William Penrose Miller, who was 76 now and retired. After World War II, Bill Miller had gone into construction on Long Island, at first building houses and then adding brokerage services. In the postwar building boom he prospered modestly, but then he was a modest man, less interested in building an empire than in spending time with his family, especially with his young daughter after his first wife died. Two years after she died, Bill Miller was remarried to May Roberts, a widow the Millers had known as a neighbor. She'd seemed a kind of aunt even while Dede's mother was alive, so to call her Aunt May was natural and easy.

When Dede opened the Manhattan office, her father began to phase himself into retirement, dividing his time between a condo in Palm Beach and their house in Westhampton. In recent years his pattern was to drive south right after Thanksgiving and stay there until mid April. It was about the trip north that Dede thought Aunt May was calling. She was wrong. Bill Miller had been having severe stomach pains that just wouldn't go away, and May had finally gotten him to a doctor. The preliminary diagnosis: maybe an ulcer, maybe worse. There'd have to be more tests, perhaps an exploratory operation. Her father hadn't wanted to tell her at all, but May thought she should know, especially because it would delay their trip north.

Dede's immediate response was that they should come up to New York to see doctors here. His father would have none of that. He liked their internist, had confidence in him. Besides, he hated the city.

"I'll come down there." Dede said.

"Not now," May replied. "He'd just be alarmed. First let's see what they find. Let's hope there'll be no reason for you to come down at all."

CHAPTER 11

When Herb finished reading the letter, he kept it clutched tightly in his hand, until finally, realizing what he was doing, he put it on the table and started smoothing it. This was a document that had to last the rest of his life.

For a couple of moments he did nothing but stare at the letter and at his own right hand touching it, suddenly noticing how many freckles—liver spots—whatever they were—were on that heavily tanned hand. It looked like his father's, his father's as an old man living in the Florida sun. Jake's hands would never get to look like that. They would stay young forever. Like the picture.

The silver-framed eight-by-ten black-and-white photo of Jake that stood in his den was the same one that had been in their room in the Bronx. It was a typical photo taken after basic training, a time when GIs were feeling tough and hardened and cocky, their smiles not yet shadowed by what lay ahead. So innocent, Herb thought. And so young.

The ringing of the phone snapped him to attention. He got to his feet, opened the sliding doors leading into the living room and headed for the phone. Marian was always leaving those doors open; he was always closing them.

"It might rain," he'd say, and she'd become exasperated.

"It won't rain! This is California!"

She was right about that and about what she was really saying: that he was 30 years out of New York, yet he still lived there.

He carried the phone back out onto the deck, sliding the door shut behind him. It was Joe Wiggins.

"Where are you?" he asked. "Hiding in the bushes, watching for my mail to arrive? I just got your letter . . . no, no, it's not a bad time; it's a very good time."

Herb listened, nodding and staring at the letter in his hand. When Joe stopped, Herb said, "I got another letter today, Joe, from someone you know . . . knew. It doesn't matter. Another time. What matters is, I've been thinking about it. I want to do it, Joe. I'm going to do it." They talked for a long time before he hung up, leaving Wiggins startled but happy.

Wiggins was 73; 40 years ago he'd seen the end of big bands coming and started teaching saxophone and clarinet while putting himself through college. He'd used the network of musicians to get his first teaching job and in time worked his way up to become head of the Long Valley State Jazz Studies Department, one of the best in the country. Now retired, he was fund raising for them.

Herb had intended to contribute, but what he'd just promised on the phone had startled him as much as it had Joe. Herb heard himself saying he'd give two million dollars toward the new building, which would be named the Jacob Ellinson Jazz Studies Center.

He suddenly wished Marian were here to share this with him. Five years ago, he'd given a half million to the synagogue his father had gone to in Miami Beach. Marty Ellinson, who as a young man had gone to synagogue twice a year, on Rosh Hashanah and Yom Kippur, had as an old man become religious. Well, maybe Herb would, too. He'd worried about what Marian would think when he told her about the half million.

"It's not our last dollar, you know," he'd said.

That had hurt her. "Oh Herb, for God's sake, I'm proud of you. Your parents were so proud of you; you were such a good son."

"I was all they had. I guess I was always trying to make up for Jake." Five years ago, and he still remembered it, he'd gone into his . . . thing. Probably that had helped push her away. Probably he should have stopped, but he'd kept going. "You know, I never could make up for Jake. I was at their bedsides when they died. Pop . . . when was it, '70? And ma, three years ago. My pop's last words were: something, something . . . 'you and Jake.' And the last thing ma said—the absolute last thing—was 'Jacob . . . Jacob.' At least with pop, I got co-billing." He'd said it with a smile.

Her answer had showed a touch of anger under the patience. "You were a wonderful son. No one could have been better."

"But they never got over Jake."

"They?" The anger had bubbled up. "For God's sake, Herb! How about you?"

"Maybe if we'd had kids, Emily and I . . . I know it must get on your nerves . . ."

She'd tried a laugh. "Some wives are jealous of other women. Did you ever know one jealous of a man who's been . . . gone . . . 40 years?" She almost never spoke Jake's name. Then she'd looked at him and sighed. He'd wondered then if it was getting to be too much for her, this man 16 years older than she, this man and his dead brother. "He was a great musician. And your hero, and your parents' favorite. It happens in every family, there's always a favorite."

"It's not that they didn't love me . . ."

"Of course not! Your mom was always so full of joy when you arrived. It was all there in her face. And so proud of you."

"Maybe I'm jealous of him because he died at a moment of perfection. He was young and strong and handsome. Unspoiled. He'll always be that; he'll never see wattles under his chin and liver spots on his hands and all the rest that goes with getting old. And he believed in something. It was easy, right, back then. Nobody thought it was sappy."

"How many million people died in that war?" she'd asked. "Is that in all those war books you read?"

"Forty, fifty million. Only 290,000 Americans. We were lucky."

"Lucky. Only 290,000 Americans."

"It's crazy! I know it! And lots of them died horribly. And you say, maybe for me, in a band, travelling around, getting overseas, with the excitement but not the danger . . . For me, it was a great time. But read the books. For those guys in combat, the times were awful, not only the killing, but the cold, the heat, the rain, the snow, the mud, the sickness, the pain, the fear. It was miserable. But it was the most memorable thing they ever did! The thing they were proudest of! And even the people back home! You don't remember; you were just a baby. There was such spirit. Because the people knew who they were for and who they were against. They had something to believe in!"

Just thinking about it agitated him. He got up and walked to the edge of his deck, and stared at the placid ocean. We were right to believe in it, he told himself. The death was terrible; ask the Ellinsons. You never got over it. Terrible, but not meaningless! Not that war. Don't let anyone try to tell him that war didn't make a difference. There was a difference between us and the Nazis and the Japs, a reason we should win and not they. Sure there was a lot of propaganda, but it wasn't all just propaganda. There was something to believe in.

Herb turned around, walked back, sat down, told himself to stop talking to someone who wasn't there. Like an old man. He thought of those brave kids who'd study at the Jacob Ellinson Jazz Studies Center, those kids swimming against a tidal wave of rock. He didn't know how they could do it, growing up in an age where no one had anything to believe in. What did kids have to care about now? A new Mercedes? A condo in Aspen? A little more coke up their noses? That drivel they call music? How could life be precious to them, when that's all they had to live for?

Life was precious to Jake.

Finally, Marian's patience would give out.

"Herb, do you envy him everything? Everything?" she'd said. "Do you even wish you'd died back then, like him?"

"I thought about it. The answer is no. For lots of reasons, For one thing, if I had, I wouldn't have you."

She'd stared at him as if she didn't quite believe it.

"It's true!" he'd insisted. "It's also true I'm glad I was around to help my folks."

"But you would have traded your life for his if you could have. Wouldn't you? And you really believe that if your parents had the choice . . ."

He remembered how that had hit him, how long it had taken him to answer. "I guess if . . . no, I won't even say it. Their prayer always was, let both sons live. They never would have thought of making a choice."

"Then I'm more selfish than they were. I'm glad it was you who lived."

"You would have loved Jake," he'd told her, trying to be light about it. "He could have taken you away from me anytime."

"Oh, Herb!" She'd become furious. "Why do you think so little of yourself? He died. That was terrible. You lived and made a wonderful success of your life. Stop measuring yourself against him! Stop asking for his approval! He's dead!" And she'd stormed off, pushing open the sliding doors he'd just closed.

Thinking back to five years ago, he realized that was the beginning of the change, a change that left him wondering what he should do about her, and himself. Now he had a project: a woman who, once upon a time, Jake had loved. June Hopkins, from Long Island. Who, once upon a time, had perhaps been pregnant. After all, what else could Jake have been talking about in the letter? Herb would find her. But how? Al Breecher had sent the letter to her and it came back. Where would she be? Was she dead or alive?

Again, Herb stood up. This time he ambled down to the beach, back around the side of the house, then inside, into the den. To the picture, which was where, he knew, he'd been headed all the time. One thing he'd never told

Marian was how accustomed he'd become to talking to the picture.

And he always got an answer. It was in Jake's smile, which was saying something Jake had actually said so often.

"You can do it, kid."

That's what he got from Jake that he never got from his parents. They were fearful people, people of small expectations. The children of immigrants who still had their parents' mentality: that this country didn't belong to them. Jake was a new generation, a real American. He believed there was nothing he couldn't do.

Herb stared at the self-confident soldier, 21 years old, face frozen in that fraction of a second nearly half a century ago.

"I can do it, Jake. I will do it."

Jake smiled at him. Herb stared back, still asking for his big brother's approval.

CHAPTER 12

Winter, early 1941

President Roosevelt announces a program to build 200 freighters, "Liberty ships," to help Britain. The German U-boat force is still small, only 22, but sinks 76 ships in January alone. The Blitz continues to batter Britain.

In Washington, the War Department authorizes the formation of the Provisional Parachute Group at Fort Benning, Georgia, to be commanded by Colonel William Lee.

Hit records: "We Three," the Ink Spots; "There I Go," Vaughn Monroe; "Song Of The Volga Boatman," Glenn Miller; "Amapola," Jimmy Dorsey, vocal by Bob Eberly and Helen O'Connell.

It is a gray, ice-cold day in January when Jake finally escapes the goodbyes of his parents and heads for what they call the subway, but which in their part of the Bronx is actually elevated. He carries a large suitcase in one hand and his trumpet case in the other. Herb, who is walking him to the station, has a smaller valise and a paper bag with sandwiches, fruit, and cookies prepared by Millie.

Herb's hands are freezing through his woolen gloves. Jake, wearing neither gloves nor hat, doesn't seem to mind the cold. And he walks at a pace that Herb, with a far lighter load, has trouble matching.

Herb looks over at his brother. At 17 and a half he's grown to within an inch of Jake's five-feet-ten, but he never can escape the feeling he is looking up at Jake.

"You scared?"

"Who me?" Jake gives a tight laugh. "Just peeing in my pants, that's all. New things scare me, Herbie. They scare the hell out of me. That's why I do 'em."

"Why? If they scare you?"

"You know the difference between a coward and a brave man, Herbie?"

"One is scared and the other isn't?" The thing that frightens Herb more than anything else is making a mistake in front of his brother.

"No, Herbie. They're both scared, but the brave man does what he has to anyway; the coward doesn't. If nothing scares you, that doesn't make you brave, it makes you a nut! Now, you know what your job is, kid?"

"What, Jake?" Herb asks eagerly.

"It's up to you to cheer 'em up, remind 'em it's only a four-week trip and then I'm back . . . for a while. Tell 'em some of those bad jokes."

"You're the one tells the bad jokes, Jake."

"Well, this is your chance, kid! Tell 'em the one about the German piccolo player."

"The piccolo player?"

"You know. You've got to tell it with a German accent. Dere I vas mit my goddamn piccolo!"

Herb looks puzzled. "How does it go?"

"He's complaining. He says when the orchestra plays for dukes and princes, if they like the music, they fill the musicians' instruments with silver or gold. So the piano player does real well, and the tuba player, et cetera. And dere I vas mit my goddam piccolo . . . See?"

"Yeah, it can't hold much gold, but what's so . . ."

"It's not over yet, Herbie! Then this one prince hates the music and tells them to shove their instruments up their asses. But the piano player can't, it's too big. So is the tuba. And dere I vas mit my goddam piccolo!"

"You want me to tell that joke to ma?"

Jake just laughs. They are at the long iron staircase of the elevated station. He turns to his younger brother. "I'll send you a postcard with another one."

"It'll have to be short, on a postcard."

"I'll write small. Or I'll send two cards."

He sets down his big suitcase, and with the trumpet case still in one hand, puts his arms around his brother. "Take care of everything at home. See you in four weeks."

"Yeah." Herb doesn't know what to say. "You take care of yourself. Don't forget to write to ma. She'll be worried."

Herb feels the strong arms of the brother who embodies everything in his world that is wonderful, who is adventurous, talented, strong, and despite what he says, fearless. He says, "You'll be great, Jake."

Jake lets go of his brother, "I'll blow their brains out. Either theirs or mine. Now give me that."

He reaches for the valise. "I'll carry it up," says Herb. "You've got . . ."

"No, no, kid, it's OK." He grabs the big suitcase and the bag of food in one hand, the smaller one and the trumpet case in the other. "You take care of everything, OK?" Without waiting for an answer, he turns and starts up the staircase. Herb watches him take the stairs two at a time. Then he is through the doors and out of sight.

On the train from the Bronx to midtown Manhattan where he is to board the band bus, Jake softly whistles "How High The Moon," a tune Benny Goodman recorded the year before; it suits Jake's spirits. He is soaring with excitement, the fear he told Herb about is submerged in it. Buddy Benson isn't the Goodman band, but it isn't a bad group either, especially if Jake can work his way into Buddy's Boys, the sextet within the band that plays up-tempo numbers. That isn't going to be easy. The sextet has trumpet, trombone, and sax or clarinet, plus the back line of piano, drums and bass, and of the band's three trumpet players, Jake is decidedly the junior man, and also, he knows, the best man. Swede Olsen, a man of about 30, is first trumpet. Swede has beautiful tone and great phrasing on ballads, but he doesn't swing. The third trumpet, Ted Cowan, a couple of years younger than Swede, is the more likely competition. Cowan is the "hot" trumpet, who solos on the up-tempo numbers. He has a lot of flash and screaming high notes, but he can't improvise worth a damn. What he does instead is use other people's solos, which fans don't hear or care about, what with all the high notes and gimmicks he throws in. Jake will blow him away if he gets the chance.

So there is confidence mixed with the fear as he walks up the subway steps into the daylight at 50th street and Broadway and heads toward the bus with the four big B's on it. When he sees the musicians standing alongside the bus, talking and laughing, all knowing each other so well, so sure of themselves, he feels a jolt of apprehension. Joe Wiggins introduces him around.

The Buddy Benson Big Band is made up of three trumpets, three trombones, two altos, two tenors, plus piano, drums, bass and guitar. Then there are Cindy Laine, the girl singer, and Buddy himself, who once was a fair clarinet player, but now holds the instrument in his hands more than he plays it.

Jake recognizes most of the men, knows that some of them are damned good. Johnny Black, the piano player, was fired by Goodman, but then so were some of the best men in the business. Benny is famous as a hard man to work for. The story goes that he always has three bands: the current one, the one he's just fired and the one he's about to hire. But having Goodman alumni speaks well for a band. Though Goodman may fire many a good musician, he rarely hires a bad one.

Swede Olsen gives Jake an easy hello and a big meathook of a hand to shake. He squeezes Jake's hand hard with his thick fingers, and Jake squeezes back. Olsen looks at him, surprised. "Hey, you got a hand there, kid!"

"You, too, Swede. And you've got the sweetest tone in the business." Swede likes that. Jake will get along fine with him.

Ted Cowan is another matter. He is a short beefy man, with a thick neck and a florid face that gets theatrically red when he hits high notes; he feels threatened by Jake, and it shows in his eyes. As they shake hands, Jake suddenly feels sorry for him. I don't blame you, Jake thinks as he watches Cowan, You're afraid I'm gonna blow you out of your chair, and you're right.

The 14 musicians will ride on the bus, along with the bags, instruments and equipment. The driver doubles as band boy, looking after the gear. Benson himself travels in his own car, with the band manager, who drives, and Cindy Laine. She is a pale pretty blonde, an appealing combination of the schoolgirl and the sexpot, but none of the men minds her travelling separately; having her on the bus would inhibit the freedom of their conversation, which is free indeed. Pat Riordan, rotund but called Bones, as many trombone players are, says things like, "You're not supposed to swear in front of ladies—or Cindy, either." Impugning her virtue is a running gag with the guys, only Jake doesn't know how much of it is kidding, how much true, and how much sour grapes.

Bones is the band wit and prankster; every band has at least one. Some of his practical jokes are legends, like the time he called 30 bass players, told each he had work for him and asked him to meet him on a midtown street corner. Then he stood and watched from a nearby window as the 30 of them, with their bulky instruments, stood milling around on the corner, until someone caught on. Bones enjoyed that one even after the musicians' local ruled he had to give each of the 30 a day's pay at scale.

Jake goes around shaking hands, finding it hard to believe he's one of them, a real professional musician, in a big band. As they're about to board, a Buick sedan pulls up, driven by band manager Fred Handel, with Cindy Laine alongside him and Buddy Benson in the back, sitting like a potentate, his jowls soft over the stiff collar of his white shirt. Benson waves to his musicians without getting out of the car, but Cindy Laine jumps out and goes around hugging them. The disparaging is forgotten; they seem genuinely glad to see her.

Up to now, Jake has seen her only on the bandstand, in a formal gown, elaborately coiffed and made up. Without the makeup, her pale hair pulled back in a ponytail, a sweater and pleated skirt replacing the gown, she looks astonishingly young to him, younger than he, though she's been with the band for three years. She is also much smaller than he thought, barely 5-3, and when he takes the hand she holds out to him, it feels as small and delicate as a child's. Holding her hand, looking down at her, takes his breath away.

She looks up into his light blue eyes and feels the first shudder of excitement she's felt around the band since those very first days when every moment was romantic. And romance is what she wants. Cindy Laine, born Laskiewicz to a Polish father and Irish mother in Springfield, Massachusetts, showed singing talent when she was 10 and couldn't wait to use it to move on to a more exciting life than the one at home. To be a band singer was her dream, but now that she's been at it for three years, it's become as routine as being at home, and a lot more strenuous. Being on the road with 15 men is about as romantic as having no man. Same old wisecracking musicians; same old Buddy Benson, who pretends to protect her like a father but really has a thing for her. If there's one thing she knows, it's when a man has a thing for her. Now there's this good-looking new trumpet player with the strong handshake and the blue eyes.

"Hi," she says, "welcome to the Buddy Benson traveling circus. I hope you're going to play pretty for us." She leans into him and makes more of a show of confidentiality than Jake thinks she has to. But he loves it. She smells of talcum powder, like a baby. He'd like her to stay real close for a while so he can keep on smelling her.

"We could use some new blood in this band," she says, and she grins at him.

He grins back. "I've got plenty of new blood. In fact, it's all new."

She turns to Wiggins. "Joe, this . . . boy . . . bears watching."

"Just keep watching, miss," says Jake, who's thinking that this is off to a very good start.

"I don't get to ride with the menagerie," she says. "I'm in the cage with the lion, the king of the beasts. But I'll see you when we get to Pittsburgh."

"And I'll play pretty for you."

"We'll see." Then she decides she's given Jake enough, and turns away, but not before flashing him another big grin. Maybe, she says to herself as she goes off, this won't be just another road trip.

"Watch it, kid," Joe warns the new trumpet player.

"She's cute," Jake answers.

"Like the sign says, danger."

"I thought it said, dangerous curves."

"Listen, Jake . . ."

"I hear you, Joe. I like danger. And I like curves."

"The road" is an apt term for touring. Whether going by bus, car or train, a band seems to spend more time traveling than doing anything else. Occasionally they get to spend a week, or even two, in one place—the better known the band the more likely the long stay. But more often it's a few days, most often a one-night stand. Bus rides between jobs seldom take less than four or five hours and until the union limits single legs to 400 miles, they can run over 12 hours. And on the roads connecting small towns, even a 400-mile trip can take a bone-rattling ten hours or longer.

The typical routine is to play the job, climb aboard the bus, try to get some sleep on the road, arrive at the new town, check into the hotel or rooming house, maybe try to grab a nap, then set up at the ballroom or pavilion or theater and play. If they are staying in that town for a second night's work, or have the next night off, the men may get a decent night's sleep. If they have to move on to the next job, it's back on the bus and on the road. It is a young man's game. In the entire group, Benson himself is the only man who's near 40; three or four others are around 30, the rest in their 20s.

Jake puts his head back on the seat and closes his eyes, remembers the smell of Cindy's talc. He can't wait to get to Pittsburgh. They arrive in the dark, at about 7, pull up to a little hotel named the Eldorado. The musicians grumble about it. They gripe incessantly; it will prepare Jake for the army. To Jake the place doesn't look so bad. His room is small, neat, its rose-patterned wallpaper fading into a pale and pleasant pink. There is a single bed with iron headboard, a maple dresser, a chair of dark wood with seat upholstered in gray and red, a sink, and, two doors down the hall, the toilet and bath. He drops his stuff, hardly has time for a quick dinner with Joe and two other musicians before they are on their way to Jake's first night of work.

The Three Rivers Club is a roadhouse on the outskirts of Pittsburgh, a 20-minute bus ride from the hotel. It is a huge, sprawling place that can hold 300 people at tables around a large semi-circular dance floor. Its decor is vaguely rustic, knotty pine, with ten-gallon hats nailed to the walls and wagon wheels of various sizes hung from the ceiling.

The band is booked into the Three Rivers for two nights, Friday and Saturday, and a national radio hookup is in place to broadcast its music both nights. The 4Bs plays mostly ballads with vocals, which have been successful on a level one notch below that of bands like Goodman, Miller, and Dorsey. On a Friday night in early 1941, even though the effects of the depression linger, people like to go out and dance; the big roadhouse is jammed when the musicians start filing onto the bandstand.

The band uniform is royal blue blazers, pale blue slacks, white shirts, and rose-colored bow ties. Although some of the men sneer at them, Jake is proud to put his on. Buddy wears a white dinner jacket and maroon slacks, and Cindy, no longer the pale blonde girl with a ponytail, now glitters in a strapless gold gown which pushes up her small breasts to make more of them than is there. Her golden hair is looped and coiled on top of her head, her fair skin highlighted by rouge and lipstick and her green eyes accented by eye shadow and mascara.

Her style is typical of the girl singers of the day, unadorned and cute, but as Jake looks at her he realizes she's not selling vocals, she's selling romance, fantasy. And he for one is ready to buy. He accosts her on the bandstand.

"How could anyone not play pretty for you?" he says, "You look . . . sensational!"

She takes a couple of beats before answering. "Thanks. Just another night on the job . . . Jack."

"Jake."

"Oh, right," she says, and starts to turn away.

"It's OK," Jake replies quickly. "Don't apologize now. Save it for later, when I buy you a drink."

Her eyes widen, then she lets out a short laugh and turns away. She hasn't said yes, Jake thinks as he takes his seat. Nor has she said no.

Waiting for the start of the first set, Jake shuffles through the music on his stand, though he has looked it over ten times on the bus. He keeps shaking spit out of his trumpet, though he knows there isn't any in there, keeps bringing the mouthpiece to his lips, blowing softly to keep his embouchure warmed up.

Swede looks over at him. "Relax, kid, you'll be all right."

"Yeah, sure. I know it." He blows a few more notes, gives the horn another shake, looks out at the customers staring expectantly up at the band. Jake has seen it many times before; they are waiting for the magic to begin. Now he is one of the magicians.

It isn't until he actually plays the first notes of the first tune, "You'll Never Know," that he begins to relax, and then he gets swept along by the sound, by the collaborative creation of music. Knowing he's part of it gives him chills. This is what he's dreamed of, being up on the bandstand, the musicians around him—guys who've played with Goodman!—the people out there looking toward the bandstand, listening for the magic.

By the time they get to "All The Things You Are," Jake is ready to show off a little. He has a small solo, only four bars, but he gives it a touch of that silvery Harry James brilliance. Cindy Laine, standing there, silently rehearsing the lyrics she will sing on the next chorus, looks at him. She thinks he's good, he can tell from the look. He winks at her quickly, and just as quickly, she turns away.

After a 45-minute opening set, the band gets a 15-minute break, and most of them go out into a long hallway next to the ballroom to smoke. Jake looks for Cindy, spots her talking with Benson. He waits. When the bandleader moves away, Jake moves in. He doesn't want her to get away.

Chatting with Buddy, Cindy keeps an eye on Jake. When Benson leaves, she stands in place, pretends to be lost in thought, pretends not to see him, all the while making herself available, giving him time to get to her. Come on Jake, she says to herself, come on.

"Hey, Cindy, how was I?"

"You blended in OK, Jack."

He grins at her. Now she's toying with him, which he likes.

"Jake," he says. "But that's all right. Call me anything you like . . . as long as you don't call me late to breakfast." He heard a drummer on a job say that a few months back and he liked it.

"Oh, Jake," she says, opening her green eyes wide. "You're a wisecracker. I didn't think you were."

"Oh yes you did."

"Now look . . ." She's trying sternness. That's OK with him, too.

"You didn't tell me what you thought of my solo."

"Gosh, I didn't notice you had one."

She won't beat him; Jake is as sure of himself now as he was playing the solo, "Oh yes, you did. 'All The Things You Are.' I was playing it for you."

She nods, not quite sure how to handle this new boy. "Wasn't that sweet of you."

"I thought so." He looks straight at her and quotes the lyrics. "You are the promised kiss of springtime that makes the lonely winter seem long."

"I know the words," she says. "I sing them. You noticed, I suppose."

He's winning; he can feel it. "How could I not? It was beautiful. You're beautiful. The promised kiss of springtime."

"It's still winter, Jake. Pay attention."

"Yes, but springtime is coming. The promised kiss." He goes back to the lyrics. "You are the angel glow that lights a star." Then he parodies. "We'll have our drink tonight at the hotel bar."

She makes a show of her amused disgust. But as she turns away, she cannot help smiling. This is a little like what she used to dream of back in Springfield.

He plays out the rest of the night, saying to himself: she'll be there. He walks into the bar, sits on a stool; it's a strange milieu to him. If the drinking age is 21 in Pennsylvania, he can be stopped, which would be embarrassing to a man on the make. He tries to look old, turning a pair of hard eyes on the bartender, who is not the least bit interested in challenging his age.

"What'll it be?"

"A beer." Jake tries to sound like he's said it a hundred times.

As the bartender draws the beer, Jake looks around. It's a run-down place, dark wood and old leather, but welcoming, warmer than the rest of the hotel. At both ends of the room and along part of the opposite wall are rows of dimly lit booths. At the moment only one is occupied. In it he can make out Billy Parkins, the guitar player, along with one of the trombonists, Bert somebody—Jake was introduced to him so quickly he didn't catch his last name—and a third man Jake can't see but figures must be in the band, too.

It's just as well, Jake tells himself, that Cindy isn't there for his first sip of beer; he doesn't really like it, grimaces at the bitterness of it, then waits, tries a second sip, which is no better. He hopes she won't be too long; the less beer the better. Ten minutes later she climbs onto the stool next to his, saying nothing.

"I'm glad to see you," he tells her.

Her eyes earnest, she launches into a speech. "I feel I should warn you. You have to be very careful about some of the people in the band. They're just awful, they'll tell such terrible stories about people. Stories that aren't true at all."

She is begging him to believe her, and he does. "But why . . ." he asks.

"They're jealous."

"Jealous of who?"

"Would you order me a whiskey sour, please?"

"Oh. Sure." The bartender is there waiting, and nods before Jake can ask.

"You don't know what it's like to be the only woman on the road with all those men." Cindy wants to tell her story. When the drink is put in front of her, she takes a sip without missing a beat.

"Some of them think that just because you're in this business, that means you're . . . which I am *not*."

"Why would they think that?" Jake is drunk with her nearness, her smell, her eyes, her pale hair and skin. With her. "Anyone can see you're not."

She is grateful for that. "Some men are just not very nice, and if you don't do what they want, they try to get even by saying nasty things."

"Nobody said anything."

"Well, I'm just warning you. My reputation is very important to me, and you mustn't believe. Promise?" Their hands are very close on the bar, and she puts her left hand on his right. He looks down; her hand is white and soft and small, barely covering half of his. On the fourth finger is a cheap silver friendship ring with a small zircon in it. On the bandstand her bare shoulders and the tops of her breasts arouse him. Now the hand and its pitiful little ring arouse his protectiveness.

"Anyone gives you trouble . . ." He balls up his fist.

"Oh, thank you!" The green eyes open wider. He is ready to take on Joe Louis for her.

"How old are you?" he asks.

"Twenty-two," she answers.

"I'm 23," he offers, lying to match what he figures is her lie.

"This your first band?"

"Nah," he says. "Played with lots of 'em around New York."

"Oh. Which ones?"

"Uh . . . none you ever heard of."

"Well, Jake. It's Jake not Jack, right?"

"Right."

"See? Jake, you're a real good trumpet player. I mean it. And I'm glad you're my friend. I need a friend." As she says it, she squeezes his hand with hers.

He wonders if she's playing some game, but with the arrogance of youth, he doesn't care. She will fall for him. She makes his heart beat fast, and therefore she will fall for him—it has to happen. As he puts his big hand on top of her tiny one, their heads are very close together, so close he thinks he can hear her breathing. He would like to time his inhaling to match her exhaling, so he can suck in her breath.

CHAPTER 13

On a Thursday night Tru told Dede he was going out to Southampton the next morning for the weekend. "Major client. Wants to play a round at the National. Want to come?"

"Oh, I can't. Too much work. I wish I'd known sooner." She was startled; weekends were a time they tried to save for the family.

"He called me this morning to say he was coming in . . . from Cincinnati, of all places. Couldn't get out of it. It's a bother."

She thought his casualness a bit too elaborate, idly wondered how much it bothered him, if it would have bothered him more had she said, yes, I'll go.

He was still asleep when she left for the office at seven the next morning. She plowed through her work, not taking calls, not stopping for lunch, waving Rita off when she offered to order a sandwich. At about 3, Rita buzzed to say that a Mr. Kenneth Glass was on the line. Automatically, the words "take a message" came out, before she corrected herself.

"No, put him on."

"Just wanted to see if, at the end of your work day, you wanted to spend an hour being asked questions."

"I've got so much work," she replied, "I'll have to say no."

"Angry about the other night?"

"No." But her voice was cold; he heard it.

"Tell you what, here's my home number. I'm here working. If you find you have some time later, give me a call."

She quit work at 7:45, went back to her apartment, poured herself a glass of white wine, started looking through the *Wall Street Journal*, slapped it down, faced the fact that Tru's departure bothered her more than she'd supposed. She got to her feet, found Ken Glass's phone number. As she dialed she looked at her watch. It was nearly 8:30. On the third ring, she heard his deep voice saying hello.

"It's Diana Miller. I realize this is rather late . . ."
"Not at all. Have you eaten?"

They met at the Madison Pub at 9. She had changed into jeans and decided to leave them on, threw on a blue blazer over her T-shirt. When she walked in, he was already seated in a booth, reporter's notebook on the table in front of him. She had to walk down four steps from the entrance and as she did, she saw him examining her, spotting the jeans, taking them in. It reminded her of going off to high school dances, walking downstairs in the Garden City house, with her date waiting, watching her while she watched him watch, so wanting his approval. She hadn't felt like a high school girl in a while.

He got to his feet. "Hi. Dynamo in jeans." He put out a big hand. She took it.

"My Armanis are all at the cleaners."

"Leave them there. You can't improve on that." In the dim light she could feel what she hoped he couldn't see, a blush. *New York Times Magazine*, she reminded herself. Watch out.

"Thanks. Is a blue work shirt the writer's uniform?" She sat across from him, glad to have the jeans tucked away under the table.

"No, just very useful. I save a buck and a half a shirt. Take them right out of the dryer and put them on without ironing. Can you tell?"

"Not at all. Except for the wrinkles."

His grin crinkled.

"But you look terrific in them."

"The least you could say after what I said about the jeans," he replied, then hesitated. "You are not turning out to be what I thought."

"Explain."

"How does it get turned so you're always interviewing me?"

"Perhaps because you say more provocative things."

"Well, say some provocative things."

"Are you going to pick on me again?"

"I am sorry about the other night. Glad you didn't tell me to buzz off."

"Look, let's be honest. You want the story, for your reasons, I want it for mine. But I don't want to be savaged. It's so easy to make a woman in business look bad. Hard. Aggressive."

"I don't savage people. Not even capitalists. Why not trust me?"

"You know and I know," she said, "that sensationalism sells."

"And here I am wearing wrinkled work shirts. Think I wouldn't rather be wearing Turnbull & Asser? And having dinner at the Four Seasons?"

"Would you rather?"

"Really? No."

"You seem quite content."

"No use kvetching."

"Doing what?"

"A Jewish word. Means to complain."

"You're Jewish."

"Yes. Didn't you know that?"

"You don't look it."

"What does it look like?"

"Don't. Please."

He leaned to her. "Look, don't take this the wrong way. It would not astonish me if you had a touch of well-mannered anti-Semitism in you. Lots of well-mannered people do."

"Nearly half my brokers are . . ." She stopped herself short, "Yes, maybe I have. Add it to the list. Can't wait to see it in print."

"I said, trust me. Now let's eat, drink, and be honest."

He ordered a hamburger and a beer, she a spinach salad and a glass of white wine.

"Another salad. Is that how you keep that absolutely splendid figure?" he asked.

"I do eat carefully. Which is not to say I accept the premise of the question."

"You have a marvelous figure. You're also extremely good-looking."

"Please don't."

"What a funny combination you are. So businesslike, so . . . almost arrogant. Then tender, like a girl. I'd imagine you'd be awfully accustomed to physical compliments. Yet you practically blush."

"You may not believe this, Kenneth, but no one's complimented me that way in a long time."

"I do find it hard to believe. I imagine that every morning your husband would say to himself, how did I get so lucky as to wake up next to *her*?"

"Please change the subject."

"All right. Tell me about the real estate business."

She spent an hour on it; it was blessedly neutral, calmed the ruffled waters.

Later, when they were standing out on Madison Avenue, she said, "I don't know what to say about the . . . God, I don't even know what to call it . . . the Jewish . . . thing."

"As long as you don't burn a cross on my lawn." She started to look upset, so he added quickly. "I don't have a lawn."

"That is not funny."

"What am I supposed to say, Diana? Don't be an anti-Semite or I'll never talk to you again? If I said that to everyone who had a touch of anti-Semitism, it would cut my circle of friends drastically, including a few Jews. Let's just go by it."

"All right." She put out her hand. He enveloped it in his, held it as he said, "I'll look forward to talking with you soon, Diana. I really mean that." Finally he let go.

Walking home, she thought, uncomfortable or not, how lively conversation with him was, how bright he was. Jews were so smart, she said to herself. And just what was that, she wondered, a compliment or anti-Semitism?

Back in the apartment, there was a message from Aunt May. Please call, no matter how late.

Early the next morning, on the first flight she could get, she was on her way to Florida. Her father had stomach cancer; it was widespread and inoperable, and though radiation and chemotherapy were planned, the prognosis was dim.

Her father. The man who'd taught her how to swim in the backyard pool, who, much as he hated "the city," had taken her to Central Park, the Bronx Zoo, Radio City Music Hall, who'd faithfully attended her tennis matches. The man who'd tried so hard and so well to be father and mother to her, who'd helped her with her homework, pored over those picture books of World War II with her, told her about the war and his own army experience, which was limited to stateside duty as a supply officer.

Like so many children, Dede had watched her father go from a big strapping man who towered over her to a middle-aged man her own height to a stooped septuagenarian who looked up at her. But she wasn't prepared for the man she saw in the private room at the hospital in Palm Beach. Aunt May warned her when she met her in the corridor. It wasn't enough. This man, sedated, festooned with tubes, barely conscious, was a man beyond saving. She stood alongside the bed and held her father's gnarled, spotted hand.

"Dad?"

Bill Miller opened his eyes, looked around, closed them as if the effort were too much and then opened them again to stare at her. Because of the tubes, he couldn't speak, but she thought she saw a passing sign of recognition in his eyes. Then he weakly squeezed her hand. Gently, she squeezed back.

For minutes, hours, she wasn't sure, she just sat holding his hand. I'm no good at this, she said to herself, then realized few people were. How do you handle this? Dede was used to dealing with problems, finding answers, but there were no answers this time. At last she felt her father's weak grip on her hand relax. She could see the regular breathing of a sleeping man; she patted the hand and took hers away. Then she turned to May, who was sitting in a chair behind her.

"It's the painkillers," May explained. "They'll cut them down soon, and you'll be able to talk to him."

Dede stayed a week, spending long hours at her father's bedside while trying to run a business over the telephone. Her decision to go back to New York came after a talk with her father's surgeon, a small dapper Southerner named Horner who, May assured him, had interned at Johns Hopkins and was good as anyone in the country. Bill Miller had only a few months to live, Dr. Horner told her with that detached sincerity so many doctors mastered. They'd decided against radiation or chemotherapy; it was pointless. The only thing to do was make her father comfortable for as long as—the doctor hesitated—there was. Dede, May, and Dr. Horner together concluded there was no point in Dede's staying around. She'd return to New York and fly back down again when—again it was the doctor who supplied the words—it became necessary.

When Dede stopped by on her way to the airport, the tube was gone from her father's nose and though still sedated, he looked a little more alert. This time when Dede took his hand, the return clasp was steadier.

"I'm headed back to New York, dad, the work is piling up, but I'll be back real soon."

Bill Miller nodded, then managed, "How long have you been here?"

"A week, dad."

"Oh."

"Now you take care of yourself. And do what the doctors tell you."

Her father nodded; his clouded brown eyes looked straight into her blue ones. He knew. She could see it. She leaned over and kissed him, then straightened up. Still, they held hands. Bill Miller's mouth opened. His murmured words were, "You are my flesh and blood. I don't care . . . you are."

Then, exhausted, the old man closed his eyes.

CHAPTER 14

On the morning Alexander Mackenzie was to arrive, Herb was up even earlier than usual, going through drawers and boxes for mementos of his brother—letters, childhood photos, report cards, clippings about the Buddy Benson band and the battles Jake had been in, medals and ribbons—telling himself he was doing it for Mackenzie. He was lost in them when Marian walked into the study to see why he hadn't come to breakfast.

"The orange juice is getting cold." It was one of her little jokes, which these days, he was usually grateful for. But he was startled and, against his will, feeling guilty at being caught looking through Jake's stuff.

"I was just . . ."

"Don't you want breakfast?

He hesitated. "A private detective is coming over this morning."

Her eyes got wide and he suddenly realized . . . but no, she couldn't think that. If he wanted a detective for *that*, he would meet him somewhere else, and certainly not tell her about it. What should he say? No, it's not to tail you. It's for something you'll dislike only slightly less. It's for Jake.

"I want to find the woman Jake wrote the letter to."

"Would you like your coffee in here?" she asked.

"Why yes, that would be fine." But he was surprised at how fine it actually wasn't, surprised at how much he still wanted her, how much he longed for the days when she—what? Cared more for his past? Pretended to care more? He'd settle for either.

"Would you like some eggs, too?"

"No thanks. Just coffee, a piece of toast. Thanks . . . dear."

She left and again he looked down at the page of the scrapbook he'd been staring at. Under transparent plastic was a large black and white photograph from a magazine. It was taken late on June 5th, 1944, the eve of D-Day. Paratroopers in battle dress were waiting to board planes which would drop them behind German lines in Normandy. In the foreground was General Eisenhower. He was seen in right profile and seemed to be speaking, his attitude pugnacious, his face grim. The men listened, some helmeted, most faces blackened. He gestured with a right hand that was almost clenched into a fist as he spoke to a tall soldier who stood at attention. On the soldier's left shoulder was the Screaming Eagle, the insignia of the 101st Airborne, Jake's division.

Herb had stared at that picture and others of the same scene dozens of time before. He had examined the faces carefully through a magnifying glass, dwelling on each face. Looking for Jake. Never finding him. There were about 8 million Americans in uniform at the time of D-Day. Of those, 14,000 were in the 101st Airborne and 2,400 in the division's 502nd Parachute Infantry Regiment. What made his obsession with this picture so strange was that he knew the men in it were from E Company of the 502nd, not from Jake's H Company. So close, but not right. Yet even knowing that, he could not stop looking. Who knows, maybe Jake had been at the same airport, scheduled to board a plane nearby, happened to be walking by? He kept looking at those men, trying to see how many he could count: 17, perhaps an 18th. And he could not stop thinking that perhaps one of those men in the background, barely visible, might have been Jake.

He shut the scrapbook and stood up as Marian returned to the room, set down the tray with coffee and toast. They stared at each other, each wanting to say something, neither saying it.

"Thanks."

"When will he be here?"

"Soon. You're welcome to join us."

"I've got to run some errands."

"Of course."

Mackenzie was a small man in his late 40s, a couple of inches shorter than Herb and weighing no more than 140 pounds. He wore a tweed jacket, gray pants, white button-down shirt with striped tie, and shoes with oversized rubber soles. Once his hair had been red; now what was left had faded almost to gray. His face had the almost sour look of someone with indigestion, but when he smiled, the pale blue eyes lit up and a kindly man was looking at you.

He smiled when Herb said, "I thought you'd be a bigger man."

"I don't do body-guarding. Not personally. But I can supply them if you need them. That's not . . ."

"No. As I told you on the phone, I want you to find someone."

Before he showed the letter, Herb went through the scrapbooks to explain who Jake was and what had happened to him. When he apologized for the excessive detail, Mackenzie joked gently, "You're paying me by the hour."

"It's worth it," Herb said.

"My mother lost a brother in the war. An uncle I never knew." said Mackenzie. "He was in a Scottish Highland regiment. The Scots are the greatest fighters in the world . . . you can look it up." His eyes lit up and a boy peeked out from that weary face. "We'll work out a price adjustment."

"You remember the war?"

"Not really." The detective sounded almost apologetic. "I was born in '42."

Herb shook his head. "How did the world get so young?"

"Young? Nearly 48?"

"Just wait."

Mackenzie gave a short laugh. "What choice do I have?"

Finally, Herb got to the letter. Mackenzie read it slowly. "All right if I take it to make a copy?"

"I'll make one and send it to you. I'd rather not let it out of my hands." Herb looked at him. "You understand."

Mackenzie nodded. "Absolutely."

"That address in Hicksville, Long Island," Herb said, "it's obviously a dead-end."

Mackenzie seemed amused. "A dead end? Obviously? I've been in this business for a few years. I've found there's no such a thing as a dead-end. There are always traces. Only most people, like Mr. Breecher from Dubuque, can't find them. That's why you pay me and not him."

As he left his parting words were, "It's a pleasure to work for someone who doesn't want a spouse tailed."

The letter had come at a perfect time for Herb. Ellinson Production Services now belonged to Global and he knew, despite the consultancy fee, they really did not need him around. For the first time in his life, Herb had plenty of time to go along with his money. Now he had two projects: Jake's building and June Hopkins.

Two days after Mackenzie's visit. Herb was standing with Joe Wiggins on a stretch of sloping lawn, looking at the spot where the Jacob Ellinson Jazz

Studies Center would stand. Wiggins had long ago given up the drinking and hard living of his early band days. He was a health faddist, tee-totaller, vegetarian, and fitness enthusiast who swam and worked out every morning. He was heavily tanned, kept his head shaved, and wore a short-sleeved shirt to show off what was remarkable muscle tone for a man of 73.

"You really keep in shape, Joe."

Wiggins slapped his flat belly. "I've become a nut. You've heard of Brazil nuts and hazel nuts and macadamia nuts. I'm a California health nut: no fat, no cholesterol, no brains. A long way from the Etemore and that lousy cherry pie. Not to mention the booze. Jake wouldn't know me." He looked into Herb's eyes. "Gee, I . . . does that bother you?"

"Hell no," Herb answered. "I think things like that all the time . . . Jake this and Jake that. When we got to this place I said to him, 'Jake, you'd like it here.'"

Wiggins pointed to the far end of an imaginary building. "There'll be a bandstand right about there. Just wait'll we get a dozen kids up on it, wailing and punching away. Can't you just hear 'em? Jake would love that. That would turn him on. He loved playing with the band, Herb. There was nobody else loved it as much. The rest of us, you know, we were a little older, we'd done it a little longer, we were a bunch of cynics. To say you actually *enjoyed* it wasn't cool." He laughed. "Did we say cool back then?" Neither man remembered.

"Jake, he just got a thrill out of making music," Wiggins went on. "The same the last day he played as the first. How long was he with the band? About a year and a half?"

"Nine months."

"Was that all? I would have thought . . ."

As they spoke Wiggins was leading Herb up the grassy incline where the building would stand. Halfway up they turned and looked down at the campus spread out before them in the valley that gave the school its name. The scene was green and sunny and peaceful, a picture postcard, had the buildings not been so modern.

"Nine months, that's all," Herb said. "Nine months, nearly 50 years ago. Speaking of long ways, this is a long way from my alma mater, the City College of New York."

"Not to mention mine, the school of hard knocks," Wiggins answered, staring out at the view. "Know what our school colors were?"

"Black and blue," Herb answered with a smile. "I haven't heard that in 50 years."

Fifty years. The two old men stood there and looked off into the distance.

"'All The Things You Are.' That was his first solo. Did you know that, Herb?"

Herb nodded, managed to speak. "He wrote to me about it. God, he was excited." His voice sounded like a croak to him. "I still have the letter."

Wiggins slapped Herb on the back, gently. "In a few months we'll have a groundbreaking ceremony. I'll have the school's big band here. They'll knock your socks off. They're going to play 'All The Things You Are.' I've got the old Buddy Benson charts."

For several minutes the two old men stood silently on the sunny slope, each looking out over the valley. Finally, Herb said, "I'm going to be here for that, Joe."

"I hope Jake will too. That he'll look down and say, those are my kids. Do you believe in that, Herb?"

"What?"

"Heaven. Life after death."

"It gets easier every year."

CHAPTER 15

Spring-Summer, 1941

The Battle of the Atlantic continues; the toll from German U-boats grows. The U.S. begins to supply Britain with war materiel under the Lend-Lease Act. On June 22nd, Germany invades the Soviet Union.

At Fort Benning, Georgia, the army activates the 502nd Parachute Battalion.

Hit records: "I Hear A Rhapsody" and "High On A Windy Hill," Jimmy Dorsey; "There'll Be Some Changes Made," Benny Goodman; "Daddy," Sammy Kaye.

From the Three Rivers, the Benson band goes into Ohio, never spending more than one night in any hotel, not getting a single good night's sleep in a week and a half. Jake's playing is being noticed. In the big band performances, there is virtually no improvising. Everything is played from the written arrangements called charts. At first, Jake has to feel his way. Though he is an excellent sight-reader who can pick up a written piece of music and play it flawlessly the first time, there is more to an ensemble sound than playing all the right notes. It takes a new sideman a while to mesh, to learn the phrasing and the dynamics that give a band its personality. Until he learns, Jake holds back.

As the second trumpet, Jake has virtually no solo work except for an occasional four-bar bit like the one in "All The Things You Are." But even four bars, read from a chart, leave room for display, and as Jake feels easier in the band, he makes more of each chance, opening up his tone to make it more brilliant, coloring the dynamics, letting his accent slide across the beat. One night in Canton, Ohio, he improvises a very small variation on the solo as written. When he finishes, he looks to his left quickly to Ted, who shows no reaction. From his right, he gets a quick wink from Swede; then he glances at Benson, who is not looking his way at all.

The next night, in a Columbus theater, he takes the variation a bit further. This time he draws some applause from the audience, and a glance from Benson. When the set is over and they are backstage, Benson waves him over.

"What is that you're playing, kid?"

"The trumpet. Buddy." Jake gives him a big smile; Benson doesn't smile back.

"I wrote those charts myself. Sorry if you don't like 'em."

Jake stops smiling. "It's not that I don't like them. They're fine." Actually he thinks them dull. "It's just that . . ."

"Then do me a favor Jake, play 'em the way they're written."

They don't do "All The Things You Are" again until two nights later in Cincinnati. Jake not only plays it straight, he wipes away all the shading and coloring he's given it, flattening it out to the way he did it the very first time, in Pittsburgh. It draws no applause.

When Benson approaches him after the set, he half expects to be chewed out for making the solo so bland. "Is that the way it's written?" asks Benson.

"Note for note, so help me," Jake answers.

"I like it your way better. Play it that way, and give me a copy so I can put it in the charts."

"It's not written down, Buddy. I just . . . improvise." He isn't sure he should use the word. "It's fresher than when I play the same thing all the time."

Benson gives him a hard look. "OK. Four bars, that's it. And don't go wild." Then he holds out a piece of music. Jake takes it and looks at it: the band's arrangement of "One o'Clock Jump," an up-tempo instrumental that Basie and Goodman have made a hit.

"You want to try the hot solo?"

"You bet, Buddy!"

"Not tonight. Tomorrow. I wanna tell Ted first."

When they get on the bus that night, headed for Dayton, Jake can see by the look on Ted Cowan's face he's already been told. There is a stifled fury that mottles Cowan's skin, and in his eyes there is fear, which makes Jake feel rotten.

He sits down next to Cowan. "I didn't ask for it, Ted. Honestly."

When Cowan tries to speak, his mouth is so tight with anger and tension he can barely get the words out. "No. You didn't ask for it. But you pushed for it. Your kind is real good at pushing."

Jake would not ordinarily let that go, but this time he feels too much pity for Cowan.

"I didn't push for it. I'm sorry, Ted. I understand how you feel." As Jake speaks, he begins getting up to look for a more congenial seatmate.

"Just get the fuck out of here," Cowan says in a voice still hissing with hatred. And as Jake is turning away, he spits out, "Jewboy."

Jake turns back, leans down to Cowan and puts a fist near his face. "I feel bad for what happened, so I'm going to give you that one, Ted. Just one. That's all you get."

When Jake sees the fear come back into Cowan's eyes, he can't help feeling sorry for him again. He takes a seat next to Swede.

"Are you?" asks Swede.

"Am I what?"

"A Jew."

"Yeah, what about it?" The hostility he wanted to show against Cowan now sounds in his voice.

"Easy kid. Nothing. Just curious." Jake sees in Olsen's broad face no animosity and no fear; he figures the Swede for a tough man. "I was with the Ben Pollack band, kid."

"Some of your best leaders were Jews, huh?" Jake answers.

"That's not what I mean. Take the chip off your shoulder, Benny Leonard."

"There've been good Jewish fighters since Benny Leonard."

Swede laughs. "OK, Barney Ross. All I meant about Ben Pollack was, you know who was in that band with me?"

"Benny Goodman."

"Yeah, him too. But he played sax and clarinet, so I wasn't worried about him. By the way, I'll tell you something. I heard Benny pick up the trumpet a few times and just fool around on it, and if he wanted to, he could worry me real easy. But the guy I'm talking about was Harry James."

"All that commercial stuff," says Jake deprecatingly.

"The sweet, corny stuff sells, Jake. So he plays what sells. But don't kid yourself; Harry can do it all. He can improvise; he can play hot. God, can he play hot. I remember the times I had solos taken away from me and given to James, who was maybe 19 at the time! It's part of the business. If you stay in it long enough, some day some kid'll come along and take your solos away."

Jake doesn't say no, but his face shows he doesn't believe it.

"Just wait, Jake. Just wait."

It isn't until Akron, the Starri-Nite Ballroom, that he can do the hot solo, which goes on for 16 bars. He pushes too hard on it; he is too eager; he can tell even as he plays it. But the audience applauds, and applause is Buddy Benson's success-meter. Later he says, "Attaway, kid. Go get 'em."

Even Cindy likes it. "You really can play, Jake!" she tells him.

"And you thought I was just a lover."

"You're terrible. You really are terrible."

Their eyes lock as she says it; he knows she doesn't think he's terrible at all. And he would take on the world for her.

Only Swede puts it in perspective. "You don't have to do it all in one night, kid."

Ohio is a relentless string of one-nighters. It's not until they cross the border into Indiana and drive to Muncie, that they have a day off before playing two nights in a local ballroom. In all that time, though Jake sees Cindy every day, he never gets to spend more than 15 or 20 minutes at a time alone with her—breakfast in a diner or a cup of coffee before going to work. Each day seems to be spent half on the bandstand and half in the bus. And much as he's already heard about the travel, the fatigue, the bad food, he comes to find out for himself something no one has told him about: the total lack of privacy. You are always with people, on the bus, on the bandstand, at meals. And when you do have private time in your hotel room, you're usually too tired to do anything with it but sleep on it.

They've no sooner gotten to Muncie and checked into the hotel than Jake goes and knocks at Cindy's door. He hears her walk to the door and ask, timidly, "Who is it?" The small voice makes him want to put his arms around her and protect her.

"The world's greatest trumpet player," he answers.

The door opens; she's standing there, smiling.

"Oh," she says. "I was expecting Harry James."

"Why settle for second best?"

Her smile widens. She has a bathrobe on. Her hair is pulled back in a ponytail. She looks 15. And she is glad to see him; it shines in her eyes.

"Harry can't make it, so I'm taking you out to dinner."

"You are?"

"If you ask nicely."

Looking at her, he is convinced she is pure and innocent and waiting for him and he is crazy about her.

"You're a sweet kid, Jake, you really are. But . . ."

"Just listen. We've got the night off. I don't want to have dinner with the guys, again. You must be even sicker of it than I am." The technique is to keep talking, not give the girl a chance to say no. "What we're going to do is have a date, a real date, as if we were human beings, not musicians."

"I'm not a musician, I'm a singer."

He reaches out and touches a finger to her nose. "The best. Gorgeous, too. You're going to dress up real nice and I'm going to take you to a restaurant where no one knows you're a famous singer and I'm the world's greatest trumpet player. We'll have a couple of whiskey sours, and . . ."

She starts to laugh. "You never had a whiskey sour in your life!"

He knows then she won't say no, and he can't keep from beaming at her. "Are you kidding?" he says. "Had to give 'em up. Doctor's orders."

"Sure," she says.

"Seriously. They make me too irresistible to women. Doctor says it's dangerous."

"I'm really scared," she says, looking him straight in the eye. He wants to kiss her. So he does, lightly on the lips.

"Jake!" She tries to make it indignant.

"Be ready in 20 minutes."

To seal the agreement, he kisses her again, quickly. "And that's without the whiskey sours."

"You mustn't do that!"

"Twenty minutes." He turns and walks off, half waiting for her to shout "no!" after him. All he hears is silence.

Twenty minutes later, he's back at her door, a dozen red roses held behind him, wearing his best clothes, a tan checked jacket, brown pants, with a white shirt and red tie.

The flowers entrance her. Even before unwrapping them, she stares at them and smells them. Then, carefully, she tears the paper off and turns them and looks at them and smells them again. There is a chipped ceramic pitcher on the one bare table in the room; she half fills it with water, and one at a time carefully places the roses in it, smelling each one as she does, saying nothing. Finally she turns to look at him. Her eyes glisten.

"Jake, this is the first time in my life, my whole life . . . a man has ever brought me flowers. Me, personally. As a person. You understand? Not as a singer." She walks to him and kisses him on the cheek.

At dinner, it takes only one whiskey sour to get him high. "Hey, these things taste good, really good!"

"You sound like you never had one before," she teases.

He reaches across the table and takes her hand; she doesn't try to pull it away. "I never have had one before. Look, when we're like this, the two of us, with none of . . . them around, let's tell the truth. You know, the whole truth and nothing but the truth. OK?"

She is instantly on guard. "What do you mean, do you think I haven't . . ."

"How old are you?"

She looks at him, wide-eyed, unsure. Right then he wouldn't have been surprised if she'd said 15.

"How old are you?" she asks back.

"I'm 20," he says.

"So am I."

"How about that? We're the same age! I was 20 in September, how about you?"

"April."

He raises his glass. "Hey, here's to an older woman."

She looks at him hesitantly. "This coming April."

He laughs. "You're only 19!" Then he sees her redden. "That's OK! It just means I have to take better care of you. You're just a teenager!"

She answers hotly. "I knew I shouldn't tell you the truth."

Jake grabs her hand across the table. "Listen, I always want you to tell me the truth. And I promise to do the same to you. OK?"

Her eyes are wide. He squeezes her hand. She squeezes back, without saying anything.

"OK?"

She looks frightened. "Who are you to ask me to make promises? You're just some kid who comes along . . ."

"Just some great trumpet player who's nuts about you."

That makes her feel better. "Oh, we don't have much of a swelled head, do we, Harry James?"

"Make it Bunny Berigan." No matter how triumphant James' success, Jake thinks he is too commercial.

She looks down at her left hand as if noticing for the first time that he is holding it, and it makes him look down, too. He stares at the friendship ring she wears; the shabbiness of it makes his heart go out to her. Her hand is so small, pale, forlorn; on the nails, red polish has begun to chip. As if she can read his eyes, she pulls the hand gently away, puts it in her lap.

The waiter serves them two steaks; on each plate is also a scoop of mashed potatoes with a puddle of gravy in it and another scoop of canned carrots and peas.

The food brightens her. "Oh boy," she says, smiling at him, "doesn't this look good!" He sees the 15-year-old again, but then 19 isn't all that far from 15. He watches her cut off a piece of steak, dip it into the gravy. Then, looking quickly up at him, she puts it into her mouth. Jake watches her chew.

"Don't stare at me!" she says, her mouth still full of steak.

Jake covers his eyes with his hands, but opens his fingers to look, so she can see him looking. She giggles.

"I wasn't kidding when I said I was nuts about you," he says.

"Will you eat?" she answers. "Your food is getting cold."

For awhile they eat in silence, Jake looking at her steadily, she lifting her eyes from time to time to meet his and then quickly lowering them to her plate again.

Suddenly, quickly, she says, "You are a real good trumpet player, you know."

"Ho hum. Now tell me something I didn't know." Then he leans forward intently. "Honestly. I do know. I'd be lying if I said no. And I'm going to be the best. The best, Cindy."

To his surprise that upsets her. "Big deal! So what? So you'll be the best. What'll happen then?"

"What'll happen? I'll get to play for Benny, maybe."

"Good. I'll come see you at the Paramount."

"Hey, Cindy, I'll take you with me!"

"What do you know about playing for Benny? You think it's so wonderful?"

"Playing for Benny means being the best!"

"For how long?" She shakes her head at his naiveté. "Did you ever hear of the ray?"

"The ray?"

"Ask any of the guys who played for him. Ask Johnny Black," she says. "You're playing and suddenly Goodman stares at you. You know there's something wrong, that he doesn't like something, but you don't know what it is. He doesn't tell you. Just gives you that look, the ray. Next thing you know, you're fired."

Jake can't understand why she is getting so upset. "He won't fire *me*. And if he does, I'll start my own band. You'll be the singer."

"It'll still be the road," she says. "It'll still be the grind and the cheap hotels and the lousy food . . ." She stops. "I mean, this is great, Jake," and in fact, she has cleaned her plate, "but, you know . . ."

"What do you want, Cindy? A rose-covered cottage?"

"Yeah. That's exactly what I want. Wait till you've been doing this for three years, instead of three weeks, and see what you want."

He pauses to drink the last of his second whiskey sour. By now his head feels very warm and light, as if it could take off and float away from the rest of him. It is not a bad feeling. "I'm going to want to make music the rest of my life, Cindy. When I get out of the army . . ."

"Are you going into the army?" she asks, alarmed.

"There's a draft, you know, when I hit 21 in September . . . but it'll only be for a year, and when I get out, I want to be the best. Like Berigan . . . or James. And then I'll get you a rose covered cottage."

"Stop it!"

"I mean it," he says, reaching for her hand. She draws it away.

"You're such a kid."

"I'm older than you are."

The frightened look comes back, "Don't tell them that. They think I'm 23. I had to lie when I got the job. I was only 16."

"Now I have you in my power." He says it to be funny. She starts to cry.

"Hey, I was only kidding!"

They both pull back; the early talk has gotten too intimate too soon. For the rest of dinner they stick to subjects like the music and the stops ahead. In front of her room, when he puts his arms around her to kiss her goodnight, she presses her slim body against him so he can feel her small breasts and her abdomen and pelvis and thighs thrusting at him. She lets her mouth open slightly when he kisses her, just for a moment, then closes it again.

The last thing she says before going into her room is, "Please don't tell anyone. Please!"

"You mean that I'm nuts about you?"

She just closes the door.

"I love you," he says softly, as he walks to his room. He's trying those words out; they feel right.

A week later, on a night off, they make love for the first time. They have dinner, walk back to the inevitable dingy hotel. This time she takes him into her room. They kiss; she sinks down onto the bed with him. His body is on top of hers; he feels the softness of her thighs, surprising to him because she is so slim. She feels the hardness of him, thrusts herself up at it. He touches her breasts; she offers no resistance. When he starts to lift her skirt, she stops him.

"Jake," she says, "I have to tell you something." Something had happened to her a year ago on the road, something with a musician. One no longer with the band, she says, which he's not sure he believes. She had some whiskey sours. He invited her into his room to show her some new charts. They had some more drinks. She was dizzy. He forced her onto the bed, she too lightheaded to realize what . . . then he was on top of her, big and heavy and very strong. And then he . . . she was too young and too drunk and too scared and too weak to stop him. He did it. She hated it; it hurt. It was the first time, the only time, and it was terrible. Then he went around telling people, making up stories, a lot of lies, things she never did.

Jake understands; she is explaining in advance what she fears he will find when they make love: that it is not her first time. For Jake and Cindy, as was common in the 1940s, there is only one acceptable explanation for an unmarried woman's loss of virginity, and that is rape, a woman overpowered and penetrated against her will.

At 20, Jake has made love to several girls and been in love, or so he thought, with a couple. But until now, no one girl has ever fit into both categories. He's always expected the girl he loves to be a virgin. Now it turns out she isn't. He doesn't care. She's Cindy.

He tells her, "You didn't love him and you didn't want to do it," as he takes off her underpants and then removes his trousers and shorts. "So that doesn't count, what counts is that I love you and you love me." Then he lies on top of her, and she opens her legs, and wraps them around him as he slides into her.

She does not enjoy it. Yes, she loves him, but they are not married and the sin of it still haunts her. After it, though, they feel very close, almost like being married. But it doesn't become a regular thing; the road is too unforgiving for that. Sharing a room is out of the question; finding time for privacy is as difficult as it was before. And Buddy Benson's policy absolutely prohibits liaisons between the girl singer and the musicians.

With brief respites at home—which delight his family, but leave Jake itching to be back playing—the ordeal of the road goes on, eased for Jake by Cindy and by Benson's decision to move him into Buddy's Boys, replacing Ted Cowan.

1941 moves from spring into summer heat, and since air conditioning is found only at movie theaters—which announce it with big banners saying things like "COOL AS A POOL," or "DELIGHTFULLY AIR COOLED," the letters hung with icicles—the dances move outdoors, to hotel roofs or to open-air pavilions, often on the water. At one of those pavilions just west of Cleveland—The Lakeview, which looks out on Lake Erie—the band is playing for a fraternal organization and they get a blessed 45-minute break while speeches are made and awards presented. Jake and Cindy walk out onto the porch that circumscribes the old wooden building, then down a flight of steps to the lake. They see a long wooden pier and, arm in arm, walk out onto it. The building is on a promontory which thrusts into the lake, and with the additional length of the pier, they feel almost as if they're at sea. To their right, the lights of Cleveland form a long low arc along the shore, with an illuminated blur in the sky behind. To their left, smaller clusters of lights stretch toward Lorain and Sandusky, two stops that lie waiting for them as they head west. A crescent moon is partly covered by clouds, giving the lake a dark, mysterious depth, broken only by the lights of passing boats.

"Just think how great it would be," Cindy says, "if we could come to all these places, see all these sights . . . without having to go up on that bandstand . . . ever!"

"Are you kidding?" he says. "It would be terrible! The bandstand, the music, that's what it's all about. Do you think I would be here in the . . . boondocks . . . at all, without the music?"

"I suppose you'll call Springfield the boondocks too," she says.

"It's your hometown," he replies. "And I'm going to love it."

When they get back to New York after this trip, Jake is going up to Massachusetts with her, to meet her parents, her kid brother, two younger sisters and her aunts and uncles and cousins.

"One thing, Jake . . ." Anxiousness shows in her eyes.

"Uh oh," he says. "Am I going to like this? I'm not, am I?"

"Please, Jake." She wants his approval in advance.

"Go ahead; tell me."

"When you're in Springfield, don't say anything about . . . let's not talk about religion."

"Why? Is your family ashamed of being Catholic?" His little joke. He knows very well what she means, and she knows he knows. All she can do is stare at him, imploringly. Usually those big green eyes looking up from that little girl's face are enough. She doesn't have to ask anything. He gives it before she asks. Not this time.

"Jake, they're not bad people. It's just that . . ."

"They don't know I'm Jewish." He tries it and looks at her, waiting. She is hoping her big eyes will do the trick. Not this time.

"Do they?" When she remains quiet, he takes his arm from around her shoulder. "You didn't tell them. You said you would."

"Well . . . honestly, it's hard to work into a letter. I tried! There was just no place it seemed . . . natural."

"You just put it in there, any old way. 'By the way, my boyfriend's a kike!'"

"Jake, that's really unfair!"

"You've still got three weeks to tell them."

"It would be better if they met you first . . ."

"What is this, like I'm hiding something? A nut in my family?"

"Please, Jake, I can't help it! Older people have prejudices. They'll get used to it. In the end they won't care . . . all they'll care about is that I get married in church."

She says it casually, as if it were understood. Jake can't believe what he's hearing. "Who do you have in mind for the groom?" He stares at her. "Do you really expect me to get married by a priest, in a church?"

"You said you're not religious! You said you never go to your church." She is frantic; he has no consolation for her.

"You call it a temple or a synagogue. We call it *shool*. It's not a church."

"I'm sorry! Whatever it is, you never go to it, you said that yourself!"

He puts his hands on her slim shoulders. "Oh, Cindy, Cindy! Did I ever give you the idea I would marry you in a church? I can't believe I did. If I did I'm sorry. I will never marry in a church. Never! It would be . . . betraying my people. Look, even if I never go to a temple, I'm still a Jew. The Jews are my *people*."

She shrugs off his hands, turns and walks back toward the shore. He catches her, again puts his hands on her shoulders, but she won't stop walking.

"Listen!" he says. "We love each other . . ."

"The only way I can get married is by a priest at a mass. In a Catholic church. Otherwise I might as well say goodbye to my family."

She turns to look at him. Her eyes are stricken. There are few things in the world he wouldn't do to make her feel better. She's picked one of them. When she sees there's no yielding in him, she heads for the pavilion. Jake plays the set angry. Cindy sings it red-eyed. When it ends, Jake walks out to a far, dark corner of the big porch. He's standing there, his anger now replaced by bleakness, when Buddy Benson walks to him, Cindy in tow.

"Look," the bandleader says. "People told me about the two of you. Let's say I looked the other way. Now I've got a girl singer comes out onstage with her mascara running; I've got a trumpet player sounds like he wants to blow down the walls of Jericho. I can't have that in my band."

Jake looks him in the eye. "You're right," he says. "It's not professional. It won't happen again. No more running mascara. No more walls tumbling down. Right, Cindy?"

She nods. Benson shakes his head, no.

"I'm not making myself clear," he says. "I've got a rule, you both know it. No fooling around with the girl singer."

"We're not fooling around. We love each other." Jake looks at Cindy. Again, she nods.

"You still don't get it. Nothing—no romance, no nothing—I don't care what you call it—with the girl singer in my band. You want to stay with the band, nothing goes on between you. You want romance, fine. Good. God bless you. Live happily ever after. Only not in my band. That's your choice."

Jake puts an arm around Cindy; this time she doesn't shrug it off. "OK."

"That's better." Benson smiles the smile of a winner.

"We made our choice. We're leaving the band." Jake squeezes Cindy's shoulders to keep her quiet.

Benson's mouth drops open for a moment, before he says, "That's it?"

"Look, Buddy. We can find lots of work, with lots of bands. Where are you going to find a horn player and a vocalist as good as we are?" He stares hard at Benson. "You know I'm right."

Benson does know Jake is right, but he can't back off. "Look, I got a rule . . ."

Jake helps him. "We'll be very private about it. The band won't see a thing; you won't see a thing. We're talking about true love here, Buddy. You're not going to stand in the way of true love, are you?" Jake tries a smile, then adds: "No one will see a thing."

Benson grabs his chance. "If I see anything . . ."

"You won't," Jake assures him. "Will he, Cindy?" She shakes her head no. "Nothing," Jake adds. And to make it easier for Benson, he ceremoniously removes his arm from her shoulder.

"OK," Benson nods and starts to walk off. After two steps he turns back. "By the way," he says. "We're booked into the Paramount. Last week in September." Jake watches till he's gone, then grabs Cindy in a bear hug and crushes her.

"The Paramount! The *Paramount*, Cindy!"

She looks up at him. "The way you did that, Jake . . . you're wonderful!" She puts her arms around his waist and holds on tight. The problem is forgotten for the moment.

It's after Labor Day when the band comes back to New York City. The bus lets them out at Broadway and 50th Street and Jake takes Cindy to Grand Central so she can get a train to Springfield. The confrontation with Buddy and the elation of the Paramount job have put a temporary patch on their wound. But neither thinks that under the patch any healing is going on. Tacitly, they've agreed not to talk about religion or marriage; Jake will not go to Springfield to meet her family.

In the lofty, magisterial space of Grand Central they stand very close to each other as they read the schedule of departures, then wait on line to buy a ticket. Burdened by suitcases, they still manage to walk arm in arm to the track for her train. They embrace avidly and stare into each other's eyes.

"I love you, Cindy."

"I love you, too!"

But the operative truth is not in the crushing hug or in the pledges, it's readable in their eyes and each reads it correctly. Please, say her eyes. I can't, say his. She boards the train and he loses sight of her.

At home, after the embracing and the tears, he has to wait 45 minutes before Herb asks him where the band plays next.

"The Glen Island Casino this week," he says, knowing that's impressive enough, a stop for all the famous big bands. He draws this out, "Then we have a week off. I'm going to clean out the refrigerator ma, so beware."

"I'm really frightened," she answers, beaming. "I'm scared to death. I forgot how to cook."

"And then," Jake goes on, not wanting the drama of this moment to be sidetracked by any talk about food, "Starting the 22nd, we play a week at the Paramount." He pauses, looks around.

"You're kidding!" shouts Herb.

"The Paramount?" Marty says.

"I don't mean the Strand," Jake replies, beaming.

During Buddy Benson's week at the Paramount, the movie alternating with the live stage show is "Our Wife," starring Melvyn Douglas, Ruth Hussey, and Ellen Drew. The doors open at 9:30 in the morning and the last complete show starts at 11:30 at night. That means the band will play five times a day. Headlining the live bill for the week will be Danny Roberts, an old vaudeville comic who now has a popular weekly radio show. Right under his name on the huge Paramount marquee is THE BUDDY BENSON BIG BAND; under that in smaller letters, "With Cindy Laine."

On opening day, all the Ellinsons are up early. Jake must be at the theater by 9, along with all the other band members, so they can familiarize themselves with the bandstand, get a pep talk from Buddy and then dress and warm up for the performance. For the occasion the band has been fitted out with new uniforms: blazing scarlet jackets, pale blue trousers, white shirts, navy blue ties with white polka dots.

The price of a ticket before 1 p.m. is 25 cents, which entitles the purchaser to stay all day if he wishes, for six screenings and five stage shows. The Ellinsons plan to be there in time for the 11:30 live show, see the movie, and then stay to see the band and the comic a second time. They emerge from the Times Square subway station at 11:00, buy their tickets and are standing in back of the Paramount, ready to run down the aisle to get three seats down front as soon as the movie ends and the house lights come up. They find seats in the sixth row center and prepare for one of the magical moments of the Swing Era—when the bandstand, which is recessed below the level of the orchestra seats for the movie, begins to rise, and even before the band can be seen, the sound of its theme floats up and out, a brilliant live contrast to the canned movie soundtrack. To emphasize the band's danceability, Buddy uses as a theme the Irving Berlin ballad "Change Partners," which they play with more bounce than the way Fred Astaire sang it in the movie "Carefree" a few years earlier.

First the sound. Then the band, lights glittering off the instruments, Buddy playing a few token notes on his clarinet before turning to the audience to smile while waving his hand at the band in what passes for conducting. On the Paramount bandstand, the rhythm section sits stage right, piano, bass, drums, and guitar. Downstage center, the four reeds—two alto saxes and two tenors, all of whom can double on clarinet—sit on the first riser, with the three trombones on the second and the three trumpets on the top. Downstage left, Cindy sits on a chair, her blue sleeveless gown, splashed with golden sequins, carefully arranged and displayed around her. Buddy stands downstage center, clarinet in his left hand, leading the band with his right.

For Herb, the band rising out of the pit is thrilling enough. Now, seeing his brother there on that top riser, he is enraptured. He casts a sidelong glance at his father, whose eyes are bright with excitement, and beyond to his mother who, despite herself, has tears rolling down her cheeks. At first, Herb takes it all in in a kind of daze. The theme over, he hears Buddy say something unctuous about how great it is to be at the Paramount and then introduce a tune that the band has recorded and folks have been kind enough to make a hit: "All The Things You Are." In a few bars Herb can hear just how smooth and professional the band is, turned into velvet by months of playing together. And then Jake stands to play his solo, which from its modest four bars has by now been expanded to 16. His playing just jumps out at them. The band has deliberately been playing legato to carry the melody along smoothly, to make the creamy Kern tune even creamier—until Jake attacks, tonguing each note so crisply that when he reverts to slurring for the last few bars, the audience applauds almost in relief.

Marty turns to Herb and says "Wow!" It comes out more like a sharp exhalation of breath than a word.

"He's good, pop, isn't he?" Herb asks.

"I had no idea!" Marty answers, and turns to Millie. "What a talent! What a talent your son has!" He leans over to kiss her cheek, tastes the salt.

The tears are pouring down Millie's cheeks now, she's given up trying to wipe them. "He got it from you," she answers and takes his hand and squeezes it.

Now Cindy is at the mic to sing "All The Things You Are," and Jake comes down front to play a muted obbligato behind her vocal. As he watches them, Herb wonders if she isn't the girl Jake spoke of. After all, on the road, what other possibilities are there? And suddenly, for the first time, mixed in with the adoration, Herb feels one little stab of envy of his older brother, his talent, his glamor, his girlfriend, his self-assurance on the stage of the Paramount in the flashy new uniform. Jake has everything!

The number gets a big hand. When it dies down, Buddy says, "That's scintillating Cindy Laine on the vocal and our own young man with a horn, Jake Ellinson, playing sweet and hot behind her." When Cindy and Jake take hands and go into their bows, Herb applauds so violently, Marty looks to make sure he isn't hurting himself.

After three ballads, Benson calls on his sextet, Buddy's Boys, to play two numbers. It is a traditional jazz configuration: trumpet, trombone, and clarinet, with a back line of piano, drums, and bass, but to the Ellinsons, it's Jake and five other guys. First they do the classic they've done so many times on tour, "Indiana," and then Cindy joins them for a jumping "Fascinating Rhythm," again with Jake behind her, echoing her phrases and playing variations on them.

While the band takes its bows, the Ellinsons confer in whispers. They decide Cindy is not only cute, but solid musically, that Johnny Black is absolutely tops on piano, and Joe Wiggins surprisingly good on clarinet. And Jake . . . Jake is great. Herb's praise is not surprising, neither is Millie's; he's her son, after all, even though he has, for the time being, chosen the wrong career. Marty's reaction is something else. Though he's never played the Paramount, he's been through the wars, on the road, filling in with the best of bands, sitting alongside the best musicians. He knows quality. And this September day in 1941, for the first time, he is sure his son can be a big band star.

Its numbers done, the band stays onstage to provide music and supportive laughter for Danny Roberts. Then the stage show is over. As soon as the band—again sounding "Change Partners"—descends into the orchestra pit, the Ellinsons leap from their seats and make their way backstage.

In the bustle of stagehands, musicians, and visitors, Jake introduces his family to the band, then walks Cindy up for introductions. He is holding her hand to lead her, but when they stop, he doesn't let go.

"I want you to meet the best girl singer in the world," he says to his family. "And the prettiest."

Millie, Marty, and Herb all get the message.

"You're a wonderful singer," Marty says.

"You really are," echoes Herb. What both of them really mean is: So you're the one! All Millie says is, "A *shayna maidel*." Though she knows Yiddish, she rarely uses it.

"It means you're a beautiful girl," Jake says. But Millie is saying more, sending a message: We're Jewish, my son Jake is Jewish, don't forget that. Just to make sure it gets across, Millie adds, "Oh, you don't understand Jewish?"

Cindy's and Jake's answers come out simultaneously.

"No, Mrs. Ellinson, I'm afraid I don't."

"No, ma, she doesn't."

"So, Jake will teach you a few words."

Millie has taken this introduction completely off track, which is where she wants it.

"A few words is all I know, ma."

"You know plenty!"

"How did you start as a singer?" Marty asks, and they get back on track, but Millie has made her point.

Then the Ellinsons hurry back out to their seats for the movie and Cindy goes to her dressing room to change for the second show. When she emerges, she's wearing a gauzy red chiffon gown that seems to float along with her as she walks.

"You look like an angel," Jake tells her, but her mind is on something else.

"You see, your parents feel the same way as mine." It comes out softly, as if she were now accepting the certainty that two sets of parents can't be wrong.

He puts his hands on her slim upper arms, just below the puffy sleeves of the gown. "I'm not going to let my angel fly away. It's our lives, not theirs."

"My mother says you don't only marry the man, you marry his family, too."

Jake snorts. "It's the kind of thing my mother would say."

"Mothers are not dumb, you know."

"No. But they're old fashioned. Times change. New ideas arrive. People don't only stick to their own kind." He's still holding on to her arms, looking straight into her green eyes. "The wedding ceremony doesn't really matter, honest it doesn't! Think past it. Think of us, in our own apartment, our cottage, rose-covered, just the way you want it. The two of us, that's all. We visit our families once in awhile. Once in awhile they visit us. We're separate from them, living our own lives. We're us, not *them*!"

From everything he's said, she seizes on one thing. "If the wedding ceremony doesn't really matter, then we could marry in church."

"Is that all you can think about?"

"I better go back to my dressing room. I don't want my eyes to get red before we go on." She turns and walks quickly away.

The next day he hardly sees her between shows, and when he goes to her dressing room after the last one, she is gone. He raps at the thin plywood door. And again. When there is no answer, anger rumbles through him. He wants to confront her, expecting . . . expecting what? In truth, he sees no way out of their impasse.

Wednesday is his birthday; he is 21, a full-fledged adult. He expects a present and a lot of fuss from Cindy. Yet at the theater that morning, she does not appear until the band is all in place and ready to come up out of the pit. Jake, on his birthday, is not about to go after her, asking for attention, but when she disappears right after the show, he starts looking around for her. Again she doesn't appear until just before they go on, walking onto the bandstand with Benson, the two of them talking intently. He tries to catch her eye; she avoids his, he can see.

When the second show is over, he is determined not to let her get away. He leaps from the bandstand and goes after her as she heads for her dressing room. He calls to her, she does not hear him, or pretends not to. Finally, he seizes that slender upper arm he has held so many times.

"Why do I get the feeling you're ignoring me?" He tries to make it light, but as she turns to him, her eyes tell him lightness is not the order of the day.

"Happy birthday," she says, making it sound a little like a prayer for the dead. "I bought you something." She takes his hand to lead him to her dressing room; when he tries squeezing hers, he gets no response.

On her dressing table sits a small, gift-wrapped box, which she hands to him. "Thanks," he says. "Do I get a kiss, too?" Yes, he does, but behind her kiss there's no one home. Jake opens the box. In it is a 14-karat gold tie clasp in a style currently popular: a clip that goes on the shirt, attached to it a loop of chain through which the tie is placed. On the chain hangs a small golden trumpet.

"I hope you like it," she says in a small voice.

"I love it," he answers, trying to make of this a happier occasion than it is. "It's great!"

"I couldn't think of anything else," she adds. But in fact, she has something else for his birthday, a bombshell.

"Jake," she begins it, "I have something to tell you."

"A birthday surprise," he says, a chill setting in.

"I'm going with Tommy Dorsey," she blurts out, nervous and fearful and anxious to get it over with. "I'm going to sing with the Pied Pipers, and Sinatra. Tommy's promised me some duets with Frank. Even some solos."

Jake feels as if he's been hung up in a meat locker. "Boy. That is a surprise. Congratulations." His mouth is frozen along with the rest of him. He has trouble forming the words. "How long have you known?"

"He asked me a while ago, and I said no. Then he asked me again, and I said yes. Yesterday." Even at this eleventh hour there is a mute appeal in her eyes, if only Jake would . . .

"He's got a great band," Jake says. "And Sinatra and the Pied Pipers . . ."

Her eyes still ask as she says, "I thought it would be best."

"When do you leave?"

"At the end of this week."

"That's pretty quick," he manages, his lips still so tense they'll barely move. "Hell, I'll be in the army in a couple of months anyway."

"That soon?"

"Sure, why not?" To his consternation, Jake finds himself close to tears. All he can trust himself to do is shrug.

"I'll miss you," she whispers.

"And that's it. I'll miss you. And goodbye."

"It's impossible."

"What about . . . never mind."

"Please don't. It's hard enough."

"OK. I'll miss you, too. Goodbye." He forces the words through his frozen lips. Then he picks up the tie clasp. "Thanks for the present." He walks out of the dressing room, out of the theater, onto Broadway, hurls the tie clasp down at the first sewer he sees. It doesn't go down; it lands on the grating and drapes over it. Jake kicks at it savagely until he can force it to drop into the darkness. A cop looks at him strangely.

He fights his way through the week, show by show, day by day. On Saturday Jake is sitting in the musicians' big dressing room when Johnny Black sticks his head into the room.

"Jake, somebody here to see you."

Jake's heart jumps and thuds as he gets up. It will be Cindy. She will act out the scenario he has been fantasizing for three days now: she's said no to Dorsey; she loves Jake and can't live without him; they can marry wherever he wants.

Instead of Cindy, Jake sees a tall man with rimless glasses. Johnny Black once worked for him and he's asked Johnny to introduce him. His smiling lips form the most famous clarinet embouchure in the world. It is the King of Swing, Benny Goodman.

"I like your playing, Jake," Goodman says in the slight Southern accent he has assumed as an overlay on the sound of his native Chicago.

They chat for awhile, then Goodman, who has a reputation for being, if not rude, oblivious to amenities, takes Jake's arm and walks him off as if Johnny weren't there.

"In a couple of months," Goodman says softly, "I'm going to be needing a trumpet player. Are you interested in joining the band?"

This is as close to feeling good as Jake has come since Wednesday. "You bet! The only problem is, I may be getting another offer."

Goodman seems displeased. "Really?"

"From Uncle Sam," Jake says quickly.

"Oh. Yes. Happening to a lot of boys. Let's see where things are in a month or so."

With that and not another word, Goodman slaps Jake lightly on the shoulder and leaves. One of Jake's fantasies is realized. But all he can think about is Cindy. The farewell that he half dreads and half wants to provoke, never happens. On Sunday, with one stage show still to be played, Jake finds an envelope on his dressing table.

Dear Jake,

Buddy gave me the last show off, so when you read this I'll be gone. It's hard for me to put it into words, but this is best for both of us. It wouldn't have worked. You can't understand how much certain things mean to me.

That's about all, except, I love you. I really do.

It's signed, "Love, Cindy;" the "i" in Cindy topped by her characteristic little-girl circle. Jake crumples the note fiercely and slams it into a wastebasket with the same ferocity he used on the tie chain.

The next weeks are the most miserable in Jake's 21 years. Even the review in Metronome, which is warm toward the band and singles Jake out for praise—"a young trumpet man with the lyricism of Berigan and the flair of James"—cannot break through the gloom. He mopes around the house, carefully polite and totally uncommunicative. His parents wonder, until Marty spots a headline in Variety, which he reads to Millie: "Warbler Cindy Laine Ankles 4Bs For TD."

"Ah hah!" Millie says. "I'll bet—I'll bet *anything*—that's the problem!"

Three weeks later, Benny Goodman's manager phones, to ask Jake to join the band. But that same morning, in the mail, he has gotten his induction notice.

CHAPTER 16

On the plane back to New York Sunday evening, Dede could think only of her father's words: "You are my own flesh and blood."

Of course she was! Why should he even say it, along with the, "I don't care; you are"? It was as if he were denying something. Or had the painkillers put words together for him, words he didn't mean at all?

Tru was at the apartment when she got back. His questions about her father were proper and remote. He'd always been as respectful toward Bill Miller as Tru could be to people who were outside the stockade that guarded his world. Dede wanted the chance to tell him about her father's words. He didn't give it to her.

"Let's have a glass of wine while we talk about the Goth," he said. "Come on into the kitchen."

She followed him, watched as he took a bottle of soave out of the fridge, opened it, and poured a glass.

"I want you to talk some sense into Mary Wheatley. She will not give up on her idea of getting a Jew in."

"I told her I would not support her. I told her no club should be forced to take anyone it didn't want."

"Well, now she's approaching other people. She is an embarrassment to Roger. If she were my wife, I'd take her across my knee and wallop her."

"Then she ought to be glad she's not your wife."

"Of course, some women like to be spanked . . ."

When that failed to get a rise out of her, he added, "Do you know what else she's said? That you would be a perfect candidate for first woman in the Goth. Now who could have put her up to that?"

"I said the same thing about women I said about Jews."

"Well, something put the bee in her bonnet. Or wherever the bee is." He had another mouthful of wine.

"Are you disappointed, Tru? Do you want me to be for Jews and women in the Gotham?"

"You're a real estate entrepreneuse, Dede, not a shrink. Skip the nickel and dime analysis and stick to selling apartments! And for God's sake, warn Mary to stop!"

"Or else, what?"

"Or else . . . one spring night you girls will show up for the annual bash and find yourselves chatting with a bunch of men in skullcaps. And I know how much you'd like that!" He picked up the wine bottle along with his glass, stood there and stared at her, quizzically. "Were you hoping for a spanking?" Not waiting for an answer, he turned and walked out of the room.

Over the next two weeks, she met several times with Ken Glass for long interview sessions. For one day, he followed her through a series of meetings and went with her while she and a broker showed an $8 million Fifth Avenue penthouse duplex on which Penrose Miller had an exclusive. Afterward, in the lobby, she mentioned the problem of getting a prospective buyer approved by the building's board.

"What are the reasons a board will turn someone down?" he asked.

At once her guard went up. "First, the buyer's financial condition. No building wants someone who is in over his head, can't handle the maintenance and the assessments. Then they want someone who will be a good neighbor. No wild parties, no loud noises, no hordes of the wrong kinds of people going to and fro."

"Wrong kinds of people?"

"The same kinds you'd consider wrong, Kenneth," She said it sharply.

He started to say, you mean stodgy WASPs? Then decided against it. "Are there certain buildings you will not show to . . . certain people?"

She sighed. "Of course. For lots of reasons. I'm interested in doing deals. I'm not a social worker." She wondered if she should have said that.

They walked out of the building on a cool, gray spring day. She was wearing a blue silk skirt and cream-colored sleeveless blouse. To her surprise, she found herself dressing more carefully on days he was to interview her. He stared at her.

"I can see the tan line on your arms where your tennis shirt sleeves usually end."

His words seemed almost too intimate to her. "I'll have to work on that."

He smiled the crinkly smile at her, put his notebook into an outside pocket of his lumpy tan corduroy jacket. "I hate to say this, but . . . I think I've got enough material. They're pressing me for the piece, so I've got to sit down and pound it out."

"I imagine that's the hard part."

"Well," he said, looking straight into her eyes, "the meetings with you certainly were the easy part. In spite of . . . everything."

"I thought you were very gentlemanly." She heard herself sounding very formal.

He laughed, gently. "Uh oh, that means I wasn't tough enough. I told you I wasn't a hatchet man."

"Thank you for that."

"Thank you for spending so much time with me."

They shook hands. He turned to go.

"If you have any questions . . ." she said.

"I'll call you."

"And if I find myself listening to any special music . . ."

"You call me." A last look and he was gone.

She wasn't sure what had put them off the track. Was it her reaction to his being a Jew? Or his being one? Oh well, it didn't matter, did it? He had kept his promise not to dig for dirt. She was going to be in the Times magazine. Why did she feel such a letdown?

One night two weeks later, as she and Tru were lying in their king-sized bed, reading, a call came from Aunt May in Palm Beach. Her father was dying. She got the first flight down the next morning and reached the hospital by noon. He was heavily sedated, lying there unable to speak, his face pocked with the concavities gouged out by age and illness. He knew her, looked at her with brown eyes that had faded measurably since the last time, and was able to squeeze her hand with a dry, feeble grip. As if waiting for her, he died two hours later, still holding her hand.

William Penrose Miller was buried next to his parents and first wife in Garden City. The plan was to sell the Westhampton house and, eventually, the Palm Beach house, too. May would settle in Palm Beach, but in a condo, where upkeep would be less demanding on a 73-year-old woman.

For several weekends after the funeral, Dede drove to Westhampton, spending long days rummaging through the oversized old beach house, deciding which few things to keep and what to do with the mass of furniture, clothing, books, papers, and just plain junk—boxes and boxes of it—the Millers had accumulated over a lifetime. The quantity of stuff to be gone through was daunting. A lot of it was her father's business records, most of which were labeled and could be disposed of quickly. It was the older cartons, smaller, unmarked, she paid more attention to, and it wasn't until after several hours of sifting through dusty papers that she admitted to herself she was looking for something.

She wasn't sure if it was prescience or perversity that made her spend her 45th birthday rummaging through dusty cartons instead of going out to dinner with Tru and some friends. But it was on that Friday evening in May she found it: a photo album in a moldy old box in the basement. A strip of paper glued to the cover said: "England, '43 - '44."

In it were pages of snapshots, dominated by images of her mother. She was in uniform in most of them, and most were dated, from her arrival in March 1943, to her departure in December 1944.

Had it not been for her father's words and her birthday, she might never have done the simple arithmetic. Bill Miller spent the entire war as a supply officer at Fort Dix, New Jersey. She was born on May 25, 1945, which meant . . . she counted back nine months . . . she'd been conceived in August, 1944, when her mother was in England and her father was in New Jersey.

CHAPTER 17

Two weeks after Herb's visit to the Long Valley State campus, Alexander Mackenzie arrived carrying his scuffed attaché case, his face showing nothing. Herb walked him into the living room, motioned for him to sit on the sofa, took the chair near him. Mackenzie put his attaché case on the coffee table, opened it, and pulled out a pad of yellow foolscap.

"You might want to sit next to me, Mr. Ellinson. There are some things I want to show you."

"Sure! I'm glad you have something to show me." Quickly, Herb moved to the sofa. For a moment or two, Mackenzie looked at him.

"Come on, for God's sake!" Herb's outburst surprised even himself. "Sorry, Mr. Mackenzie, but this is . . ."

"I know. I'm sorry. I've been thinking about just how to present this in the best way. I suppose I should just plunge in." He looked down at the pad. "All right. June Hopkins. She was born in Hicksville, Long Island, in 1918. Became an RN. Enlisted in the Army Nurse Corps in 1942, shipped to England in early 1943, then sent home at the end of '44. On March 20th, 1945, she married army Lieutenant William Penrose Miller, and on May 25th, 1945, she gave birth to a daughter, Diana Penrose Miller, in Garden City, Long Island. June Hopkins Miller died in 1953, also in Garden City. Cancer."

Herb sat there, trying to digest all of this. Mackenzie must have seen something funny in his eyes. "Shall I go ahead?" he asked gently. "Do you have any questions?"

"Are you saying this . . . Miller . . . was the father of the child?"

"Biological father? No, I'm not saying that. He certainly played the role of father, but she was in England for all of 1944, and he was stationed at Fort Dix, New Jersey. Is it possible that he travelled to England during that time, or that she came back to the states for a visit? It's possible. Not likely; there was a war on."

"I remember," said Herb. "Jake, on the other hand, was definitely in England at that time. His regiment arrived in the fall of '43 and stayed till D-Day, June 6th '44."

"Well now, hold on." Mackenzie interrupted. Again he looked at the pad. "Diana Penrose Miller was born on May 25th, 1945. Which means she was conceived in . . ." He ticked off the months on his fingers, "late August of '44. If Jacob Ellinson left on June 6th . . ."

"His division was brought back to England in mid-July, to their original camps, and they stayed until mid-September. It fits."

From his case, Mackenzie took out a black and white glossy. "This is the child that was born to the Millers in May of 1945, which makes her 45 years old now. Diana Penrose Miller. Quite a big deal in New York."

Herb took the picture and searched the face. He saw a good looking woman with eyes set wide apart, a regular nose, strong jaw, hair cut short. A woman who might be related to the Ellinsons, but certainly not someone whose resemblance would stop him short on the street.

"Could this be Jake Ellinson's daughter?" Mackenzie asked.

"Maybe, maybe not," Herb replied. "Nothing definitive either way. What do you mean by quite a big deal?"

Mackenzie flipped a page on his pad. "Owner of one of the city's biggest real estate firms, active in Democratic politics, member of a couple of exclusive clubs, Fifth Avenue address, summer house in the Hamptons, lots of money. June Hopkins's daughter has done very well. Here."

Again, the detective reached into his case, this time coming out with a copy of *The New York Times Sunday Magazine*, folded open to an article titled "Speaking With Two Voices."

He handed it to Herb. On the open page, he saw a picture of the same woman, this time in color, tanned, the eyes light blue, the hair dirty blonde with highlights that might be natural or subtly streaked, a woman to whom black and white photos didn't do justice.

The sub-head of the story read: Diana Miller runs a household and a major corporation. Which is easier? "Neither," she says.

Herb started reading.

"With the voice of an entrepreneur, Diana Penrose Miller commands one of the city's biggest real estate firms and speaks out in the world of Democratic politics. With the voice of a wife and mother, Dede Miller cares for a family and manages a Fifth Avenue apartment and a Southampton beach house. No one handles the change of voices more adeptly than this authoritative, strikingly attractive woman. Yet she is the first to say, it is never easy.

"'I'm always on guard to make sure the transitions are made,' she reflected one day in her sunny Madison Avenue office. 'I've been in the business world for 22 years and married for 19 and the mix still doesn't come naturally. I don't think it ever will.'

"Ms. Miller, who is 45 and looks a decade younger, would seem to have what millions of women in this country long for: marriage, career, success, looks, wealth, power. She is sole owner of Penrose Miller Associates, a huge real estate sales and management company—and industry talk has it she is planning a merger that could make her company even bigger. Her voice in the Democratic party is so persuasive, she could be asked to run for the Senate . . ."

Herb looked up. "A big deal is right."

"Not a niece to be ashamed of," Mackenzie said. "If she is your niece."

Mackenzie sat patiently as Herb scanned the rest of the article, until his eye found a paragraph near the bottom:

"When she's not on the go, which is seldom, Ms. Miller plays tennis with her husband, Wall Street investor Truman Martindale, and jogs with her 18-year-old son James. Yet no matter how crowded her schedule, she remains active at St. James Episcopal Church, taking a leading role in its programs to help the poor and homeless."

"So she is not Jewish," Herb said.

"The Millers were churchgoers in Garden City," replied the detective, "and apparently so is Diana Miller."

Herb sighed, handed back the article. "She's rich; she's social; she's an Episcopalian. Doesn't sound like an Ellinson."

In answer, Mackenzie pulled from his briefcase another 8 by 10 glossy, and handed it to Herb. As Herb stared at it, his eyes widened, and he turned it over to look at the reverse side.

"Where did you get this?" Herb finally asked.

"I hired someone to take it."

"Who do you think it is?"

"I *know* who it is," replied Mackenzie. "Diana Miller and Truman Martindale's son, James Miller Martindale. Sometimes called Jimmy, sometimes Jim."

The photo showed a lean boy in shorts, T-shirt, and running shoes, standing on a track, his hands on his hips, his feet slightly apart and pigeon-toed. Though he was very thin, his shoulders were broad and the muscles on his arms defined.

Herb kept shaking his head.

"Who do *you* think it is?" Mackenzie asked.

"Who took this picture?"

"Someone I hired."

"Can you vouch for it?" Herb asked it without looking up from the picture.

"I wasn't standing alongside him when he took it," the detective replied. "I can sure vouch for the photographer. Why?"

"When was it taken?" Herb's eye remained fixed on the picture.

Mackenzie took the glossy, turned it over and pointed to something Herb hadn't spotted, a date, written in small numbers in pencil. "Nine days ago. I don't get . . ."

"Are you sure?" Herb turned the photo right side up again and stared at it.

"I don't hire people I can't trust. Yes, I'm sure. Who do you think it is?"

"My brother. Jacob Ellinson."

The next day Herb was on a plane to New York.

He went straight to the Carlyle to check in, then without even stopping to unpack, headed for Central Park, where, according to Mackenzie's report, he might be able to spot Jimmy Martindale at this time of day.

The warmth of the afternoon was fading with the sun and Herb turned up the collar of his tan silk jacket as he sat on a bench in a corner of the park's Great Lawn, watching a lone runner on the asphalt path that bounded the athletic fields and grass. The path was more than a half-mile around and Jimmy kept circling it, alternating a fast lap with a jogging lap. By now, the rest of the team had stopped, one by one heading out of the park and back to school, until Jimmy was alone, his strong, skinny legs relentlessly driving him around the path.

He wasn't sure when he first noticed the man in the tan jacket sitting near the Shakespeare theater. At that hour on a spring day there was no shortage of people in the park, but as it got later, more of them, mothers and nursemaids with young children, high school students, old people reading newspapers, left the park. The man in the tan jacket seemed to be in his 60s, better dressed than most of the men in the park, not reading or anything, just watching him, although making a point never to stare at him when he got close.

His coach warned him not to over-train; some of his teammates thought he was nuts. To him it felt right: the strength, the speed, even the tiredness. Finally he told himself, just one more lap, this time starting slowly and gradually accelerating so he could end on a high. Tired, but the best kind of tired, he finished a final lap, noticing the man in the tan jacket still there as he headed out of the park.

A half hour later, his hair still wet from the shower, he walked out of school and over to Central Park West. There on the corner, looking for a cab, stood Marcy Tillman. His heart thumped; Marcy was a junior, new to the girls' cross-country team and one of the best looking girls he'd ever seen, if not the best; not tall, but with a slimness and proportion that made her seem to be. She was tanned from running, eyes blue and set wide apart in a heart-shaped face, hair like corn silk, tied in a ponytail that whipped around when she ran. A solid runner, middle of the team this year, maybe top three next year. Not a star, but running wasn't everything. Not when it came to her, anyway.

He walked up to her, telling himself: be cool.

"Thanks for waiting," he said as he got close.

"Waiting?" She was trying to be cool too.

"You mean you weren't?" He tried not to be nervous. "I was just hoping. We haven't officially met, but I've seen you run. You're terrific. I'm Jim Martindale."

"I *know*." He liked the way she said it. "I'm Marcy Tillman."

"I *know*." He tried to imitate her, and she got it. For just a moment they stared at each other.

"I was trying to catch a cab. I promised my mom I would take one if it started to get dark and I was alone."

His smile widened. This was perfect. "Well, you're not alone anymore. I'm headed over to the East Side and I've arranged for my bus to pick us up at 86th."

"Your bus?"

"Well, yes, but I let other people use it too. Just charge enough for expenses. Where do you live?"

"79th between Park and Lex."

"Hey, I live at 74th and Fifth. We're practically neighbors. From now on you'll never have to go home alone."

They walked south on Central Park West to 86th. The euphoria of having just run and of being alongside her kept his feet from touching the pavement all the way to the bus stop.

On the other side of Central Park, Herb Ellinson walked slowly down Fifth Avenue in the spring evening, watching the lights go on in the city that had once been the center of his world. New York City still seemed to him a majestic place, the park flanking him on the right, on his left the solid wall of buildings, ahead of him the lights of the midtown office towers.

When you lived in a Malibu beach house, New York became some place you read about—a place of intractable deficits, pervasive filth, despairing ghettos, and frightening crime. You forgot how thrilling it could be just to walk down Fifth Avenue. But the thrill he felt now was about more than just the city. It was about an 18-year-old boy who was, without question, his nephew, his brother Jake's grandson. Herb saw it in more than just the face. It was in the expressions, the shape and attitude of the body, the movement, the pigeon-toed stride.

He'd told Mackenzie it *was* Jake. Well, it could have been. Jake had not been as tall as this boy, and a bit more muscular, but aside from that . . . just uncanny.

On an impulse, Herb stopped at a sidewalk phone and made a call he hadn't intended to make till the following morning: to Diana Penrose Miller. It was after six; he half expected no one would be there.

"It's personal," he told the secretary. "I think I may have some information about Ms. Miller's family."

At once she was on the line. "You say you have information on my family, Mr. Ellison?"

"Ellinson, with an n," Herb corrected. "If your mother was June Hopkins, yes, I may have information for you. And you may have some for me. Could I meet with you? It's the kind of thing that isn't easy to deal with over the phone."

Herb was at the Bemelmans Bar in the Carlyle, eyes on the entrance, when Dede walked in. For a moment, the two stared at each other, Dede seeing a thin older man dressed in the softer, pastel colors that went with the California sunshine, Herb seeing a tall, strong, handsome woman who seemed glamorous yet businesslike in a beautifully tailored navy pants suit and carrying a slim leather briefcase. Even if Herb had not known about her, he would have said: here is someone used to being in charge. And yet there was something open, inquiring, in the blue eyes so close in color to his own.

Herb began as soon as they both sat down. "I have information about your family which may surprise you. If true. It's possible it isn't, although I doubt that."

Dede nodded, and hesitated before saying, "Does it have something to do with my father?"

Now it was Herb's turn to be surprised. "Yes. Have you been contacted by someone else?"

She told him about her father's last words and her mother's photo album.

From an envelope Herb pulled a copy of Jake's letter to June Hopkins. "This was written in December, 1944, to your mother by my brother, but never mailed."

Herb sat and watched as she read. When she looked up he said, "Of course the 'news' could be many things, but . . ." Herb pulled from the envelope two photos. He showed the first to her.

"You know who that is."

"Of course. My son Jim."

"Now look at this one." He handed her a picture of Jake in shorts and singlet, taken when he was on the CCNY boxing team.

"This is a picture of someone who was stationed in England in 1944, when your mother was there. It's the man who wrote the letter. My brother, Jacob Ellinson."

She stared at the picture, and all she could say was, "Incredible."

CHAPTER 18

Winter, 1941-42

German forces reach the northern suburbs of Moscow, within sight of the Kremlin. The Soviets begin a massive counterattack.

On December 7, Pearl Harbor is attacked. The next day Roosevelt makes his famous "a date which will live in infamy" speech. In quick order the Japanese attack the Philippines and Malaya, and Germany and Italy declare war on the U.S.

The War Department authorizes the formation of four parachute infantry regiments, one of them the 502nd, which is to be activated on March 2, 1942 under the command of Lt. Col. George Van Horn Moseley.

Hit records: "Green Eyes," Jimmy Dorsey; "Chattanooga Choo Choo," "Elmer's Tune," and "String of Pearls," Glenn Miller; "I Don't Want To Set The World On Fire," Horace Heidt.

Sunday, November 30th, the day before Jake's induction and one week before the attack on Pearl Harbor, is a grim day at the Ellinsons'. Millie goes about her household routine elaborately, tight-faced, saying almost nothing, occasionally daubing a cheek as if to wipe away a tear. Jake is trying to cheer her up. His father is trying to keep the peace. Herb can only watch this drama being played out, powerless to affect it, his nerve endings tingling at the tension. Though the evening is cold and blustery, Marty suggests that Jake join him in a familiar ritual, a walk to buy ice cream.

"Give us a chance to talk," says Marty. "Who knows when we'll have another chance. It'll probably be a few weeks before they'll even let your mother come to make your bed . . ."

Jake laughs, as much in appreciation of what his father is trying to do as at the joke.

"Who made your bed when you were in, pop?"

"My mother wanted to. She didn't get to, either."

Jake puts his hand lightly on his father's shoulder as they walk along the empty street. Marty is three inches shorter than his son, stocky, thick-shouldered; Jake can feel the bunched muscles below his father's neck.

"I'll manage, pop. One of our trombone players was drafted a few months ago. He wrote to Buddy that after being on the road, basic training was a picnic. And the food was better."

He expects his father to be amused; he's wrong. Marty pats the hand on his shoulder. "Won't be too long before we're in the war. That won't be any picnic."

"You think we'll go in?"

"We have to. The Nazis have taken over Europe, and it looks like they're going to run over Russia. The Japs are out to do the same thing in the Pacific. Korea, Manchuria, China . . . and they're just getting started. We can't let the dictators take over the world, even if they're willing to leave us alone. And believe me, they won't leave us alone."

"At least the Japs aren't against the Jews."

"No, not specifically. That's Hitler's department. But it's not just a question of the Jews; it's a question of the whole country, America. You must never forget, Jake, in the history of the world, there's never been a country as good for the Jews as America. Not since biblical times, when we lost our homeland. Look at how the Jews have done in this country! We've got a Jewish governor in Albany. A Jewish Secretary of the Treasury in Washington. A Jewish Supreme Court justice. We've even got a Jewish king . . . of swing."

Marty smiles at his own little joke. "If there's anybody that should be saying prayers for this country, it's us. What the Nazis are doing to Jews, everyone hears about. But we mustn't think that's so unusual, that it never happened before. In Russia, in Poland . . . have they got anti-Semites! Why do you think your grandparents came to America? Believe me, Jake, for us, America is the *goldene medina* . . . the promised land."

"*Weltanschauung*. Know what that is, pop?"

"A philosophy, an outlook on the world. You think because I never went to college . . . ? I read, Jake."

"All I meant was . . ."

"You can learn a lot just reading. There's almost nothing you can't learn."

"I know, pop. All I wanted to say was you're the only one I know who has it. The only one who looks at the big picture. I learned so much from you."

The two men have reached the candy store but don't go in. Marty looks up at his grown son.

"I hope I can give you something. I know what I haven't been able to give you. Not that I haven't wanted to . . ."

"Stop it, pop! You gave me music! You gave me a . . . *Weltanschauung*!"

Marty shakes his head sadly. "No. My boy, Jacob. My eldest son. I am a liar! I may talk about the problems of the world. But when I try to look at the big picture, all I see is you and Herbie. I try to worry about the world, but all I can worry about is the two of you. In my mind, I care about the British and the French and the Russians and the Chinese and . . . everybody. In my heart, all that I care about is, nothing should happen to you. And to Herbie, when his turn comes. That you two should be all right. Some *Weltanschauung*."

Marty reaches for his son, to hug him. Jake can see the tears in his father's eyes.

"I'm gonna be all right, pop. You'll see." Father and son are hugging each other. Jake can barely choke the words out.

The next day, Monday, December 1st, is cold and bleak. And gray, as only a day in a drab neighborhood like theirs can be. Eleven months earlier, on an equally cold, gray January day, there was another leave taking. But for Mildred Ellinson today is infinitely worse. Going on the road is one thing; those dangers she knows something about. About the army and its dangers she knows nothing and so is free to imagine the worst. She is crying as he walks to the door, this time carrying only a small bag with a few personal belongings, as he's been instructed to do by the induction notice that begins with its famous salutation, "Greetings . . ."

Even the contents of the small bag occasion an argument. Mildred wants him to take a trumpet, to show he's ready to go into a band. Jake refuses. Finally, a compromise. He puts a mouthpiece in the bag, so he can play someone else's horn if the chance comes.

At the door, Mildred holds onto her son as if she were still considering physical restraint. "Be careful," she says. "Jacob, Jacob. Don't do anything dangerous. Don't let them make you!"

"I'll tell them," Jake says. "I'll say it's my mother's orders and anyone who disobeys will have her to deal with."

"Now's not the time to be funny," his father warns gently.

Jake heeds him. "Ma," he says, "I'll be careful. Don't worry. And I'll be all right. It's not as if we're in the war. Anyway, who's going to hurt me?" He makes a threatening fist, half in jest, half in youthful invulnerability.

As he did 11 months earlier, Herb walks Jake to the elevated train station. The day is even colder, the wind fiercer. Halfway down the block they meet Mrs. Steinberg, whose younger son Stan is a friend of Herb's and whose older son Sidney has already been drafted. She is carrying a full shopping bag and hurrying along as fast as she can, but she stops to say hello.

"Want me to carry that for you, Mrs. Steinberg?" Jake asks. Herb marvels at how cool his brother is, not even worried about being late to the army!

"I'm almost home," she answers. "What a day, I wouldn't send a *vildeh chaya* out on a day like today." A wild beast. "Go home, boys!" she enjoins.

"Can't," says Jake cheerfully. "Places to go, things to do. Right, Herb?"

"Yes, right."

"Everybody these days is going and doing. So go, do. Just don't catch cold. Everything's all right at home?"

The boys nod simultaneously.

"So say hello for me." And she hurries on.

As soon as she is gone, Jake turns to Herb. "Hello." "Hello," says Herb in return. The two brothers laugh. Then for several minutes they walk side by side in silence.

"What's on your mind Herbie?"

"You scared?"

"Peeing in my pants!"

"Seriously."

"What should I be scared of? Bullets? Bayonets? Bombs? Grenades? Poison gas?" Jake laughs again. "You're always scared, kid, with something new. A little anyway. It's normal."

"Think you'll get in a band?"

Jake shrugs.

"Mom will be awfully upset if you don't."

"That's your department, Herbie. Make sure she's not upset. And write to me regularly. Let me know what's going on."

Herb nods. They walk along in silence. Herb has his hands jammed into the pockets of his wool jacket; Jake does not deign to warm his hands. One, red-knuckled, holds the small bag he has with him. "I guess they give you gloves," Herb says.

"Are you kidding? The best of everything!"

"I'll find out soon enough, I suppose."

"They're not taking them till 21, Herb. By the time they get to you, I'll be a general. You won't have a thing to worry about."

They're at the foot of the stairs to the train. Jake turns to his brother. "Take care of everything at home. It's up to you."

Herb wants to tell his brother he loves him, but he doesn't. He just puts his arms around him and hugs him. Then, without another word, Jake turns and runs up the stairs. Herb stands there, watching the bounce in his stride. At the top Jake turns, gives him a wave and a big, confident grin, then goes through the door and disappears.

Herb will always remember the parting look that says: How could anything hurt me? *Me!*

That afternoon Jake is again aboard a bus, this time not with a band but with a bunch of draftees as green as he. This time headed not for one-night stands in the Middle West, but for Camp Kilmer, New Jersey.

When uniforms are issued, these men, virtually all from the Northeast, but beyond that as different as can be—WASPs from Vermont, Italians from New Jersey, Irishmen from Boston, French-Canadians from Maine, Poles from Connecticut, Portuguese from Massachusetts, Jews from New York, graduate students and high school dropouts, rich and poor, short and tall, skinny and fat—all begin to look a little more alike, and like it or not, suffer the same routine: getting up before anyone should have to, falling out for formations, marching to the mess hall, doing KP and most of all, waiting for basic training.

On the first Sunday of his army service, Jake and some other guys are sitting around in the barracks, listening to a New York Giants football game on the radio, when they hear the news about Pearl Harbor.

"Yellow Jap bastards!" shouts one man.

"What about Germany and Italy?" asks another.

"They'll stay out of it if they know what's good for them," someone replies.

"No they won't," says Jake.

"Yeah, how do you know?"

Because my father told me, Jake wants to say, but it doesn't sound grown-up enough. So he just says, "Watch."

Four days later, on December 11th, Germany and Italy declare war on the United States.

Jake sits around at Camp Kilmer for four weeks before being sent to Fort Benning, Georgia, in January, 1942, for basic training. After a train trip and a bus ride, Jake and a busload of buck privates, lugging overstuffed duffel bags, are ordered out of their buses in the inky, freezing night and into a long, big-windowed barracks which, with its bare bulbs, is somewhat brighter than the night and barely warmer. Two long rows of double-decker bunks stand at right angles to the sidewalls, with an aisle down the middle.

"Everybody grab yourself a sack," shouts the corporal who leads them in. "You got ten minutes to make it up before we go to chow."

The men scramble; Jake gets himself a lower bunk, pushes his bag underneath it and starts making it up, when he hears a voice.

"Jake? All right if I sleep up on top?"

Jake looks up and sees Phil Epstein, a chubby, bespectacled man a year older than he, who lives a block and a half away from him in the Bronx, yet someone he knows only slightly.

"Hi, Phil. Let's see. Do you have a reservation?"

But he can see Phil is too scared to be amused by anything, so he adds quickly, "Sure!"

The men have been divided into platoons alphabetically for basic training, which puts Ellinson in the first platoon, along with Epstein. As they begin the ordeal of basic training, Jake realizes he has a ward in Phil, who is frightened, clumsy, and inept at everything military, from physical training to drill to marksmanship to bed making. One evening Phil sits on Jake's bunk; Jake would just as soon skip the intimate conversation that's coming, but he knows Phil is miserable.

"Jake, this place is strictly for *goyim*."

"I don't understand Yiddish," Jake replies angrily. Jake knows the word well enough; it means gentiles. He's angry at Phil's weakness, not his Yiddish.

Phil doesn't get it. "I mean, this is no place for a Jewish boy from the Bronx,"

Jake gets up on one elbow: "Have you heard the news, Phil? There's a war on!"

"I know there's a war on. What does that . . . ?"

Jake doesn't want to get into this; he wants to rest in the few minutes before they're called to the mess hall. But he's in it now. "It means no one wants to be here! Except maybe for a few R-As who found a home in the army! All these guys, Italians, Irish, whatever they are, want to be home. This is no place for anyone! The war is not just theirs; it's ours, too. Maybe more than theirs, because Hitler is after the Jews more than he's after anyone else."

Phil is taken aback. "Gee, Jake, all I'm saying is . . ."

"The Jews have got to be here. And I hate to see a Jew look like a . . . *schlemiel* . . . in front of *goyim*. Make the best of it, Phil; everybody else is."

Phil rises, looking even more dejected, and starts to climb up to his bunk. Jake gets to his feet, and looks at his unhappy fellow Jew from the Bronx. "I'll help you, Phil, honest. Just do the best you can and don't complain."

But Phil is not soldierly. It takes him a week, with Jake's help, to learn to dis-assemble and re-assemble his M-1 rifle. Jake gets it in two days, the New England farm boys in a half hour.

As they approach the end of basic, an obstacle looms that is legendary for trainees: the infiltration course. The men must climb out of a trench and crawl through a course that simulates combat. Mock explosions go off around them as they attack an objective. Most fearsome is the live ammo from machine guns fired at a fixed height of three feet above the ground. At least that's what the trainees hear; no one can actually vouch for the height of the fire, or, indeed, that real bullets are being used. But if the purpose of the course is to scare the hell out of the men, it works. As they wait to crawl out into the trench, there is more nervousness than Jake has yet seen in his couple of months in the army. With Jake's apprehension is mixed a thrill of anticipation; he can't wait to get out there. He doesn't believe the stuff about the machine guns; he figures if there are real bullets, which he doubts, they're more likely being fired six or seven feet above the ground, not three.

When the time comes to start, Phil is petrified.

"Suppose I stand up?" he whispers to Jake.

"Why would you stand up?" Jake asks.

"Panic!" says Phil.

"You won't panic."

"Look at my hands." In his right, Phil holds his M-1. He extends his left; the fingers are quivering as if each had a life of its own.

"All right," says Jake. "Here's what you do. You go into that trench right next to me. You climb out of it when I do, right next to me. You crawl alongside me; do exactly what I do; stick with me. OK?"

Phil does exactly as he is told. The two crawl the length of the course, with machine gun fire rattling overhead, punctuated by the deeper booms of simulated artillery shells and grenades. They both emerge dirty but unscathed, as does everybody else. They will never know if the ammo was real, and if real, at what height it was being fired.

On a Saturday night, two weeks from the end of basic, Jake goes with some men from his platoon go to a big rec hall on post, where the division band is playing for a dance.

A rare sight meets them: females. Red Cross volunteers and local girls brought in from nearby towns. Hundreds of GIs are packed into the hall, most just milling around, others paired off with women on the dance floor, doing a dreamy fox trot to a syrupy arrangement of the Tommy Dorsey hit "I'll Never Smile Again." Jake is not really interested in dancing; he's not very good at it, having spent most of his time playing the music others danced to. He is hungry for live music; this is the first time he's been in the presence of a band since he was inducted. He pushes through the mass of uniforms that surrounds the dance floor, works his way up close to the right side of the bandstand where the reeds and brass sit. In the jacket of his dress uniform rests his mouthpiece, warmed by his body heat and ready.

He spots a trombonist he once played jobs with around New York and a reeds man who worked with the Sammy Kaye orchestra, both competent pros. As he stands and listens, Epstein approaches with three other guys from the platoon, Kevin Fitzgerald, a Bostonian; Tony Calabrese, who's from Perth Amboy, New Jersey; and Jim Archer, from Poughkeepsie, New York.

"What do you think of the band?" Phil asks. "I told these guys you were a professional musician."

Jake shrugs; he doesn't want to put down fellow musicians. "They're all right. Probably haven't been playing together very long."

"What instrument you play?" Tony asks. The men are now virtually shouting at each other, because the band has gone into a thunderous version of the Jimmy Dorsey hit, "Green Eyes." Jake points to the three trumpets.

"Trumpet."

"You as good as those guys?" asks Tony.

Jake laughs and shrugs.

"Well, are you?" Tony is persistent.

"Some of them are pretty good, some . . . aren't," Jake finally replies.

"You better?" asks Tony.

"Yeah, I'm better."

"You going into a band after basic? What a deal that would be!" says Kevin.

The number is over and Jake goes up to say hello to the musicians he knows. Phil heads over to the warrant officer who leads the band and in a couple of moments the two approach Jake.

"This guy says you're a musician," says the warrant officer.

"The best," offers the trombone player.

"Who'd you play with?" asks the warrant officer.

"Buddy Benson, The big band and the sextet. Goodman asked me to join his band. But I also got an invitation from Uncle Sam."

The warrant officer is now interested. "Do you have a horn? Want to sit in?"

"All I've got is this." Jake reaches into his jacket packet and takes out the mouthpiece,

"I'll get you a horn," says the bandleader. "Why don't you look through our book, find something you want to play."

Jake leafs through the arrangements, comes to "All The Things You Are."

As he sits down, he's nervous and very excited, holding the horn in his hands, the other musicians around him, the crowds out there waiting for the magic. When the number begins, he's surprised at how easy it is to get back in the groove. In the second chorus, he gets the nod and goes into a solo that is supposed to be eight bars long but turns into 16, when the leader gives him the go-ahead. The solo is modest; Jake hasn't played in months. But he knows how to make it creamy and appealing and he gets a big hand when it's over, especially from the four men in his own platoon.

When the number is over, the leader gets over to him quickly, "You want to play in this band?"

Jake hesitates before saying, "Sure."

"Where are you now?"

"Basic," Jake answers. "Next to last week."

The warrant officer says, "Write down your name, rank, serial number and your unit. I'll see what I can do."

Two weeks later, basic training is over and orders come down. Most men are assigned to the infantry, scores of names on one set of orders. Not Jake. Only one name is on his orders.

At home, Herb is finishing his sophomore year at CCNY. With the war on, the draft age has been lowered to 18 and he will be called up at the end of the school year, a month away. Mildred and Marty Ellinson, bowed under the weight of Jake in the army and Herb on the way, get news that makes them rejoice. Jake has been assigned to a band!

CHAPTER 19

"My father." Dede said it as much to herself as she did to Herb. "Jacob Ellinson."

"A poor Jewish musician from the Bronx." Herb spoke almost casually.

"What?"

"Yes. A big band trumpet player. Extremely good one."

"A Jew?" He saw the blood drain from her face.

"What's the matter?"

"My father . . . was . . . Jewish."

"Yes."

"That makes me half Jewish."

"I guess it does."

"That . . . can't be!"

"It is, I'm afraid."

To Herb she looked as if she'd just heard her family had died, instead of been discovered. "Traditionally, under Jewish law, you're not a Jew unless your mother was," he said, not sure why, not sure whether to feel sorry for her or be angry at her.

"Mr. Ellinson . . . it's not a question of . . . It's just that, suddenly . . . I find I am not who, what, I thought I was."

"You're exactly the same person you were before," Herb said

"No."

"Well, look, we don't know for a fact that my brother was your father . . ."

For a moment a surge of hope went through her. She hated herself for it but it did. Then she said, reluctantly, "Those two pictures . . . how could he not be?"

"It's more than just the pictures. I watched your son running in the park. His body, his pigeon-toed run, the way his arms swing . . . It's uncanny. But there is one thing . . ." Herb hesitated, hating the possibility of losing the family he'd just found. "Jake had a rare blood type. A-positive."

She stared at him. "So have I."

"Then I guess I've brought you what you obviously consider bad news."

"Please, understand . . . nearly half my brokers are Jewish . . ." Her own voice sounded feeble to her.

"And some of your best friends . . ."

"No," she answered. "None of my best friends."

"Well, then, maybe you're going to lose some of your best friends."

"Perhaps more than that."

"And maybe you're thinking, why did this man have to show up with this news?"

"This is a shock to me. A tremendous shock. That's all I can say."

"And to me. First to find I have a niece, the only child of my only brother, the only member of our family left in your generation. And then to find she is a WASP. And an anti-Semite. Are you an anti-Semite, Ms. Miller?"

"No!" She sat quietly for a moment. Then, "Someone else called me . . . yes, perhaps I am."

Herb got to his feet. "I'll be in New York two or three more days, at the Carlyle. If I don't hear from you, I'll go back to California, and never bother you again."

Please understand! She wanted to say.

How could you deny Jake? he wanted to say. How could anyone deny Jake?

They each said goodnight. He turned and left.

She walked back to her apartment in a daze. In the library Tru was holding a drink and reading the *Wall Street Journal*. He looked up.

"Any new worlds conquered?"

"I have just discovered something," she began. She didn't know how to tell him. Wanting not to, yet having to, her first words were as blunt and clumsy as they could be. "My father was a Jew."

As she told him the story, he sat there, face impassive, eyes cold. When she finished, still he sat, sipping from his glass, while she looked at him like a criminal waiting for a judge to pronounce sentence.

Finally: "How long have you known?" His voice sounded dangerously mild.

"I told you. I've just found out."

"How long have you suspected?"

"Tru!"

"I've suspected for awhile myself."

"What are you talking about?"

"I've never known *our* kind of woman to be so . . . pushy. As it turns out, you're not our kind of woman, are you? But then, you always were a bit beyond the pale, weren't you? As I remember, Garden City is slightly outside the pale. Isn't it?"

"Does that make me a leper?"

"We don't allow them in the Goth either."

"Am I supposed to laugh at that?"

"Am I supposed to laugh at being married to . . . ?" He got up from his easy chair. "I'm going to bed."

Later, lying awake, she realized that Tru's reaction, which had made her so furious, was not all that different from her own. They were both anti-Semites, she was just a bit more polite about it. Now these two anti-Semites were confronted by a Jew in their midst.

She was falling off to sleep when Tru sat up in bed. "Dede, I've been thinking."

For an instant she hoped it was going to be all right. He was going to come through for her.

"Who knows about your father, besides us and this man from California?" he asked.

"I don't really know. No one else, I suppose."

"Certainly none of our . . . people. Well, why don't we just . . . forget about it? No one need know. We can just go along as if . . ." He shrugged.

Anger coursed through her. Confusion. "But we'll know, won't we? About the Semitic skeleton in my closet? We'll never forget. Especially not you."

He'd always been able to read her with dismaying accuracy. "No more or less than you. Don't lie to yourself. You don't want to be a Jew anymore than I want you to be one. You love what you have, as much as I do. Perhaps more, because you came by it later. Well, let's try to keep what we have. Let's both try to forget what we've just learned. The cold light of morning will tell you I'm right. Think it over." He lay down again.

She lay there, thinking it over. To her consternation, she realized he was more right than she could bear to admit. Keep quiet and they would still be the dream WASP couple who had the best-looking son, went to the best church, belonged to the best clubs. Most people lived with some lies. All she had to do was let Herb Ellinson go, make believe he'd never been there. It took her a long time to fall asleep.

†

At the Carlyle, Herb lay awake. He thought it a bitter irony that the one person in the world he had ever known to reject Jake was his own daughter. True, she did have the honesty to admit being an anti-Semite and the grace to be embarrassed by it. But he wanted more: To find a family, for him, and for Jake. To make his revered older brother proud of him, which, after all, was the thing he'd wanted above all other things, all his life. So now he'd head back to California, bringing nothing, returning to Marian and their . . . problem.

The next morning as Dede sat putting on the touch of mascara and lipstick that was as close as she came to makeup, Tru, still in his pajamas, walked to her, bent over, kissed her on the jaw. Neither had said a word about last night's revelation.

"It's not too bad a life we have, Dede, is it?"

"Not too bad a life," she echoed. She knew what he was really asking: Do we have a deal? That question she didn't answer.

"See you tonight at the Blanchards'. The invitation says drinks at 6:30."

But so elaborate and varied were the hors d'oeuvres at the Blanchards', who lived on Park, just four blocks north of them, and so lively the chatter, that at 9:30 most of the 30 or so guests were still there and still chattering. Harding and Margaret Blanchard had invited people in honor of Harding's brother, Preston, who was in the middle of a messy divorce and moving back into the city from Greenwich.

Mostly they were in their 40s, WASPs, the men tall and fit, the women slim, tanned, and good looking. For the first time since she married Tru, Dede felt herself examining them from a distance. They were a handsome bunch, she thought. She hadn't been born one of them, in Garden City, as Tru never ceased pointing out, to a short, plump, brunette mother and, she now knew, a Jewish father. But she had joined them, and she could think of no group she'd rather belong to. If indeed she still belonged.

A cluster of people surrounded "Press" Blanchard, who, however difficult his divorce, was at the moment making cocktail party capital of it.

"She said her lawyer, someone named Cohen, wanted to see my 1040s. I told her, Babs, his messiah will arrive before my 1040s do." He paused for laughs, which he got. "I'll be damned if I'll let any Jew lawyer see *my* tax returns!"

Dede managed a frozen smile; she would have done nothing more if Press, who had earlier admitted having a "thing" for her, hadn't put an arm around her and said, "If you and Tru ever split, my darling, two bits of advice. One, call me first thing. Two, do not hire a Jew to represent you. You'll both end up paying him alimony."

Having spent the day willing herself not to think about Herb Ellinson, she suddenly imagined him there, imagined his humiliation at hearing Press. Then, suddenly, it was not his humiliation, but hers, and she spoke loudly enough so that everyone in the cluster, including Tru, could hear.

"I wish you wouldn't say things like that, Press. My father was a Jew."

For three or four long seconds, Press was rendered speechless, before managing, "Oh, Dede! I . . . well . . . you're different. You're a great gal, anyway." The cluster melted away. That was not supposed to happen at one of their cocktail parties. After all, one of the comforts of their crowd was that you could say the kind of thing Press had just said without being embarrassed.

When Dede said to Tru, "I'm going home," he nodded coldly and stayed on. She was in bed when he came in. He said nothing as he put on his pajamas, nothing until he was about to put out his bedside lamp. Finally he snapped, "I take it then your answer is no." Then he shut off the light.

The next morning before eight she called the Carlyle.

"This is Diana Miller." Groggy, Herb had trouble recognizing the name. "I would like to talk with you."

That evening when he emerged from the elevator on the 17th floor of 951 Fifth, Dede was standing at the apartment door. He walked into an elegant foyer which led to a living room decorated in what seemed like a compromise between the cool modernity of its furnishings and the traditional fussiness of its accessories—puffy pillows, Chinese vases, clusters of family photos.

"Mr. Ellinson, for two nights I've lain awake, almost all night, thinking."

"So have I, Ms. Miller."

"Try to imagine my shock when I found out who my father was."

"Not who he was. What he was. A Jew."

"Yes. All right. A Jew."

"Now try to imagine my shock when I find my only brother's only child—my niece—and she, in effect says, I don't want to be that."

"That is not what I'm saying. I have to be who I really am."

"But who are you, really? Daughter of a Jew from the Bronx? An anti-Semitic East Side WASP? How did they say it on the quiz show: Will the real Diana Miller please stand up?"

"You're a very smart man, Mr. Ellinson."

"What is it you want, Ms. Miller? I told you if I didn't hear from you I'd leave and never bother you again. Isn't that good enough? Do you want to stay a WASP with my blessing? I can't give you that."

Now she had to take the step from which there'd be no going back. "No," she answered. "I've already told the truth to my husband and my son. And others."

"I can't imagine it would be such a big deal to them."

"I couldn't have either. But it is. To my husband. And others." She thought of Press's embarrassment, the wide eyes on the faces in last night's cocktail party cluster.

"You're wishing I'd never shown up on your doorstep . . ."

"I've spent a few moments doing that, yes. I may do it again. Right now I want you to meet my son. I want you to help me, Mr. Ellinson."

"Will you call me Herb?"

"Herb, my friends . . . and family, call me Dede." She held out her hand. He took it. They did not shake hands, just held them, for a few seconds.

"Let me get Jim. My husband is . . . not here."

She walked off, leaving him there, waiting. Waiting for Jake to appear. In early '45, when the news came about his brother, he was touring with a Special Services band in England and got compassionate leave to be with his parents. The army even got him aboard a cargo plane for the trip home. His main feeling was not grief; it was disbelief. Not Jake. No. Jake had promised. Sitting on those unyielding bucket seats amid the whine of the props and the roar of the engines, he fantasized that it would turn out to be a mistake, and when he got back to their apartment in the Bronx, Jake would be there, giving him that grin with all the muscles around the mouth, muscles Herb supposed had come from playing the horn.

It felt so real that when he got home he actually looked for his brother. Instead there were his parents, bent by a sorrow that would never again allow them to stand straight. For them it was the sorrow that remained; for Herb it was the fantasy. Back on duty, in the barracks or rehearsing, something would grab his attention, a noise, a voice, a footstep, and he'd look up, suddenly sure it would be Jake walking in grinning, saying, "You didn't believe it Herbie, did you?"

Over the years, the fantasies recurred less often and less vividly, but without disappearing. Occasionally they could still make Herb tremble and look to a door or down a street. And wait. In all his years of fantasizing Herb had formulated dozens of speeches he'd make when Jake appeared. Now, here was Jake in sweatpants and a T-shirt, and Herb could do nothing but stare. The boy was taller, but that was the only difference. Everything else was . . . Jake. Standing there, looking, Herb barely heard Dede.

"Jimmy, this is Herb Ellinson."

Still in a daze, Herb saw himself reaching out to this boy, grasping a hand that was surprisingly big and strong for the rest of him. A hand like Jake's.

"Hello, Jimmy." Herb felt like a fool staring at this boy. His brother. What he wanted to say was, this is some sort of joke, isn't it, Jake? Where have you been? His eyes began to mist. He willed control over himself, forced his eyes over to Dede, looking for help.

She beckoned them both to the sofa, and sat on one end of it. "Why don't you show Jim the pictures?" she suggested gently.

With shaking hands he managed to remove the photos from the envelope, first handed the boy his own photo.

"That's me," Jimmy said. "Where did you get it?"

"Had it taken a few days ago." Then Herb handed him the one of Jake.

"Is that me, too? No . . . it isn't . . . CCNY on the shirt. Is this . . . ?" Jimmy didn't know what to call him. Nor did Dede.

"Yes," was all she said.

"What do you think of all this?" Herb asked.

Jimmy thought for a moment, then smiled. "It's a little like a fairy tale, where it turns out a child is really a . . . what do they call it? A changeling. Really the son of a king or a prince."

"Your grandfather wasn't a king or a prince," Herb answered, "But he was a hero."

"A hero!" The boy said it with eyes bright. "All right!" Thank God, thought Dede, we have someone in the family who's not a bigot. She touched her son's shoulder, "I love you, Jimmy. Isn't he a handsome boy, Herb?"

"Oh yes!" said Herb, just as Jimmy said, "Oh, mom!" She cooked pasta for the three of them. They toasted each other with diet Coke. When Herb left, he hugged both of them, this time unable to will the tears away.

The next morning Dede and Herb drove up to the Westchester cemetery where Jake and his parents were buried. She felt strange as her Mercedes glided under the Star of David on the wrought-iron arch over the entrance. Like most cemeteries around New York City, this one wasted no space. Fathers, sons, mothers, daughters, aunts, uncles who may have kept their distance in life, lay shoulder to shoulder for eternity. Close to the Ellinsons on one side was Mildred Ellinson's family, the Goldens. On the other side, a family named Samuels, whom the Ellinsons had never known. Two polished gray granite headstones marked the graves of the Ellinsons. Mildred and Marty shared a double stone, and to their left lay Jake, the stones marked only by large Stars of David, names and the years of birth and death. Mildred Ellinson, the last of the three to die, lay, at her request, in the center of the family, Jake on her left, Marty on her right.

"And there," Herb pointed to a small space to Jake's left, "is a place for me."

"Not California?"

"California is a place to be young. Sometimes I think I've already outstayed my welcome."

For a few minutes they just stood there. Then he picked up two small stones, walked to the graves, in the Jewish tradition put a stone on each, whispered to Jake, "You should see your daughter, Jake. And your grandson." Even as he chided himself for being a foolish old man, he added, "Maybe you can."

She kept a respectable distance, let him return to her. When he was back, she asked, "Why did you put those stones there?"

"An old custom. To show you were there. I'm not sure whom you're showing, other people, or God, or the person who is . . ." He couldn't bring himself to say buried, ". . . resting there."

She bent over, picked up a couple of stones, then looked to him. He nodded. She walked to the graves, put a stone on each. As they walked away, neither spoke, but he put an arm around her shoulder.

When she got home Jimmy was reading while thundering rock music shook the walls. He read her look correctly and turned it off.

"That better?" he asked with a grin.

"How about Frank Sinatra?"

He looked surprised. She had never before requested anything but silence. "Sure!" He walked to the stack of CDs, "I think he's filed under antiques."

"Ha ha."

While "All The Way" and "Strangers In The Night" sounded softly in the background, she told him about her ride with Herb.

"You seem kind of shook up, mom."

She nodded. "You don't seem to mind at all."

"I guess I'm not as hung up on the Jewish thing as you are. And . . . now I can tell you something I couldn't tell you before. Marcy Tillman? The girl at school?"

"The one you're . . . fond of?"

"Her dad, Dr. Tillman. He's Jewish."

"What do you mean, you could never tell me before?"

"You or dad. Because of the things you said about Jews."

"Jimmy, I . . ."

"It's all right. But don't tell dad."

She nodded, started to ask why not? But she knew why. "I'm having dinner with Herb Ellinson tonight. Why don't you invite Marcy and come with us?"

"She's gone to Fire Island for the weekend, with her family."

"Then you come."

"All right. Cool." She walked to her tall, strong son and hugged him.

In his room at the Carlyle, Herb turned on the news, took his shoes off and sat on the bed with a copy of the *New Yorker*, going through the Nightlife section to see if there were still any jazz names he recognized. Near the end of the listings one popped off the page. At an Italian restaurant in the Village, a place where, according to the magazine, "the food is respectable and the piano players formidable," playing through tomorrow night was, "Johnny Black, a hardy veteran of the Benny Goodman band and other rigors of the Swing Era." Johnny Black! Who'd played in the Buddy Benson band with Jake! Herb picked up the phone to tell Dede he'd found a restaurant.

Rienzi's was a small place, two steps down, on the ground floor of a brownstone on 12th Street between 5th and 6th. When they walked in there were five or six people at the bar, and about a dozen of the 20 or so tables were occupied. Black was in the middle of a set; the room was quiet. This was an older crowd which had come to listen to the music, not talk through it. Dede saw a little man at the piano, baggy faced, hair dyed a vivid brown, who sat hunched over the keyboard, expressionless, eyes closed as he played. He was in the middle of the ballad "You Go To My Head" and never looked up as the maître d' walked Herb, Dede, and Jimmy right past him to a table against the exposed brick wall.

For the rest of the set the three sat silently, letting the piano music wash over them, Herb amazed at the freshness and facility of this musician who had to be in his mid-70s. When it ended, Herb waved the maître d' over, "Would you tell Johnny Black an old friend would like to say hello?" A couple of minutes later Black shuffled to the table, moving like a man who never walked unless he absolutely had to.

"Always glad to meet an old friend, even if it's for the first time." Like most club performers, Black had a line of patter that was cordial yet impersonal, to keep customers happy at a safe distance.

"We are, actually, old friends," Herb replied. "Have a seat, let us buy you drink, and I'll tell you about it." Obediently, Black sat down.

"Just a cup of coffee, thanks," he said. "Doctor gave me a choice. He told me, you can drink. Or, you can stay alive. Guess which I picked?" He laughed, then coughed. "Gave up smoking, too. So we're old friends, eh?"

"We played together twice. In '43, I think it was," Herb told him. "Once on 52nd street, the other time at Rainbow Corner, London. I was in an army band, you were on a USO tour."

"Jesus!" Black's eyes got bigger. He realized Herb was not just one of those guys who thought a drink could buy friendship with a performer. "What did you play? I'm sorry I don't remember . . ."

"Tenor. Herb Ellinson, Johnny."

"Holy . . . Jake's brother! I don't believe this!"

"Such a long time, Johnny. And yet, that night in London, I remember it so well. You kept feeding us scotch. I was never so drunk in my life."

Black shook his head. "Jake's brother! My God!" For a moment, he sat, silent, then seemed to force himself back, to the present, to the table at the little Village restaurant. "Those were some times. The air was . . . charged." He looked to Dede. "It was. You wouldn't believe the excitement! Of course, for guys like Jake . . ." He let his voice trail off.

"Johnny," Herb said, "This is Jake's daughter, Diana Miller. And his grandson, Jimmy."

"No kidding? But . . . Jake never . . ." He grasped Dede's hand, and then for the first time looked right at Jimmy. And kept looking as he shook the boy's hand.

"Look at this kid! How long has it been since Jake and I . . . London . . . that was the last time." Talking to Herb, he never stopped staring at Jimmy.

"December it was, '43," Herb said. "The last time for me, too."

"That was, what? Nearly 47 years ago. God, that's a long time, but isn't this kid the spittin' image of Jake?"

"The spitting image," echoed Herb.

"I don't believe any of this," said Johnny. He turned to Dede. "I never knew Jake had any children. But with *him* how can there be any doubt? You had a great old man there. You must have been just a kid."

"I wasn't born until five months after he died."

"Ahh. So you never knew him. Well, you missed a great guy. I'm sure your mother told you."

Dede shook her head.

"Jake Ellinson! Ahh. What a guy. Tough. A bit of a temper. But good natured; he had a smile you never forgot. Cocky, and you know what? He was as good as he thought he was. What a musician! A lot of trumpet players with the big bands back then sounded like they were dipped in honey. Sweet and sticky. Jake played like . . . how can I put it? Like champagne. Light, sharp, clear, crisp. How he could attack a note! He reminded you of Bix Beiderbecke. You can still hear it on the old Buddy Benson records. But you've probably heard them a thousand times."

"Not yet," answered Dede.

Black turned to Herb. "Hey! Herb! How have you allowed this to happen?"

"It's a long story. We've been out of touch."

"Well. Let's see, it's . . . Diana. You had a great father. Believe me, everybody in the band loved him. And Jake with the ladies, wow!"

"He had a real thing going with the vocalist, Cindy Laine, didn't he?" Herb asked.

Black looked at Herb quizzically. "Yeah, she sure had a soft spot in her heart for Jake Ellinson. When he . . . it took her a long time to get over it. If she ever did!"

"Whatever happened to her?" Herb asked.

"Didn't you know?" Black's look turned mischievous. "A fate worse than death. She married me."

"You're kidding!"

"Forty-something years and three daughters later, he asks me if I'm kidding." Black looked at Dede almost wistfully. "Life takes some funny turns." For a moment he seemed lost somewhere. "God! Just wait till she sees this kid! Come to think of it, I don't know if I want her to. She spends enough time going around singing 'All The Things You Are.'" He looked to Jimmy. "You know that tune?"

The boy shook his head no.

"Well, you ask your uncle here to give you a tape of the Buddy Benson recording. Jake's solo on it was a thing of beauty. And Cindy did the vocal pretty good. In fact, she still does." The thought put a smile on Black's face. "Hey!" he said with a burst of enthusiasm, "I'll play it in my next set!"

That night, after the last set, after the goodbyes with Herb and Dede and Jimmy, Johnny let himself into the co-op apartment on the West Side that he and Cindy had bought after their daughters left the nest and they sold the cottage in Westchester. Cindy was sitting up in bed half reading a book, half watching an old movie on cable. She kept her hair blonde, and as small compact women often do, she'd aged well, helped by a face-lift nine years ago, a present from Johnny for her 60th birthday.

He sat on the bed next to her. Up close, he could see the lines of age re-emerging through the face-lift.

"How come you get better looking each night I come home?"

"Well! To what do I owe this charm?" She tried to sound skeptical, but he could tell from the way her eyes lit up, she was very pleased. She stroked his hair.

"I just had it done," he said. "How does it look?"

"If I didn't know, I'd never guess,"

"Not only gorgeous, maybe blind, too, but I love you."

He leaned over and kissed her on the lips.

"My goodness, pretty soon you'll be having your way with me! What's gotten into you?"

"It was some evening."

"Really? Good house?"

He shrugged. "All right. Half filled. They're keeping me on for another week. Don't pack yet."

Two of their three girls lived in Southern California and wanted them to move out there. Johnny promised to "as soon as the jobs dried up." But Cindy knew he hoped they never would. So she was being patient; she didn't like the dirt of the city, the crime, the hostility, the weather, but she was being patient.

"So what happened?"

He looked at her, wondering why, after 40-something years, he should hesitate about telling her. "I saw Jake," he said.

"Jake? Jake who?"

"How many Jakes have you known?"

Did her face get pale, or was he imagining it? "That's impossible!" she said. "Jake!"

"It was his grandson."

"No," she said. "Jake never . . ."

He nodded. "Did you know Jake's brother, Herb?"

"I met him."

"Well, Herb was there. And Jake's daughter. And the boy, the grandson, who looks so much like Jake, you wouldn't believe it."

He told her the story, then added, "I told them, Cindy takes one look at that kid, she'll want to run off with him. I was joking." He leaned in and kissed her cheek. "Wasn't I?"

She looked at the 77-year old man with the glowing brown hair and pulled him to her. "Jake was in my life and out of it a long time ago. You are my life."

Later, as she lay awake, listening to the puffing sounds of Johnny asleep, she wondered what Jake would look like at . . . he was a few months older than she, which would make him nearly 70. Would the muscular body have turned soft and frail like Johnny's? Would the lean face have gone baggy, the silky dark hair turned white, or disappeared?

Jake. So long ago, she had almost forgotten. She wasn't sure whether it was the forgetting or the remembering that made her start crying.

The next morning, a Sunday, Dede decided to drive out to Southampton, unannounced, sit down with Tru, come to some sort of understanding.

Next to Tru's Porsche in the driveway stood a jaunty little red Volkswagen convertible. She walked in the front door, called out, got no answer, kept going to the terrace in back, walked toward the dunes. In a hollow, she saw Tru on a blanket in the vivid June sunlight. He was rubbing suntan oil on the back of a tawny blonde who was lying there totally nude.

Quietly she walked back to the Mercedes, started to get in, then stopped. She went to the Porsche and then to the VW, took the keys from both ignitions, threw them as far as she could out in the dunes, then got into the Mercedes and drove back to the city.

CHAPTER 20

Spring-Summer, 1942

With the Battle of Midway in the South Pacific, the tide of war begins to turn. The Marine First Division lands on Guadalcanal.

In Europe, the Nazis formulate "the Final Solution to the Jewish Question" (die Endlösung der Judenfrage, often just "The Final Solution") and begin mass shipments of Jews to concentration camps. British and Canadian forces raid Dieppe on the French coast and learn a bitter lesson about an amphibious assault on a defended port, a lesson they remember in planning the invasion of France.

On August 16, the 101st Airborne Division is activated at Camp Claiborne, Louisiana. The 502nd Parachute Infantry Regiment is attached to it.

Hit records: "Don't Sit Under The Apple Tree," Glenn Miller; "Tangerine," Jimmy Dorsey; "I Don't Want To Walk Without You," Harry James; "The Jersey Bounce," Benny Goodman.

In mid-1942 the 502nd Parachute Infantry Regiment exists more on paper than it does in the flesh and bone and muscle of the young men who will give it life. The men must be found. They will all be volunteers: athletes, renegades, hard cases, men trying to prove something. To prepare for combat, they will undergo some of the toughest training a soldier has ever been put through. An Airborne Command order establishes standards of fitness: "the ability to make a continuous foot march of twenty-five miles in eight hours, a five-mile march in one hour and a nine-mile march in two hours, *with full equipment.*"

Jake's regimen at Fort Benning is so much less demanding he is embarrassed by it. The musicians are attached to a Special Services Unit in which almost everybody has some link to show business: actors, singers, dancers, comics, musicians, directors, producers, designers—all people with enough talent, ingenuity, connections or luck to find a safe haven from the dangers of war.

Like everyone else, they have to fall out at 6 a.m. for the morning formation. At that point their schedules diverge from those of other GIs on the post. The band performs four or five times a week, for USO shows, dances, parades; in addition, it rehearses five days a week for either an entire morning or afternoon. The rest of the time the musicians are on their own.

Jake has plenty of spare time to brood about Cindy. He gets a letter from her, filled with love and unyielding determination about the rules for marriage. He broods about something else, too. All around him he sees men training for combat. That's what the army is all about, or should be. The idea is to beat the Japs and the Germans, not play tame charts at officers' club dances. The idea is to be a warrior. One day the simmering discontent is brought to a boil.

Men in Special Services eat in a huge consolidated mess hall that also serves meals to a wide range of other troops. Jake, just finishing lunch, is sitting near another band member, Hyman Siegel, a bass player from Brooklyn, who is talking to a broad-faced Pfc. across the table from him. Jake sees his face getting red; voices are raised. Suddenly the other soldier, who wears the insignia of an infantry regiment, spits out the word "Jew." Jake stands and walks over. Siegel is saying, "I'm doing my share! That's where I was assigned!" Agitated and frightened, he looks to Jake hopefully.

"What's the matter, Hymie?"

"Jake, this anti-Semite . . ."

"Oh Jakey!" the soldier says. "Jakey! Another Jew with a soft job! You want us to fight for you, isn't that what you want . . . Jakey?"

"Ignore this dumb fuck, Hymie. You finished eating? Let's get out of here."

"Jakey and Hymie stay here while everybody else goes to fight to save the Jews from Hitler. But not Jakey and Hymie!"

The infantryman taunts them as they walk off. Outside the mess hall, Siegel looks at Jake. Before he can say anything, Jake snaps, "From now on, fight your own battles!" He storms off, leaving the bass player bewildered.

That night when they climb onto a bandstand at a service club, Jake walks over to Siegel. "Sorry, I'm kind of jumpy," he says.

"It's all right," answers the bass player. He knows that though Jake avoided a fight, he also saved him from at least a taunting, maybe worse.

"The thing is," Jake says, "maybe he was right. We should be the first ones over there fighting."

Siegel's eyes get wide. He is a frail man, narrow-shouldered and sunken chested, who smokes steadily; Jake wonders how he manages to lug his bass fiddle around. "Hell, Jake. Like I told that anti-Semite . . ." This time he pronounces it in Yiddish: AHN-tee seh-MIT. ". . . they assigned me to the band."

"It's OK, Hymie. I didn't mean you."

The leader, Warrant Officer Junior Grade Leon Goodley, is staring at them. Jake claps Siegel on the shoulder and goes to his chair, I meant me, he says to himself as he sits.

A few days later, outside a PX, he encounters the infantryman who harassed Siegel. The soldier is walking with two friends; he looks at Jake, trying to place him.

"You don't remember me," says Jake. "I'm the musician. Jakey. Now do you remember?"

"Oh yeah, Jakey. Still here, huh? Not overseas winning the war yet?"

"You're still here, too, I notice," says Jake, planting himself firmly in front of the man.

"I'm going soon enough. Now get the fuck out of my way."

Jake doesn't move. "Walk the fuck around me."

The soldier pushes Jake, who responds with a right hook to his face, sending blood spurting from his mouth. His two friends charge Jake, who knocks one down with a punch. The other is much bigger than Jake and he tackles him, carrying him to the ground. Jake is taking a heavy pounding from the three of them when another soldier intervenes, pulls the big man away. Jake rolls the others off him and is dragged away by the man who helped him.

"You're a pretty good fighter," the soldier says to Jake. "But you can't take on three guys." The rhythm of those few words tells Jake he is an Italian from New York. He introduces himself as Pasquale Buonaventura, "but everyone calls me Patsy." Not only is he from New York, but from Arthur Avenue in the Bronx, the heart of an Italian neighborhood that's a half-hour walk from Jake's home.

"You want a cup of coffee?"

"Thanks, but I go on duty in an hour."

"Doin' what?"

"I'm in a Special Services band; we're playing at the NCO club tonight."

"You don't play the saxophone or somethin' like that, do you?"

"Trumpet. Why?"

Patsy points to Jake's mouth. "You got a problem. Your lip is split open like an overdone hot dog."

Jake's adrenaline rush has been so strong, he hasn't noticed anything beyond a vague throbbing in his lip. He puts his hand up, feels the split and the blood on his chin.

For the next week or so the band will have to manage with two trumpets instead of three. For now, Jake goes to the PX for a cup of coffee with Patsy. His mouth is beginning to swell.

"On my block, that's what we call a fat lip!" says Patsy good-humoredly. "What are they gonna have you do while it's gettin' better?"

"Why, nothing." Jake is surprised at the question.

"You mean, that's all you do, is play the trumpet in a band? You don't do nothin' but that?" Jake nods. "What a deal! What a soft deal!"

Jake agrees, and part of him is ashamed of it. "What do you do?" he asks.

"I'm training to jump out of an airplane."

"While it's in the air?"

"Yeah, how else?"

Jake wonders if he's being kidded. "Well," he says, "it's something you don't have to do more than once."

"I better get to do it more than once," Patsy says.

"Seriously . . ."

"Ever hear of paratroops?"

"Guys with parachutes! Who jump from planes!" His own words excite Jake. "What's it like, parachuting from a plane?"

"Ain't got to that yet. They're still too busy torturin' us."

"What?"

"I'm talkin' about the training. Compared to what we do, basic was like . . . like playin' the trumpet in a band. It is the worst. You can't believe what they put you through."

"How did you get stuck in something like that?"

"I volunteered."

As Jake soon finds out, everyone in paratrooper training is a volunteer. With nothing to do until his lip heals, he hitches a ride on an army truck and goes out to watch the trainees in action. In the spring of 1942, the army is struggling to get the program going. Men are coming and leaving every day, the arrivals eager for action, the departures men who have found their bodies, minds, or spirits not up to the systematized torture inflicted by order of the War Department.

Some men are still being physically hardened, others being taught the rudiments of jumping; others are already jumping and performing tactical exercises. Men are being put to the test. Could Jake pass? It takes ten days for his lip to heal; during that time he makes several trips out to watch the paratroopers train. Each time the question grows: Could I get through it?

The day comes when he is ready to report for duty. He shows up at a practice, carrying the horn he has been issued by Special Services. He approaches the bandleader. A Chicagoan and a public school music teacher in civilian life, WOJG Leon Goodley is a mediocre musician, but a fine bandleader—hard-working, well organized, fair, and good-natured. He looks at Jake, examines his lip. "Ready to blow?" he asks.

Jake shakes his head no.

"Give it some more time. Meanwhile, I've been thinking. You said you wanted to try doing a few arrangements . . ."

Suddenly Jake is tortured. Why in hell does he have to offer that now? Jake has always wanted to try arranging. For a moment . . . but no, he's decided.

He thrusts the trumpet case forward. "I'm quitting."

Goodley's mouth drops open, then he starts to laugh. "Pfc. Ellinson, I've got news for you. This is the army. No one quits."

"I'm not quitting the army. I'm volunteering for the paratroops."

Goodley just stares at him for a while. "The . . . paratroops? Those maniacs at the other end of the post? Who jump from planes and break their legs? Your lip's better. Now your brain needs fixing."

He and Jake stare at each other. Goodley smiles. "All right, what's bothering you? You know we try to work things out around here."

"Nothing's bothering me. You're a good guy. I like you. I just don't want to be in the band anymore."

Goodley grabs Jake by the arm, walks him over to one of the benches along the wall, sits him down. "Jake, how old are you?"

"Twenty-two."

"I'm not quite old enough to be your father, but I'm going to talk to you like one anyway. You are such a fine, fine musician! The best I've ever worked with. Why do you want to get yourself killed?"

"I don't want to get myself killed."

"Those guys are headed for suicide missions, Jake! You shouldn't be wasted on that, you've got too much talent. Music makes people happy! Doesn't it make you feel good to see how happy they are?"

"I love to play!"

"Then . . . is it because you're Jewish? Do you think you've got to get Hitler singlehanded?"

"Maybe. Partly . . . No, that's not really it."

"Then what is it, for God's sake?"

"Those guys in paratrooper training, they're trying to find out what kind of men they are . . ."

Goodley lets out a big sigh. "And a lot of them will die trying."

Jake nods. "I guess so."

"But not you, huh?" the bandleader snaps angrily.

Jake shrugs. "I'm not the type that gets killed."

"That's what they all say, you damned fool!"

"Look, Leon, I really like you, and I appreciate what you're trying to do."

Goodley's mouth is set and hard. "Then you'll appreciate what I'm *not* going to do. I'm not going to release you. I'm going to say you're essential—which you are! You're not going anywhere!"

Jake shakes his head no.

"You'll thank me!"

Jake hands him the horn. "I won't play for you anymore. Have me court martialed. See if that'll do anyone any good."

Goodley thrusts the horn back at him. "OK, I'll have you court martialed!"

"OK." Jake refuses the horn. The men's eyes lock and hold.

"You stubborn son of a bitch!" Goodley is shouting. Jake has never heard him raise his voice before.

"That's what my mother says," Jake answers softly. "But not in those exact words." Goodley's concern touches him.

Goodley lets out a breath; he can see Jake will not yield. "Tell you what, you play for another week, while you think this over. If you still want to go, I'll let you." He drops the horn in Jake's lap. "You stupid, stubborn son of a bitch." He gets up and walks away.

One week later, he agrees to release Jake and two weeks after that Jake moves over to a training platoon in the Airborne Command. A Special Services truck driver gives him a lift to his new home on sprawling Ft. Benning. It is across the Chattahoochee River, which marks the boundary between Georgia and Alabama; airborne training takes place in what is called the Alabama Area of the post. To Jake, his new home looks very much like the old: a drab wooden barracks that is stifling in summer and freezing in winter. Standing in front of the barracks in the bright July sun is a group of his fellow trainees. Jake joins them, leaning against the building, listening to men talking about where they're from, why they've volunteered, when he hears a voice.

"Hey, Pfc!"

Jake wears the single stripe he has been given as a band member. This distinguishes him from most of the others, who are still buck privates, entitled to no stripes. He turns, sees a sergeant, short, thick-necked, wide-shouldered, slim-hipped, sandy hair cropped close, pants bloused above paratrooper boots. Standing there, hands on hips, he could have jumped off a recruiting poster.

"Get over here, Pfc!" Jake walks to him. "Give me 25."

It's been awhile since Jake has had to do pushups; they were not part of the routine for an Army musician. He drops down and does 25. As he finishes the last, but before he can rise from the pushup position, the sergeant yells at him.

"Hold it, right there! Know what they were for?"

"No, sergeant!"

"For leaning against the building. Around here, nobody leans against anything. Ever! Got that?"

"Yes, sergeant."

"Now give me 25 more!"

The second 25 are tough; Jake barely manages them. This time he gets to his feet without the sergeant stopping him.

"Know what they were for?"

"No, sergeant."

"You walked over when I called you. Around here, nobody walks. You double-time. Everywhere!"

"Yes, sergeant!"

He continues to stare at Jake. Jake, not sure what he wants, stares back.

"What's your name, Pfc?"

"Ellinson, sergeant!"

"I'll be watching you, Ellison."

Jake, accustomed to that mistake, is wondering whether to correct him, when the sergeant turns away and looks at all the men.

"I am Sgt. Cody and it is my job to turn you miserable misfits into the meanest, toughest, fightingest soldiers in the world. In other words, paratroopers! Pfc. Ellison, I want you to go into the barracks and tell the others to get their asses out here! Now how are you going to do it?"

"On the double, sergeant," Jake knows he should stop there, but something makes him add, "And no leaning against the barracks." He turns and starts running.

"Ellison!"

Jake stops and turns. "I see that 50 pushups haven't taken all the smartass out of you. Let's see how much you got left. Gimme another 25."

As Jake begins to struggle through another set of pushups, Sgt. Cody sends someone else into the barracks to get the other men. When they emerge, he shouts, "All right, fall into three ranks facing me."

The first 15 pushups are tough for Jake, the next five painful, the last five agonizing. He gets to his feet.

"Fall in, Pfc. Ellison! On the double!" Jake finds a place in the ranks. "Like I said, I'll be watching you, Ellison!" Jake decides this is definitely not the time to correct him.

So begin 13 weeks that make Jake's earlier basic training seem like a stroll through the Botanical Garden in the Bronx. Six mile runs before breakfast. Twenty-five mile hikes at night, cross country, with full field equipment. Obstacle courses, rope climbing, marksmanship, calisthenics, weapons training, plus the usual army mix of drilling, KP, and inspections.

And hand-to-hand combat. The men assemble in T-shirts with Sgt. Cody in front of them.

"OK, today we start teaching you how to kill a man with your bare hands. Now I need someone to help me in a demonstration. Someone who thinks he's real tough."

Cody starts looking around; Jake tries to make himself invisible.

"Pfc. Ellison, why don't you come up here?" Jake double-times to the front.

"How'd you like to help me out?"

"Yes, sergeant."

"Does that mean you'd like to?"

"Yes, sergeant." Jake is determined to avoid provocation.

"You don't sound real eager."

"Yes, sergeant!"

"You any good at fighting, Pfc. Ellison?"

"I did a little boxing in college, sergeant." Jake was in fact on the CCNY boxing team, but as soon as the word "college" is out of his mouth, he'd like to have it back. Too late.

"A little boxing in college? Oh, how smashing!" Cody is trying something that to Jake sounds like a kind of English accent. He figures the sergeant is conjuring up a privileged Ivy League education for him. He wants to say, hold it, I'm just a poor kid from the Bronx! But he knows this is a no-win situation. He stands there and waits.

"Well, I want you to try a little of that Marquis of Queensberry stuff on me. Come on; come at me. Give it the old college try."

Should Jake attack Cody half-heartedly, he's in for trouble. Should he do it successfully, he's in for even more trouble. He approaches the sergeant throwing a looping punch. The next thing he knows, he's flipped sideways and onto his back with a force that stuns him. He lies there unable to move. Cody puts his foot on Jake's chest as he talks to the men.

"You see! This is where the rules get you! We're not talking about college boys at play here. We're talking about killing or being killed! We're talking about some Jap or Nazi bastard gouging out your eyeballs. Slitting your throat. Cutting your balls off. Sticking a knife in your belly and slicing it open till your intestines come spilling out. And what'll you do? Lay there and tell him, 'I say, old chap, that's against the rules, you know.' There's only one rule: get that sonofabitch before he gets you."

With his foot still on Jake's chest he goes on. "All right, now we're gonna teach you a few tricks so the other guy's guts will be decorating the ground, not yours."

Only then does he take his foot off Jake. He looks down at him surprised. "Hey, what the hell are you doing down there? Get up and get the hell back in formation!"

Jake is paired off against a tall, lanky soldier toward whom he directs all the anger he feels toward Cody. The sergeant strolls around, watching, correcting, haranguing as the men, in pairs, go through the unarmed combat drill. Cody reaches Jake as he has his opponent face down on the ground, Jake's knee on his neck.

Cody sees Jake's face suffused with blood and anger. "Like to be doing that to me instead of him, right, Ellison? Good! Think of me every time you kill a Jap or a Nazi! I'll be honored!"

When the class is over, Jake's tall opponent says, "Perhaps I should have told you this before, but I am not the enemy. I wish you wouldn't try to kill me; we may be related. My name is Ellison, too."

"Mine is Ellinson, with an extra n," Jake replies.

Kent Ellison, a charming, sardonic WASP snob, is also from New York City, yet from another world: the Upper East Side, prep schools and Ivy League colleges. He is a jazz fan, and when he discovers Jake is a musician, he is delighted, even though he doesn't think much of Buddy Benson. Jake doesn't mind that from someone who has actually heard of Armstrong and Berigan, and even Jake's idol, Bix Beiderbecke. Kent and Jake get bunks next to each other and like so many GIs they spend what little free time they have talking.

One summer evening they are sitting on their bunks in the few minutes of respite allowed them before lights out, Kent says, "Hey, Bix . . ." He's begun calling Jake that, and after several requests that he stop, Jake has given up. "Do you suppose you'd ever be able to stick a knife into some German or Jap and slice him open the way they've taught us?"

"If the sonofabitch were coming at me with a knife or a gun, I'd have no trouble whatever. If he were lying there asleep, that might be something else."

"And . . . what would you do?"

"With a German I'd think of what they were doing to the Jews. With a Jap, Pearl Harbor. Or maybe I'd just imagine it was Cody."

Kent doesn't smile. "Might you think that somewhere the poor guy has a mother and father who love him and want him home safely?"

Jake shakes his head no. "I'd remember that I have a mother and father who love me and want me home safely. You'd think the same thing."

"Would I?"

"Come on, Kent!"

"Does everyone have to have a mother and father who love him?"

"Are you saying you don't?"

"Not if it upsets you. My sister, though, I'd think of her. I do believe she'd actually miss me."

No one Jake knows has ever suggested his parents didn't love him. He doesn't know what to say. "Then think of your sister. Or what about a girl? Do you have a girl?"

"Do you?" Kent stares at Jake with his big hazel eyes and smiles the smile Jake can never quite fathom. Is Kent being pleasant? Is he making fun of him?

"Kind of. At least I had one. Now . . . I guess not. How about you?"

"Tell me what happened."

"Listen Kent, you keep asking all the questions, and not answering any."

"My life is just . . . uninteresting, Bix! You . . . you've been on the road with a band. Tell me, is that girl involved with music?"

Jake gives in. "Yeah, the singer with the band."

"That's fantastic! Right out of Hollywood! But really, it just demands a happy ending!"

Jake shakes his head no. "She wants to get married in a Catholic Church. I won't do it. I'm Jewish."

"Jewish?"

"Yeah. What about it?"

"Hey, don't get pugnacious, Bix. All I meant was . . . those blue eyes. Jews don't have blue eyes!"

"My mother has blue eyes. My father has blue eyes. My brother has blue eyes. I think you're nuts, Kent."

Kent unfolds his lanky frame from a sitting position and stands over Jake, "You think I'm nuts? You, a trumpet player with an army band, volunteer to get yourself killed in the paratroopers? And you think I'm nuts, Bix?"

"You got it wrong. I told you before: I volunteered to kill. Not be killed."

He finds himself enjoying the lessons in killing, and the phys ed. and the weapons and tactics. But to him, indeed to all the men, the jumping is the centerpiece of their training. There is a lot of technique to be learned: how to leave the plane, maneuver the chute, land, collapse the chute. The teaching starts on the ground and bit by bit the height increases: an 18-inch platform, a five-foot platform, a 34-foot tower where you slide down a wire leading to the ground, simulating the shock of a parachute opening. Then a free jump from the 250-foot towers copied from those at the 1939 New York World's Fair. A trainee is harnessed to a chute, hoisted to the top of the tower, and cut loose. For the first time he can feel what it's like to be floating free under an open chute. All of this leads to that climactic moment, the first jump.

As they get ready for it, another buddy has joined with Jake and Kent. Al Breecher, from Dubuque, Iowa, is a short wiry man who weighs no more than 135 pounds, yet has astonishing strength and stamina, gained working long hours on his family farm. Again, music is the connection. At night back home, Al listened to live big band broadcasts on radio. Once, he tells them proudly, he actually saw the Benny Goodman band, in person, when it played Dubuque. He has a huge collection of big band records, among them a few by Buddy Benson, and he is overwhelmed when he finds out Jake actually played the trumpet solo on "All The Things You Are." Simple, relatively uneducated, Al is a mechanical genius, capable of repairing all his family farm machinery, and a whiz at tasks like taking apart and re-assembling anything from a rifle to a BAR to a machinegun or mortar.

These three, who in civilian life might never have met, let alone become friends, are drawn together by music and bound fast by the adversity of airborne training.

After 13 weeks, Jake's platoon becomes part of H Company, Third Battalion, 502nd Parachute Infantry Regiment, 101st Airborne Division. The physical training gets tougher; the rivalry among the companies of the 502nd meaner. H Company sets a division record when it covers 145 miles in a 57-hour march, going the first 33 miles in 11 hours, cross country and over back roads at night. The jump training builds to that day when the men will step out of a plane into thin air, with only a chute between them and oblivion. The closer they get, the higher the toll of injuries: strains, sprains, and breaks. And deaths, when chutes don't open at all, or open partially—becoming "streamers," which send men hurtling to their deaths. The area around the dispensary that cares for paratroopers is called Malfunction Junction and is frequented by hobbling men, in bandages, in casts, on crutches.

H Company's first jump comes on a September day, warm and breezy, the sky studded with puffy clouds, wind close to the 15 miles per hour considered the maximum for a safe training jump. On tables in a huge packing shed, they pair off to pack their own chutes—carefully. Jake and Kent team up, knowing their lives are riding on the procedures they've learned and practiced. They board trucks for the ride out to the field. The warm breeze buffets them. Jake's throat is so dry he can barely talk, but then nobody is talking. The men pile out of the trucks and sit on benches, waiting their turn to board a C-47, the same kind of plane that in 21 months, on a June night in 1944, will carry them into battle.

To Jake's right sits Kent, to his left Al. He looks at Kent, who is pale and grave. Just for a moment Jake can look inside to the frightened boy, then Kent sees him staring and his face closes down. When Kent says, "Play something, Bix," his voice is so hoarse it is almost unrecognizable. Jake does not even trust himself to speak, he just whacks Kent on the knee with the palm of his hand.

Then he looks to Al on his left. "Ready to go, Al?" he manages. He can see that Al needs no jollying; he is imperturbable, as always.

"Guess so," Al responds. "Just going over it all in my mind. Right from hooking up to the static line to collapsing the chute after you land."

"Wait a minute," Jake says, "You collapse the chute after you land? You sure?"

For an instant, Al stares at Jake to see if he is serious. Then he gets it. "You really are a card, Jake."

"And I ought to be dealt with."

Al's face creases in a grin. "A card. Dealt with. That's a good one."

Jake scans the faces of the other men, feels better seeing that they all look as frightened as he feels. To add to the tension, there's a delay, a wait for the wind to die down a bit. Finally, they board the plane, which has been sitting in the sun and is now stifling.

They buckle into safety harnesses for the takeoff, sitting in two rows, one on each side of the plane, facing each other, main chutes on their backs, emergency chutes on their chests, 12 of them in what's called a "stick," plus a two-man crew and instructor.

Someone breaks the tension. "What time do they serve the beer?" Everybody hoots, out of gratitude rather than amusement.

"If they don't pretty soon," someone replies, "I'm leaving." This gets a big laugh. Someone else says, "Whatsamatter, you gettin' jumpy?" Louder laughter. They're loosening up a bit, until the plane comes to life with a sputter then a roar. The faces tighten again. The plane starts to taxi, reaches the end of the runway, turns and begins gathering speed for the takeoff. The faces are frozen. For Jake and many of the others, this is not only a first jump, it's also their first flight.

Jake is afraid to breathe. Finally, he feels the C-47 lift off the ground. Through a window, he watches them clear a stand of trees by what he thinks a dangerously small margin. He tries to swallow, cannot manage it. He sees the earth grow smaller, receding beneath him. The instructor, a master sergeant, tells them it's all right to unbuckle their safety belts, to smoke if they want to. Jake, who never smokes, takes a cigaret when the man across the plane offers it, tries a few puffs, coughs, stubs it out.

Now, Jake tells himself, you just follow the jump routine that's been drummed into you, drill after drill. Do what you've been taught. It's just like the training . . . except . . . Then the door slides away and he can look out at the vastness of the sky, see the miniatures below them: the tiny tufts of a woods, the thin line of a road, the silver ribbon of the Chattahoochee river. Just like practice, except . . . out there is nothingness, waiting to be jumped into. He is jolted to attention by the order from the jumpmaster, the words no paratrooper will ever forget:

"Stand up. Hook up."

The men get to their feet, snap the hooks on the static lines coming from their chutes onto the cable running overhead. They check their own equipment, then each checks the main chute of the man in front of him.

Over the roar of the plane, the jumpmaster barks, "Sound off for equipment check!" And Jake hears the numbers shouted, until behind him Al shouts, "Five, OK!" And he follows with "Four, OK!," hearing Kent's "Three, OK!" and down the line. In close formation, they move up to the door and wait.

A red light goes on over the door. Two minutes to go. They can hear the plane slow. Kent shouts, "Good luck, Bix!"

"You, too!" Jake turns his head. "Good luck, Al!"

"Same to you, Jake," Breecher answers.

The jumpmaster shouts, "Are you ready?" A hoarse cacophony of sounds answers. From the jumpmaster; "Stand in the door. Close up! Tight!"

The green light comes on over the door, and then the jumpmaster is out the door. As one man, the others shuffle up. Then a second is out. Jake trying to remember everything, remembers nothing. Kent is in the door. And gone. One instant Jake is there, too. Then he is out into thin air. The prop blast hits him, he remembers to start counting, but by the time he finishes "One thousand, two thousand, . . ." he can feel the canopy of the chute rattling out of its case, then the jolt that threatens to take his body apart as the chute opens and blossoms with air.

He's floating. He's alive. He looks up to check his chute. It is open, working, beautiful. He grabs the risers and twists to get his back to the wind. Around him he sees other chutes, steady in relation to his, so he knows he's all right. He can feel himself beginning to smile. Not for long, for now the ground is coming up at him, fast. He tries to remember: look at the horizon, chin in, feet together, knees slightly bent. While he is going over that, the ground hits him hard. Knees flexed, fall to the side. He lands the way he's been taught, and for a moment lies there, stunned.

But in one piece. He collapses his chute and gets it off. He feels himself grinning. He's done it! He's a paratrooper! Not officially, it takes five jumps to qualify, but he's done it! There will never be another jump like this one. Not until France. The four others needed to win him his paratrooper wings are uneventful, even the night jump, which is scary in a whole new way.

By the time the 502nd is shipped to Fort Bragg to join the rest of the division, he is a full-fledged paratrooper, with the high boots, the wings pinned to his jacket, the $50 a month extra pay, and the contempt for ordinary infantrymen, MPs, and all military types other than airborne.

Into early 1943, the grueling training goes on, now with a new emphasis on combined exercises to teach the units how to function on a battalion, regimental, and division level. All of this leads to maneuvers, mock warfare with real jumps, and real casualties. During one of these exercises Jake sees death for the first time. He has just landed from a jump and is collecting his chute. He takes a moment to watch a planeload of men jumping; the sight never ceases to astonish him, the chutes billowing out, the troopers floating to earth. Then, suddenly, a streamer—a chute that comes out of its case but fails to open. He cannot stop watching, he sees the reserve chute start to open, but it is too late; there is no chance for it to inflate. Jake has heard men describe the sound of a body hitting the ground: "like a watermelon splitting open." And he would think, but I've never heard a watermelon split open. Now he knows. He starts toward the body, when he thinks of one verse of a paratrooper song sung to the melody of "Battle Hymn of the Republic:"

There was blood upon the risers, there were brains upon the chute,
Intestines were a' dangling from his paratrooper suit;
They picked him up still in his chute and poured him from his boots.
And he ain't gonna jump no more.

Jake edges closer, dreading what he may see. Yet the man might be alive and needing help. Then he spots an ambulance racing across the field. He is grateful; he won't have to go any farther. He watches a couple of medics leap from the vehicle, run to the body . . . and stand there transfixed. One of them puts his hand to his face.

Blood upon the risers, Jake thinks. Brains upon the chute. Intestines. Poured him from his boots. The medics just stand there. Through the tall grass, Jake spots a pair of boots; he wants to see no more. He heads back to collect his chute. That's what these maneuvers are for, he reminds himself, not only to teach fighters how to fight, but medics how to tend to the wounded and injured . . . and mortuary people how to . . . do whatever they do to bodies. There are specialists for everything in the army.

Now the men are trained, qualified as jumpers. What remains is the chance to fight. It comes as a jolt to the 101st to learn that will come later rather than sooner. In July of 1943, their airborne rival, the 82nd, takes part in Operation Husky, the invasion of Sicily. The men of the 101st, toughened by month after month of training, are envious and angry. Like the others, Jake takes the army decision to send the 82nd into combat first as a personal rejection. It is a Saturday afternoon, the men have a half-day off from training and they are sitting in the barracks. Jake, edgy, restless, is complaining. Breecher, listening, merely shrugs as he lovingly polishes his boots.

"Doesn't anything ever bother you, Al?" Jake snaps. "Don't you ever complain or get angry or disappointed?"

"No use complaining," Al answers calmly.

Jake just shakes his head. Kent looks at him, waiting. Finally Kent says, "Well?"

"Well, what?" Jake asks, impatiently.

"'No use complaining.' 'I Got Plenty O' Nothin'.' 'Porgy and Bess.' Music. You remember music?"

"Vaguely."

"Hey," Al says. "There's a USO show over at division tonight. A band, a vocalist, dancing. How about going over there?"

"Might be just what Jake needs," says Kent. "Music hath charms to soothe the savage breast."

"I thought it was beast," Jake says. "Savage beast."

"Well, you're wrong, Bix. Although in your case, beast would be more like it."

On the bandstand at the fieldhouse is the 502nd Regiment band, The Swing Eagles. Though the members have been through airborne training, they are musicians, not parachute infantrymen; in Jake's letters home, he has become one of them, to account for his transfer from a division band at Benning to the 101st at Fort Bragg.

The first act in the USO show is four girls who tap dance and do high kicks, which the men love, especially the high kicks. Next comes a comedian, Stony Brooks, a minor league Bob Hope, telling minor league jokes about army food, discipline, training. Jokes about women. Jokes about towns near the post.

"You know the difference between Fayetteville and hell, don't you?" Eager, waiting for the answer. "People die and go to hell. Nobody's dying to go Fayetteville." A lot of hooting.

"Now speaking of hell . . . or was it Fayetteville, why do I always get those places mixed up?" Jake can just hear him changing the town name and using the material all over the country, ". . . let me go completely in the other direction, and introduce you to a little bit of heaven. She's the lovely singer you've heard with the Buddy Benson Band and more recently with TD, the great Tommy Dorsey." Jake's heart thuds. "You probably know her hit recording of 'All The Things You Are,' and she's sung on coast-to-coast radio and at leading theaters across the nation, like the Paramount in New York City. She's blonde; she's beautiful. She's the kind of girl every GI would like to bring home. Especially if there was no one at home. Here's Cindy Laine!"

Jake is taking deep breaths. Kent turns to him. "That the one?"

"That's the one."

Al, not knowing the story of the romance, leans across Kent to Jake. "Cindy Laine, gosh! You must know her!" Jake just nods.

Cindy comes on to feverish applause, slim and young and adorable in a long, tight sequined gown, strapless to show slim shoulders and arms, her small breasts pushed up to invent the barest of cleavages. Her hair is very blonde and coiffed elaborately on top of her head. She has too much makeup on—how many times has Jake told her about that!

She starts with an up-tempo "All Of Me" that makes the troops howl and then goes to ballads the rest of the way. "The Nearness Of You," "I Don't Want To Walk Without You," "I'll Be Seeing You" and finally "All The Things You Are."

Musically, the performance is ordinary, but she is not trying to make music, she is trying to caress the soldiers, and at that she is brilliant. By the time she finishes Jake knows that somehow he must see her. In the huge fieldhouse, trailers have been set up as dressing rooms and fenced off by a string of sawhorses, the single opening guarded by an MP. As Jake approaches the MP, prepared to plead for entry, he sees a soldier in fatigues off to the side come out from between two trailers and simply jump the low barrier and walk off.

Jake changes direction, walks to the spot where the soldier emerged, nonchalantly leaps the barrier and disappears between the trailers. He strolls among them until he sees a door with a star and a paper sign taped on it: Miss Cindy Laine. He walks up four steps to the door and knocks.

"Who is it?" The voice makes him catch his breath.

"The world's greatest trumpet player," he says.

The door opens in a flash. She's in a dressing gown, her makeup wiped off. Wide-eyed, she looks 16, just as she did standing in front of the bus that first time he met her.

"Just look at you!" she reaches out and strokes the paratrooper wings pinned to his chest.

"Look at you. Like a little girl."

She throws her arms around him, puts her face in his chest. "Don't worry," she whispers. "I won't spoil your uniform. The makeup is off."

"And you look great that way." He has his arms around her and he's crushing her.

"No criticism!" she says.

"No criticism, you're perfect. 'You are the angel glow that lights a star. The dearest things I know are what you are.'"

"I didn't sing it all that well."

"You sounded great. Like you were singing it to me."

"I was."

"I bet you say that to all the soldiers."

She looks up hurt. "No!"

"I was just kidding. I love you."

"Oh, Jake! I love you, too."

"Can we spend the night together?"

"They're taking us off to another show somewhere. I've got to be ready in 15 minutes."

"That's enough time."

She giggles. "Yes, Jake, but hurry."

"Won't take hardly any time at all." She giggles again.

They make love with him sitting on the tiny sofa in the trailer and her straddling him. She sighs, "oh, oh." It takes hardly any time. For him, anyway.

"They'll be here any minute," she says afterward. "You won't get in trouble?"

"I know the general."

"Seriously . . ."

"Seriously, I'm going. I've really missed you."

"Oh Jake, I wish . . ."

"Maybe after the war . . ."

"If only we could . . . oh, I love you!"

"I love you, too. You have to try and . . ."

"Let's not even talk about it now." She puts her arms around him and squeezes him with a ferocity he never knew she had. "Remember this," she says. "No matter what happens. No one will ever have my heart but you. No one. Ever."

When he gets back to the barracks, Kent and Al want to know where he went.

"Dropped in to see Cindy Laine." He tries to make it sound as casual as he can.

"Did you get a little?" Kent asks.

"Shut up!" Jake glowers at him. "That's the girl I'm going to marry."

"Gee, that's great!" says Al. "You and Cindy Laine! When are you going to do it?"

"He means, get married," says Kent with one of his sardonic smiles.

"Watch it, Kent." To Al, Jake says, "We've got a problem: she's Catholic and I'm Jewish."

"You? Jewish?" Al cannot seem to take this in.

"You sound like you don't believe it."

"I never met a Jew before," Al says with honest astonishment. "I never even saw one."

"You saw Benny Goodman, didn't you?"

"Benny Goodman?" echoes Al, disbelieving.

"And Artie Shaw. And Irving Berlin. And George Gershwin. And Jack Benny."

"No!"

Al's eyes are wide; he is so innocent, Jake finds it hard to be angry with him.

"And Louis Armstrong," offers Kent.

"Come on!"

"Cut it out, Kent," says Jake.

Al is thoroughly confused. "You're both kidding me."

"He is," Jake says. "I'm not."

"You'd never know, would you?" says Al, naively.

Kent shakes his head gravely. "There's a new horn-removal operation."

Al appeals to Jake. "You're not kidding me, are you?"

"No, I'm not. Ignore the cynic."

At mail call a week later, Jake gets a letter from Cindy. Beside the protestations of love it contains a copy of her USO schedule. She writes to him every day; he writes to her when he can and phones her every Saturday afternoon.

During one of those phone calls a few weeks later, he tells her he's getting a two-week leave, which delights her, and then has to report to Camp Shanks, up the Hudson River from New York City, for shipment overseas, which frightens her.

"What will you do on your leave?" she asks from Camp Claiborne, Louisiana, where she will sing for the troops.

"Spend some of it with my folks. Spend some of it with you."

"Oh, Jake, just tell me when and where. I'll be there."

"I'll have to figure that out. Can you just leave the troupe?"

"I'll go AWOL."

"Picked up a little army slang, eh?"

She laughs over the phone. "Soldiers comes up to me and say they want to go AWOL with me. That's how I found out what it meant. At first I thought it was something dirty!"

"It is," says Jake.

"No, Jake! It means taking off without leave."

"I know what it means. What they have in mind is dirty. You suppose they're thinking about sightseeing?"

"You're the only one I want to go AWOL with!"

Jake's problem is, where to take her. Kent solves it. "Why don't you come with me?" he says. "Do you know Myrtle Beach?"

"She's a dancer, isn't she? I didn't know you hung around with girls in show business."

"When you put a trumpet to your lips, Bix, the world lost a very bad comedian. It's a town on the beach in South Carolina . . . about 150 miles from here. My grandmother has a beach house there that nobody ever uses."

"You, me, and Cindy?"

"It's a big old place. I won't even know you're there. And vice versa."

The plan is made. Cindy will get to Myrtle Beach by train. The two men will hitchhike there; GIs in uniform are never denied rides. They will meet at the train station, where a local who serves as the house's caretaker will pick them up and drive them to the beach.

On a windy August day, the three of them get out of an old Plymouth, wave goodbye to a leathery old man who has been introduced by Kent only as Fred, and stand looking at a sprawling house of weathered shingle, its ground floor encircled by a covered porch. Around them are Jake's and Kent's barracks bags, Cindy's two well-travelled suitcases, and six bags of groceries and drinks.

"You must first see the house from the dunes," says Kent. He leads them to a path through the dune grass.

"What about the stuff, just sitting out there?" Jake asks after they've taken a few steps.

Kent looks up. A few high, white strands of cirrus clouds interrupt an otherwise blue sky. "It's not going to rain," he says.

"I wasn't worried about rain," replies Jake.

Kent smiles. "I know." He waves for the other two to follow and continues up the sandy path, stopping when he gets to the point where the dune drops off to the beach.

"Look around," he orders. Jake and Cindy obey. To the east, the calm Atlantic stretches to the horizon; to the north and south, unbroken dunes; the house and the narrow road are the only intrusions into this pristine realm.

"Talk about boondocks," Jake says.

"No telephone," says Kent. "No newspapers. No heat. No hot water . . ."

"What?" Cindy squeals.

"We have an outdoor shower and a separate water tank for it that sits out in the sun. Most any summer afternoon you can have a warm shower. But the best way to bathe is in the ocean. Just take your bathing suit off and walk in with a bar of soap. It's very cleansing, physically and spiritually."

"You mean naked?" Cindy asks.

"The nearest house that way," Kent points north, "is about four miles. And the other way . . . God knows. About three miles that way there's an inlet, the road dead-ends."

"And you two?"

"I won't look," Kent answers. "And Jake, well I assume he's allowed to."

Cindy blushes as only a pale-skinned blonde can. "No!"

"Well, then," he tells her. "You can't watch when Jake and I go skinny-dipping."

That gets a giggle out of her.

For a few minutes they stand looking out at the ocean. The only sounds are the rhythmic murmuring of the low surf and the high call of the gulls. Jake has been to the beach; he has watched the surf, heard the gulls. But solitude like this is completely new to him. He cannot encompass the idea that for all this shore, there are no people. He stares at the house, its porch glowering, its eastern second story windows dark as the afternoon sun moves west.

"Who lives here?" he asks Kent.

"No one, really. My grandmother—granny Purvis we quaintly call her, to differentiate her from granny Ellison—used to spend some time here. She is from Charleston, you see. But none of her northern progeny want to come here. They prefer Maine in the summer and Palm Beach in the winter. She was thinking of selling it, but, well, there's a war on."

"So I've heard," Jake says. "Maybe I could rent it sometime. For our honeymoon." Cindy grasps his hand.

Kent looks at the two of them, standing side by side. Jake can see a look of envy, of sorrow, come over his friend's face. Jake is touched, almost frightened, by its intensity. Then, quickly, it is gone.

"I think something can be arranged," Kent says. "Provided you don't ruin the neighborhood by skinny dipping!" He starts down off the dunes. "Hey, we'd better get our stuff in the house before somebody steals it!"

On the second floor of the house, the bedrooms are strung along a long hall, one huge corner room at each end with windows on two sides, two large bedrooms in the middle along the ocean side and a series of small guest rooms, maid's bedrooms and storerooms on the back of the house. When Kent shows Jake and Cindy to the big room at the southern end and says, "why don't you take this one? I'll take the one at the other end, so we won't run into each other." Cindy seems upset.

"We're not married yet," she says.

"Shh," Kent says elaborately, putting a finger to his lips. "It's all right, I won't tell."

Jake can see Kent doesn't realize she's not joking. He catches Kent's eye, looks toward the adjoining room. Kent picks it up smoothly. "Or if you two would prefer separate rooms, take these two."

That evening, Kent lays a fire in the brick fireplace.

"People don't realize," he says as he works, "just how cool it gets at the ocean, even on a summer's evening." After he gets the fire going, he drops into an old easy chair next to the soft, faded sofa where Jake and Cindy sit side by side.

"Hey, this is really great of you," Jake says. "We'll remember this for a long, long time. In 50 years, when we're sitting around—the four of us, with lots of kids and grandkids . . . we can look back to the good old days."

"Makes a pretty picture," Kent says, almost mockingly. "Right now, all the picture needs is some drinks—and music. Drinks first."

He walks off to the kitchen and soon returns with three tall glasses, hands one to Cindy, one to Jake.

"The choice is simple. Gin. That's all there is. And some quinine water. Very English. Cheers!"

They all sip at their glasses. Jake is vaguely aware of an edge, an aroma, to the gin, and is pleased by the bittersweet edge of the tonic.

"Now for the music." Kent walks to an old wind-up phonograph set in a cabinet, the bottom part of which is storage space for records. He looks through the stack of 12-inch 78s.

"Again, not much choice. No Bix, no Benny, no Billie, not even Buddy Benson," he announces. "Granny Purvis is a purist. She offers you only Bach or Beethoven, 'Bach for the glory of God,' she says. 'Beethoven for the glory of man.' What'll it be?" Kent asks, then answers himself. "Let's make it man."

He puts a record on the machine, winds it up, and places the needle on the record. "Beethoven's Sixth Symphony. The Pastoral. Perfect for the country, but honestly, more for meadows and streams and mountains than for the seashore. The man should have been more thoughtful."

For a while they just sit in silence and listen, motionless except when Kent gets out of his easy chair to change the record, rewind the machine, or refill their glasses.

"I like these, they taste pretty harmless, though," Jake says as he drinks.

"Ah, Bix. The last words of many a good man. Gin is very potent. Be careful. Uncle Sam needs you for the big invasion."

"Is that a military secret?" Cindy asks. "They warned us about asking our boys in uniform for any military secrets."

"No military secret at all," answers Kent. "There's going to be an invasion of Western Europe . . . France. There simply has to be."

"And will you be in it?" Cindy asks as if the idea had never occurred to her before.

"They're not shipping us over to go sightseeing," Jake says.

"Or play in a band," Kent adds mischievously.

"That's where you should be!" says Cindy, now thoroughly alarmed. "Not where you can get killed!"

The "harmless" gin is making Jake feel very warm. "Kent and I are not going to get killed."

"How do you know?" Cindy asks.

"Yes, Bix," echoes Kent, "How do you know?"

"Because we didn't sign up for it," says Jake. "You have to sign up for it."

"Be serious!" shouts Cindy, also feeling the gin.

"All right. We're not going to be killed, because . . . we're not the type that gets killed. You can tell by looking at us."

"This is no time to be funny, Jake!"

Kent looks at Cindy solemnly. "That's where you're wrong, my dear. This is no time to be anything else."

Jake raises his glass. "Here's to being funny."

"To everybody getting through the war safely," offers Cindy.

"To a marvelous week," says Kent, "Let's not think of anything but the week ahead. And let's make it superb!"

Going to bed, Cindy insists on the charade that she and Jake are sleeping in separate bedrooms. They go to their three rooms and close their three doors. Moments later, Jake sneaks out of his room into hers. As he slides into bed next to her, she actually says, "Did Kent hear you?"

"Oh, Cindy, for God's sake!"

"Jake, I've told you, please don't take the name of the Lord that way."

"All right," he says, resignedly. "No. Kent did not hear me." He puts his arms around her, kisses her.

The days are magical, the weather perfect; the time is spent lying in the sun, swimming in the ocean, walking along the beach, riding the bikes they find in the shed next to the house, sitting in front of the fire, drinking gin. For Jake and Cindy, making love, last thing at night, first thing in the morning. Jake wonders if Kent knows when they do it, thinks about them doing it, wishes he were doing it, too. Kent offers no clues.

On the afternoon of the fifth day, a visitor arrives. Having reached a compromise on the bathing suit issue—he will wear one except when actually in the water, she will close her eyes as he makes the transition—Kent and Cindy are on the beach. Jake, not being a good swimmer and not enjoying it, is sitting on a canvas chair near the house reading "For Whom The Bell Tolls." He enjoys Hemingway, likes the manliness of the heroes and the clean economy of the writing. It reminds him of the way Bix Beiderbecke played the cornet.

His reading is interrupted by an uncommon sound: an automobile, the first they've heard since the caretaker drove off. He walks around to the front of the house, sees a man getting out of a foreign sports car. The man pulls a leather gladstone bag from the front seat and turns and sees Jake.

"Well . . . hello," he says. Jake isn't quite sure what he means, but he knows it isn't just hello.

"Hello," Jake answers.

"I'm Tony Graves." Tony Graves is a few years older than Jake, very tanned, his hair bleached white by the sun. He looks like a model in a clothing ad. Right now he is staring at Jake alertly.

"I'm Jake Ellinson."

When he hears the name. Graves breaks into a grin, "Are you a cousin?"

"You mean of Kent's? No. My name is Ellinson with an extra n. We're in the same company in the army."

The guardedness returns. "Where is he?"

"On the beach. With my girlfriend."

Graves brightens up again. "I'll run down and surprise him." He drops his bag and goes off across the dunes. A few minutes later Cindy comes back.

"Who is that . . . Tony?"

"A friend of Kent's I guess."

"Kent didn't seem very glad to see him."

Cindy describes the scene: Graves amused at seeing Kent and Cindy; Kent annoyed and kind of embarrassed, wanting to know what he was doing there. Graves saying he'd heard that Kent was using the house, so he drove up from Charleston and expected a better welcome than the one he was getting. That's when Cindy decided she'd leave them alone, said she was going back to the house for a drink of water.

"He's real handsome," Cindy says. "But he sure knows how to make a girl feel low. He just looked right through me!"

Dinner is a model of tense civility, eaten with two bottles of red wine brought along by Graves. Jake and Cindy don't really like wine; they sip theirs reluctantly. Kent and Graves more than make up for them, and as they empty both bottles, the civility frays.

"I thought that poor Kent would welcome the company, here all alone before being sent overseas to defend his country," says Graves, ostensibly to Jake and Cindy, but looking at Kent.

"How did you find out I was going overseas?" Kent asks.

"Your mother told me."

"My mother?"

"Yes! Mother. Mere. Madre. Mutter. The lady who brought you into this world."

"Why were you talking to my mother?"

"Because I wanted to find out how my buddy was!" He looks at Jake. "Isn't that what you call them in the army . . . your buddies?"

"That's right," Jake answers. "Are you in the army?"

"No. I'm not in the service. For medical reasons. Kent could have been exempted, too. But he wanted to fight for his country."

"Tony is trying to do his share on the homefront," says Kent, who has been uncharacteristically quiet. "Help the troops in any way he can. However, now that he knows we here are being well looked after, he will drive back to Charleston first thing in the morning and help keep the mighty war engine humming."

"Oh, are you in defense work?" Cindy asks. Jake says nothing. He knows some kind of game is being played, but isn't sure what it is.

"Kind of. I'm in the family business."

"The Graveses are in many businesses," Kent offers.

"Yes, we have been very fortunate."

Then the four of them are sitting there staring at each other, as if simultaneously, they have all decided that the fabricated conversation is not worth the effort. Decisively, Graves jumps to his feet.

"Listen you two," he says to Jake and Cindy. "I'm going to help Kent with clean-up. You two are relieved of duty."

Cindy starts to protest, until a gentle squeeze on the arm from Jake stops her. "All right," he says, "We'll go have a look at the stars and then go to bed."

"Hit the sack," Graves supplies. "Isn't that the way you say it in the army."

"Sometimes," Jake answers. He leads Cindy out onto the beach. It is a clear night, the moon's reflection shimmers on the ocean, the stars are brilliant, as they can seem only when far from city lights. They sit with their backs to the dune, his arm around her.

"This is so far from . . . everything," she says, "it's hard to imagine that somewhere Buddy is leading the band, and people are dancing."

"And Ted Cowan's face is turning purple," Jake laughs.

"Ted is dead," she says.

"What?"

"He enlisted, in the Marines, right after Swede did. They sent him to Guadalcanal, and . . . he was killed in action. He got a medal; they said he was a hero."

"Jesus." She stares at him. "Sorry." Jake shakes his head. "Ted, poor Ted. I wish . . . I caused him a lot of pain. I didn't mean to, but I did."

"He wasn't a very nice guy," she says. "I'm sorry to say that about the dead, but he just wasn't. He was a bad person."

"Not bad enough to deserve dying." Jake is surprised at how choked up he is. "You're right, he wasn't a nice guy." Saying that doesn't make Jake feel any better. "At least he died a hero!" he says fiercely, trying to make it all right. "'Nothing in his life became him like the leaving of it'. That's not quite right. It's Shakespeare, but I think I got it wrong. You've got the idea, anyway."

"I really don't think I understand that," she says timidly.

"Ahh, it just means he lived wrong, but he died right."

"Big deal. He's just as dead. I don't want you to die, in any way."

"I'm not going to, I have this feeling. They say that some men sense they're going to get it. I'm not going to. Not me or Kent or Al. We're going to be all right. To bad Al isn't here. You'd like him."

"I like Kent. That guy Tony, though. What's wrong with him?"

"Cindy, I think he's queer."

"He sure is!" Then it dawns on Cindy. "Hey, do you mean queer . . . like . . . a fairy, a fruit?" She lifts her arm and lets one hand dangle limp at the wrist. Jake nods.

"What about Kent? Is he?"

"No! They don't take queers in the service! Definitely not!"

The next morning, when they wake up, Graves is gone. Jake thinks he remembers hearing the sounds of men's voices arguing in the night, but isn't sure if he dreamt it. Kent never speaks of Graves again, to excuse or explain him. The day after Graves leaves, the caretaker comes to drive them to the station; they catch a train to Columbia, South Carolina, where they make a connection to New York.

On the train, Jake takes out the trumpet mouthpiece and buzzes softly into it, long tones to strengthen his embouchure, triple-tonguing to keep his attack sharp. A week in New York lies ahead. He thinks of 52nd Street, of sitting in with the guys; realizes how much he misses all those instrumental voices coming together to make music. This week may be his last chance in a while.

Cindy's head rolls to his shoulder; she has fallen asleep. Very gently, he strokes her hair.

CHAPTER 21

"I'm 45. I was born the same month the war ended in Europe, and one month after Roosevelt died."

Dede punched out the words, taking her time, using choppy gestures that reminded some people of John F. Kennedy's, careful not to cross the line from forceful to masculine. She enjoyed persuading an audience, having all eyes on her, feeling the power. Here the audience included New York City's mayor, a U.S. Senator, three Congressmen, and about three dozen major Democratic contributors, members of the Democratic Issues Symposium, all sizing her up as senatorial material. The DIS was a group of entrepreneurs, executives, lawyers, bankers—all wealthy Democrats, all interested in counterbalancing the weight of the professional politicos by using the power of their purses.

"The youngest people who even remember Roosevelt and World War II are pushing 60! Roosevelt was a great President, but we must stop using his name as if it were a magic wand. Nostalgia is no substitute for ideas! Glenn Miller and his orchestra were great. But young voters today are listening to . . ." She hesitated; she could think of no current equivalent. Then she realized that was working for her. She grinned. "You'll have to fill in the blank there, I don't know what passes for popular music these days." A chuckle came from the room; she could spot no one there under 40. "I should have brought my son." Another chuckle. She thought of what she'd told Ken Glass: I don't have time to listen to music these days.

She could see that the current president of DIS, Robert Stinson, was not joining in the laughter. Stinson was a wealthy lawyer who basked in the soubriquet, "adviser to Presidents," although there hadn't been a Democratic president to advise in some time. In the years since Jimmy Carter, he had served as counsel to a couple of Senate committees and occasionally made the evening news as a stern interrogator at corruption hearings. Washington clout did him and his midtown law firm no harm. Now in his late 60s, Stinson was a rainmaker whose name and contacts brought in national and international clients and earned him an extravagant income.

Stinson didn't like Dede. She was too new on the political scene, hadn't paid her party dues, and worst of all was being talked of as a senatorial candidate. For all his acumen and power, Stinson was not being mentioned at all. He was a small, dour man and an unappealing public speaker. Most of him was shrewd enough to know he was not a winning candidate, but part of him wanted to be asked.

Forty-odd people, seated at six tables, sat listening to her in the private dining room of a New York club that had neither the cachet nor the restrictive policies of the Gotham. When she finished, she waited for questions, and for Stinson. The adviser to Presidents held off until she'd fielded questions on tax policy, the deficit, economic relations with Japan, and crime in the cities. Then he got to his feet.

"Diana, your husband is a member of the Gotham, which, unless I am mistaken, excludes Jews, blacks, and women. How serious a liability do you think that would be to a Senatorial candidate?"

"Bob, the Gotham is his club, not mine. Am I my husband's keeper?" She was unsatisfied with that answer even as she gave it.

"No, but you are his wife," he shot back. "Remember Geraldine Ferraro in '84. A lot of us think she paid for the sins of her husband . . . if there were any sins."

She nodded. Then it came to her. She realized it must have been percolating in her mind for some time, but she was as surprised as anyone in the room when she heard herself say it aloud. "Bob, I am doing something about the Gotham. I am applying for membership. Not only as a woman. I have learned recently that my father was a Jew."

There was a hush. Stinson was stopped dead in his tracks. She stood there asking herself, what made me say that? I have just set fire to the bridge across which I might have run back to Tru and the WASPs' nest. Yet she felt good watching the escape route burn and crumble. Now she was publicly committed.

"If I am denied membership, I'll take them to court."

She waited. "Any more questions?"

Silence.

"Then, thank you for giving me this time."

Applause. People got to their feet; Dede wanted to be sure to shake the hand of every man—and the two other women—in the room. First the Mayor came over. "Good speech," he said. He was a handsome, light-skinned black man, with gentle eyes that always seemed to be responding to bad news. "We need candidates who can bring people together."

"Mr. Mayor, I strongly agree with what you say and what you've been working for. We need citizens who can bring people together, at every level. From the sidewalks of New York to the White House."

Her platitudes pleased the Mayor a lot more than they pleased her. "Good. Good. We must talk more soon," he said. "And if there's anything I can do . . ." He shook her hand and moved off. Candidate or not, she remained a substantial contributor to Democratic campaigns and the Mayor paid her all the deference her money had earned.

The Senator, a six-foot-two-inch leprechaun with white hair and mischievous blue eyes, had been standing behind the Mayor, listening as he awaited his chance to congratulate her. They'd known each other a long time.

"You sound like a Senator already," he said with a grin.

"That bad, huh?"

"Not bad, not good. Senatorial." He turned serious. "The question is: why do you want to go through it?"

"I don't know that I do. If I do, it's to make a difference, to help people."

His look said, let's not kid each other. Then he replied, "That's not enough, not nearly enough. You have to want it. Need it, need it badly."

"What do they call it, a fire in the belly?"

"I'd place it a bit south of there," the Senator said, his eyes dancing.

"I won't ask where." She knew he wouldn't let it go at that.

"It has to be as satisfying as an orgasm. Well, almost." The Senator, divorced for two years, was one of New York's, and Washington's, most notorious flirts.

"Why hasn't anyone put it that way before?" she asked.

"I promise you this. If you should ever surrender to the urge and join me in Washington, you will be without question the best looking woman on Capitol Hill."

"To some folks that might sound a bit sexist."

"If that means being an old-fashioned admirer of beautiful women, I plead guilty. But then what would you beautiful women do without us?"

"Why do I get the feeling you're dangerous, Senator?" She pretended to take his flirting seriously; she didn't want to hurt him.

His smile broadened. "By the way, congratulations on the *Times* magazine piece. It beats a million bucks worth of TV spots."

"I thought I sounded awfully . . . hard."

"Diana, nice guys finish last. You sounded like the kind of candidate who'd get my support. And just think of where you stand now with the Jewish vote! If anyone ever discovered I had some Jewish among the Irish, I'd be so grateful!"

He was shaking her hand, preparing to leave: "Oh, and that thing about getting into the club. Great move! When did you think it up?"

"About five minutes ago."

His eyes widened for a moment, "Who's running your campaign? I want to meet him!" Without a pause, he adroitly added, "Or her."

"What campaign?" she asked. He winked as he turned away.

Back in her office she called Mary Wheatley, told her about the club and her father. Now the world would know. "So I'd be applying as a woman and a Jew. Can I count on your support?"

Mary did not seem happy to hear the news. "Actually, I had in mind putting up Bob Broffman . . ."

Now Dede understood Mary's burst of social conscience. Broffman was a senior partner in a Wall Street investment-banking house, a graduate of Andover and Princeton, what some people called a "white shoe Jew." His WASPy wife was Mary's closest friend.

"With me you'd be killing two birds . . . And it would make it easier for him, once I got in."

"Do you think you can?"

"Mary, I don't start something expecting to lose. Will you help me?"

A long pause. "Yes. Yes, I will." The voice was frightened.

Dede began her campaign with a letter to every member of the club, saying it was time to open the Gotham to women and to "others" and, for the benefit of the few who may not have known, that her father was a Jew. Tru's copy went to the Southampton house where he was now spending most of his time. The day after he got it, he appeared at Dede's office, immaculate in a gray seersucker suit, blue button-down shirt, striped rep tie. In the late morning his bright blue eyes were clear. He seemed so big, so handsome, so formidable.

"What a surprise," she said.

"Have a few appointments. I'm headed back to the country this afternoon." "The country" was what Tru's people called the place that outsiders called "the Hamptons."

"I need a couple of minutes." With her it was always, do you have a couple of minutes?

"Of course." She stood, walked from behind her desk and led him to the tan leather and chrome chairs that stood around a coffee table. He tossed his fine slim briefcase onto the table; she wondered what he had in it.

"The full treatment, as if I were one of those biggies . . . Rudolph or Bronstein or Frischberg." He let his voice take on just a touch of Jewish intonation as he spoke the big real estate names; Tru was very good at accents.

"I don't think that kind of stuff is funny anymore, Tru. What do you want?"

"You're trying to punish me, and the Goth, because you're Jewish. It's not our fault, you know."

"Fault? It's not anybody's fault. It's not as if I have a disease."

"You'll never get in. As a woman or a Jew. You'll only harm yourself by trying."

"Is that advice? Or a threat?"

"How much business do club people throw your way each year? I'm told it's 50 or 60 million."

"That is a threat! My God, Tru, is the club thing so important to you?"

"My lawyer will be getting in touch with you."

She was having trouble breathing. "Lawyer?"

"Divorce lawyer."

"It's not just the club, is it? It's because of who I . . . turned out to be."

"And the way you're going around proclaiming it. I gave you a way out. You decided not to take it."

She tried to stay cool, but the words jumped out. "And how about the blonde you were greasing up in the dunes? Where does she fit in?"

"You've been spying on me."

"Entirely by accident."

"The car keys!"

She nodded. "Did you find them?"

"Had to have new ones made."

"Too bad."

"What a . . . tacky . . . thing to do."

"What would you call that session in the dunes?"

"Find yourself a divorce lawyer."

"Nineteen years, Tru. Is this the way it's done?"

He was trying to stay controlled as he got to his feet and picked up the attaché case, but the fury showed in a pinched, white look around his mouth and nose. "The article in the *Sunday Times*," he said. "You obviously snowed him. But even he caught the bitch in you."

"Goodbye Tru." She said it to his back.

For a few minutes after he left, Dede just sat in the easy chair, stunned. Nineteen years. Before she could do anything about them, the tears welled up in her eyes, overflowed. Quickly she swiveled her chair around so that through the open door Rita couldn't see her crying.

Eyes reddened, she tried to confront the work on her desk, shuffling pieces of paper, forcing her attention to them, only to have her mind drift off, to her Jewish father, to the blonde in the dunes, to the repugnance of a divorce, to the sudden shambles of what was for so many years a perfectly ordered life. She wasn't sure how long she'd been sitting there when the phone rang and Rita told her that the *New York Times* writer was calling. She took a deep breath and reached for the phone as if it were a lifeline.

"Curious as to what you thought of the magazine piece."

"I've been meaning to call you. You're a marvelous writer."

"Now tell me what you thought of the piece."

"It's . . . too complicated to do over the phone, really."

"Perhaps over a drink."

"Yes, we could." It wasn't until he asked that she realized how much she wanted him to.

"How about this evening?"

"That would be fine."

The Madison Pub was her idea. As they sat down in a booth, he told her, "I had something a bit more upscale in mind. Something more . . . you."

"That's what I didn't like about the article."

His crinkly smile was just a bit tight. "You don't waste any time. One of the things I admire in you."

"You were very clear about the things you didn't admire." The old waiter brought them a bottle of Valpolicella, struggled to pop the cork. Ken motioned for him to fill both glasses.

"Here's to being honest with each other." They held up their glasses.

"Well, you were certainly honest."

"Funny. A friend of mine who read it said I must have a crush on you. I of course denied it." He looked to her for a reaction, got none. "The friend, by the way, is divorced, very rich, great skier and tennis player, houses in Southampton, Aspen, and Jamaica—at last count. Handsome macho stud. Wanted your home number."

"I hope you didn't give it to him."

"I told him you were happily married." Again he looked to her. Again her face gave away nothing. "His name is Denny Knight. Charming. Relentless. Irresistible. He'll find you, unlisted number or not."

Dede shook her head. "I can't imagine how he could be attracted to the woman in the article. Hard-nosed, ambitious snob."

"Didn't I say things like: smart, straightforward, knock-out blue eyes, great face, body like an Olympic athlete? Maybe you and I didn't read the same article."

"My husband said even you caught the bitch in me. Which article did he read?"

"*Even* I, huh? Sounds like he was projecting. Projecting is when you put your attitudes into . . ."

"I know what it is! That is a cheap shot."

"You're right, I shouldn't have said it."

She was getting to her feet. "I'd better leave before this goes any further downhill." What she wanted to say was, after Tru, I came here for stroking, not whipping.

He sat there, slumped, watching her go. What he wanted to say was, Denny was right; I do have a crush on you.

Walking home she realized she never had the chance to tell him about her Jewish father.

She lay in bed that night thinking about Jacob Ellinson, about all the Jewish jokes she'd laughed at—and told, although her accent, unlike Tru's, was not very good. About being called a snob by Ken Glass, an anti-Semite by Herb Ellinson, a bitch by her husband. About how alone she felt. She didn't fall asleep until 1:30. At 7:30 the next morning, Roger Wheatley phoned, wanting to take her to lunch, to talk about Mary, and the club.

†

They met at a little Italian restaurant on 53rd Street, east of Third. Roger was a couple of years older than she, stocky and muscular, a college lacrosse star who never forgot he was an athlete. In his perfect world all men were jocks and all women cheerleaders. He seemed always to be flexing his biceps; his light gray pinstripe suit was tailored to show off the breadth of his shoulders. His hair long, straight, and disciplined, managed just a touch of an insouciant curl as it reached the back of his thick neck.

"I'm really sorry to hear about you and Tru," he began.

"Things will work out," she answered, taking care to sound noncommittal.

"I've always thought of you as the golden couple. People would hold their breath when you two walked into a room. How we all envied Tru!" His eyes were trying to lock with hers; hers kept refusing. "Men will be lining up outside your door." His eyes added: I'd like to be one of them. Men don't waste any time, she thought.

"I've got so many things on my mind, Roger. That is not one of them. Now, I know there's something you want to say."

"This isn't easy . . ." He sipped nervously from his water glass.

"Sometimes one has to do difficult things."

"I have nothing against Jews, Dede. Sure, I've said some things . . ."

"We all have. Including me, which I regret."

She looked at her watch, so he could see her doing it. He hesitated, brought his hands together, interlaced the thick fingers.

"Mary is not going to help you."

Now when her eyes locked on his, he knew seduction was not the issue. "What changed her mind? Or should I say *who?*"

"We talked it over. I told her now is not a good time to rock the boat."

"Is there ever a good time, Roger?"

"People don't like to be pushed. Your letter was very . . . ill-advised."

"Funny, a lot of members who wrote to me don't seem to agree with you. Do you know George Whitman?"

"Used to be club president. Older man. Spends a lot of his time in Maine."

"He said the executive committee is empowered to call a general membership meeting on important issues, to get what he called 'the sense of the membership.'"

Roger nodded. "He sent me a copy of his letter."

"You're the chairman, will you . . ."

"We're not planning to."

"I should imagine it's preferable to a lawsuit."

"Dede, why are you doing this?"

To rock your prim, smug, neatly trimmed boat, she said silently. To get back at Tru for his anti-Semitism. And his blonde in the dunes. To make up for all the nasty things I've said about people like my father . . . about people like me. To show everyone I'm not ashamed of who I am. Everyone, including myself. "Because it's time," she said to him.

"You'll be turned down."

"Then I may have to sue."

"We meet all the requirements for a private club, the courts can't touch us."

"That's not what my lawyer says." Pure bluff, but she knew it made clubs nervous. "And when the suit is filed, just think of how the newspapers and TV will jump on it."

Roger searched her face for a sign she was bluffing, or joking. He sighed. "Suppose we considered a membership meeting?" He was a corporate lawyer and always ready to negotiate.

She thought for a couple of moments. "If you call the meeting, I'll agree to abide by a membership vote. If the majority goes against me, I'll withdraw. If the majority supports me and I'm not admitted, I go to court."

They stared at each other. Poor Roger, she thought. Twice rebuffed—on the club and on the other purpose of the lunch. On the street afterward, he gave the other a last try. With his muscular hand wrapped around hers, he said, "Whatever our differences, I regard you as one of this town's great women. Anytime you want to have a drink, or need a shoulder to lean on, I have strong shoulders. You know what I mean."

"Yes, Roger. I know what you mean."

When Herb walked into the house in Malibu, there was a letter from Al Breecher on the hall table. Amanda Ellison Turnbull, the sister of Al's and Jake's buddy, Kent Ellison, had gotten in touch with him through the 101st Airborne Division magazine. Al was sending along her address and phone number; Herb might like to have them. He would. So would Dede Miller.

Marian was out on the deck, reading a novel by some Englishwoman; she never seemed to run out of English women novelists. Herb changed into a polo shirt and a pair of shorts and stretched out on a chaise next to her.

"Well, I've found a family," he told her.

"And . . . ?" She put her book down and stared at him.

"They are . . . different from what I thought. Look, Marian. Somehow Jake got between us. Maybe if I'd had a family of my own, he wouldn't have. Maybe now, because of his daughter and grandson, I can put him to rest. I just wish you were with me on this. I wish I could have shared the entire trip with you."

She stared across at him, "I missed you." She reached out a hand to him; he took it and squeezed it.

"Why don't you put on a tape of your brother's," she said.

He smiled his thanks to her. "I'll put on Count Basie, he had a better band." He got up, went into the den to find the Basie tape, stopped at the photo of Jake, stared at it.

"I found your daughter and your grandson. I hope you're proud of them." What he wanted to say was, I hope you're proud of me.

CHAPTER 22

Summer-Fall, 1943

The Allies cross the Strait of Messina from Sicily and land on the toe of the Italian mainland. Six days later, they establish a beachhead up the coast at Salerno; troopers of the 82nd Airborne are dropped within Allied lines as reinforcements. Heavy Allied air raids continue against Berlin and other German cities. Soviet forces, attacking all along the Eastern front, retake Kharkov.

Hit songs: "Comin' in on a Wing and a Prayer," The Song Spinners; "You'll Never Know," Dick Haymes; "Sunday, Monday, or Always," Bing Crosby; "All or Nothing at All," Harry James, vocal by Frank Sinatra.

On an August night in the Bronx, with the temperature high and the sky light until after eight, the schoolyard teems with neighborhood kids. As Jake, in uniform, barracks bag slung over his shoulder, goes by the schoolyard of Public School 50, which he attended from kindergarten through the sixth grade, Benny Waxman is the first to run up to him. Benny is 16. His older brother Al is Herb's age; they were in the same high school class and were drafted at the same time.

"Hey, Jake! Where you headed?"

"Hi, Benny. Home."

"I mean overseas, or something like that?"

"Not sure. And if I was, I wouldn't tell you. You know what they say, 'a slip of the lip might sink a ship.'"

"Count Basie, right?" To the kids in the neighborhood, the Ellinsons are the ultimate resource on musical matters, the court of last resort, used for resolving arguments and settling bets.

"Duke Ellington, I think . . . but I don't get to listen to music so much these days. How's Al?"

"They shipped him to the Pacific. All we got is an APO number."

"Well, when you write to him, tell him I said hello."

"Yeah. Hey, what's that?" Benny points to the paratrooper wings pinned to Jake's jacket. By this time a half-dozen other boys, trailing Benny, have surrounded Jake.

"Oh, this." Jake fingers the wings. "You get this for jumping out of airplanes." There is a hush.

"You mean, with a parachute?" one of the boys finally ventures.

"Parachutes are for sissies," Jake says.

"What?" Benny shouts. Then he sees Jake smiling at him. "Come on!"

"Yeah, with a parachute."

A kid Jake barely knows, who can't be more than 10 or 11, pipes up. "You ever shoot a machine gun?"

"Yup."

"How about a pistol?"

Jake nods, smiling.

"A tommy gun?"

"Uh huh."

The kid holds an imaginary tommy gun in his grimy little hands and imitates its sound with a staccato bark, "Ah-ah-ah-ah-ah-ah."

"How many Japs and Nazis you gonna kill, Jake?"

"Plenty, don't you worry."

Benny gives Jake a very grown-up look. "You scared they're gonna shoot you?"

"Nah, you kidding? We're gonna lick those Nazis and Japs and then come back home and play stickball. And when you kids see us coming, you better get off the field!"

That gets a howl. In the densely packed Bronx, the right to a schoolyard playing field starts a lot of fights, which the older boys invariably win.

Then he's on his way again. In two minutes he's ringing the bell. The door opens. His mother is standing there, a little grayer, older, softer. Her moist blue eyes stare at him.

"Am I late for dinner?"

"Marty! He's here!" she calls. Then she starts to cry and puts her arms around him.

Without even bothering to look, she says, "You got so thin!"

"I gained five pounds since I went in, ma." He says that futilely. He never goes anywhere for more than a day without, in his mother's eyes, losing dangerous amounts of weight.

His father comes running, behind him . . . surprise: Herb, who has taken some leave time to see Jake. Jake throws his arms around as much of the family as he can encompass. He is home. He doesn't know when he'll be home again.

That night, carrying their horns, Jake and Herb head for 52nd Street and the Unicorn, which is a particular favorite of younger musicians, because it encourages them to sit in and it gives them a break on drinks. It is dark, deep, and narrow, a bar on the right side, a tiny bandstand beyond that, with tables along the left and in the rear. Billy Garafola, who is part owner, maître d', and bouncer, stares at the two soldiers in uniform. His expression changes as he spots their instrument cases, then changes again as he recognizes the Ellinsons.

"Hey, a sight for sore eyes! So many soldiers come in here, they all begin to look alike. You guys want a table?"

"Looks pretty crowded." Herb says.

"Always room for you guys. Gonna sit in? Wanna be near the bandstand?"

"Who's playing?" Jake asks.

"Johnny Black, drums, and bass."

Jake's eyes light up. "Johnny? Damn! Put us on the piano bench with him!"

Billy laughs. "We'll make it the next best thing."

"We're four, though."

"Hey, we stretch the walls!"

Billy does the next best thing; he stretches the tables. Tiny disks covered with dirty checked cloths seat anywhere from one to six people. That becomes the limit only because no more than six glasses can fit on a table. Though it's rumored that the Unicorn also serves food, as required by law, nobody Jake and Herb know has ever dared to test the rumor.

Billy leads them to a table directly across from the empty bandstand, pushes people on both sides away and seats Jake and Herb. They wait for Kent and Al Breecher, who has arrived from Iowa and is staying with Kent for the last three days before they report to Camp Shanks and shipment overseas. When Kent and Al walk into the club, with them is a tall, broad-shouldered blonde girl.

"I knew Kent was holding out on us about a girlfriend!" Jake whispers to Herb as they walk up.

She is almost as tall as Jake, her fair skin tanned by the sun, her hair—pulled back in a short ponytail—so blonde it is almost white. In that frame, the brightness of her eyes, which are a blue-green, is startling. She is wearing a pale blue linen blouse and cream-colored linen skirt.

"I'd like you to meet my sister Amanda," Kent says. She surprises Jake by reaching out to shake his hand; hers is long-fingered and strong.

The five of them are squeezed around the table, Amanda between Jake and her brother. Jake can feel the solid length of her thigh against his. The contact is unavoidable given the size of the table; that doesn't make it any less sexual. Jake is both aroused and embarrassed by it.

When she says, "I asked to come along at the last moment. I hope I'm not crowding you," he's not sure if she's teasing.
He shakes his head no, "In the army you get used to being jammed in with lots of people. None of them as pretty as you are." That kind of compliment is Jake's way of taking control in a conversation with a girl. He is used to lowered eyes, a blush, a half-whispered thank-you.

Not from Amanda. "I'm glad someone thinks I'm pretty! Be sure to tell my brother. He says I'm too horsey."

"He's a rotten judge of looks."

"But a good judge of friends," she answers.

"Gee. Thanks." She's stopped Jake in his tracks, just the way he tried, and failed, to stop her. He likes it, kind of. "Remind me to tell Kent he's nuts to call you horsey. What is it anyway?"

"Someone who likes to ride."

"Are you 'horsey?'"

She grins at him. Her teeth are white and perfect. "Yes. I just don't want to look it." Jake is enjoying this. But he's still not in charge; she keeps turning it on him. He tries again.

"I just can't figure out," he says, staring at her, "whether your eyes are green or blue."

"Depends on what I wear. With this blue blouse, they look blue. With green, decidedly green. Perhaps more green. Yours, on the other hand, are an unmistakable, heavenly blue."

"And when you're not wearing anything?"

"Gee, I never thought to look! But I will. You'll be the first to know." She almost laughs at him. Jake leans across her and speaks to Kent over the din of the room. "How come you never told me how good-looking your sister was?"

Kent gives Jake one of his patented sardonic looks. "Just yesterday she was a freckle-faced kid, with pigtails, glasses . . . and braces. Then I came back on leave and all at once, by God, she was beautiful!"

"I never wore glasses!" she says heatedly, sounding 18 again. Just then the small, frail form of Johnny Black makes its way from the rear of the club to the bandstand, followed by his drummer and bass player. Johnny sits at the piano and plays a few opening chords before he spots Jake and Herb sitting directly in front of him. He gives them a big grin and goes into "Stardust," followed by a jazz waltz arrangement of "Falling In Love With Love." After three more numbers, Johnny looks to Jake and Herb, and mimes the words, "Want to sit in?"

Johnny introduces them, and the five play, "Taking a Chance On Love" and "April In Paris." Then Johnny surprises them by saying, "I had the pleasure of playing in the Buddy Benson Band with Jake Ellinson, and I can tell you he's not only a great trumpet player, he's a pretty fair vocalist, too. Jake, how about singing something?"

Jake can count on the fingers of his hands the number of times he's sung with the band, and mostly that was horsing around on rhythm numbers. But now people are applauding, especially, as he notices, Amanda.
He looks at Johnny. "How about 'Them There Eyes?'"

Jake is not much of a singer. His voice is husky; he can't sustain long notes, doesn't even try, and like most instrumentalists, he sings the way he plays. In his case, it's with a crisp opening attack followed by a clean sustained note, ending in a faint vibrato.

He aims the lyrics at her, changes them to "You better watch out green eyes if you're wise." He's looking straight at her when he sings, "They sparkle, they bubble, they're gonna get you in a whole lot of trouble. You're overworkin' 'em, there's danger lurkin' in . . . them there eyes."

This time she lowers her eyes. That's more like it, he thinks.

After the set Johnny joins their table. "Hey, you guys look great in uniform!" he says, after the first mouthful of a double scotch and water. "The lady here and I are the only ones in civvies."

"Some people have all the luck," says Kent.

"Hell, I want to do my part," Johnny says, clearly offended by the idea he'd prefer to be a civilian. "I'm 4F. They told me I have a heart murmur and the worst eyes and the flattest feet they ever saw. They said I could make 4F three or four times over! Like 12F or 16F! I said, take me and I'll play piano for the troops. Like I'm doing now, only in uniform! They wouldn't do it."

"Must be plenty of work," says Jake. "Not that there isn't always plenty of work for Johnny Black."

"Too much work," Johnny answers. "Rooms packed every night. People drinking, over-tipping you to play sloppy sentimental songs, spending money like there was no tomorrow."

"Perhaps there isn't," Kent says.

"Huh?" Johnny says, "isn't . . . what?"

"A tomorrow."

"Stop it, Kent!" Amanda snaps.

"I never been to college," Johnny says. "In fact, don't ask to see my high school diploma. But I know this much, you gotta go along thinking there'll always be a tomorrow."

"If I could play piano the way you do, I suppose I'd be a lot cheerier about tomorrow," Kent says. "My God, you're wonderful! You can almost make Bix here sound like a singer."

"Hey, he's good," says Johnny cheerily. "For a trumpet player! He's no Cindy Laine, though. Speaking of which, you two still . . . close . . . Jake?"

"Yeah, well, we have our ups and downs. She's coming to see me tomorrow, to say goodbye." The look of disappointment just slides across Amanda's face. But Jake sees it and is pleased.

"This guy," says Johnny, nodding toward Jake, "has got all the luck. Great trumpet player, and he's got the greatest gal in the music business."

"I didn't know anyone in the band liked her," Jake says.

"The guys were just jealous. She wouldn't give any of us a tumble. Then you came along."

"De gustibus non est disputandum," says Amanda.

"Don't know it," says Johnny. "Hum a few bars and I'll fake it."

"It's Latin," Amanda tells him. "It means some girls have strange tastes."

"Hey, you don't know me well enough to be jealous!" Jake is grinning.

"Wishful thinking," Amanda replies.

But Jake now has an edge and likes it; he turns to Johnny. "I can't blame the other guys for going for her."

"I was as jealous as the rest of them," the pianist replies. "If I only had a uniform, with wings on it."

Jake feels Amanda's leg moving away from his. For the rest of the evening, she virtually stops talking to him, until they leave the club, pushing their way through the unending stream of people, mostly men in uniform fighting their way in, looking for somewhere to forget the war for a few hours. When they are out on 52nd street, standing in a muggy August night, she looks at him, her eyes on the same level at his.

"If you and your brother and your . . . singer friend . . . would like to come to dinner at our apartment tomorrow night, we'd be pleased to have you."

"Gee thanks," he says. "That's nice, but Cindy and I . . ."

". . . want some time for yourself," she says coolly. "I understand."

"We have some places to go. Thanks anyway."

A little after nine the next morning, the phone rings. It is Cindy. Jake knows there's something wrong; she's supposed to be on an 8:40 train to New York.

"Jake . . ." Her voice is lifeless, choked, near tears.

"What's the matter?"

"My parents . . . I'm not coming down."

"Why? What about your parents?" He knows exactly why and what.

"What we're doing is wrong."

"What? Loving each other?"

"They say if you loved me you would marry me in church, the right way." He almost doesn't recognize her voice. Trying to control her crying, she sounds cold and constricted.

"They say that. And what do you say?"

"I have to marry in my faith. If you loved me, you would."

"Do you hear me telling you, that if you loved me you'd have to get married in a shool?" In his anger, Jake uses the Yiddish word for synagogue.

"It's different. You never even go to one of those . . . things."

"But I'm still one of those people!" He knows this is pointless. "Look, Cindy, you're not coming down here to get married, just to say goodbye! Don't they know that?" He realizes his anger is not against her but against them—her parents and whoever, whatever, is behind them, forcing her into line.

"They don't want me to see you. They don't want me to . . . do things, you know, unless I'm married."

"And it doesn't matter to them that I'm going overseas?" He lowers his voice. "That I could . . . that something could happen to me?"

"Oh Jake . . ."

"And what about you? You don't care enough to tell them you're coming to see me? No matter what they think?"

"They say no. I don't know what to tell them . . ."

"Tell them to go to hell!" Jake slams down the phone, walks into the kitchen where his mother is doing the breakfast dishes. He sits at the table and says nothing. His mother keeps working as if not noticing he's there, until without turning she asks, "So who should go to hell?"

"I really don't want to get into it, ma."

"No, don't get into it. Soon you'll be gone for . . . who knows how long. It would be terrible if you told your mother what's going on in your life." She turns off the water in the sink, wipes her hands on a towel. Then goes to the refrigerator, takes out a bottle of milk, pours a glass, carries it to the table, where she puts it in front of Jake.

"Drink. I've got those cupcakes, with the vanilla icing, the kind you like."

"I've just had breakfast, ma."

That doesn't stop her from putting a cupcake on a plate and giving it to him. "Get some nourishment . . . while you can!"

"They don't starve you in the army, ma."

"Then how come all your clothing hangs on you?"

"Oh ma, for God's sake."

"Don't holler at me. I'm not some girl who doesn't want to get married in shool!"

"You were listening."

"Who could help it? You were hollering!"

Jake takes a drink of milk to shut himself up. But she can see. She reaches up to kiss his cheek, then turns back to the sink. "Still with the shiksa singer?"

"I love her. Her parents don't want her to marry me, because I'm Jewish and I don't want to get married in church."

"They're right! She should marry a Catholic boy in a church; you should marry a Jewish girl in a shool."

"You left out nice. Nice Jewish girl."

"Nice would be nice. Nice would be better than not nice. But Jewish is a must."

"We love each other."

"Yes, and the first fight you have, she'll call you a dirty Jew."

"Ma, that's something out of the dark ages!"

"Pardon me, I never went to college. Believe me, there's a lot you can't learn in college."

"I didn't mean . . ."

She turns back to him, puts her hand on his muscled forearm. "Listen to me. Jacob. It's the best thing. What's the rush to get married? You'll forget her. You'll come back; you'll find a Jewish girl." She smiles a girlish smile; her blue eyes twinkle. "Yes, a nice Jewish girl."

That smile touches his heart; he puts his hand on hers, pats it gently. She clutches his hand fiercely. "You should only come home safe. The rest we'll take care of later."

"I told you not to worry."

He puts his arms around her and gives her another hug. Then goes to the boys' bedroom and practices his horn for an hour. It does not blow away the anger. He goes to the phone, calls Cindy. A woman's voice answers.

"Who's calling?"

"Jake Ellinson."

"I'm sorry, she's gone out."

Jake does not believe that for a moment. "When will she be back?"

"I don't know. Look, it's better if . . . she won't talk to you."

"I'm going overseas tomorrow, Mrs. Laine!" Then he remembers, the name isn't Laine. But he doesn't give a damn about correcting himself.

"You two will forget each other. It's all for the best. Please don't call again." She hangs up.

Bursting with anger, he picks up the phone again, dials. Again a woman answers.

"Amanda?"

"Yes?"

"It's Jake. Ellinson."

"Oh! I was about to call you, to tell you how much I enjoyed the evening. You and your brother are such wonderful musicians. And you're really quite a good singer, too."

"Yeah, Bing is worried. Frankie boy is trembling."

"Well, I liked it. You should learn how to take a compliment."

"Lot of things I should learn. Look, my plans have changed, and if that invitation to dinner tonight is still open . . . No. Alone."

At eight that evening, dressed in his khakis, he arrives at the entrance to 111 East 72nd Street. He hesitates, then walks into the lobby, where a uniformed doorman accosts him.

"May I help you?"

"I'm going to see the Ellisons."

"Your name?"

"Jacob Ellinson."

The doorman, aloof and forbidding in gray, with military cap and white gloves, allows his expression to change when he hears the name. He picks up the phone.

"There's a Mr. Ellison to see you."

He listens, then looks at Jake as he hangs up. "This way, sir." He walks Jake to the elevator, which is open, with an operator standing ready.

"Ellison," the doorman orders, and Jake is wafted up to the ninth floor. The Ellisons's door is open and Amanda is standing there barefoot, wearing a blue cotton blouse and white skirt. She puts her hands on his shoulders and kisses him on the cheek.

"I'm so glad you could come."

"I see what you mean by the blue," he says.

"The blue?"

"Your eyes. The shirt makes them look blue."

"I hope you like blue eyes," she says as she takes his hand to lead him through a large, high-ceilinged, marble-floored entrance foyer. To his right he can look into an immense dining room, with a long massive table of polished oak. Ahead of him is an even bigger living room with a marble fireplace; on its floor a Persian rug dominated by burgundy, navy, and shades of tan and cream; in it a profusion of traditional furniture. On the wall opposite the fireplace hangs an oil painting of a striking young woman who is clearly Amanda. On both sides of the portrait, built-in shelves, some of them with glass doors, hold books, vases, plates, and other *objets*. Around the fireplace stand a sofa and easy chairs, covered with chintz in a subdued pattern of rose and tan. Under the windows on the far wall is another sofa. Small tables stand alongside the sofas and chairs, on them framed photos. Jake has never seen this scale and opulence anywhere but in a museum.

"I'm slightly overwhelmed," he offers.

"We're glad you like it."

"Where are the . . . we?"

Still holding his hand, she walks him to the sofa that faces the fireplace. She sits, taking him with her.

"I'm going to light a fire. I know it's warm, but I love a fire so."

"It is warm," he says, but Amanda has already gotten up and begun to lay the fire.

"Where is everybody?" he asks, again, as she works.

"Mom is on Nantucket. Father has not lived here for some time." She lights a match, puts it to the paper and kindling, and watches as the flames take hold.

"How about Kent and Al?"

"Oh, they went out to some bars, to hear jazz."

"Without me?"

She curls her legs up on the sofa. Her bare knees and lower thighs, considerably tanner than her face, are showing. She takes his hand again. Those eyes, now blue, definitely blue, bore into him.

"They asked to be excused." She smiles at him.

"They went without me, and asked to be excused? I don't believe you." He smiles back as he says it.

"Well, ah . . ." She is encouraged by his smile. "I told them you'd called to say you and your girlfriend couldn't meet them. You had . . . other plans. They understood."

"Why?" Jake asks, but knows the answer. Right now he doesn't know how he could ever have thought those eyes were anything but blue.

"Because I wanted you all to myself."

"I'm flattered. Most of the time I'm the one who . . ."

"Chases the girl. Not the other way around."

"You're so beautiful, boys must chase you all the time. Why are you doing it?"

"Because you're not chasing me."

"You haven't given me a chance!"

"Besides, my brother is your best friend. And you have a girlfriend."

"I'm not so sure about the girlfriend."

"You must have lots of girlfriends."

"No."

"Then this one is special. Say no."

"Yes."

"Tell me what is special about her. Is she a simply marvelous singer?"

"She's a very good singer. She's no Billie Holiday."

"What then? Tell me."

"Let's change the subject."

"All right. Know what? We've got Billie Holiday records. I'll put some on. We've also got a changer, latest thing, so you can play several records without having to stop what you're doing. Isn't that marvelous?"

In a couple of minutes the sound of an alto sax playing "I Cried For You" comes through the speaker.

"That's Johnny Hodges," Jake says. "One of the greatest. He plays with Duke Ellington."

"I forgot I was with an expert. Does the expert like champagne?"

"Never had it. My drink is whiskey sours."

"You'll love it. I'll be right back." she starts off, stops, turns back. "Don't go 'way!"

Leaving Jake to listen to Billie Holiday, look at the fire, wonder at the room, the apartment, and the girl, and think confused thoughts about Cindy, she returns in a couple of minutes with the champagne in an ice bucket in one hand and two glasses in the other. She pops the cork, fills the glasses, hands one to him, stares into his eyes. Then holds her glass up to clink his.

"Here's to us," she says and sips the champagne.

"Anyone ever tell you you're a tease?" he asks.

She ignores that. "If someone makes a toast, you must drink, or it's bad luck."

He has to laugh at her. "Have I ruined everything?"

"Well," she says, looking very serious, "there's a way it can be fixed." She takes another sip of champagne, and before he can move, she leans forward and kisses him on the mouth. Her lips part; he can taste the champagne. She forces her tongue between his lips, which doesn't take much forcing. Then he is drinking the champagne from her mouth. It is a while before they separate and she sits back on the sofa.

"That's the only known way to keep the bad luck away."

"I don't think it's all gone away." He leans to her and they kiss again.

"Oh," she says, when he lifts his face. "Oh oh oh."

He sips the champagne. It is fizzy, weightless. Not of this world.

"Like it?" she asks.

"Uh huh."

"Like me?"

"Uh huh."

"Happy to be here?"

"Uh huh!"

"Even without your girlfriend?"

"I never met a girl as nervy as you are."

"Don't you see, I have to be! You're leaving tomorrow!"

"It's not the end of the world."

"Haven't you heard, fella? There's a war on. Who knows what will happen tomorrow?" Almost without pause, she throws a change of pace at him. "Are you hungry? Or can we sit here for awhile and finish the champagne?"

"I'm not hungry." In fact, he's had a full meal with his parents and Herb at 6. That's dinnertime for the people he knows.

"Do you see that rug in front of the fire?" she asks. For the first time, he looks down at it.

"God, a bearskin rug," he says. "I've seen 'em in the movies. But never in real life."

"My father shot him on a hunting trip in Alaska. At first I couldn't stand to look at him, poor thing. My mother had to keep telling me, those are not his real eyes, they're just glass! Finally I outgrew that. And now when I look at it . . ." She pauses. "May I be absolutely honest?"

"Aren't you always?"

"Oh, you've noticed!" She hesitates. "Do you know what I think?"

Jake holds off for a moment, then says to himself, what the hell. "Let me guess," he says. He gives her a chance to say no. When she doesn't, he goes ahead.

"You want to make love on it. Right?"

"Yes."

"You want me to take off your shirt . . ." He reaches over, takes hold of her blouse at the waist and begins to lift it. She holds her arms over her head to make it easy. He tosses the blouse behind the sofa. She's not wearing a bra; all the girls he knows wear bras. Her breasts are small for a girl her size, the nipples pale pink.

"You want me to kiss your nipples." He leans forward and takes first one nipple in his mouth, then the other. He can hear her taking deep almost sobbing breaths.

"You want me to lift you . . ." He gets to his feet, reaches down, picks her off the sofa. "Carry you to the fire, put you down . . ." He places her gently on the bearskin. "Then undress you all the way." The skirt has buttons down the side, which makes it easy. He grasps the waist of her silk underpants; she lifts her hips so he can slide them off more easily. She is stretched out, her skin white where she wears a bathing suit, slightly tanned to the outlines of tennis shirt and shorts, and deeply tanned beyond that. Her pubic hair is so blonde it is almost colorless, her thighs looking every bit as strong as they felt the night before.

"Then you want to watch me get undressed so you can see how excited you make me." He takes his clothes off and stands over her. She can indeed see how excited he is. She reaches her arms up, and he drops down on top of her. She puts her arms around his back and kisses him. Suddenly, she rolls over so that his back is on the rug and she's on top of him.

"May I ask you something really, really special?" she says.

"Two reallys, huh?"

"Could we make love with me on top of you, so I can see the fire, and the rug, and you?"

"Anything you want."

She sits up, straddling him, looking at his penis standing straight up in front of her body, then raises herself and puts him into her. As she slides up and down on him, she gets her wish, seeing him and the bearskin and the fire. But in the end, she closes her eyes.

Billie Holiday is singing "Easy To Love."

Afterward, she just stretches out on him, until he rolls her over and makes love to her with him on top.

Later she wants to lie on the rug, naked. She leaps up only to turn the batch of records over and get the champagne. Then she sits down between his legs, both of them facing the fire.

"Sex and champagne," she says. "It makes you feel like heaven, like you could just take off and fly away." She drains her glass.

"If champagne could make anyone fly, you'd be about ready."

"This is a special, special evening. I just want to sit here with you, naked. And make love. Forever and ever and ever, hallelujah!" She is high, and sounds it.

"What do you suppose Kent would think if he walked in now?"

She giggles. "He'd probably be jealous!"

Jealous? He asks himself. Of whom? He doesn't like either answer.

They make love again before they dress and have dinner. As he stands at the door, ready to leave, he says, "The champagne and the food were delicious. Not half as delicious as you."

"Do you suppose we'll ever do this again, you and I?"

He looks into her eyes a long time before answering, softly, "Haven't you heard, young lady, there's a war on."

She throws her arms around him and hugs him. "Remember this evening, will you? No matter what happens!"

"Forgetting it would be hard." He kisses her lightly on the lips, starts to turn away, stops, "Hey, I forgot to notice what color your eyes were!"

For his farewell dinner, Millie has used the entire month's meat rationing coupons, on steak. As usual, she overcooks it.

"How soon do you think you'll ship out?" asks Marty as they eat.

"Don't know," Jake says. "They don't tell us. Military secret, you know. Like where we're going, they don't tell us that either. But I hear the chow is great aboard ship, French chefs and all that."

He's trying to get a smile, or some reaction, from his mother, who is strangely silent. He gets nothing. "Of course, not as good as your chow, ma!"

"Chow? What kind of word is that? Like chow mein?"

It's not what Jake wants, but it's something. "It's an army nickname for food."

She nods, returns to her silence.

"Look ma, nothing will happen to me. I've got too much to do when the war is over. Besides, who'd want to hurt a musician? With a few exceptions, of course. There are a couple I'd like to hurt myself."

This time she just stares at him, not even bothering to react to that little try at levity. The weary blue eyes are knowing and resigned, as if she no longer has the strength to resist the might of the U.S. Army and the machinations of her son.

Once again, there is the walk to the door, this time with Jake in uniform and carrying his barracks bag, and Herb and their parents in a semi-circle around him.

"Everything's going to be all right, you'll see. I'll be home before you know it." He hugs both of them. "Before you know it."

His mother looks up at him and says only, "Jacob, Jacob."

Then he is gone, he and Herb taking that walk to the subway they've taken so many times before. It is a hot, muggy day in late August, the schoolyard packed with youngsters relishing the last days of their summer vacation. Jake stops for a moment, watches.

"Look at them. Kids playing. War, no war, doesn't make any difference to them. That's the great thing about being a kid. You don't know how much you don't know. And you don't care. Hey, isn't that Red Kleinman's brother . . . what's his name?"

"Stanley," Herb supplies. "You heard about Red . . ."

"No!"

"Missing in action. He was stationed in Australia, with the Army Air Force. He never came back from a mission. They're hoping . . ."

"Red," Jake says. "Toughest kid on the block." He smiles sadly. "Except for me. If there's any guy who'll make it, it's Red." He lifts his barracks bag to his shoulder and they start off. For a block or so they are silent. Then without looking at Herb, Jake says, "Kid, if anything happens to me . . . nothing is, but if anything does . . . you've gotta work specially hard to make sure they . . ." He doesn't have to say who they are; ". . . come through it all right. You've gotta make it up to them."

Herb says nothing. Jake looks to him. "Herbie?"

Finally, he answers. "Jake, I'll never be able to make it up to them. You know that. So you better make sure nothing happens to you."

"Look, I'm saying this . . . just in case. A guy can get hit by a car crossing the street." Jake claps his free hand on his brother's shoulder. "It's great to have a brother like you. Someone I can count on." Herb, 20 years old, a private first class in the United States Army, is like a ten-year-old kid again, bathing in the warmth of his revered older brother's praise, so touched by it he wants to cry.

"You know you can count on me, Jake. Always."

In answer Jake just squeezes his brother's bony shoulder. They walk along, Jake's hand on Herb's shoulder, until they reach the foot of the stairs. There they stop, turn to each other.

"Take care of yourself, kid. I love you."

"I love you too, Jake. Don't let anything happen to you. Please!"

"That's a promise, kid!"

Jake turns to head up the stairs of the elevated station. Herb remembers their two other farewells at this spot, when Jake left to go on the road and, less than a year later, to be inducted—remembers how he stood there, wondering why he didn't walk to the top of the stairs with Jake. This time he says, "I'll go up with you."

"It's all right, Herbie."

"No, I want to."

And they start up, Herb barely able to keep pace with Jake, who, barracks bag on his shoulder, takes the iron steps two at a time. At the top, Jake says quickly, "Don't forget to write, kid."

"I won't. Don't you forget either." Jake claps Herb on the arm with his free hand. Herb wants to hug his brother, but he doesn't. Jake is at the door when he looks back.

"Hey, you're 20! I can't call you kid anymore!" Then he is through the door and out of sight.

Four days later, on September 4th, 1943, 2400 officers and men of the 502nd, along with other units of the 101st, board the SS *Strathnaver*, a British tub originally built to sail only in coastal waters. Re-fitted as a troop ship, she is designed to carry 4300 men under crowded conditions; nearly 6000 are packed aboard. She sails the next day and six days later docks at St. John's, Newfoundland, doesn't sail again until the 26th and then immediately returns to port for repairs. It's not until October 6th that they're loaded aboard a replacement ship, the *John Ericsson*, which has much improved accommodations. They sail late that night, join a convoy the next day, and on October 18th, they dock at Liverpool.

By train and truck, the 502nd is transported down to the southwest of England. They settle into the town of Chilton Foliat, in the county of Wiltshire where it borders Berkshire, about 75 miles west of London, 25 miles north of Stonehenge. Chilton Foliat is every city boy's dream of an English village, with thatched roofs, narrow cobblestone streets, sheep and horses in the fields, hogs and chickens in the barnyards.

Their quarters are not nearly as picturesque: The men sleep on straw mattresses in Nissen huts which are freezing in winter and torrid in summer. The accommodations are matched by the food, almost none of which is fresh—the eggs and milk powdered, the potatoes dehydrated.

The training gets tougher and tougher: marches, physical training, classes in machine guns, mortars, BARs, grenades, mines, demolition, field problems, tactics. Night problems. Jumps.

After fighting it for a couple of weeks, Jake caves in and writes to Cindy, about how he'll come back after the war, get into the Benny Goodman band, then organize his own. How they'll work out a way to get married and have kids and take them to the zoo and the Paramount, the way his parents took him. It is a letter full of longing and optimism and hope, the letter of a boy far from home. It takes three weeks for an answer to come from Cindy. Neither his optimism nor his hope is reciprocated. It would be better if they made up their minds to forget each other, she writes, better if they did not write to each other any more. He can see, or wants to imagine he can see, her parents looking over her shoulder as she writes, dictating the words. Angry and despairing, he tears the letter into pieces.

The next day they begin a cross-country training exercise, in which his platoon has to circle an objective over wooded hills and take it from the rear. Jake is demonic as he climbs a steep slope, charges over the crest and races down the far side. One foot slips out from under him and he begins to tumble, catapulted forward by the weight of his pack. Trying to get his legs under him, he feels something twist in his right knee. He manages to get to his feet, but can barely put any weight on the right leg. After a while a medic gets to him, decides nothing is broken and leaves him to his own resources. He spends three hours hobbling back to his barracks. The next morning, the knee is so stiff and painful, he cannot walk on it at all. Sgt. Cody, who does not believe in pampering a paratrooper, refuses him transportation. "We ain't going to have any chauffeurs behind enemy lines," he says. "You better get used to it." All Jake can do is put an arm around Al Breecher's shoulders and let the powerful little man practically carry him to the infirmary.

He sits and waits for an hour and a half in a room full of injured paratroopers. Finally he is sent into an examination room. Standing there is an Army nurse who appears to be in her mid-20s. She has dark brown hair, brown eyes and what used to be called an hour-glass figure: petite, slim-waisted, yet bosomy, with ample hips. Just looking at her makes Jake feel a lot better.

On the radio a lethargic band is playing "Stardust."

"What seems to be bothering you, Pfc?"

"That arrangement for one thing," Jake replies. "They're supposed to be getting people to dance, not putting them to sleep."

"We're very busy," she says, very businesslike. "We don't really have time for New York wiseguys. Do you want to come back when you've defined your problem more clearly?"

"My knee. I thought you might have noticed when I came hopping into the room."

"Take your pants off."

"My name is Jake Ellinson," he says. "I always like to introduce myself before I take my clothes off." He reminds himself to be careful.

"I'm Lieutenant Hopkins, Pfc. Ellison." It is not so much an introduction as a pointed reminder of their ranks.

He undoes his belt, unbuttons his fly, drops his pants. "Shorts too?"

"That won't be necessary. Sit up on the table."

He gets up on the table, legs in front of him. "It's the right one."

"I can see. It's a bit swollen." She begins to probe his knee.

He winces.

"How'd you know I was from New York?"

"The accent and the attitude."

"Thanks."

She looks up, surprised. "For what?"

"For the compliment."

She smiles faintly, and presses at his knee with what he thinks may be unnecessary severity, "Brooklyn?"

"No, the Bronx. You from Brooklyn?"

"My family is from Flatbush, but my parents moved before I was born."

"To where?"

"Long Island."

"Where on Long Island?"

"Did you come here to have your knee checked or to cross examine me? It seems to be a sprain. You'll live to make the world safe for democracy. If you get to your feet, I'll wrap it with an ace bandage."

He stands up, and when she sits on a low stool to work on his knee, her head is exactly at the level of his crotch.

"Oh boy," he says after a moment or two.

"Too tight?"

"That's not it."

"What's the problem?"

"Well," he says, beginning to be embarrassed. "We're in real serious training, and we don' t get much of a chance to be near women . . . not this near,"

As he speaks, she looks up from his knee.

"Pfc. Ellison!"

"It's Ellinson, with an extra n. I'm sorry. I can't help it."

"I can finish wrapping it with you sitting on the table."

As he climbs up again, the sound of the Benny Goodman band comes over the radio.

"Now that's dance music," he says, grateful for the distraction.

"Benny Goodman," she says. "'Don't Be That Way.'"

"Good for you."

"Don't be patronizing . . . Pfc."

"Listen, lieutenant. Music is my business."

She taps his knee. "You're finished."

"Gee. I was just getting started."

"Call me when you get to the Paramount."

He mimes putting a telephone to his ear. "Oh, Nurse Hopkins. It's Jake Ellinson calling."

"It's Lieutenant Hopkins, Pfc. Ellinson. Are you telling me you worked at the Paramount? As a musician?"

"I can't tell jokes worth a damn. And those usher's uniforms are too tight for me. Music is what I do. Did you ever hear of the Buddy Benson Big Band?"

She makes a face. "Buddy Benson!"

"Everybody's a critic! Suppose I tell you that just before I got drafted, Benny Goodman asked me to join his band?"

"Put on your pants and stop trying to impress me. Anyone can talk big."

"Do you know the Rose & Crown?"

"I've actually been in it, so don't make any wild claims." He thinks she is now somewhat amused, and interested.

"Do I look like the type?"

"Definitely."

"I'm hurt. Stop by the Rose & Crown Saturday night and I'll see if I can really impress you."

The Rose & Crown has been awakened from its amiable drowsiness by the war, which has brought a flood of men and women in uniform to this rural part of southern England. In late 1943, more than a million Yanks have been poured into the confined vessel that is Britain. There are places, especially pubs, where the mix is not a happy one, where the American and British military detest each other, and the locals detest both. The Rose & Crown has no problems. The few British troops in the area don't seem to favor it, which leaves it to the Yanks and the locals, who co-exist happily, if sometimes boisterously. Jake drops in whenever he can, not for the warm beer, which he likes even less than cold beer, but because he's made welcome by the locals, jolly and uncomplaining people who like to chat, drink and sing along with the piano player. The piano is an ancient upright, badly out of tune. Harry Ashford, who plays it, is, during the day, a chemist—the kind Americans call a pharmacist. He is an unsophisticated player, but he has a good ear, a lively sense of tempo, unending enthusiasm, and he knows the basic chords. Listening or singing along, Jake suspends his professional judgment and just has a good time. When Harry and the other regulars ask if he'll play for them, he avoids it by saying, truthfully, he has no horn.

But this Saturday night, he'll change that. Kent and Al are headed for the town of Swindon, about 15 miles away, in pursuit of what they hear is a jazz band. They are surprised when he tells them he's not going. Instead, he borrows a cornet from the 502nd band and heads for the Rose & Crown.

He looks through the crowd, fails to see Lt. Hopkins, takes the horn out of its case, waves it as he makes his way through the bar crowd to Harry. Jake and Harry amuse themselves with wildly inaccurate caricatures of each other's accents.

"Look wha' I got 'ere, 'arry, you old bloke," Jake says.

"What's dat, ya mug ya?"

Jake puts the horn to his lips and goes into a British favorite, "Smiles." Soon everyone in the bar is singing. After a couple more sing-along standards, Harry says, "Hey, dese mugs wanna hear a solo, Jake!"

"No, old chap," Jake replies. "We're in this together, pip pip and all that!" He leads Harry into "White Cliffs of Dover." They're halfway through when Jake spots walking to a corner of the bar, Lt. Hopkins, with another woman in uniform. As he plays, he tips the horn in her direction. She looks at him and nods, barely. When the entire bar has roared its way through "White Cliffs," Jake puts his hands out to quiet the crowd.

"In response to popular demand," he announces, "I'm going to play a solo. This is a song popularized by the great Harry James. It's dedicated to a special friend, who's been a fan of mine since the days of the Paramount in New York."

He does the instrumental "Ciribiribin," which was a big hit for James a few years back, playing it with lots of grace notes and flourishes and drawing tremendous applause. Then he asks Harry to go into "Tipperary" and as soon as everyone starts singing he slips away from the piano. He is headed for Lt. Hopkins at the bar, but taking the long way around; the army does not favor an enlisted man's fraternizing with a female officer. The pub is aroar with "Tipperary" as he makes his way toward the lieutenant and her friend. He can see her looking around. For him, he hopes. He works his way through the smoky, noisy room and gets very close, almost touching her, before he speaks.

"Now are you impressed?"

She is startled, "A paratrooper who can actually live up to his bragging!" she says, then turns to her friend. "Cynthia, this is Jake." He's pleased; she's dropped the rank and remembered his name.

"Hello," Jake says. He puts out his hand to Cynthia, who takes it and for a moment or two holds it.

"Hi," Cynthia says. "I was really impressed. June tells me you actually played at the Paramount!"

He smiles. "June got it right. For a week in '41. Benny Goodman came to see us, wanted me to play for him. But Uncle Sam booked me for a command performance."

He stares at Cynthia. She is auburn haired, with pale skin, a tiny turned-up nose and purple eyes that radiate lots of sexual come-on and little intelligence. Jake suspects at once she is a bore. Cynthia confirms it by saying, "Boy, can you make that trombone do tricks."

June is accustomed to Cynthia stealing men away. She is watching to see which way Jake will go.

"Thanks," Jake says, "Even though you got the instrument wrong."

"I did? Oh dear!"

June is smiling.

"Ask June. She knows," Jake says.

"It's a cornet," June replies.

"Now I'm impressed!" Jake says. "Can I buy you two ladies a drink?" Though he makes the offer to both, his eyes meet June's as he speaks, and the deal is sealed. It takes two drinks before Cynthia gets it and spots a couple of Army doctors she wants to chat with.

"Was it something I said?" Jake asks when she leaves.

June just smiles. "You know damned well what it was."

"Do you mind?"

"If I did, would I be standing here?"

"I'm flattered."

"Good," she says, nodding. "Keep on being." She offers him a cigaret. He shakes his head no, lights hers.

"Hey, you are one sharp lady," he tells her. "You sure you're not from the Bronx?"

Now she grins at him. "No, but I took my nurse's training at Columbia-Presbyterian."

"Not far from where I went to school . . . City College."

"They used to give us a hard time on the subway."

"I apologize for them," Jake says.

"Harmless Jewish kids. I had the feeling if I ever said to one of them, come on over to my place, he'd faint."

Jake's eyes harden. "I'm Jewish."

"I know that," she answers.

"I'm not harmless."

"I hope not."

"I wouldn't faint if you said, come on over to my place." He stares at her.

"It just happens," she says, "I've been assigned quarters in a charming house on the edge of the village. The room's barely big enough for a small bed and a large bottle of scotch. Tiny but private. I guess it was a maid's room. Even has its own entrance."

Together they steal out the side door into the quiet and the chill of the English night. From the pub to her small bedroom is a five-minute walk, their way lit by a moon that is almost full. That is their only light, for this village, like every other in Britain, is totally blacked out to thwart the German bombers that still visit regularly.

After she makes sure the blackout curtains are drawn she turns on a lamp and lights another cigaret, offers Jake one; again he shakes his head no. While she tends the small coal stove, he looks around. The room is smaller even than the hotel rooms on the road, but far more attractive. It is papered with a hunting pattern and the minimal free floor space is occupied by a throw rug that picks up the dominant maroon of the wallpaper. The bed is barely larger than a twin, puffed high with an enormous quilt and brightened by a string of colorful pillows. On the table is a framed headshot of an army officer.

"You get this room all to yourself?"

"All of it," she answers.

"It beats 20 guys to a Nissen hut," he says fervently.

She walks to where a mahogany wardrobe stands against a wall. It is a beautiful piece; clearly it once stood in a much grander bedroom and was moved here during some past redecoration of the house. She opens it and takes from the top shelf a bottle of scotch and two glasses, opens the bottle, pours a couple of fingers of the liquor into each glass and hands one to him.

"The only thing this room is too big for is the stove. I don't think I'll ever be warm again till the war is over."

He raises his glass to hers and clinks it. "To being warm," he toasts.

"To being warm," she answers. He sips at his glass; she drains hers in one swallow. "Would you believe that back home I never touched this stuff?" she tells him.

"What would he say?" Jake nods in the direction of the photograph. By this time she has more scotch in her glass, another cigaret in hand. She raises her glass to the picture. "Here's to Lt. Bill Miller, who would disapprove. But Bill, there's a war on!"

"A straight arrow, huh?"

"The original. The kind of man every red-blooded American girl would want to marry. Should want to marry."

"Including you?"

"Don't I look like a red-blooded American girl to you?" She notices his glass. "If you don't like that stuff, don't waste it. Jews don't drink, do they?"

"Hey, what is this?"

"Relax, Jake Ellinson, I didn't invite you over here to make anti-Semitic remarks."

He takes another sip of the scotch. It reminds him of the toothache drops his mother once administered on a weekend when they couldn't find a dentist.

"What did you invite me here for?"

She walks to him and kisses him on the mouth. The scotch takes on a new bouquet.

"First, to tell you the rules. You see Bill Miller over there?" She turns him to the photo. "Do you know what he actually said to me before I shipped out? He said, 'June, I will remain faithful to you. And I hope you will save yourself for me.' Imagine that?"

She walks over and pours herself some more scotch. "Tell me, is there someone you promised you'd be faithful to?"

He shakes his head slowly. "She turned down the offer."

"Ah. But you know what, Jake?" Her eyes belie the smart-talking woman he's been listening to. "After the war it will work out. You will find a way."

Again he shakes his head no.

"Yes, you will," she insists, "And you know what will happen to me after the war?"

"What?" Jake thought she was getting drunk, but now he sees a focused intensity in those eyes.

"I will become a virgin again. And Bill and I will live happily ever after." She walks to the photo and looks down at the man she promised to be faithful to. "So we will have to remember the happy ending that's coming for each of us when this war is over. But meanwhile, Jake, I need someone to remind me of New York. Of the Paramount and the Strand and the Capitol. Sitting there in the dark and watching the bandstand rise. Jake, did you really sit on that bandstand?"

"Five times a day for a week."

"Will you tell me about it? And about the clubs on 52nd Street?"

"All about it."

"And will you help me keep warm?"

"Snug as two bugs in a rug."

"Just till the lousy war is over and I get back to central heating—that's all! That must be understood! Then I become a virgin again."

"That is understood."

June walks to the picture of Bill Miller. She picks it up and kisses it. "Please remember, Bill, there's a war on." Then she turns it away from the bed. She comes toward Jake and puts her arms around his neck. He stoops slightly to put his arms around her waist, straightens up and lifts her off the floor. Then, squeezing her tightly, he carries her to the bed.

He awakens in the middle of the night. She lies next to him, a light film of perspiration on her slender shoulders and soft neck; he has kept her warm. He kisses the arm that is folded up so that her hand rests under the side of her face, then slips out of bed, dresses in the dark and gets back to his barracks.

Kent and Al know Jake has something going. He swears them to secrecy; an enlisted man shacking up with a female officer can be dangerous. Aside from Jake's visits to June, the three buddies spend most of their time together—nights at the pub and occasional visits to London, sometimes with passes, sometimes without them.

But on most free nights it's their "local," The Rose & Crown, where Jake gets to know and cherish the people of Wiltshire. Harry Ashford, the piano player, becomes a special buddy. He's in his late 50s and he and his wife live in an apartment above his apothecary shop, where two small empty bedrooms are kept ready for the return of the two sons who are in the British navy.

On the weekend before Christmas, Jake has a three-day pass. The plan is for him and June to go to London, see the sights, dance, listen to the swing bands. Then comes bad news: June has pulled weekend duty at the infirmary, a last minute fill-in for a nurse who's sick. Jake goes alone, catches a ride on a 2 and ½ ton army truck crammed with GIs headed for the big city. He finds a room at a small hotel just off Piccadilly Circus that is reserved for enlisted men. On a bulletin board in the lobby, he reads of a big dance that evening at the famous GI club, Rainbow Corner, on nearby Shaftesbury Avenue. As he enters he can see onstage a USO touring band backing a singing trio in one of the big hits of late '43, "All or Nothing at All." Sitting at the piano is the man who in late August bemoaned being 4F and hoped he would be able to get out to entertain the troops: Johnny Black.

After the set, Jake bulldozes his way through to Johnny, who throws his arms around him. When the hellos and the exclamations of surprise and happiness are over, Johnny says, "Wanna hear a coincidence? You'll never guess who came up to me right here two nights ago to say hello!"

"Ah . . . Benny."

"Naah. Benny wouldn't say hello. He and I know each other well enough not to be on speaking terms."

"Come on! Who?"

"Well, the guy plays tenor. Real good. But talent runs in his family. His brother plays trumpet."

"Herbie? You're kidding!"

"They shipped his band over two weeks ago. He says he wrote to you."

"I never got it!"

"They're playing at a dance tomorrow night. Some big hall in the East End. I wrote it down, 'cause he asked me to come and sit in. We'll go together. Got a horn?"

"No, but I've got a mouthpiece in my hot little pocket."

"I'll find you a horn. What a surprise it'll be to him. We'll blow the place down!"

The East End dance hall is cavernous; only the low ceiling would keep it from serving as an airplane hangar. The lights are dim, the air a haze of cigaret smoke. Tonight it is packed; perhaps 500 girls and women are in it and they are outnumbered three to one by men in uniform. As Jake and Johnny try to make their way to the bandstand, they pass men in the uniforms of Poland, France, Holland, Belgium, Norway, Denmark, and all the British Commonwealth: Canada, Australia, New Zealand. Lots of Brits, of course: Army, Royal Navy and Marines, RAF. And the dominant group, the Americans. The walls are lined with MPs, most of them American, with their armbands, white helmet liners, trousers bloused over boots, clubs hanging from white web belts.

Virtually all of the women are on the dance floor, while the huge surplus of men circle on the fringes, shouldering each other aside, scouting the dancers or positioning themselves to make a move when the number is over, or for the more impatient to cut in while it's still going on.

Herb is sitting down front on the bandstand, two other sax players alongside him, playing a languid "As Time Goes By." For a while, before Herb spots him, Jake is able to examine his kid brother. Herb seems so young, so fragile, thinner now than ever. Every family, Jake thinks, especially every Jewish family, must make a commitment to fighting the Nazis, even at risk of life. How happy he feels that it's he who is doing that for the Ellinsons!

Herb looks up from his music stand for a moment, to see, standing just to the left of the bandstand, Johnny Black and, staring at him, grinning, Jake! His eyes meet Jake's, he wants to smile back, but a tenor sax embouchure will not allow it, so he turns toward his brother and nods, instrument and all. When the set is over, Herb and Jake rush to each other, Herb with his sax still hanging around his neck, Jake carrying the borrowed trumpet in its case.

"I don't believe it!" Herb says.

"I didn't believe it when Johnny told me you were here! You sounded real good, Herbie, smooth!"

Herb makes a deprecating face. "Know how many times we've played 'As Time Goes By'? I did get kind of nervous when I saw you. You look great. You actually look like you put on a little weight."

Jake looks at the ceiling, "Ma? Did you hear that? Put on weight!" He slaps Herb on the shoulder. "How are you holding up?"

"It's exciting, Jake. All the excitement, none of the danger. Sometimes I think I'm cheating."

Jake scowls, jabs a finger at Herb's chest. "Hey, you're important right where you are. Just look at the faces of the GIs while you're playing. You stay right in that band!"

Herb's eyes ask: then why not you? Jake's eyes admit nothing.

Before long Jake, Herb, and a very good trombone player Jake has never seen or heard before, backed by Johnny and bass and drums, are playing uptempo numbers that have the jitterbugs lindying madly. Then the crowd packs in and just listens. The six of them are swinging. For a pleasurable and poignant moment or two time freezes and men in so many different uniforms can forget what it will lead to when it resumes ticking. They finish to a roar of approval. As Jake walks off to the side, a few strides behind Herb, he hardly notices the tall officer who approaches him.

"Hello, I'm Colonel Egan."

Jake looks up, sees the eagle insignia that mark him as a full or "bird" colonel, as opposed to a "light" or lieutenant colonel who wears silver leaf. The man thrusts a hand out, which Jake shakes.

"You are a remarkable talent."

"Thank you, sir."

"I'm head of Army Special Services in London. We could sure use you in a band!"

Jake smiles. "No, thanks!"

"Think of how good that would make your folks feel, knowing both their boys are in a band, instead of one of them being . . ." He takes in Jake's airborne badge, ". . . in the paratroops, aiming to get himself killed."

This man knows how to play it.

"I'm not going to get myself killed, sir!" But he's got Jake thinking, that this is a last chance, that the colonel is right, his parents would be so happy. Colonel Egan sees it. "Tell you what, if you change your mind, just have your brother let me know."

†

Late the next afternoon, the brothers say goodbye. They stand in Piccadilly Circus, at the famous statue of Eros that's been boarded up to protect it from the bombing. Around them, men and women in the uniforms of dozens of nations stream by and the hookers, the "Picadilly commandos," are patrolling in force.

As the brothers hug each other, one of the women shouts, "Eh, don't you fancy ladies?"

"Hey, get lost, ladies," Jake shouts back.

With a few catcalls and gestures, the hookers keep going.

"Take care of yourself, Jake."

"Don't I always? You too, Herbie."

"Ma wrote that she got a picture of you with a band. It made her happy. You know, if anything happened to you . . ."

"I told you, nothing will happen to me!"

They hug again and Jake hoists his bag to his shoulder and starts off. For a few minutes Herb watches him go. Then he decides, for the first and only time in his life, to disobey his brother. He will find Colonel Egan and ask him to get Jake assigned to a band.

Christmas eve comes to Chilton Foliat with damp cold and drizzle. Jake and Kent are sitting in their barracks, waiting for Al to arrive so the three can visit the Rose & Crown. Tomorrow, all but a skeleton force have the day off. The locals have mounted a tremendous effort to make sure that every GI is invited to someone's house for Christmas dinner; Jake, Kent, and Al will be guests of Harry and Mavis Ashford in their apartment above Harry's chemist's shop. Friends will be coming by afterwards and a rousing sing is in store.

Al walks into the hut with his usual poker face. "Smile!" Jake tells him. "We've got the day off! Tomorrow's your big holiday!

Al throws himself on his sack. "I pulled guard duty tomorrow."

"You're joking," Kent says, knowing well that Al doesn't joke.

"No. They posted it a few hours ago."

"Oh hell," Kent says.

"Somebody's got to do it," Al replies.

"For God's sake, don't be so accepting!" Kent almost shouts.

"Doesn't do any good to get angry. On a farm you work every day."

"You're not working tomorrow," Jake says. "I'm replacing you."

"No, Jake . . ."

"No nos. It's not my holiday. I always feel funny hanging around you Christians on one of your big days, anyway."

"Jake . . ."

"Besides, you'll pay me back. I give you one of these damned miserable, bone-chilling English winter days, and you'll give it back on the sunniest, most beautiful day in spring."

"Spring . . . say, isn't that when Passover happens?" Kent offers.

"Right!" Jake says. "You'll make it up to me on Passover! And, Al . . . you sucker . . . Passover lasts eight days!"

For an instant Al looks startled, till Jake says, "You only have to pay me back one!"

"Jake, I'll pay you two," Al says.

Jake balls up his fist. "Hey, I'm no Shylock!" The three men laugh.

Jake spends his stint of guard duty along the perimeter of the 502nd's encampment, rain dripping through the protection of his poncho, cold water seeping into his sodden fatigues. He's heard it never gets very warm or very cold in England. He's had no chance to test the first. But on this Christmas day, he's ready to dispute the second. Maybe it's not much below 40, but for miserable frigidity it will do. The idea of danger or death has never put him off, but if at a moment like this someone were to offer him a job in a band, or a warm, dry assignment doing anything, he might accept. When he gets off guard duty, he drops by Harry's house, where dinner is long finished.

"Just want to pay my respects, as one musician to another," he tells Harry. "I'll bet I missed a great time!"

The middle-aged man gives him a long, affectionate look. "That was a very Christian thing for you to do."

Jake starts to set him straight, then decides it's not worth all the trouble. "That's me!" is all he says.

Harry walks to an old bookcase, on which is sitting an object wrapped in newspaper and tied with a ribbon. He takes it and hands it to Jake.

"Got a little something for each of the boys," Harry says modestly. "Wrapping's not all it should be. But, have you heard? There's a war on!"

Jake unwraps the newspaper to find a small, beat-up old silver cornet that's been carefully polished. He feels tears coming to his eyes. All he can do is grab Harry and throw his arms around him.

"It's not in the best of shape," Harry says.

"It's just great!" Jake answers. He puts it to his lips and plays a scale on it. In truth it does not sound too bad at all. "Just great! Harry . . . I'll take it with me. Everywhere!"

On New Year's Eve, he is called to company headquarters, where a corporal behind a desk tells him that orders have come through transferring him to Special Services.

"Request permission to see the CO, corporal!"

But Capt. Chuck Smith is not prepared to dispute a bird colonel, so, orders in hand, Jake double-times over to regimental headquarters and tells the sergeant major he must see the regimental commander. The sergeant major is not accustomed to having a Pfc. ask to see the colonel. Jake is explaining why, when Colonel George Van Horn Moseley himself walks in, and Jake just wheels and addresses Moseley. The worst they can do is throw him into the stockade, and that at least will have the effect of jamming the machinery of the transfer.

"Colonel, sir! If I don't get to talk to you, the regiment is going to lose a good man!"

The sergeant major is seething, the colonel curious. "And who is the good man?"

"I am sir!"

Colonel Moseley's attention has been grabbed. He waves off his sergeant major and leads Jake into the part of the command tent that has been sectioned off as his office. Jake tells him the story, shows him the orders. "Ole Moe" Moseley asks Jake who his platoon sergeant is and then tells the sergeant major to get Sgt. Cody over on the double.

Cody, standing at attention in front of a bird colonel, manages to give Jake a murderous look.

"This Pfc. says he's a good man, sergeant. Is he right?"

A hesitation. Then, "Yessir!"

"Tough?"

"Yessir!"

"Real tough?"

"Yessir!"

"Dammit, sergeant, stop yessir-ing me! Some desk jockey wants to transfer him to a band! He wants to stay here and get himself killed. That proves he's dumb, but how tough is he?"

"Tough, sir. A boxer, sir."

Now Moseley gives Jake a new kind of look. "Like to fight, huh?"

Jake's answer is oblique. "I'm good at it, sir."

"Worth keeping?" Moseley is talking to Cody again.

"Yessir!"

"You've got a damned limited vocabulary, sergeant, but I get the message. Lt. Moore!"

An aide comes running in. Moseley hands him the papers. "This transfer is denied. We've got a job to do that needs tough men. OK, Pfc . . . what's your name?"

"Ellinson, sir."

"OK, Ellison, you get to stay, you damned fool."

"Thank you, sir!"

"Thank me by killing as many of those Nazi bastards as you can get your hands on. Sergeant, take him with you. Dismissed."

"Yessir!" Jake and Sgt. Cody shout it together.

When they get outside, Cody yells, "What the hell was all that, Ellison!"

"Not my fault, sergeant. Some colonel heard me play trumpet, wanted me for a band."

"What are you: a trooper or some fairy musician?"

"I'm a trooper, sergeant! That's why I . . ."

"Why'n't you just come to me?"

"Because Capt. Smith said . . ."

"I said, why'n't you just come to me?"

"What could you have done?"

"What could you have done, *sergeant*!"

"What could you have done, *sergeant*?"

"I would've torn up the goddamned orders and if any of them special service queers come around, I'd've run my bayonet up where they probably would've liked it. Now, you double-time your ass back to the company area!"

"Yes, sergeant!" Grinning, Jake takes off.

†

The men wait and prepare for Operation Overlord, the invasion of France. In late May, units of the 502nd begin to be trucked from Chilton Foliat to the rows of tents waiting for them at the Greenham Common airfield, where they will be quarantined to keep plans of Operation Overlord from leaking out.

On the night before the Third Battalion is moved, Jake meets June at the Rose & Crown. Everything has taken on a new charge; the air is heavy with invasion talk. They all know what's about to happen, although none of them knows when. She is sitting at a table in the corner of the main room, sipping at a glass of stout, smoking a cigaret; she is never without a cigaret. Harry is toying with the piano; he looks up when Jake walks in. His eyes want to tell his American paratrooper friend something, but he doesn't know what the words are. Finally, not trusting himself to speak, his eyes never leaving Jake's, he gives him that characteristic British thumbs-up gesture. Jake just stops and claps Harry on the shoulder.

"Keep playing pretty, Harry. Tonight's a good night for pretty music." Jake realizes as he uses the word twice that pretty is a description of music he picked up from Cindy. He hasn't written to her in a long time, and he's resolved not to think about her. Did I ever know a girl named Cindy? he asks. Did I ever play in a band? Was I ever anybody but a paratrooper? No, he tells himself. No. No.

There is a glass of stout waiting for him on the bar, put there by Freddie Pawling, the owner. Jake carries it to June and sits across from her. They lift their glasses and clink them.

June sips at the stout. "I hate this stuff." Big slow tears bulb from her eyes, roll down her cheeks; she puts a hand up to wipe them away.

"It never made you cry before." That almost gets a smile out of her.

"I've got a new bottle of scotch at my place."

"I've got to be back."

She nods. "How is your knee?" she asks. The injury turned out to be a badly strained ligament; he's been in twice to get the knee taped.

"Getting better every day."

"You should not be jumping on it. All I have to do is put in the papers . . ."

"You must be kidding." His anger at her suggestion surprises him.

"You could be a liability to the men around you."

"Hey, let's talk about something else. What's with the tears? The fatal Ellinson charm strike again?"

"I used to wonder how men could face things like . . ." She lets the sentence trail off. "Now I know what it is. They're children! Too young and stupid and egotistical to realize. Anything could happen to them."

"How many times do I have to tell you, nothing's going to happen to me!"

"They've been briefing us to get us ready for . . ." She takes a drag of her cigarette.

"I think they call them casualties."

What she wants to tell him but doesn't is that the pessimistic estimate of casualties in the two American airborne divisions jumping on D-Day is 75 percent. The most common estimate is 50 percent: one out of every two men from the 101st and 82nd will be killed, wounded, or captured in the attack.

"Yes," she answers almost mockingly. "Casualties. What a nice clean word. As if they were something you just filled out forms for. You haven't seen the . . . casualties, Jake. I have. Boys from the fighting in North Africa and Italy. When they go off, they put that hard look in their eyes. Just like you. Nothing can harm *me*! But when they come back paralyzed, or with a leg blown off . . . or with their crotches shot away, yes, that happens, too! You know what else is gone? That invulnerable look in their eyes! Know what you see instead? 'I want my mommy!'"

"It must be tough for you to face that," Jake answers somberly, sidestepping her message.

June lights another cigaret from the stub of her last one, her hands fumbling as she does. "I can handle it; it's my job. But I tell you Jake, I couldn't handle it if one of them was you."

He shakes his head. "One of them is not going to be."

"You're so strong, aren't you! Know what a hand grenade can do to all those muscles? Or a mortar shell? I don't want to see anything happen to those wonderful muscles, Jake. Or that lovely circumcised penis. For God's sake, Jake, please!"

"Please what? Don't get killed? I'm going to try my damnedest not to, I told you! You see, Junebug, you did the smart thing: got engaged to a stateside supply officer. You know he'll be safe."

"You're a rotten bastard to say that!" She stubs out a cigaret, lights another.

"A rotten egotistical bastard. You can't stand it that I haven't told you I was crazy about you!"

Jake smiles, reaches over, takes her hand. "Funny, I thought you *were* crazy about me."

She puts her other hand on his, strokes the hard, leathery back of that muscular hand. "I don't want to see you carried into my hospital, Jake. I couldn't stand that."

"OK! I'll request a hospital up north. I hear the nurses there are all blondes."

"Don't be funny." Her big brown eyes stare at him. "And don't let anything happen to you. That is such a stupid thing to say, isn't it? As if you have much control over it. But I'm saying it anyway." Her eyes drop, fix on his outstretched hand, which has taken hold of hers.

"Maybe if you told me you were crazy about me, I could see to it I didn't even get a scratch."

Without looking up, she almost smiles. "Promise?"

"Promise."

She strokes his hand, still doesn't look at him. "I am crazy about you, Jake."

He takes the hand he's been holding, lifts it to his mouth and kisses it. "Maybe we could find a half hour to go to your apartment. For a drink of scotch."

Once the men are trucked to the airfield at Greenham Common, there is no going anywhere. The tents stand in a field which is surrounded by barbed wire and guarded by MPs. They are now aware of their mission, so they are allowed no contact with the outside world.

Behind them now is the relentless physical training: the marches, the running, the pushups, the jumping jacks. Behind them the classes in tactical problems, in explosives, in weapons. By now the men all know how to handle machineguns, mortars, BARs and bazookas, although most of them are not assigned those weapons; they know how to operate German weapons, should they capture any. Every rifleman knows how to use explosives to blow up a bridge, a house, or a tank tread, although most will not be carrying explosives.

They have been thoroughly briefed—on the terrain they will have to traverse, the locations of their objectives, the opposition they are expected to face. The briefings are so thorough and wide ranging, it is said a private in the airborne knows as much about his mission as a colonel in the regular infantry.

Now time hangs heavy. They are free to bask in the sun, and to feast. The food is lavish, with treats like fried chicken and ice cream and fruit cocktail. When Kent says they are like cattle being fattened for slaughter, the men laugh, knowing there is some truth to it. The 502nd band plays at meals; at other times the loudspeaker system blares the hit records of the day. Jake and his scarred silver cornet are always in demand, to play sentimental ballads like "You'd Be So Nice To Come Home To" and "I'll Be Seeing You." One night, while a bugler sounds taps, Jake plays harmony and variations. Except for one officer, who calls it a profanation of a sacred bugle call, the men all love it.

Men shoot craps or play cards. Not being a gambler, Jake takes part in the pick-up baseball games, goes to the movies, writes to Herb, to his folks. Breaks down and writes to Cindy. Many times he answers Amanda's letters. Only one is ever sent, the others he tears up. He is intimidated by her lyricism, by her nakedly expressed feelings.

Some men have their heads shaved. H Company decides on Mohawk haircuts. The job is done by a Texan named Amby Garner, who claims he once worked as a barber, but who butchers them.

Chutes are checked and re-checked. Rifles are broken down, cleaned, oiled, reassembled, then broken down and cleaned and oiled again. Knives are sharpened and tested and sharpened again; some men will carry three or four of them, plus machetes. Jake has only his bayonet, jump knife, and a substantial pocketknife, which he can reach easily and use to cut himself out of his parachute harness if he has to. He's learned from training jumps that the harness's five buckles often do not respond the way nervous fingers want them to.

The men are sharp, aggressive, ready to fight. Over-ready. Tempers are honed as fine as the knives. Impromptu boxing and wrestling matches start everywhere; sooner or later, each turns into a vicious brawl. Jake is a particular target because he is known to be a boxer. A corporal named Butkowski, from G Company, is always challenging him. Jake always refuses.

One evening after dinner, he corners Jake. "C'mon," he says. "I just wanna see how a pro does it."

"No," Jake says. "Besides, I'm not a pro."

"You know what I mean. Am I too big for you? That it? I won't use all my weight."

"Why don't you just forget it?" Jake tries to walk around Butkowski, who holds his ground and puts up his hands in boxing stance.

"Show me how you block a jab," he says, shooting his big fists out at Jake, aiming at his chest and shoulders.

Jake deflects a couple with his forearms. With no warning, Butkowski wings a roundhouse right at Jake's head. Jake slips his head to the side and the fist misses, but the big forearm slams against the side of Jake's head.

"Cut it out, goddamnit," Jake yells, and pushes the corporal away from him. The other man pushes back; he is 25 pounds heavier than Jake and very strong.

"You're a creampuff," Butkowski says, and charges at Jake, who meets him with a jab and then a right hook that breaks his jaw. Butkowski will spend D-Day in a hospital in the south of England. His company commander complains to his H Company counterpart. Capt. Smith bucks it down to Sgt. Cody, whose only action is to say to Jake, "Save it for the Krauts, will you."

The men are issued ammunition and grenades, rations, French invasion francs and the little toy crickets they will use as signals when they land: each emits a tinny click when it is pressed in and another when released. One double click is the challenge, two the response. They also learn the passwords: "Flash" as challenge, "Thunder" as response.

On June 4th, they are packed and ready to go. They are given a sumptuous last meal, which turns out not to be their last. Stormy winds and rain force a delay. With the weather still bad, but a meteorologist's promise of improvement, an agonizing General Eisenhower decides to go the following day. D-Day is now set for June 6th. The men of the 101st and 82nd will be the first Americans in France, landing shortly after midnight, six hours before the landing craft scrape onto the beaches. On June 5th, again they are ready. This time there will be no cancellation. The men of Company H blacken their faces. They eat a meal, this time stew, nothing lavish, their last in England for some time. For some, their last ever.

In late afternoon, they begin boarding the trucks which will take them to their planes. Tied to the side of Jake's web belt is the cornet. As they climb aboard, the 502nd band is playing one of its favorites, a song Jake detests, "Holiday For Strings." The men are enveloped in silence. The only sounds, other than the band, are the clanking of equipment and the occasional grunts or curses as the men hoist themselves and their loads onto the trucks.

Finally, Jake bursts out, "I hate that song!" The men, seeking any excuse to break their silence, roar. "What would your preference be?" Kent asks him. The men in the truck, hearing that, chip in with suggestions. One yells "In The Mood." Another, "Remember Pearl Harbor."

"'Show Me The Way To Go Home,'" says one. That gets a huge laugh.

But Kent tops them all. "How about 'Let's Call The Whole Thing Off,'" he shouts. A roar of laughter ends very quickly, as if all at once they realize the thing will not be called off.

Now the trucks are moving. Jake waves to the band, most of whom he knows well by this time. I could be standing there with them, he tells himself. He stares at the row of men sitting across from him. He knows what they must be thinking. All volunteers, they are all having their own variations of his thought: I could be somewhere else. It is evening when they pull up near the row of C-47s that will ferry them to the Cotentin peninsula of Normandy. The men climb down from the trucks; their main and reserve parachutes and equipment are unloaded and each man makes sure he has what belongs to him. They check their gear carefully. They are all issued airsickness pills and cardboard containers in case the pills don't work. Then they sit on the ground, wait, watch the sun set. They are quiet if not tranquil, waiting for dark; on June evenings in the wartime's Double British Summer Time, there is light in the sky until after ten o'clock.

As far as Jake can see, planes are lined up and ready, men lined up and waiting to board them. Jeeps with officers in them are scurrying around. One races up to Capt. Smith. A major leans over and talks to him. Then the jeep hurries off. Smith gets to his feet, barks, "On your feet! Fall in, on the double!"

Troopers leap to their feet, grateful for a break in the waiting. "Listen to this!" shouts Smith. "General Eisenhower is in the vicinity, visiting the troops, and he's headed this way. I want you to look good, How Company!" Even as he says it, Jake can see a string of jeeps headed their way. In the second one is Ike. The jeeps move slowly by them; Ike waves at them, flashes that famous smile and gives them a thumbs-up sign. Instinctively, though they haven't been told to, the men break their formation, crowd toward him, cheering. The jeep slows, but does not stop. Disappointed, they watch as it moves away, then comes to a stop further on, at E Company of the Second Battalion. Ike gets out and the men are soon clustered around him. Jake's company can see him talking. Then the general gets back in his jeep, which moves off and out of sight.

The men of H Company walk back to their places and sit down. People have run out of things to say. There is silence, then the roar of airplane engines starting up, and the voice of their platoon leader, Lieutenant Pete Sobchak: "All right, get ready to board!"

Now wearing all their gear, including both chutes, the men are bearing loads of 125 pounds or more. Sgt. Cody is the first of Jake's stick to board. In the doorway of the plane, he turns to the men gathered below, pulls his big paratrooper knife and brandishes it in front of him.

"See this knife?" he screams. "I promise you that before this day is over, I will bury this in the heart of some goddamn Nazi bastard! Are you with me?"

In answer, the men roar like animals, then follow him on board. With the help of the men ahead and behind, each of the 16 in their stick is hoisted aboard the plane. Awkwardly, each manages to waddle to the low benches running along each side of the fuselage. There they sit, two rows of eight, faces blackened, staring at each other. Talking would be difficult over the sound of the engines, but no one seems inclined to talk.

Men light up cigarets; Jake sees he's the only one not smoking. Even Al is puffing away. This is the closest to nerves Jake has ever seen him show. Jake looks at the others: a first lieutenant, two sergeants, two corporals and 11 Pfcs and privates. If the pessimists are right, 12 of them will be killed, wounded, or captured in the battle ahead. If the optimists are right, it will be only eight.

The engines go from a throaty roar to a higher pitch that's almost a whine as the bulky C-47 begins to lumber down the runway, laboriously picks up speed, and finally lifts off the ground. They are in the final hour of Monday, June 5th, 1944. By the time their boots touch French soil, it will be June 6th.

CHAPTER 23

"Mrs. Turnbull, Diana Penrose Miller. We haven't met, but my company represented you in the sale of your apartment."

"Why Dede, I am a bit disappointed . . ." The cultivated voice at the other end of the phone was redolent of Park Avenue, boarding school, and the Seven Sisters colleges, which got the cream of the young women in the days before all of the Ivy League went co-ed. "Nelson and I were at your wedding. My family has known the Martindales for ages."

"Forgive me. I should have remembered. One doesn't really have one's wits about one at a wedding."

"I was teasing. After all, it was . . . 20 years ago?"

"Very good. Nineteen plus."

"The fact is the Ellisons and the Martindales have always been rather . . . distant. I remember our surprise at having been invited."

Over the phone, Dede liked her at once. "You do have a remarkable memory," she said.

"Widow ladies my age have little to do but remember," she replied. "Unlike career women who have such exciting lives—and get written up in the *New York Times Magazine.*"

"Oh dear. I am not quite the person you read about."

"Please don't disappoint me again, Dede. I admired and envied the woman I read about. Made me wish I'd been born 20 years later."

When Dede said she wanted to meet with her, Mrs. Turnbull was delighted, but added she had no plans to buy or sell an apartment.

"It's about something else entirely. May I wait until I see you to tell you?"

"You may indeed," she answered. "Any little *frisson* of suspense is most welcome."

She invited Dede for a drink at the "small" apartment she'd bought after her children moved out and then Nelson died. On a high floor of a

Fifth Avenue building, it had a majestic view of Central Park to the west and the Manhattan skyline to the south. With a huge living room, dining room, study, and maid's room, it was small only in having only two master bedrooms. Dede knew that even before seeing it, knowing as she did the layout of virtually every line in every "good" apartment house on the upper East Side. What surprised her was the starkness of the living room. She'd expected a room overstuffed with age and memories: fussy furniture, pictures, trophies, bric-a-brac. They were scarce. In a silver filigree frame on a side table stood a large family photo, young husband and wife with two small girls and a boy: the Turnbulls, Dede decided. Next to it, in a plain silver frame, was a picture of a handsome long-faced young man in World War II army dress uniform. She had no doubt who that was. On the wall opposite the fireplace hung a large oil portrait of a striking young woman, more a girl, probably still a teenager, in a blue sweater and plaid skirt, blonde hair in a ponytail, light blue eyes shining out of the canvas. Nor had Dede any doubt about her.

The Amanda Turnbull who showed her into the room had silver hair pulled back into a chignon, its severity emphasizing the fineness of her nose and cheekbones. Slim and tall in black trousers and a pale green silk blouse, she was a stunning woman; her eyes now more green than the ones in the painting, a woman in many ways even more compelling than the girl who'd been captured in oils. She had to be about 65 and made little effort with makeup to hide the network of fine lines in her skin, yet Dede was overwhelmed by her beauty. She almost blurted out, oh, if only I could look like you when I'm 65. Instead she said, "What a lovely, serene, simple room."

"Thank you," the older woman answered. "I hate places that smell of age and nostalgia. I try to make the apartment look as if it were inhabited by a younger person."

"Ah, but it is," Dede said, not quite sure what that meant.

Mrs. Turnbull understood. "Compliments, and a surprise, too! Would you care for a glass of wine? I welcome any reason to open a bottle of champagne."

"That would be lovely."

While she was off getting it, Dede stared at the painting. Handsome rather than beautiful was perhaps the word for the girl. She was most struck by the boldness and clarity of the eyes, which the painter had caught in the girl and were still evident in the woman nearly half a century later.

Mrs. Turnbull came back with a bottle of Perrier-Jouet, which she opened easily and poured into two champagne flutes. "Cheers," she said as they lifted their glasses. Dede tasted a wine that was clean and light, aristocratic without flaunting it. Like Amanda Turnbull herself.

"I was admiring the portrait," Dede said.

Amanda Turnbull waved her hand dismissively. "You pay an artist to turn out a piece of flattery; this one earned his pay."

"Funny," Dede said. "I was going to say it doesn't do you justice."

"You never saw the girl," she responded.

"Ah, but I do see the woman."

"Now, Dede! I am really not much good at handling compliments. May we go on to the surprise?"

"It will take you back a long way. To World War II. Do you want to go back there?"

A change came over that bold, handsome face. Gone was the easy good humor, replaced by a look almost of apprehension. "To our family, the war was not a happy event. We lost my brother Kent, killed in action in '44, at the age of 23. There he is." She pointed to the photo. "I'm sure you didn't know any of that."

"I did know that."

Amanda's face showed surprise, but she said nothing. Dede walked to the window, from which she could see the General Motors building and the Plaza hotel. "Perhaps this is a bad idea. Does the subject still hurt?"

"I'm always surprised at how much it does, after—how long—nearly 46 years. I adored Kent. Worshipped is not too strong a word. He was handsome, charming, brilliant, cynical, in some ways the black sheep. But how we loved him! Mother and father, too, although Kent never believed they did. He particularly thought father had contempt for him because he was . . . different. And yet he was so much like any other son, desperately wanting his father's approval. That's why he volunteered for the airborne. In fact, father was so proud of him!"

She looked off into space, as if trying to spot something at a great distance. "When the news came . . . it was the only time in my entire life I ever saw father come close to crying. His eyes just filled up, and he turned away. It wouldn't do for a man to be seen crying. Right to the day he died, father kept Kent's Bronze Star and Purple Heart under glass in a special case. Like a shrine. There." She walked Dede to a table that turned out to be a glass case on legs. In it lay the medals, the five-pointed star, the heart with its purple ribbon. For a moment the two stood there, Dede at first looking at the medals, then at the older woman, who stood staring down at the case as if seeing it for the first time.

"This is turning out to be far from the kind of surprise you opened the champagne for," Dede said softly. "I'm sorry. Perhaps I shouldn't . . ."

"Of course you should." She walked to the champagne bottle, carried it to the sofa, where she refilled both glasses as the women sat. "Please, go ahead."

"Mrs. Turnbull, did you . . ."

"For World War II and Kent, it won't do to call me Mrs. Turnbull. It's—what's the term?—an anachronism. It was Amanda Ellison. Eighteen when she last saw him. Nineteen when she got the word. Call me Amanda."

"Eighteen." Dede stared at the portrait. "That's just the age you seem there."

Amanda's eyes followed Dede's to the picture. "Yes. I posed for it in the spring of 1943. It was a graduation gift from my parents. One of the few things they did together. Kent loved it. When we got . . . the word . . . about Kent, I thought, I have no right to be up there, smiling, looking so happy." She stopped herself. "Please go ahead."

"Did you know any of Kent's army friends?"

"Let me show you something. If I can find it." She stood and started out of the room. "It may take a few minutes."

Dede sat and waited, staring at the 18-year-old captured before a shadow would come over that open, radiant smile. Amanda returned carrying a photo album, which she put on the table. She flipped through the pages quickly, until she came to a large photo of four soldiers sitting in a nightclub with a girl, the girl unmistakably Amanda Ellison, one of the men equally unmistakably Jake Ellinson, a second, she was fairly sure, Herb Ellinson.

"Years ago, Dede, before your time, young women photographers would walk around in nightclubs, usually in rather brief outfits, and take one's picture, for a fee of course. It would be developed and printed by the time one left that evening—a technological marvel in the days before Polaroids. This was taken in one of the jazz clubs on 52nd Street. There I am, and that's Kent." She pointed to a handsome blond man who seemed both amused and arrogant.

"Do you remember who the others were?"

"I can't remember the name of the short fellow; he stayed with us for a few days before they all left." Then she pointed to Jake. "This one I do remember.

Indeed. His name was a lot like ours. Ellinson. With an extra 'n.' Jake Ellinson. A Jew from the Bronx. Trumpet player. And this one," she pointed to Herb, "was his brother, also a musician, played the saxophone, as I remember. They both sat in with the band that night. The trumpet player sang, too. 'Them There Eyes.' The song's been a favorite of mine ever since. 'You're overworking them, there's danger lurking in . . . them there eyes.'"

There came over her face a look of girlish modesty, and Dede got a glimpse of the 18-year-old. "Silly, isn't it, to remember something like that over, let's see, it was the summer of '43, just before they shipped out, nearly 47 years, silly. But . . . some things one never forgets."

Dede should have told her right then, but she wanted more of what Amanda felt and remembered, before she knew who Dede was. "You sound as if that other fellow, the trumpet player, made quite an impression on you. Did you know him well?"

"Hardly at all. And yet . . . well, you'll never know what it was like to be young back then, and I'll never be able to tell you. We corresponded, at least I did. He wrote to me only once. Kent wrote that he tried to many other times, kept tearing up the letters. Kent urged me to keep writing, which I wanted to do in any event."

"It was a long time ago," Dede said. "Did you save that letter?"

She thought for a moment. "I'm sure I did, although heaven only knows where it's packed away now. I can't imagine I would throw that letter away."

"That good a letter?"

She laughed, "No, actually. Stilted. Writing was not his métier. Nothing like the élan of the man himself."

"You liked him," Dede offered.

"Oh, my! I was crazy about him. So was Kent. He was the kind of boy people just took to. All that energy, that spirit. You couldn't resist him. A typical New York Jew, mind you. The accent, the way he used his hands when he spoke. The wisecracks. But, oh my!"

"So many years ago and such a strong impression!" Was this right of her, to conceal what she knew? Perhaps not, but Dede couldn't resist pressing for more.

"Yes indeed." The blue-green eyes stared at her, unafraid, like the eyes in the picture. "Wartime. A girl longing to grow up. A handsome paratrooper who has a body like . . . steel. This is more than I should be telling, but it was so long ago, and does it matter?"

Dede nodded. "It does to me. Do you still think about him, ever?"

"Oh . . . oh, yes. And I will until I die! It's strange that you raise the subject now. You see, I've given money to a scholarship fund sponsored by the 101st Airborne Division Association, Kent's old division. And I get their newsletter. In the last issue there was a request for information about Jake Ellinson. Somebody in the midwest. I dropped him a note. Of course I didn't have much to tell him."

"Don't you remember his name?"

She thought for a moment. "No, I don't."

Dede pointed to the nightclub photo. "Al Breecher. And I'm quite sure it's that man, the short one, right there."

"Dede, how in the world would you know that?"

She wasn't ready to answer just yet. Instead, she asked, "Do you suppose that some time I might look at the letter?"

The older woman was startled. "Why would you be interested?"

"It's all part of the . . . story. When you wrote to Al Breecher, that man in the midwest—actually, Dubuque—he told that man." Again Dede pointed to the nightclub photo, "Jake Ellinson's younger brother Herb, about your note. And Herb Ellinson told me."

"Why would he do that?"

Dede carefully recounted the story of the letter, and the child and how the child was tracked down. It was not until Amanda asked, again, how she knew, that knowing how melodramatic she was making this and not caring, Dede said, "The man June Hopkins married while she was pregnant with Jake Ellinson's child was an army lieutenant named William Miller. They named the child Diana Penrose Miller, nickname Dede. Jake Ellinson was my biological father."

"Oh my! Oh, Dede!" Amanda's eyes filled with tears.

"I'm sorry if this is . . ." Dede began.

The tears were now rolling down the older woman's cheeks. "No, it's I who should apologize, for . . ." She now seemed almost out of control, and Dede was alarmed. Then she tried to reclaim possession of herself. "I'm afraid you'll have to excuse me, Dede, dear . . . I . . . there's so much, but I can't. Not now. Please forgive me." She stood and walked out of the room. Dede waited. When after 15 minutes Amanda had not returned, she left the apartment.

†

While membership in the Gotham was the province of the executive committee, there was an unusual provision in the club constitution which provided for general membership meetings to determine "the sense of the membership" on issues deemed to be of major importance. It was under this provision that the meeting was called to consider Dede's letter and her wish to join the club.

She was pleased to be invited, but under no illusions as to why Roger had called the meeting: First, to avoid a lawsuit or at least delay it. Second, hoping for such a decisive No vote that Dede—and future troublemakers—would be fatally discouraged. The meeting was for discussion only; ballots would then be mailed to the members, who would have two weeks to return them.

As she was about to leave her office for the meeting, Henry Gordon, her executive VP and sales manager, dropped in.

"Got a minute?" he asked, shooting his cuffs as he stood in the entrance to her office. He was short and dapper, perfectly dressed to be a young executive in a TV commercial. He was also the best real estate salesman who'd ever worked for her.

She looked at her watch, smiled at him. "One, not two. I'm on my way."

"Won't take two. I'm a little disturbed. In the last week, we've lost three deals we should have had."

"How many times has that happened?"

"These are different. No rhyme or reason. We didn't make any mistakes, not that I can see . . ."

"Who were they?"

"Hodges. Shelburne. Matthews."

Dede let the names percolate through her mind. Hodges, Mrs. Timothy. Husband a member of the Gotham. Shelburne, Price. Member of the Gotham. Matthews, Mrs. Robertson. Widow of a former club president.

"I know why and it had nothing to do with mistakes. There may be others. Don't worry about them."

Walking to the Gotham she began to get angry. Tru, Roger, those WASP snobs, were not above turning the financial screws to get what they wanted. Just the kind of thing they'd be quick to condemn Jews for. Well, dammit, let them! There was not much she knew about her "real" father. But there was one thing she was sure of: she was the daughter of a fighter.

†

Deliberately, she arrived at the club a few minutes after the scheduled 7:30 meeting time. Chairs had been set up in the big ballroom and to her astonishment not only was every one occupied, people were standing along the sides and in back, more than 300 in all. She was, of course, the only woman in the place. As if he'd been waiting for her, Roger Wheatley walked to the lectern.

"Good evening, gentlemen. And Ms. Miller."

He outlined the situation, mentioned Dede's letter, restated his belief that the club's position would not be overturned in court, repeated his warning about how bad all this controversy was for the club, stressed that the vote would not be binding on the executive committee. Then he went on to express his own view.

"I believe in keeping the club the way it is. I am a conservative, which by definition means I favor the status quo, provided it works. Here it works very well and I see no reason to change it. I want to make it clear that my feelings are not directed against any gender, race, religion, or individual. Now I'll open the floor to discussion."

The first hand to be raised belonged to Tom Harper, a thirty-ish banker who was a cousin of Tru's.

"What's wrong with the club the way it is?" he asked, and looked around. As a sprinkling of applause spread through the room, Harper's eyes moved about, spotted Dede and fixed on her for a moment. "Then why not leave it that way? What's the expression? If it ain't broke, don't fix it." He sat down to applause that was less enthusiastic than Dede had feared.

Another pause. Then a couple of Tom Harper clones stood to sound stodgy variations on his little speech. Dede wanted them to have their say first. Seeing no one else rise, she almost took the floor, until in the front of the room, a white-haired figure got to his feet and turned to face the crowd. It was George Whitman, a former president of the club and the man who had suggested the meeting. His gray suit was lighter and tweedier than most of the gray and blue pinstripes in the room, his shirt a tattersall check, his tie a maroon knit. Retired as managing partner of an investment banking house, he no longer had to wear the Wall Street uniform, yet would not stray too far from it.

"Would it be so dreadful to have some women in the club?" he began. "Now I know most of you here like women. I've heard some stories . . ." He smiled faintly. "Don't worry, I'm not going to tell any. Then what's the problem?

Do you like to tell dirty jokes? The young women in my firm could tell you a few. Will it require a ladies room? Big deal. Would a few women and a few Jews harm the place? They might even help it. Now I don't know Dede Miller, but I have seen her around. Her letter says she's half Jewish . . . and I can tell from looking at her she's all woman." A few chuckles. Even Dede had to smile at it, sexist or not. "I for one would love to sit in any bar she's in. So let's end the possibility of a lawsuit, which would look so bad. Let's act our age. I am a member of three clubs that in the past few years have taken in women and Jews. Know what? It hasn't hurt them one whit! Let's just make sure they're the right kind of people. You've got one vote here for Dede Miller." Whitman raised his hand over his head, held it, then lowered it and sat down. He was met with a surprised silence, and an uncomfortable look from Roger.

Dede hesitated, then raised her hand, made her way to the lectern.

"Thank you for inviting me and letting me have my say. I am against quotas. I don't think any club must have X number of women or Jews or blacks or anybody. It's this club that has set quotas. The Jewish quota is zero. So is the female quota. And a lot of others I could mention. There's only one quota here that has a number attached to it: 100 percent white, Christian male. Once it was all Protestant. I'm glad that has changed. The time has come for further change.

"If someone—anyone—came to me and said I don't want you in this club because you are dishonest, or too loud, or drink too much, or beat your children, or cheat on your husband, I could accept that. But no one has, not a single soul. There's only one reason: I am a woman. And that reason existed even before you, or I, knew I was the daughter of a Jewish father.

"Think for a moment about what that says to the women in your life—your company, your family, your bed: You're not good enough, just because of your sex.

"And let's not talk about opening the floodgates. There'll be no floodgates opening. Each nominee will still be judged on merit. There'll still be a very careful executive committee guarding the gates. We all know the kind of people you want in the club. Well, then, choose them. Discriminate. On the basis of the individual, not some label. I know that most of you consider this place as part of the legacy to your sons. Just what kind of a club do you want to leave them? And what about the legacy to your daughters? Are you telling them that though they become corporate executives, or march on a picket line supporting choice, or run for Congress, or become a Supreme Court justice, or even President, that they are not and never will be good enough to join their father's club?"

She paused, took a deep breath. "I understand that someone has to move that a vote be taken to determine the sense of the membership. Not being a member, I can't do it. I hope someone will."

She stood there, looked over the group to challenge them. No one would meet her eye. Except for Tru. Halfway back and on the left, he stared back at her. For a moment, she fantasized he would stand up for her. A silly moment. He did nothing but stare. She walked away from the lectern, heading for her place in the rear. As she strode the length of the ornate ballroom, no one looked at her. The silence droned on, before Roger Wheatley walked to the lectern.

"Does anyone move that a sense of the membership vote be taken on this issue?"

Dede prepared herself to be humiliated. Then the white head of George Whitman again surfaced above the seated figures. "I so move. For reasons I've already stated."

Roger nodded. "Is there a second?"

There was no sound, no movement. She couldn't believe that no one else in the room favored admitting women or Jews. What she could believe was that no one had the guts to defy the establishment.

Then Whitman's hand went up.

"You cannot second your own motion," Roger said.

"I am not trying to," Whitman said.

"Any other motion is out of order at this time," Roger shot back.

This time Whitman got to his feet, spoke loudly. "I rise to a point of order, Mr. Chairman, which, as you know, is always in order. As I recall from my days as president of this club, neither the constitution nor the by-laws require that motions be seconded in order to be brought to a vote. It is therefore appropriate that the membership of this club, those present and those absent, be polled by written ballot on the motion I have made."

Roger looked right and left in a silent appeal for help. None was offered. No one would question either Whitman's knowledge of the constitution or his prestige. Finally Roger had to speak.

"The motion has been made. Ballots will be sent out in due course, with instructions on when they are to be returned. I remind you once again, this sense of the membership vote is merely advisory—and non-binding. Has anyone anything further to say?"

Silence.

"Do I hear a motion to adjourn?"

"I so move," came from a voice in the crowd.

"Seconded," said several voices.

"Apparently a second is not required," Roger said with bitter humor. "Those in favor."

A loud chorus of ayes.

"This meeting is adjourned."

A sea of somber blues and grays began rolling toward the ballroom's main entrance. Watching it, Dede was surprised at how many young members there were, men she had never seen before. Those she knew avoided her eyes. Some of the others looked at her quickly and looked away. A few glanced down at her legs. Boys will be boys, she thought. Then Tru walked up to her, stared down at her and while barely stopping, whispered, "I hope you're proud of yourself."

"Hodges. Shelburne. Matthews." she answered. "It won't work."

"It's just beginning," he whispered, and walked on.

Roger came by. He stared at her sadly and shook his head. She stared back. She didn't see how she could win, and right now all she wanted to do was get out of this enemy camp. But there was Whitman; she couldn't leave without thanking her ally. Scanning the crowd in vain for the sight of his white hair, she trailed in the wake of the suits, letting them carry her toward the door. As she passed the bar, she looked straight ahead. Tru would be in there, with Roger and other kindred souls, angry at the meeting and yet turning it into martini humor. She was almost past the bar when a hand grasped her elbow. Turning, wondering if it would be Roger to lament or Tru to attack, she was surprised to see the hand belonged to George Whitman.

"I'll buy you a drink."

"I was looking for you," she replied. "To say thanks. Let me buy you one."

Whitman smiled. "You can't. You're not a member . . . yet."

"And never will be."

He held on to her elbow. "Don't be so sure. What you saw in there was pure peer pressure. In the privacy of a secret ballot you never can tell what might happen. What did Churchill say? Never give in. Never, never, never.

Something like that." He shook his head. "Whatever happened to quotable leaders?" He picked up his drink from the bar and led the way to a small table in the corner. Dede could see Roger in another corner of the room, sitting with Tru and four others; she looked away.

"When I saw your picture in the *Sunday Times*, I thought it would be a story about some glamor gal."

"Stop it, Mr. Whitman, and order me a glass of white wine! I'm not too old to blush."

"And I'm not too old to be called George." He waved to the waiter, who stopped what he was doing and came over at once. "President-emeritus has its privileges," Whitman told her after he'd ordered the wine.

"It also gives you a rather detailed knowledge of the club rules," she added.

"Oh, that." He laughed. "I may be right about that. I may not. But I figured Wheatley wouldn't know anyway." The wine was in front of her. He picked up his scotch.

"Cheers."

"Thanks," she said. "Why did you do it?"

He shrugged. "Not even sure. Because I hate to see someone picked on. Because of something in the war."

"World War II?"

"What other war was there?"

"My father used to say that."

"The Jewish one?"

She hesitated. "I never met the Jewish one. But he was in the war. He was killed in it."

Whitman stared down into his scotch. "There were two problems with being in it. I mean really in it, not sitting behind a desk in Washington or somewhere. Problem One was, you'd get killed. Problem Two was, you wouldn't, you'd take off the uniform, and go home. And the rest of your life would be a goddamned anti-climax. The war was . . . the most mind-boggling experience, the greatest, most exciting, most frightening event that anyone could live through. If you lived through it. And once you played a part in it, well, everything else was pablum. Somebody at the office would come running up to you, all excited or frightened. And you'd want to say to him, you call this exciting? Have you ever commanded a line of tanks that charged into a Belgian town and tore the Germans apart, and seen the townspeople all come out to cheer you as if you were their savior? Which you were? *That's exciting!* Have you ever turned a corner and come face to face with a German Tiger tank pointing its 88 at you? *That's* frightening!"

He stared at her. "You're thinking, I ask this old guy why he helped me and he goes on about the war. What has that got to do with a woman getting into the club? Huh?"

She smiled at him and shrugged.

"It's really the Jew thing," he told her.

"I have my father to thank."

"Listen, I wish I had a guy like your father here to talk to, swap war stories. But they're all gone—dead or moved down to Palm Beach. Instead there's a stream of yuppies who come around sucking up to me because I was somebody at Pemberton, Jones." His glass was empty and he signaled the waiter. Another scotch was there almost instantly.

"That's why I wish your dad were a member of this club. I could talk to him."

"Of course he couldn't have been."

"Yeah. The Jew thing. That's what really got me going." He rapped a hand on the table. The hand was gnarled, discolored, veins standing out on it, but thick and strong, the hand of a warrior. "I'll tell you a story. April 29, 1945. I have trouble with my own children's birthdays, but that's one date I'll never forget. I was a first lieutenant, exec officer of a tank company in Patton's Third Army, when we liberated Dachau. The concentration camp. Just outside of Munich.

"We rode in; our tanks knocked down the gates. Saved about 30,000 people. They were alive, but barely. You'd never believe people could look like that and still be alive. And then there were the bodies. Oh, the bodies! Just stacked up. What a sight. Once you've seen it, there's a whole list of problems and worries you can never take seriously again.

"I was in a jeep, just looking at those bodies. I couldn't believe what I was seeing. Now, Dede, I had seen bodies, but this . . . this was . . . Anyway, one of my men came running up to me, saying they'd caught a German SS officer, one of the top men running Dachau. He insisted on surrendering to an officer. So I walked into the room where he was being held. He was your archetype of an SS man. Tall, blonde, insolent. He looked at us like we were worms, which took some nerve, considering the situation he was in. He was a Sturmbannfuehrer—that's the SS equivalent of major—and he didn't much like the idea of being confronted by a mere first looey, but it was better than a lowly enlisted man.

"There were three of us in the room. The major, myself, and a sergeant I was using as an interpreter. His name was Solomon Liebman, from Brooklyn, and he spoke some German and fluent Yiddish. I never knew this, Dede, maybe you do, but Yiddish is enough like German so that you can understand it."

She shook her head. "I haven't been half Jewish very long."

He smiled at that, went on. "I must tell you about Sgt. Liebman. He was no ordinary Jew." He stopped, looked at her; she just waved him on. "He was built like an ape, maybe 5-6, bull neck, sloping shoulders, bow-legged. Thick, hairy arms, so long his knuckles practically scraped the ground. Won a Silver Star, Purple Heart with two clusters. If there was one guy bullets would bounce off, that had to be the guy. Also, the meanest son of a bitch, excuse me for that, I ever met. I think he may have been a mobster—what do they call them? A hit man—for Murder, Incorporated. Men said that but no one ever dared ask; everyone was afraid of him. One funny thing: He'd tell you to call him Shloymee, which I found out was the nickname for Solomon in Yiddish. I thought then and I think now that Shloymee—I'm still not sure I say it right—is one of the ugliest and most ludicrous nicknames I have ever heard. Liebman knew people thought that, so he would insist on the name, just daring someone to make fun of it. I promise you, no one did.

"Well, there we were, the three of us in the room. The SS man is telling me he is assistant commandant of the camp. And he is demanding that he be treated according to the rules of the Geneva Convention, because he is a soldier who has served honorably. Sgt. Liebman is interpreting and his eyes are getting smaller and meaner with each word from this Nazi. I don't like it much myself, and so after he tells me about serving honorably, I ask, what about the bodies lying out there? Liebman translates, and the SS man answers with only one word. He just waves a hand and says, '*Juden.*' Jews.

"I'll never forget that moment, that man, and my own shock and hatred for him. They were only Jews, so what did it matter? They were not us; they were 'the other,' less than human. Denying people membership in a club is a long way from stacking their bodies up like firewood. But it is the first small step toward declaring their otherness. And the minute you make people 'the other,' you're a little bit closer to denying them their humanity.

"I never forgot it. But I went on to live my life as if it had never happened. At Pemberton, Jones we fought having women, never employed a Jew, had a few blacks in menial jobs. I didn't start that. Nor did I do anything to stop it.

Same here at the club. During the war, I was a brave man, Dede. After it, I stopped being brave. When I got your letter, I just decided, enough!"

"You were heroic," she said. "I would be honored to buy you dinner."

"Thanks, but I can't. Promised to my daughter and son-in-law and three grandkids."

"Tomorrow night?"

Whitman shook his head. "Sorry, but I'm driving back up to Maine."

"You didn't drive down just for this, did you?" she asked.

"I most certainly did. Nine hours and well worth it."

"I'm touched," she said simply.

"Good luck on getting in. I'll do everything I can to help. I mean that." Whitman raised his glass and touched hers.

"Thanks," Dede said. "By the way, what happened to the SS major? Did he get his Geneva convention rights?"

"As it turned out, he met all the requirements for a war criminal. He could have been hanged."

"But he wasn't?"

"No, he wasn't." Whitman hesitated.

"Why not?"

"It's a story," he said slowly, "some people don't like to hear."

"I would like to hear it," she said.

"After the interrogation, I had to arrange to ship him off to a prison compound. So I headed for the next room, to use a field telephone. I said to Sgt. Liebman something like: look after him, or take care of him . . . words I concede might have been misunderstood. At any rate, I was out of the room about ten seconds when the most blood-curdling scream came from it. I ran back in. There was the SS man lying on the floor, his throat cut from ear to ear, blood just pumping out of him. Liebman stood over him, holding the hunting knife he always wore in a sheath on his belt, blood dripping from the knife.

"He looked up and said, 'He tried to jump me.' In his eyes was that same look he had when he told you to call him Shloymee, and dared you to make fun of it."

"What did you do?" Dede asked.

"Nothing. I didn't see what happened. Maybe the German did try to jump him. I couldn't say. Maybe I had subconsciously told Liebman to do it, by the words I used and by leaving him alone with him. Besides, a lot of that went on. These were men who had seen their buddies killed, and were themselves used to killing without a moment's hesitation. There was a lot of frontier justice meted out back then. The truth is, I half wanted to kill the bastard myself. Maybe if I'd been a Jew, I would have."

Later, when Dede got up to leave. Whitman said, "The problem with modern life is there's so little chance to find out if you've any bravery in you at all. So if the chance comes along, you've got to grab it. I think that's what you did."

"I'd like to think that, George. But the truth is, it was forced upon me. By my father."

She walked home thinking about the SS officer, the sergeant named Shloymee, and the bodies stacked up like cordwood. She realized that had she been in Europe back then, one of those bodies could have been hers.

Next morning at the office she looked over that day's calendar. The evening's activity was a black tie dinner to benefit the New York Youth Association, a patronizing upper-class WASP charity that helped inner city youngsters. They had her check, they didn't need her presence; she picked up the phone and cancelled, went back to an empty apartment to try an evening with no company, no plans. Waiting for her was an urgent message from Mary Wheatley.

Reluctantly she called back.

"There's something I must tell you," Mary said, "Want to meet me for a cup of coffee or something?"

"How about a jog? I must get a little exercise."

"It's nearly eight."

"It's such a beautiful evening." Dede was looking out over Central Park as she held the phone to her ear. "If we run around the reservoir, there are lights . . . and lots of people."

It wasn't until they were out on the reservoir track that Dede remembered how slow a jogger Mary was. She was petite, took tiny, deliberate, ladylike strides. Now Dede knew how it felt for Jim to run with her.

"I . . . I feel terrible about the club," Mary said as they made their way north on the one-and-a-half mile jogging path bordering the irregular outline of the park reservoir. "Are you angry with me?"

"You have to keep the peace at home."

"So should you."

"Not anymore."

They were at the point where the track started curving to the west along the northern boundary of the reservoir. It was the darkest, loneliest arc of the circumference. "I always get nervous up here, Dede."

"It's all right, there are lots of people." In fact there were not as many as Dede thought there'd be. She expected a stream of runners. Instead there were separated beads of them. Dede could hear Mary's labored breathing, as if she were trying to get the oxygen together to say something.

"I'm sure Tru would forgive and forget."

"Forgive and forget what? That I'm half Jewish? That I want to get into the club? You're the one who said I'd be perfect for it."

"That was before . . ." Mary said. They traversed the east-west arc of the track, which then veered to the south down the west side. "I'm glad we're past that stretch," she added.

"Before you knew about the Jewish part?"

"No!" Mary sounded hurt. "Before I knew how seriously the boys would take it. How . . . fanatical they are about the Goth."

"They're not boys, Mary, and we're not girls. We shouldn't be so afraid of them."

Mary turned to look at her, running even more slowly than she had been. "They're not fooling around, Dede. They're out to get you." She lowered her voice. "They're sending a letter . . ."

"I can't hear you! We're not being followed; it's all right!"

"They're sending a letter to every club member, telling them to use some other real estate broker, someone they call 'a friend of the club.' Tru told Roger, 'hurt her business, that's all she cares about.'"

"That's not all I care about!" Dede's voice sounded shriller than she intended. "To hell with them." Mary didn't know what to say and Dede had nothing more to say, so they ran awhile in silence.

Finally Mary spoke, "I suppose this is a bad time, but I'm really sorry about the item in the *Post* this morning. It was so tacky."

As Dede kept running, her stomach ground to a halt. "I haven't seen the *Post*."

"Oh, Dede, I shouldn't have . . ."

"But you have. Tell me what it was."

"On page six. Something about the split marriage of handsome Wall Streeter Tru Martindale and . . . they call you 'real estate queenpin.'"

"Queenpin. How clever. Is that it?"

"Also." Mary hesitated. "How Martindale is trying to forget—something like that—with a blonde tennis beauty in Southampton."

Uh huh, and with lots of suntan lotion to grease the way, Dede thought.

"I'm so sorry, Dede. Really."

"It's all right."

They turned north and ran the last quarter mile up the east side in silence.

"Let's go around once more," said Dede when they got to their starting point at 90th street and Fifth Avenue.

"Do you think it's safe?"

"Anybody comes near us, I'll make believe he's Tru and punch his lights out!"

"Dede!" Mary giggled.

But as they continued north to the dark corner, Mary noticed there were fewer runners than there had been the first time around and she looked at Dede nervously.

"It's all right, Mary!"

Barely ten strides after she said it, she saw the two figures idling on the side of the five-foot wide path, standing near a lamppost which no longer gave any light. As the women got closer, Dede could see they were boys, skinny, fairly dark, possibly Hispanic or light-skinned blacks. In baggy pants, windbreakers, high-tops, they were not joggers and they were watching the two women while pretending not to.

"Dede!"

"Let's show them we see them, but are not worried, and just go right by them."

But as they got within 25 yards of the two, the boys moved to the center of the track, so the women could not get by them, Dede put a hand on Mary's arm to slow them. Surely some other runners would come by. None did.

"Excuse us!" Dede sang out, trying to sound unconcerned. "Don't stop," she whispered to Mary. But now the boys turned squarely to face them.

"Where you goin', ladies?" the taller one asked. Five yards from the boys, the women had to stop.

"Let's run back!" said Mary.

Dede was astounded at her own sudden rush of anger and adrenalin. She stood squarely facing them. "Get the hell out of the way!" she shouted. At the same moment, Mary started screaming, "Help! Police!" over and over. For a moment the shouts made the boys look uncertain. Then the moment passed and they started toward the women.

Mary's screams continued, yet, unbelievably, no other joggers appeared.

"Don't take another step!" Dede shouted. Again the boys hesitated, but only momentarily. She knew that if they ran, Mary would be caught immediately. Through Mary's screams she heard a deep male voice.

"We're coming!"

The boys heard it, too, and Dede could see them looking beyond her and Mary. Then they turned and scampered down the incline from the track and disappeared into the darkness. Dede turned back and saw a big man racing toward them like a football player covering a kickoff. He slowed when he saw the boys disappear, then came to a stop.

"Are you all right?" He was middle-aged, not as tall as Tru, but twice as broad, with huge shoulders, a thick neck and sandy hair going gray and cropped short. He was football-player handsome, his nose dented just enough to give it character; he seemed perfect casting for a Marine colonel. She could see why the boys would flee at the sight of him.

"Thank God you came, officer!" Mary said, close to tears.

"Come on," he said, "Let's run back and get you out of the park." They began to jog south.

"Are the others going after them?" Dede asked as they ran.

"Others?" he asked.

"The other policemen. You yelled, 'we're coming.'"

"I lied. I thought if I yelled, here I come, a solitary, unarmed, 51-year-old venture capitalist with two bad knees, it would not be very intimidating."

They reached the 90th street park entrance, looked around for some sign of the police, saw nothing. "I'll phone the cops," he said. "But let me run you home first." Then he stared at Dede.

"Say, aren't you Dede Miller?"

"Yes."

"I thought I recognized you from the *Times* article. I'm a friend of Ken Glass's. Denny Knight. I don't know if he's mentioned . . ."

"He has." So this was the rich, handsome, irresistible Denny Knight! She had to admit he looked impressive.

"Mary, this is Denny Knight, a friend of the man who wrote the article about me."

He stuck out a hand. Mary shook it, forgot enough of her fright and shock to look mesmerized. Adroitly, Knight contrived to run Mary home to 84th and

Park first and then continue with Dede down to her building.

"Kenneth said you would find me," she told him as they stood in front of her entrance. "You certainly managed to do it at the most opportune time. Say, you didn't set that whole thing up, did you?"

He smiled down at her, a smile of total self-assurance. "I'll bet you haven't had dinner. Why don't I come by in a half hour. Ever been to Salle à Manger?"

"Latest, hottest, best, most expensive, most exclusive restaurant in New York? Impossible to get a table? That place?"

He smiled the smile again and snapped his fingers. "Half hour. Don't dress up." She said yes because this was not the kind of man you said no to. And she did want to go to Salle à Manger.

What am I doing? She asked herself as she quickly showered. Without waiting for an answer, she threw on a tan silk pants suit and a light green blouse, hurried downstairs. She was not prepared for the Rolls and the chauffeur. Knight sat in back in a navy blazer, jeans, open shirt, and loafers. He examined her and she felt like a girl waiting for approval.

"You look great, Dede," he told her. "But then you looked great jogging."

Keep your balance, she told herself. Sweeping women off their feet is this man's specialty.

"Thanks. The article didn't use my nickname."

"It's the sort of thing I usually know," he answered, not telling her how or asking her if it was all right.

"And how do you propose to get a table at Salle à Manger on one hour's notice?"

He just snapped his fingers again.

"Be serious."

"When I turned 50, I pledged to avoid two things, seriousness and hard work, and I've kept the pledge for a little more than a year now."

"How are you going to get a table?"

"Knowing that sooner or later I'd run into you, I took the advance precaution of investing in the restaurant."

When the maître d' saw Knight he bowed almost to the floor, showed them to a large table in the front of the room. Knight was the only man in the restaurant without a tie.

He leaned to her. "This is the number two table. The number one table is occupied by the senior senator from New York. Sorry about that. I'll introduce you." Before he could, before she could say she knew him, the senator's voice sounded from the next table.

"Two old friends," came the familiar voice with the Irish lilt to it. "Denny!" he said. "Diana!"

After the obligatory chat with the senator, Knight said to her, "I forget I'm with a celebrity, as certified by the *Times Magazine*."

"And how does he know you?"

"Nothing like contributing to a campaign to put you on a first name basis." Knight grinned.

"I would have guessed you were a Republican."

"I am," he answered, the grin widening. "I hedge my bets."

Without asking, the maître d' brought a bottle of Dom Perignon. Next came the menus and with them the chef and co-owner, Michel, whom Knight introduced as "my old pal Mike."

Knight handed the menus back to the owner. "You choose for us," he said. It wasn't until both men were gone that he added, "I hope that's all right with you. You're not allergic to anything, are you?"

"Only to French food," she replied. For a moment she thought she might have shaken that magnificent aplomb, but after the merest flicker of an eye, he laughed. "*Nobody's* allergic to French food. That's like being allergic to . . . Dom Perignon."

"And *was* the whole thing a set up?" she asked a little later. "The boys, the rescue, all of it?"

He stopped the glass of champagne halfway between the table and his mouth, stared at her, burst out laughing.

"No, but it's not a bad idea. I may try it sometime."

In the car on the way home, she asked him, "What would you have done if those kids had pulled a gun or a knife?"

"I never thought about it," he said. "Heard the screams and just took off. What would you have done?"

"The way I was feeling at the moment, I'd have attacked them. And gotten hurt."

"The way you were feeling? Have anything to do with the item in the *Post*? Or the club letter?"

"Do you know everything?"

"Ken told me about the *Post*, and I've been a member of the Gotham since Yale." She liked him for not calling it the Goth. "I was a class ahead of one

Truman Martindale, who was not a friend. He was a charter member of the snobs; I was a card-carrying hedonist. My dad gave me the club as a graduation present. Never go. Worst bunch of stuffed shirts I ever came across."

Two nights later he took her to a nightclub in Tribeca, where they were the only people over 30 and not models. Three nights after that to a $1000-a-ticket black tie dinner at the Pierre, to benefit an African famine relief group. The night after that to a restaurant in little Italy where the owner hugged him as if he were an investor, although he told her he was not. She wasn't sure why she went; it was just that when Denny Knight asked it was hard to say no.

Two days after the Italian restaurant Ken called her in the late afternoon. "It's odd," he said, "that I had to find out about your Jewish half from Denny Knight."

"I've been meaning to call you. So many people have complimented me on the article. I suppose it's like a photo; no one is ever fully satisfied. Everyone has some idealized self-portrait in mind that no picture ever captures. Because it's simply not there. I wanted to tell you about my father last time, but things were ended rather abruptly."

"By you."

"Yes. And I do want to apologize. May I buy you dinner?"

"Some night Denny has left free."

"Now, Kenneth!" He was jealous; she didn't mind that at all. "How about . . ." She looked at her book, "Thursday?"

"Ahh . . . let's see," he answered elaborately. "Yes. I think I can free that time. I'll tell Barbara and George sorry."

"Kenneth, you are amusing!" She hung up smiling.

As soon as she and Glass were seated in what had become their booth at the Madison Pub, he said, "Getting swept off your feet, I suppose. They all do."

"You're sounding jealous again."

"Every man in the world with the wits to understand is jealous of Denny Knight."

"I can't imagine you'd feel competitive with him."

". . . because he's this handsome, powerful, athletic, glamorous money man and I'm . . . the opposite of all of the above."

"Do you care about things like that?"

"Hath not a writer hands, organs, dimensions, senses, affections . . . passions?"

"Shylock. Very clever. It's so . . . lively . . . talking with you, Kenneth. I almost forget my life is in turmoil."

"But now old Denny Boy has found you."

"He really gets to you . . ."

"No, no. The problem is, he gets to you." He leaned close to her. "Let me tell you something. That theatrical broken nose of his? Cosmetic surgery."

"No!"

His smile was rueful. "No. He got it playing football, or something heroic like that. Maybe even saving a fair damsel from a mugging."

"I think a little jealousy brings out the cleverness in you."

"Yeah, I get the good lines; he gets the girl."

"Don't be silly. No one's getting this girl. Not for a while."

"Put me on the waiting list."

"Kenneth . . ."

"I mean it."

They sat there, just looking at each other. He wanted to reach out and take her hand. He didn't.

On the street, just before saying goodnight, he asked, "Are you busy this weekend?"

"I'm going away."

"Where is that son of a bitch taking you this time?"

She laughed. "I'm taking myself to see my son, who's a counselor at a running camp in Massachusetts. Yes, Kenneth, I'm sure of it. Jealousy becomes you."

By 11 Saturday morning she'd checked into the New England Traveller Inn near Williamstown, changed, and was standing on the athletic field of the Gibson School, a struggling prep school trying for extra income by renting its premises as a running camp for the summer.

In t-shirt, shorts, and running shoes, she looked around for Jim. Together they'd join in a five-kilometer fun run for campers and parents. When she spotted him, there was a surprise standing alongside him. Tru, who had said he could not make it in from "the country," had decided to drive up after all.

"Good morning!" She forced it to sound bright and cheery. She would not let this turn into an ordeal for the boy.

"Decided to make the drive," said Tru.

"That's fine!" she said. "How are you? And how is the lean, mean running machine?" She put her arm around Jimmy. He was all taut bands of muscle.

"Fine, mom." Jimmy sounded awkward. Tru, his twin shields of alcohol and arrogance down for the moment, looked uneasy. Dede kept smiling, without at all feeling smiley. They were all relieved when the head counselor blew his whistle to assemble everyone for the run. In blazer, pink trousers, and loafers, Tru was obviously not dressed to run. Dede and her son jogged toward the assembly point.

"I invited Marcy and her parents to join us for dinner," Jimmy said. "I hope that's all right."

"Didn't realize she was at the camp."

"Thought I told you."

"You probably did. It's fine. This is all going to be fun, don't worry about a thing," she reassured.

The head counselor gave another blast on his whistle, and the group began to jog slowly to a corner of the athletic field, across the quarter-mile track and then onto a dirt road used as a cross-country running trail. Dede and Jimmy were at the back of a pack of about 75 people; with her following, Jimmy circled to the outside to make his way around the slower runners.

"By the way, dad is staying at the Traveller, too." The boy gave his mother a sidelong glance.

"I told you, it's all right."

"He said you were definitely getting a divorce."

"I thought you knew that."

"Not the definitely part."

The boy had moved to the front of the group of runners, at a pace that was slightly uncomfortable for his mother. "Easy, Jim."

"Sorry, mom." He slowed.

"Apparently 'definitely' is the word."

"Seems kind of sudden to me," Jimmy said after awhile. "I guess nobody cares what I think." It was a cry from his heart and it tore at hers.

"Of course we do, but . . . What do you think?"

"I think it stinks!" He picked up his pace and ran away from her as if she were standing still.

Dinner was set for seven-thirty at the inn, which was reputedly not only the best lodgings in the area, but also the best dining room. When she came down from her room, Jim was waiting.

"I'm sorry, mom. That was not a very mature thing to do."

"No. We're the ones who should say we're sorry. We're the ones not doing the mature thing. I don't want to lay blame on anyone else, but . . . it seems to be out of my hands."

"I . . . I know, mom."

"Have you talked to your dad?"

The boy spoke slowly, thoughtfully. "Dad is not easy to talk to."

She put her arms around him, could feel him tensing with the embarrassment teenage boys feel when parents show affection in public. "Just remember, both of us still love you as much as always and we hope you'll keep loving us the same way."

"Mom. Here come the Tillmans." She released him quickly.

Tru did not arrive until they were about to sit down to dinner, his eyes telling Dede he'd already had a martini or two. They got through the meal in an edgy 55 minutes, during which Tru, trying to conceal his disdain for the Tillmans, drank most of a bottle of chardonnay. By the time they were ready for goodnights, he was showing the stiff equilibrium of someone who'd become expert at concealing how unsteady he was. Standing together as if they really were together, Dede and Tru said goodnight to Jimmy and Marcy as they left for the camp, and the Tillmans as they went up to their room. Standing at the elevators, Dede said to Tru, "Sleep well."

"I'm not quite ready for that. I am ready for a brandy."

"Oh, Tru."

"Come on, first lady of New York real estate. Put down your briefcase and join me." He took her arm just above the elbow and held it tight as he headed for the bar. His grip was halfway between courtly and compelling.

"Just one," she said as she went along. They walked to a corner of the bar, sat in two easy chairs around a low cocktail table.

"Speak for yourself, Madame Chairperson."

"I was." She remembered when they were newly married, how much she'd loved going into an East Side bar with him after work, getting that light buzz, so proud to be young, good looking, and successful; so sure of their superiority. Tru ordered a double cognac, downed half of it in one gulp as she sipped at a glass of mineral water.

"Jimmy is upset at what's happening," she said.

"I've tried to make it very clear to him whose responsibility it is."

"And whose is it?" she asked.

"Now that is enough to drive a man to drink!" For emphasis, he took another gulp at his brandy. "To bring the house down around you, considering the kind of house you've been living in, is . . . I don't know what to call it but sick."

"You mean, bring the house down by being half Jewish?"

"All you had to do was keep quiet about it. Instead you go around advertising it, as if you were proud of it."

"Should I be ashamed of it?"

She watched him, wondering what was stopping him from saying yes.

"What you should be ashamed of," he said, "is being seen with that . . . lounge lizard . . . Denny Knight."

She laughed. "I don't think anyone's used that expression since World War II."

"All right, 'sleaze.' Is that more contemporary?"

"He is nothing of the sort. And I've done nothing but go to dinner with him. Nothing that I had to hide in the dunes to do!" There they were, getting into one of those nasty marital battles she'd always been so contemptuous of.

"Denny Knight never settles just for dinner. He's famous for it." He signaled the waiter, pointed to his glass.

"And what is your blonde tennis beauty famous for?"

"Nothing. And she is content that way, very happy to play the role of the woman and let me be the man. You were pretty good as a woman, Dede. As I remember. But you're lousy as a man! And you will be brought down! You will regret the club thing! Remember my words! You will be taken across our collective knee and spanked! Until you . . ." He had another gulp of brandy. ". . . beg for mercy!" Unsteadily, he got to his feet. "Look at me, Dede! I'm six-four! You're not big enough to take me on!"

"Tru, you've had too much to drink."

He lurched toward her. She jumped to her feet, stepped away from him. He put one hand on a chair to hold himself straight.

"I wasn't going to touch you, Dede."

"What about spanking me until I begged for mercy!"

"That was a metaphor."

"You should go to bed, Tru." Her moment of fright had turned to pity.

"Not until I finish my brandy."

"Then I'm going." She started to turn away when she heard his voice.

"Why, Dede? Why?"

"So that your son, who is one-quarter Jewish, will be able to get into your club. That's why." She walked off feeling terrible, for both of them.

On Sunday, knowing Tru would leave early to beat the traffic, she stayed to have lunch with Jim, trying to reassure him with more confidence than she felt herself that everything was going to be all right. She got back to the city a little after seven, dropped her car at the garage, started on the one-block walk to her building, then decided the evening was too lovely to go straight home. Instead she strolled over to Lexington Avenue, north to 86th street, then turned west, heading to Fifth. At Madison she saw a slim young woman, perhaps 30, whose animation and self-confidence caught her eye. She had dark silky hair, which swung from side to side as she spoke. Her head swiveled; her delicate hands gestured; she smiled. She seemed so immersed in the moment, so attentive to her escort, so enthusiastic, Dede at once envied her. Only as she followed the woman's eyes up to the face of the man with her, did she see it was Ken Glass.

Quickly she turned and looked into the window of a shop until she saw them cross to the north side of 86th street. Then she took a few deep breaths and asked herself why she wanted to avoid them, why the idea of Kenneth having a life, a romantic life, she didn't know about was such a shock to her.

Lying in their king-sized bed that evening, the moonlit Pacific gleaming, Herb and Marian put down their books and switched off their lights. He turned and looked at her face, illuminated by the pale light of the moon. Her bone structure was remarkably defined, unspoiled by the sagging skin and added fat that changed so many faces over 50. Yet, the lines were there, a subtle mesh of tiny cuts, extended since the last time he'd noticed. Suddenly the expression "best years of my life" hit him. She was giving him the best years of her life, growing old with him. If anything should happen to them, she would be out on her own, a woman about whom men would say, "I'll bet she used to be real good-looking." He didn't want her to be on her own. For her sake. And for his. But he was tired of this unspoken dueling, this nervous stand-off.

"Moonlight becomes you," he said. "Burke and Van Heusen wrote that for Bing Crosby. They could have written it about you."

"Thank you."

"How's your book?"

"It's a love story, you know how I like them. And yours?"

"About an infantry company in World War II."

"I should imagine there's nothing about World War II you don't already know," Her tone was carefully neutral.

"There's so much to know," he replied. "Why do you resent them?"

He heard the silence of her hesitation. Then, directly: "They make me feel like an outsider." She too was tired of circling the subject.

"*You've* kept yourself outside that part of me. The war. And the music. Deliberately held yourself outside." Should he be saying these thing now? Yes. Now. At last.

"They belong to you and your brother."

"Jake, why is it you never use his name?"

"All right! Jake. Jake! Jake! He's the wedge." Her voice, like his, sounded with an unaccustomed sharpness.

"You drove the wedge. I never wanted it there. You made me feel I had to make a choice, that it was you or Jake. I treasure his memory; he represents my family, my youth, my music. They're all gone now. Why can't I have him, and you? He's not your rival. He doesn't take me away from you." The next came out before he could stop it: "I don't go running off for five or six hours every Saturday to commune with Jake!"

"You don't believe I go to an aerobics class."

He started to do what he would usually do, say never mind, it's not worth fighting about, forget it. Not this time.

"I do believe you go to an aerobics class. But that's not all you do."

"You've been having me followed."

"No. You thought that when the detective came here, didn't you? The answer is no, never."

He waited for her to say something. When nothing came, he almost let it go. Not this time. He asked the question even as he dreaded the answer. "Well? What do you do on Saturdays after the aerobics class?"

In his dread, he'd long since composed an answer for her: I am seeing someone else. Seeing, she would say, not having an affair with, certainly not making love with. Seeing would be bad enough.

So when she said, "I'm taking a course in word processing and computers," he almost laughed.

"You are *what*?"

"Computers. Word processing."

"Why, for God's sake? I can see music, or drawing, or Chinese cooking. But computers? We don't even have a computer!"

"It could help me get a job. In case I have to be on my own."

"Are you thinking of going on your own?"

"Suppose I'm forced to? It's happened to me before."

"I'm not *before*. I promised you I would never desert you. If you want to go, I'll see that you have enough money. I don't want you to tied to me by purse strings." He waited for a reply. None came.

"I mean it, I'll set up an annuity for you. Only stay if you want to." She looked at him and this time she nodded.

"If anything does happen, it won't be because of me. I love you, Marian."

"I love you, too." She put her head on his chest and he circled her with his arm.

"I would have liked for Jake to have lived. I would have liked for him to be married and have kids, and live somewhere near us, so we could visit him and he could visit us, and have dinner, or go off on a picnic, or go to the beach. The way other families do. In a way, everything I've done or tried to do since the war, I did for him, as if he were watching me. He meant so much to me, in a way that maybe only an older brother can mean to a kid brother. Then he was taken away. So long ago. I'll never have any of those things, only the memory. So maybe I grabbed onto the memory and held it too tight. Maybe I didn't bring you into it in the right way. I don't know. All I know is, if I love you and you love me, we were doing something wrong, something we can fix."

"Can things like this ever be fixed?"

"As long as we're alive and trying, why not? While you're alive, nothing's final. The only thing that's final is death."

CHAPTER 24

June 1944

U.S. forces on New Guinea push forward against heavy Japanese resistance. In Italy, Allied forces take Rome and continue north in pursuit of the retreating Germans.

On June 6th, D-Day, Operation Overlord, the invasion of France, begins.

Hit records: "Mairzy Doats," The Merry Macs; "I'll Get By," Harry James; "It's Love Love Love," Guy Lombardo; "San Fernando Valley," "I Love You," and "I'll Be Seeing You," Bing Crosby.

As the lumbering C-47 gains altitude, Jake looks through its open door at a spectacle neither he nor anyone else may ever see again: in a darkening sky, the lights of hundreds of planes, circling until all are aloft and they can get into the nine-plane V-formations in which they will fly across southern England and over the English Channel.

The 16 paratroopers sit in rows along the sides of the fuselage. Turning briefly from the awesome splendor of the scene in the sky, Jake can see the startlingly light eyes of the men around him, gleaming from the blackened faces, eyes filled with wonder and solemnity and the conscious desire not to look frightened. Kent reaches over and taps the old cornet Jake has hooked to his belt. "Play something, Bix."

"Mouth too dry," Jake answers. Indeed, his mouth is so dry he cannot work up enough saliva to wet his lips with his tongue, worse even than on his first training jump. Part of the reason is the airsickness pills they've been given. Another part is that this is not a training jump.

Operation Overlord has been two years in the planning. At dawn, 150,000 men will begin landing on five beaches along a 50-mile stretch of Normandy coastline. From west to east, the beaches have been designated Utah, Omaha (to be assaulted by American forces), Gold (British), Juno

(Canadian), and Sword (British). The invasion armada numbers more than 5000 ships of all kinds and 12,000 aircraft. Six hours before the amphibious landings, in the dark of night, paratroopers will drop—men from three airborne divisions: the American 82nd and 101st on the western flank, and the British 6th on the eastern.

When Lt. Sobchak, their jump leader, announces, "Say goodbye to England," all who can, look through the open door and see the coastline passing below them and receding. No, this is no training jump, no exercise. This is what the training, the exercises, were for. The sky is filled with planes; there seems to be no room in it for more. Over water, they are flying at an altitude of about 500 feet to avoid radar. Over France, they will climb to 1500 as protection against flak and then drop down again for the jump.

This seems to be the lowest 500 feet at which they've ever flown; they can almost feel the ocean spray. Looking down in the moonlight, they see ships everywhere, almost close enough to reach out and touch. "Hell," a voice says, "They didn't need to give us no planes. We could've walked over to France on them boats!" Jake looks up. It is Amby Garner, the rangy boy from the Texas panhandle, who gave them such bad haircuts. He hardly ever speaks, but even the taciturn Amby is touched by this moment.

"And you'd lose your jump pay," answers Sgt. Cody, who will be the last trooper out of the plane. Several men manage a nervous laugh. In the dark, cigarets glow in the hands of everyone aboard except Jake. Now, even he would like a cigaret. Only the sandpaper dryness in his mouth keeps him from asking for one.

They can feel the C-47 climb as they reach the coast of France. They head into cloud cover. When they emerge from it, the stillness is broken. Far off they can hear the thunder, see the explosions of bombs as Allied planes assault the German coastal defenses. In a few minutes, the distant sky begins to light up with the multi-colored criss-cross patterns of tracer bullets as planes ahead of them come under attack. Then the arcs of anti-aircraft shells, culminating in the explosions and the blossoming of ack-ack fragments. The sky is coming alive with a fireworks show like no Fourth of July ever seen.

"It's beautiful!" says Al.

"Hard to believe anything that splendid could hurt you," Kent adds.

As they come into range of the machine guns and the antiaircraft batteries the fireworks grow more personal. Flak explodes near them, rocking the plane like a small boat in an ocean chop.

Now they can see fires on the ground, some started by Allied bombs, others lit as beacons by the Germans, still others planes that have crashed in flames. And now the C-47 seems to be caught by a sea that has gone from choppy to wild: they are lifted, jolted sideways by explosions all around them. Suddenly there is an angry splatting sound. Machine gun rounds are rattling through the skin of the plane. To their right there is a loud, immediate explosion. Jake looks out the door. One of the C-47s has been hit, the left side of its fuselage blown away and a wing disintegrated. In flames, it manages for an instant to hold a miraculous equilibrium. Then it plunges to earth, tumbling over and over. In it are 16 troopers whose chutes will never open, who will die without firing a shot.

The orders to all the pilots: no evasive action, no matter how heavy the fire; slow down to 120 miles per hour for the jump, at a height of about 500 feet. But most of the pilots have never been under fire, and many will disobey some or all of the orders.

No one is speaking, the roaring of the plane's engines is deafening, the firing getting heavier, the plane bouncing around like a toy boat in a hurricane. Tracer rounds seem to be cross-stitching the fuselage and just as Jake is wondering how all that firing cannot possibly be hitting anyone, there is a strangled grunt. He looks quickly. Amby Garner from West Texas has a look in his eyes like a dying animal and he is clutching at his throat. Then the grunt turns to a choking sound and he slumps forward and hits the deck in a crouched, fetal position, in a cocoon of paratrooper gear.

Sgt. Cody leaps to him, shouting, "Nobody move!" As Cody turns Amby so he is face up, Jake looks away. A moment later, he hears the sergeant say, "He's gone."

Before anybody can take this in, the red light goes on over the door. Lt. Sobchak sees it first, shouts the words they have heard so often in training.

"Stand up!" The men leap to their feet, awaiting the next order, "Hook up." It does not come. Instead, he says, "Cody, Ellinson, get that man out of the way!" Laden as they are with their own equipment, the sergeant and Jake are barely able to locomote by themselves, let alone move Garner, who with his gear must weigh 275 pounds. But they manage to drag his body forward.

"Hook up!" The lieutenant's voice rings out as soon as the body is clear of the 15 jumpers. This is their first taste of combat death: a taste they have known was inevitable, nonetheless strange and bitter when it comes. Now, however, there is no time for it to linger. Each man hooks his static line to the cable running down the center of the plane, begins checking his own equipment and that of the man in front of him.

"Sound off for equipment check!" Sobchak screams. From behind Jake first hears Cody's voice. "Sixteen OK!" Then "Fifteen OK!" After "Eleven OK!" there is a pause, where Garner would have answered. But Amby Garner, 20 years old, farm hand, eldest of five children, will never answer again. As Cody starts to yell "Goddammit!" he is drowned out by the shout of number nine, and the voices continue on down to Kent. "Five OK!" Jake feels the slap on his back. "Four OK!" he screams and slaps Al. "Three OK!" comes Al's voice. Then "Two OK" from Cpl. Rocky Forgione, and finally Lt. Sobchak: "One OK!"

"Stand in the door!" Sobchak roars, and steps to the open door, puts one hand on each side, as the stick of men closes up behind him.

They wait for the green light, "Good luck, Bix!" comes Kent's voice from behind Jake.

"See you on the ground, Ellison. Or is it Ellinson?" Then Jake adds, "See you on the ground, Al!" He slaps the smaller man's muscular shoulder.

"Good luck, Jake." Al's words are just out when the light over the door turns green and almost instantaneously the lieutenant shouts, "Follow me!" and he is out the door. The line shuffles forward. Forgione is gone, then Al, as behind them Cody is roaring, "Go! Go! Go!"

Then Jake is out, hurtling out into a night that is being lit up by explosions, fires, bursting shells, and the ceaseless multi-colored patterns of tracers. Jake forgets to shout "Bill Lee," as all the troopers are to do, in honor of the first commanding general of the 101st. He forgets to count to three, but his chute bursts open, almost separating his upper body from his lower. He is floating down, and now he can see the origin of some of those arcs of tracers. Those are German machine guns and they all seem to be aiming at him. He pulls on his right-hand risers, spilling some air out of his chute so he will slip to the right and away from the firing. Above him and to the left, he hears an explosion, looks up, sees another plane hit and losing altitude fast. Several men are able to get out, but their chutes barely open when they hit the ground. If any survive, it will be a miracle.

He looks down, the ground is coming up fast and he seems to be headed for a line of trees, but luck is with him, he just clears them, and lands hard, pain shooting through his knee. He falls on his side, sits up, looks around. He is on a paved road between two of the formidable hedgerows that serve as field dividers in Normandy's *bocage* country. They resemble earthen breastworks, as much as six to eight feet high, and from them grow impenetrable thickets of bushes and trees. They are redoubtable fortifications, from which a road or a field can be raked with fire. It is on a road like this the Germans will be moving reinforcements, so he must get out of his chute and get on the other side of a hedgerow. To remove the chute, five buckles must be unfastened, and in the tension and excitement of the moment, Jake, like many of his fellow troopers, cannot get the buckles to work.

"Shit, goddammit!" he hisses, reaches for his jump knife and begins to cut himself out. He cuts his jump suit, gashes the knuckle of his thumb, but finally he's free of chute and harness. Pain shooting through his knee, he limps along the road, crouching low to avoid being spotted, looking for a gap in the hedgerow through which he can get off this road. He finds one, pushes through, down the far side, throws himself flat, shoves a clip into his M-1. He realizes he is sucking in air so fast and hard, he is almost sobbing. He takes a moment to regroup. Not far off there is machine gun and small arms fire, but he doesn't seem to be the target. His hands are white-knuckled on his rifle; his knee hurts badly; it is dark; he is alone. He can hear the sound of anti-aircraft fire all around him, see the stream of planes still going past, see another get hit, try to right itself and, flaming, head for the ground.

For units to assemble, men at the front of the stick, who will land first, are to move in the direction of their plane's flight, while those at the end of the stick come back to meet them. It is called "rolling up the stick." Close ahead he hears a machine gun firing, but he is not sure where it is. He's alone, scared, a New York City boy in a French field at night. Near him—how near he doesn't know—are men who are trying to kill him.

But he's well trained. He knows his job. And he's alive.

When the men of the American Fourth Division come ashore at Utah Beach five hours later and begin moving inland they will have to use four causeways leading from the beach across marshland and low areas flooded by the Germans before they reach higher ground. Securing the third and fourth causeways is the assignment of Jake's Third Battalion of the 502nd Parachute Infantry Regiment. The Second Battalion's task is to capture a coastal battery of 122-millimeter guns positioned to rake both Utah Beach and the causeways with its fire; the First's is to capture the artillery battery's barracks, designated WXYZ, and to secure the northern flank.

To place the 502nd near its objectives, the plan is to land them between the two causeways, an area designated Drop Zone A. That plan, however, is one of many that will not go right in those first hours of D-Day. Of the scores of sticks of 502nd paratroopers, only one actually lands in Drop Zone A. Others drop miles away and are lost, some merely for those initial assaults, others permanently: captured, killed, drowned in the channel or the flooded marshes. Many do land close to an objective, although not their own. This pattern holds for both U.S. airborne divisions, the All-American 82nd and the 101st Screaming Eagles. As officers and non-coms move through the dark of the night of June 6th, trying to round up quorums, troopers find themselves fighting alongside men from a company, battalion, regiment, or even a division not their own, attacking an objective not their own.

Before Jake can find the other men in his stick, there is the matter of the machine gun rattling somewhere across the field from him. Staying close to the soft earth of Normandy, he begins moving cautiously in the direction in which his plane was flying, when he half hears, half sees, mostly senses, someone nearby, and he drops flat on the ground, his rifle ready. Frozen in place, he waits and listens. He knows someone is there, but hears nothing more. The other man has hit the ground, too.

Then there is the double click of a cricket. It is the sound of the little metal toy—a kind found in Cracker Jack boxes—given to all the troopers to signal with: one click-click as challenge, two in reply. Jake has completely forgotten about the cricket. He reaches for his, which was hanging around his neck; it's gone. He wonders how long before the man holding the cricket will open fire. The click is repeated. In frustration, ignoring his instructions, Jake shouts, "Click-click! Click-click! I can't find the goddamned thing!"

"Jake? Is that you?"

He recognizes the voice of Kent, shrill, as scared as he is, too scared even to call him Bix.

"No, Kent, it's Hitler. Adolf Hitler."

He can hear the figure drawing close, and though he knows who it is, he still holds his rifle ready, until he can see by the pale moonlight it is indeed Kent, who drops down beside him.

"Are you nuts, Bix?"

"Would I be here if I weren't? I'd be playing 'Stardust.'"

"Hoagy Carmichael, Mitchell Parish. Where's your cricket?"

"Refused to jump. Hopped back to England. How the hell do I know? I lost it."

"How about the password?"

"Oh shit . . . Flash. Thunder. Forgot all about that."

The two boys from New York lie in a Normandy field, in the darkness, a German machine gun somewhere in front of them.

"What do we do now?" Kent asks.

"We try to hook up with the other guys."

"And which way is that?"

"I think that way." Jake points toward the hedgerow where the German gun is. Just then more planes come over. The machine gun opens up. Both men flatten themselves on the ground. Now the tracers show them its exact location: behind the hedgerow and less than 50 yards away.

"Let's go," Jake whispers, and gets up and starts running toward a hedgerow that's at a right angle to the one hiding the German gun. Kent is right behind him. They've taken no more than six or seven steps when the gun is turned on them. Jake can hear the bullets whining past him, hissing through the grass around him, and he hits the dirt, crawls to a slight depression that offers a little protection from the fire.

"Well, what do we do?" Kent has dropped down beside him, breathing heavily. It is now clear to he is deferring to Jake, who wants to say, don't count on me, I don't know what the hell to do: I've never been through this before!

Instead he says, "Let's outflank that bastard and get him."

Jake crawls forward, Kent following. The firing has stopped; he hopes the machine gunner has lost sight of them. They cover 20 yards when they hear the click of a cricket to the right. Kent answers with two clicks, and in a few seconds a figure crawls up to them. In the darkness, Jake can make out the form of a paratrooper near them.

"Howdy doo," he says in a Southern accent. He has a round baby face and he looks to be no more than 18. "Bobby Jackson, 508."

The 508th Parachute Infantry Regiment is in the 82nd Airborne, so someone is off course here.

"Hi, Jake Ellinson and Kent Ellison, 502."

"Y'all brothers?"

"No, it's not really . . . no."

In what is to be repeated a hundred times that night, a few men, not where they're supposed to be, with no one to command them, take action on their own.

Jackson takes charge. "I'll keep him busy," he says. "Y'all outflank him." He points Kent to the right and Jake to the left.

"They said no firing before daylight," Kent offers. The idea is not to give away position by your muzzle flash. The consensus is that it is an unwise order, and it is widely ignored.

"Fuck 'em," Jackson replies. "Go on."

On a small scale, it is the basic infantry holding attack: Firing from the front pins the enemy down, while he is attacked from the flanks. Jake starts to the left, hugging the ground, crawling through the pasture, moving as fast as he can, his fear, excitement, adrenalin, all making him forget the pain in his knee.

Jackson begins firing and Jake can hear the deeper staccato of the machine gun as it opens up in return. Lying in that field with little firepower and less cover, the baby-faced boy from the 508th is drawing fire so Jake and Kent can get to the German gun.

Lathered in sweat, Jake moves even faster, until the sound of the machine gun is very close. Then, cautiously, he climbs to the top of the hedgerow, sees he is almost on top of the German gun. Two men, dug in, are crouched behind it, one firing, the other feeding a belt into the gun, with a second belt at his side. Jake hears the crack of Jackson's M-1. He is indeed keeping them busy. Then Jackson's firing stops. Jake has to move quickly, while the Germans are distracted. Nervously, he reaches for a grenade. The procedure he knows well. He has done it in training, sometimes even with live grenades: pull the pin, count to three, throw. But this is different. If it works, he'll kill two Germans. If it doesn't, they'll kill one trumpet player from the Bronx. He concentrates, pulls the pin, counts, throws, dives for cover as the loud boom sounds, shaking him with its concussion, showering him with dirt and branches. The machine gun is silent. Rifle ready, he crawls to the hole, looks. Both man have been thrown onto their backs by the explosion and are lying there motionless. One's face is gone. The other is a bloody pulp where his crotch and belly used to be. The grenade must have rolled right under them. Jake looks away. As he does, a cricket sounds.

"Flash, thunder," Jake replies.

"One will do," comes Kent's voice from beyond the machine gun nest.

"I forgot which one. Where are you?"

"Here." The voice is coming from the other side of the hole, but not close.

"Let's get back to Jackson." Jake moves to Kent and they make their way down from the hedgerow onto the field, where they pause for a moment, both breathing deeply, listening for a moment for other guns. There are many sounds of firing, none very close.

"You got them," Kent half asks. "I heard the grenade."

"Yeah."

"You saw them?"

"Yeah."

"What did they look like?"

"Not like in the movies. Let's find Jackson."

They move a few yards apart, running low across the field in the faint moonlight to the spot where they left him. Jake sees him still prone, his M-1 ready to fire.

"We got 'em!" Jake says excitedly.

When there is no answer, he adds, "Nice going!"

Still no answer. Jake drops to his knees alongside Jackson and sees the reason he is lying so still. There is a neat hole in his helmet, put there by a round from the machine gun. Jake turns him over and can see that under the helmet there is a matching hole in his forehead, no more.

"That's the way it is in the movies," Jake says softly. Kent, who has stayed at a distance, hasn't heard him.

"How is he?" Kent asks.

"He's dead."

"Jesus. What do we do?"

"We look for the other guys."

"What about him?"

"Leave him here. Nothing else we can do. We'll tell someone . . ."

"Who?"

"What the fuck is this, Twenty Questions? Let's go!" Jake feels himself exploding, unable to stop. "For God's sake, Kent! He's dead; it doesn't matter! We've got to hook up with the others! Come on!"

He rises to a crouch, moves over to Kent. "Get on your feet, stay low. Let's go." Without looking back, he starts forward in a crouching lope, headed for the hedgerow that until a few minutes before held the German machine gun. They follow the hedgerow until they find a place to get through. Jake looks through to the far side; a narrow blacktop road runs by it. Cautiously, he slides down the embankment to the road. As he is about to signal to Kent to follow, the roar of an engine is heard, and before Jake can move, around a curve comes a German truck, bouncing, swaying, moving too fast, with no lights.

"Stay there!" he hisses to Kent, and flattens himself against the embankment, grateful now for having blackened his face so that it will not reflect the faint glow of the moon. Though it passes within 10 feet of him, the truck does not slow down, the driver either not seeing or ignoring him. Jake catches a glimpse of the driver, the face that of a man in panic.

Motionless, Jake waits for following vehicles. When there are none, he signals to Kent, then crosses the road, moves along the hedgerow on the opposite side, looking for an opening to the next field. For reasons unknown to them, the sound and pace of firing picks up, so when they get into the next field, they move carefully, then pause. In the dark of this foreign land, Jake is disoriented, no longer sure how they should be rolling up the stick.

"Which way should we be heading?" he asks Kent, Kent points to two o'clock; Jake would have said 11 o'clock. That puts the two men about 45 degrees apart. From both directions the sound of firing is heavy. Jake makes a decision.

"I say we stay here, get some sleep, then move when the sun comes up and we can figure out where we're going."

"I defer to you, Bix."

Jake motions for Kent to follow as he walks into the field, hugging the side of the hedgerow, to get them away from the opening onto the road. They sit with their backs to the embankment, rifles across their legs. Jake checks the safety of his weapon. It is still on, he's never had it off, would not have been able to fire it if he'd had to. If one of those German machine gunners had been alive and functioning . . . Men are dying this night because of small mistakes. Jake has gotten away with one.

"Were you scared, Kent?"

"Why use the past tense?"

"I was so scared I thought my heart and my guts were all going to come popping up out of my mouth. I kept swallowing to hold them down."

"You know Bix, that is precisely how I felt. I suppose what would have come up, though, would just have been my last meal. I didn't let it, I'm proud of that. I'm very worried about being a coward."

"Anyone who's not is a nut. Now let's get some sleep."

"That guy from the 82nd. He told us his name. Bobby Jackson. He said, howdy doo."

"Forget him."

"Forget him?"

"He's in God's hands. We've got to worry about us."

Exhausted by the tension of the day, still sedated by the airsickness pills, they do what so many of their fellow troopers do that night. In chilly fields, with gunfire all around them, they fall sound asleep.

When Jake is startled awake by a nudge from Kent, he has been dreaming about Cindy. She is in the ocean at a place that first looks like Orchard Beach in the Bronx, then becomes Myrtle Beach, then no beach he has ever seen. She is standing in shallow water, only, as Jake walks toward her, it gets deeper and he cannot quite reach her. Strangely enough, she does not seem upset by the deepening, roughening surf; she has a faint smile on her face. Then she turns away . . .

"Jake, someone is on the road."

"What? Who?" For a moment Jake doesn't know where he is, he looks around for the ocean.

"On the road."

"Our guys?"

"I heard someone speaking English."

Jake climbs the side of the hedgerow, M-1 in his right hand, this time with the safety off, and pushes through far enough to see the men. They are Americans, about a dozen of them, wearing the Screaming Eagle patch. They are stopped on the road, while a staff sergeant speaks softly to them. Jake is so elated to see them, he shouts "Flash!" louder than he needs to. Despite the password, the men jump.

"Thunder," replies the sergeant. "Come on out and be quiet."

Jake and Kent run to the opening in the hedgerow and out onto the road.

"That all?" asks the sergeant. "Two of you?"

"That's all," Kent answers.

"What unit you from?"

"H company, 502,"

"You're going with us."

"Where to?" Jake asks.

"First Battalion objective—WXYZ—the artillery barracks."

"But we're Third Battalion, we're supposed to . . ." Jake begins.

"You're now honorary members of the First," says the sergeant. "Just do what I tell you."

They walk along the road for a few hundred yards before the sergeant moves them into an open field and spreads them out in a skirmish line, Jake and Kent on the extreme left flank, unable to hear the sergeant and having no idea what they're supposed to be doing.

To the man on his right, Jake shouts softly, "What's the plan?"

"Nobody told me nothing."

"Who's the sergeant?" Jake asks.

"Never saw him before. I'm from the 506."

They see ahead a string of stone buildings on both sides of the road. From firing ports in the near buildings, rifle fire starts to crackle. Most of the men drop into ditches alongside the road; Jake and Kent take cover behind some low hedges. The firing is not heavy, nor does it seem to be doing any damage; but it has stopped their advance.

"What's going on?" Kent asks.

"Beats the hell out of me," Jake replies.

Just then they see the sergeant, who is about 50 yards away, start forward, holding a Thompson submachine gun, staying low as he lopes along, almost casually. No one else moves. The enemy does not seem to see him. He races to the side of the nearest building, kicks in the door, charges in.

"What the hell is he doing?" Jake shouts.

"Looks like he's doing a solo, Bix."

"Looks to me like he's nuts!" says Jake. "Why aren't the guys near him moving up with him?"

The firing from the first building stops. The sergeant emerges, seems to shout something to them, what it is Jake cannot make out, and crosses the road, heads for a cluster of three buildings. From the right, they see a lieutenant run forward to join the sergeant. He has almost reached him when he's hit, falls and lies motionless.

Jake turns to the trooper on his right, "what did he say? Does he want us to move up or hold?"

But the man from the 506th, crouching, is now on his feet and moving forward at a run, although the firing has resumed and is heavier than ever.

When Jake turns to his left, he sees Kent also running forward. Jake wants to get to his feet, but his legs will not obey him; they will not launch his body into the stream of bullets rolling by. Momentarily, but what for him seems like hours, he is paralyzed. Ahead of him the firing gets too much for the man from the 506th, who drops behind a tree stump and begins firing at the near house. Kent, charging ahead, takes no more than 20 strides before he is hit and goes down. Seeing that, Jake regains control of his body, leaps to his feet, races toward his buddy. Kent is trying to crawl for cover. But there is none. Jake hears bullets hissing through the grass around him as he runs, expecting to be hit at any instant. He reaches Kent, drops to the ground. Kent is lying on his stomach, the left side of his face bloody. Near them is a slight trough in the ground that might afford some cover. Rising to a crouch, he grabs Kent's collar in one hand, drags him to the trough, falls to the ground beside him.

"You OK?"

"Hit in the shoulder or arm, not sure. Face hurts." They now seem to be lying in a hailstorm of bullets. It is only a matter of moments before they're hit. If Jake tries to drag Kent back, they're both dead men. There's only one way to go, forward, to neutralize the closest building, which has them under fire.

"You'll be all right, Kent. You're not hit bad," he says, having no idea whatever if that is true. "I'll get a medic."

Jake now knows the truth about himself. Within him is a coward, a coward who must be subdued, who must never again be allowed to surface. Go, he tells himself as if he were ordering someone else. Swallowing hard, clutching his rifle, he starts forward, races about 20 yards, bullets whizzing by him, until he spots a hedge and dives behind it. Safe for the moment, he can see the sergeant. He is at the door of the second building, unseen by the Germans, for by now the paratroopers have set up a steady fire at the building and the defenders are staying low. As Jake watches, the sergeant kicks at the door and charges into the building. Separately from the rifle fire, Jake can hear the deeper sound of the sergeant's Tommy gun; he races to the side of the building. As he gets near, the sergeant emerges, looks at him calmly.

"Come on," he says to Jake. He is now walking—so deliberately it is almost a saunter—toward a third building. Jake forces himself to go along. The sergeant points to a ditch. "Cover me."

Jake drops into the ditch, starts squeezing off rounds, flattens himself as close to the earth as he can as the Germans return fire. Meanwhile the sergeant has reached the third building, charges through the door. Again Jake hears the staccato bark of the Tommy gun. In little more than a minute the sergeant is out again, waves to Jake, who races toward him. Together they head for a fourth building. Calmly the sergeant squats alongside the wall, just a few feet from the open doorway. This man, Jake decides, has a charmed life. He will stick with him.

"The place is wide open. They're inviting us in," the sergeant says. Then from a nearby orchard, a tall lean figure appears and runs toward them. They can see he is an officer—a captain. They spot the twin A's of the 82nd Airborne on his shoulder patch; he is one of the many mis-dropped troopers that day who join the battle wherever they are. He gives them the thumbs-up sign; he is joining their assault. Ten strides from them, he is hit in the chest by a single rifle bullet and falls dead.

"Some guys got no luck," the sergeant says. "Let's go. You get alongside the door while I go in. Cover me."

In answer, Jake pulls a grenade from a pocket, mimes throwing it. "Then you go in," he says.

The sergeant nods. "Do it."

Jake walks carefully to the open door, pulls the pin, throws the grenade in, falls back to avoid the blast. Before the smoke has stopped billowing out the door, the sergeant is through the door, firing.

He emerges in a moment, rubbing his eyes to clear away the smoke. "Next case," he says. "Let's go." Jake following, he crosses the road to another cluster of buildings. There is now a heavy volume of fire, from the Germans in the remaining buildings and from the paratroopers who have crawled forward in the ditches and moved behind nearby hedges and into an orchard behind the houses. Despite all the firing, with the sergeant Jake feels untouchable. As they get near the fifth building, a corporal carrying a Browning automatic rifle comes running up. The sergeant knows him. "Chambers. About time someone showed up. Set that thing up, and keep them busy," He points to two other buildings. Jake cannot get over how calm he is.

Chambers, not feeling untouchable, hurries to a compost pile, sets up his BAR behind it, begins firing. The sergeant points to an open window, mimes the throwing of a grenade. Jake moves to the window, grenade in hand, looks inside, sees a half dozen Germans, four of them firing through the ports on the opposite side of the building, two of them sitting on the ground wounded. He hesitates.

"Do it," hisses the sergeant.

Jake pulls the pin, lobs the grenade through the window, dives for cover. A moment later, a German soldier stumbles out. The sergeant calmly fires a burst into him, keeps firing as he steps through the door. In three minutes he emerges.

"Let's go," he says to Jake, and heads for the next building, gesturing to the BAR man, Chambers, as he does. "Save the grenades this time."

They go through three more buildings, the sergeant charging in, Jake and Chambers covering him, leaving German bodies behind.

There are now two buildings remaining. Both are larger than the others, the first of them more than 100 yards away. They approach it in a ditch alongside the road, the sergeant in the lead, Jake behind him, the BAR man in the rear. The sergeant leads them right up to a window of the building. He looks in it, turns away, amazed. "Those sonofabitches are sitting and *eating*!" he says.

He points to a far door, speaks to his BAR man: "Chambers, you set up for that door. We're going in this one. When they come out that one, chew 'em up."

He waits for Chambers to make the move. Then he leads Jake to the near door. "We're going in shooting. Make that weapon *smoke!*" When Jake nods in response, the sergeant says, "Let's go."

He kicks the door open and starts firing. Jake moves in and to his right and gets off rounds from the M-1 as fast as he can. There are about 15 Germans. Some go for their weapons and are cut down; others race out the far door, where Chambers and his BAR are waiting. Jake can hear its hiccupping begin.

The final building is a two-story stone barracks with a shed next to it. It is heavily fortified and manned and its defenders are putting up strong resistance. But paratrooper reinforcements converging on it have arrived. Finally, a machine gunner firing tracers sets fire to the shed. About 30 men come running out and are hit and finished off by the surrounding Americans. The barracks itself is set afire by a bazooka. As the Germans pour out of it, 50 are killed and 30 more taken prisoner.

The barracks buildings are in American hands. Jake is standing near the sergeant, both of them exhausted. Jake has just watched a man do something that, if he hadn't seen, he would not believe. Finally Jake asks a question. He knows it's stupid, but he can't help it.

"Why did you do it?"

The sergeant stares at Jake, his brown eyes showing nothing. It seems the question has never occurred to him. He shrugs. "No one else wanted to," he finally says and then, as if put off by his own verbosity, turns and walks away. Jake does not even know his name, and will never see him again.

Jake realizes he is not only exhausted, but aching, from running into building corners, pushing through doorways, throwing himself into ditches. He must now hook up with his company, find out how Kent is and locate Al. A couple of hours later, he finds Kent at a battalion aid station, lying on the ground, his left arm in a sling and the left side of his face bandaged.

"Hey Ellison. Or is it Ellinson?"

The right side of Kent's face smiles faintly. "Hello, Bix."

"How are you doing?"

"They tell me I'm lucky. Went through my arm, tore up the muscle, without breaking a bone. And my looks may be gone. They're shipping me out of here."

"That's what they mean by a million dollar wound, buddy! England, here you come! Give my best to the gang at the Rose & Crown."

"I didn't fight it, Jake. I didn't say, no, I want to stay."

"Which only goes to show you're not nuts. Were you lying out there long?"

"Ten minutes. A corpsman from First Battalion got to me. He was great. Helped me get back here. I could hear the firing; I said to myself, that's Bix being a hero."

"Uh uh. Just tagging along. That sergeant was doing it all." He does not tell Kent about the coward inside.

A regimental medical corpsman walks up. "We're taking you to the beach, pal." He points to a horse and wagon someone has commandeered from the French. Jake puts out a hand to Kent, helps him to the wagon. Three men are on it, on stretchers. One has his face completely bandaged except for an opening so he can breathe—breaths that come in sobbing moans. With Jake's help, Kent climbs aboard, sits on the floor of the wagon, legs dangling from the back, far from the man with the bandaged face. A half dozen more walking wounded climb aboard. Finally a soldier jumps onto the driver's seat, snaps the reins and the horse starts forward, getting the wagon into motion slowly and laboriously. Kent clutches Jake's hand as Jake walks along with him.

"See you back in England," Jake says.

"Thanks Jake. God bless you."

Kent releases his hand and the wagon pulls away. Jake watches and waves, then turns and begins the search for his company and Al. In the mid-afternoon of

D-Day, after walking for an hour, Jake finds his battalion and spots Al. He is so glad to see him, he hugs him. Al looks to both sides of Jake before asking: "Kent?"

"He's OK. Wounded, in the face and arm. Didn't look too bad; they're shipping him back to England."

Breecher grins, but only for a moment. "Your friend from the Bronx, the sergeant whose name I can't say . . ."

"Patsy Buonaventura?"

"He got it. Mortar round. Lt. Sobchak was wounded; so was Cpl. Forgione, but they're going to be OK." Al lists three other names—all dead.

The two go quiet. Jake is thinking about those men, men they have known and trained with, going way back to 1942. In one day, they are all gone. Sgt. Cody doesn't give them too much time to think. "All right, you goldbricks!" he is shouting. "I want y'all to form a perimeter and dig in."

The rest of the day and the next are quiet, the troops around them no longer German, but men of the Fourth Division pouring inland from Utah Beach. On D-Day plus 2—June 8th—Jake's regiment moves south, backing up the attack on St. Come du Mont. On June 10th the regiment begins the assault on the large town of Carentan to the south. Carentan is a road and rail junction vital to the Americans to link the Utah and Omaha bridgeheads. And to the Germans, to bring up reinforcements.

Just north of the town, the road becomes a causeway as it crosses salt marshes and two rivers. Arrow straight and standing six to nine feet above the surrounding marshes, the causeway will come to be known as Purple Heart Lane. As men of G Company move over it, they come under withering fire from German machineguns and 88s on high ground to the north and from snipers in the marshes around them. They drop down to the sides of the causeway, trying to dig in or use the reeds as cover. They are stopped and begin taking heavy casualties. Battalion Commander Cole orders Jake's Company H to move up through Company G that night. By 5 on the morning of June 11th, 84 men of Company H have fought their way over the causeway and are moving along the road when, from a U-shaped group of farmhouses on the right, they are hit by heavy fire and pinned down. Col. Cole asks for artillery fire on the houses, but it does not quiet the enemy. So he orders the artillery to send in smoke, and then tells his executive officer, Maj. John Stopka, to order the men to fix bayonets and reload their weapons with full clips for a bayonet charge on the farmhouses.

The smoke arrives. Col. Cole gets to his feet, .45 in hand, to begin the charge. But once again, in the fog of war, few of the men get the order, so when Cole starts forward, firing his pistol, almost no one goes with him. As they see him, though, in ones, twos and groups they get to their feet and advance, leaning forward as if they were facing sleet or snow instead of a storm of bullets.

Al starts forward. Next to him, Jake once again forces the coward inside under control and moves with his buddy. Al is hit almost at once and falls. As he lies there, a mortar round explodes nearby, rocking him and knocking Jake to the ground and stunning him. Trying to clear his head, Jake looks to Al, sees him on the ground and trying to crawl forward.

"Al?" he yells.

Breecher looks up at him, still crawling. "I'm all right, go ahead!" As if to reinforce that, Al puts his rifle to his shoulder and from his prone position fires off several rounds at the farmhouse.

Then he shouts, "Go on! Take 'em!"

Jake can see blood all over Al's back and legs. He starts toward him, but Al, firing his weapon furiously, yells again.

"I said, go!" Then Al reaches to his belt for another ammo clip and with speed that no one in the company has ever been able to match, re-loads and resumes firing.

With Al watching, Jake must go. His head clearing from the shock of the concussion, he shoves a new clip into his M-1, gets to his feet and charges forward. He moves so fast he catches up to Sgt. Cody, who has a Tommy gun in his hands. The two men arrive simultaneously at one prong of the U formed by the farmhouse cluster and see the colonel standing there waving at them. They stop at the wall until they realize that Cole is screaming at them to keep going, for in a hedgerow alongside the house are snipers and a machinegun nest.

Cody sprays the hedgerow and points to the machinegun, signals for Jake to go to the right of it while he moves to the left, firing as he does. As Jake hurries off to his right, the machine gun does not follow him; it is turned on Cody. Jake is able to get close enough to hurl a grenade, which kills three of the five Germans in the position and stuns the others. From their separate directions, Cody and Jake charge into the gun emplacement. The two remaining Germans are trying to scramble out. Cody pulls the hunting knife from his belt, and yells to Jake, "Save your ammo!" Following Cody's example, Jake pulls his knife and leaps into the hole. The Germans, groggy from the grenade explosion, are moving in slow motion, but Jake cannot use the knife. Cody leaps on them and stabs one just above the collar bone, the second in the throat, Jake is standing upright, knife in hand, the firing still heavy from all directions, as Cody's knife rises and plunges.

"Get the fuck down!" Cody yells and Jake drops down.

"Couldn't do it, college boy?" Cody says, crouching there with the bloody knife in his hand. "Not Marquis of Queensberry?" Then he holds the knife up. "See? I promised y'all I would do this! See it?"

"I see it, sergeant."

"Now we go after the Krauts in that hedge. Follow me!"

Cody springs from the hole. He is hardly on his feet when he is hit by a fusillade of fire. He falls over backwards, knocking Jake back into the hole and landing on top of the Germans he's just stabbed. Jake scrambles to his feet, bends over the sergeant; he has been shot in the chest and throat. His eyes are open, staring at Jake. He extends his knife to Jake. Then the hand goes limp, the knife drops, hitting Jake's thigh, smearing blood on his pants.

Jake picks the knife up by the handle, holds it, not sure what to do. He starts to wipe it on Cody's pants leg, then stops, wipes it instead on one of the Germans. He looks at the knife, hesitates, then takes his own knife from its sheath, drops it to the ground and replaces it with Cody's. He looks to the sergeant; Cody's eyes are open and for a moment Jake thinks he may still be alive. But in the eyes is the stare of death. Jake hesitates, then reaches to close them. He cannot bring himself to do it.

"Goodbye, sergeant."

The Third Battalion has taken the farmhouse, but from positions around it, German troops, strengthened by reinforcements, pour fire on them. Of the 150 men of H Company who jumped into Normandy, 84 made it across Purple Heart Lane. After the farmhouse battle, 30 remain in the field.

All night and the next day the fighting rages. The key crossroads town of Carentan has still not been taken. Finally the Second Battalion comes up to relieve the battered Third. When they have withdrawn, Col. Cole takes a head count. His battalion, which at full strength numbered about 700, now has 130 men fit to fight.

On the morning of the next day, June 12th, in a pincers movement, the 501st and the 506th, with the glider infantrymen of the 327th, take Carentan with comparatively little resistance. As they stand in the town that has cost so many 101st casualties, the division commander, Gen. Maxwell Taylor, tells the CO of the 502nd that it was the dogged attack of his regiment the day before that shattered the German defenders. He will recommend Third Battalion commander Lt. Col. Cole for the Medal of Honor for leading the bayonet charge on the farmhouses.

For the 101st Airborne, the worst of the Normandy fighting is over. After several more days of mopping up, they spend nearly a month patrolling the Cotentin peninsula. On July 10th, the division is moved to a bivouac area behind Utah beach and three days later LSTs carry the men back across the English Channel to Southampton.

As they land, the band is playing "Holiday For Strings."

In the Normandy campaign the 101st has suffered more than 3800 casualties, with nearly 900 killed.

By train and truck, they go back to home base, Chilton Foliat. Jake walks into the Nissen hut that has been home for him since last October, sits on his bunk, looks at the empty bunks where Kent and Al once slept. He thinks of the voice of Sgt. Cody that they will never hear again. In this hut once shared by 20 men, three are dead, five wounded, two missing. Ten beds are empty. Everyone has made the count; no one speaks of it. The invulnerability of innocence is gone.

After dinner there is a mail call. Among Jake's letters is one from Cindy. The stationery is pink with a bouquet of roses in the upper right hand corner of the page. Just the sight of it makes him want to put his arms around her. It is written in the careful Catholic school script and the stilted locutions so familiar to him—a little girl trying to sound grown up.

> *My dearest Jake,*
>
> *I hope this letter finds you in good health. The newspapers are full of stories about the invasion and the fighting in France. Whenever I read them, I think of you and pray for your safety. There will always be a place in my heart for you, no matter where our lives may take us. This brings me to my news.*
>
> *I don't know if you heard that I went back to Buddy's band. We have been on the road steadily. The crowds are huge and they seem to love me. Do you know what they ask for most? 'All The Things You Are.' Every time we do it, I think of you.*

An older guy, Vito Massaro, has your solo. He's not bad, but not like you! That's what the band is now, old guys, 4Fs, and kids who play until they get drafted. Like the song says, 'They're either too young or too old.'

Now comes the real news. I don't know how to say it, so I'll say it straight out. Buddy and I are getting married. It turns out he's really liked me for a long time. That's why he was so angry about you and me. He was just jealous, only he never could say right out how he felt. He wants to get married in the right way. You know what I mean by that, in church. He's a good man who really loves me and wants to look after me.

It's not the same as with you, Jake. But you and I could never work things out. There's no point in saying any more. It makes me want to cry and I've already done enough of that.

Jake looks away from the letter. A fog has come between it and his eyes, like the smoke at that farmhouse on the Carentan road. He throws the letter down on his bunk, finds himself shaking with anger and . . . he's not sure what else. He strides out of the barracks, heads for the infirmary. Perhaps there he will find out where Kent and Al are. Perhaps, too, he'll find June Hopkins. Maybe she'll celebrate with him. He wants to celebrate, not get letters like that one. In the infirmary he sees a medical administration officer, a young second lieutenant, pale and blond, in an immaculate uniform, who spares him only an annoyed glance.

"No sick call until tomorrow morning," the lieutenant says.

"I'm not on sick call. I wonder if you can help me, sir?"

"I'm very busy . . . Pfc." His tone is weary and neutral, as if he is too tired either to like or dislike Jake.

"Do you know if Lt. June Hopkins is here?"

"I don't know. And I don't have time to find out."

"I wonder if there is someone who could . . ."

"We're all working our asses off, Pfc! Do you have any idea what kind of administrative mess we're trying to deal with here?"

"No I don't, sir. I just got here. I've been in France for five weeks. It was very messy there. Men with their bellies blown open and their guts hanging out. That's a mess. Men who were nothing but body parts, a head here, a leg there, a dick there. That's a real mess. Men with their brains oozing out of their skulls. You want to talk about messes . . ."

An alarmed look comes into the lieutenant's eyes. Jake sees it and is surprised.

"No disrespect, sir."

"I'll go look for her. What's your name . . . Pfc?"

"Ellinson, sir."

"Sit over there."

The lieutenant turns on his heel and walks off. Three minutes later, June comes running down the hall.

"Oh Jake!" She puts her hands on the sides of his face and squeezes gently as if to make sure he is real.

"Junebug."

"Are you all right?"

"Sure."

"Come on," She takes his hand, leads him to an examination room, closes the door. She puts her arms around him and hugs him hard. "I'm so glad to see you!"

He clutches her. "And I'm very glad to see you," he replies, surprised at how glad he actually is.

"You're sure you're all right?"

"Sure I'm sure. Don't I look all right?"

"Lt. Madigan didn't think so."

"That little jerk!" Jake grins. "As long as I look all right to you." She does not smile back. Her look is worried.

"He thought you seemed . . . on the edge."

"On the edge? Well . . . maybe. When that little . . . jerk . . . started telling me about his problems . . . I'll tell you the truth, I suddenly wanted to . . . Goddamned little second looey in his spotless uniform." Jake makes a point of sounding very calm.

"Easy, Jake." Clearly now, he can see she half agrees with the lieutenant.

"Junebug, this is such a funny war. Know what I did a few weeks ago? I threw a grenade into a room full of Germans. There were parts of bodies all over the place. Little parts, bits of tissue, bone, guts. There was so much blood all over the floor, I slipped on it, landed on my rear end. I went around with the seat of my pants soaked with German blood! And here's this lieutenant with his files and his papers. That's his war!"

Jake hears a shrill voice, realizes it is his. He stops himself, "Sorry. Maybe I am on the edge." He lets the air out in a whoosh. June takes his hand.

He looks at hers, so white, his looking like it is still coated with the dirt, the manure, the grease, the blood of Normandy, although he has washed it many times since.

"It's all right," she says softly, "If you want to talk, talk."

"Tell the lieutenant I didn't mean anything, that I'm a little . . . overwrought. That's a good word; it sounds very impressive. A guy who likes files will like it. Know what I want to do, Junebug?"

"What?"

"Tonight I want to drink that warm ale I hate at the Rose & Crown. Tomorrow I want to find my buddies, Kent and Al. Can you help me?"

"Yes, I can, Jake. I was worried about you. I'm so glad . . ."

She hugs him again; as he buries his head in her neck and shoulder, he wishes it were his mother.

That evening, he walks into the Rose & Crown to meet June, sits at a table in a far corner of the main room, its battered wood familiar to him after the many evenings he's sat there sipping at the warm ale. A new barmaid approaches.

"Where's Em?" he asks her.

"Oh, Em's gone off to a defense plant in the north. Is there something I can get you?"

"An ale," Jake says. "Not too cold." That's a little joke he and Em shared.

The girl looks puzzled. "Warm is all we've got," she answers. Then when Jake smiles at her she gets it and smiles back before going off. He is sipping the warm ale when June arrives.

"They're both at the station hospital in Swindon," is the first thing she tells him. Jake is elated. Swindon is only 15 miles up the road from Chilton Foliat. He'll go there tomorrow.

"How are they?"

"Fine. Breecher is getting out in a few days. Ellison had his arm operated on a few weeks ago, to repair the muscle. He's got a way to go."

June gestures to the waitress to bring her a glass like Jake's. When it arrives, she sips at it.

"I really believe I'm beginning to like this stuff."

"I'm not quite there yet," Jake replies.

She puts a hand on his. "Oh Jake, your friends are so lucky! The casualties are pouring in. Some of them . . . it's just heartbreaking. Just being around them, day after day, gets to be more than I can bear. What it's like actually to be one of them—to be 19 years old, lying there with your legs shot away—I can't imagine. They look into my eyes, asking for something—something I can't give them."

"You know what they're asking for." Jake tries a smile.

"It's not funny!"

"Speaking of being close to the edge," he says, lightly. "I'm not the only one needs some time off."

"I have a week's leave coming," she answers, looking at him.

"So have I."

"There's a house in Cornwall," she says. "It belongs to an English doctor I know. He said I could use it, anytime."

"Even without him?"

She smiles. "Even without him."

"With another guy?"

"He didn't specify. Of course, neither did I." She laughs, squeezes his hand, takes hers away. Invasion or no invasion, the rules about officers and enlisted personnel remain.

"I've been dreaming. That you would come home safely. That we could spend some time there, far away from everything, everybody. Can my dream be coming true?"

Suddenly the words in Cindy's letter surge through him again, so strongly he feels a physical ache. June sees it on his face. "Not possible?"

"Look," he says. "I just got a Dear John letter from my girl. She's marrying someone else. So there'll be a ghost going with us. If you can handle that, you've got a deal."

As she reaches out and shakes the hand he has offered her to seal the deal, the piano starts playing. "Cue the music," he says.

"It will be such fun!" she exults.

"I've got to pay my respects to the piano player. Keep my drink warm."

Jake takes his horn, walks up behind Harry Ashford, who is playing, for what must be the 10,000th time, "White Cliffs Of Dover." This time there is a strange despondency to it.

Jake puts on his most spurious British accent. "I say, old chap, do you know 'White Cliffs Of Dover?'"

Without turning, Ashford answers, "Never heard of it, Yank." Then the voice registers. He swivels on the piano bench.

"Why, ya mug ya! Ya made it back in one piece!"

"I had my lucky charm with me," Jake holds up the horn.

Harry is on his feet. He puts his arms around Jake, crushes him in a bear hug.

"You're going to do more damage to the horn than the Krauts could," says Jake, grinning.

Harry lets go, steps back, puts a thick hand to his face to wipe his eyes, tries to compose himself. "A sight for sore eyes! And your mates?"

"In the hospital, at Swindon, but OK. Can I buy you a drink?"

"No, thank you, lad."

That, and the piano playing. Jake knows something is wrong.

"Everything all right?" Harry's face has the answer. "The boys OK?"

"I'm afraid Bobby, the younger, is no longer . . . with us."

"No longer . . . ?" Jake is hoping he has misunderstood.

"Mavis says, gone to heaven. She's sure he has. I hope so."

"What happened?"

"He was in on D-Day. His minesweeper was clearing the way for our lads off the beach. Struck a mine. All hands lost."

Harry puts a hand to his forehead as if to shade his eyes. Jake can see his pain in having to tell the story. Fresh pain—it's only been a few weeks. He thinks of all the families. Amby. Sgt. Cody. Bobby Jackson from the 508. The tall captain from the 82nd, who got a bullet in the heart. And Patsy Buonaventura from Arthur Avenue—so few blocks from the Ellinsons in the Bronx. All of their families, getting the news and trying to cope with it, having to tell about it, over and over, and trying to cope with that, just as Harry is now.

"And how is Mavis holding up?" Jake asks. He remembers those two tiny, orderly rooms in the Ashford apartment over the apothecary shop, each of them standing at attention, waiting for a son to come home to it.

"Tough as leather," Harry says. "But then she's got religion to help her. I wish I had. What do you think, Jake? Has the lad gone to heaven?"

Jake doesn't want to say no. "If there is a heaven, Harry, I guarantee you there's a special place in it for men who died for their country."

"A special place, eh? It must be getting bloody crowded these days. Still, it's a lovely thought. Let's play something, Jake."

Not looking at Jake again, Harry turns to the piano, goes into a halting intro to "I'll Be Seeing You." Jake picks up on it, plays it as a slow, moody ballad, his quivering lips producing a new kind of unintended vibrato. He tells himself he's just rusty.

The next morning Jake hitches a ride to the hospital at Swindon; he finds Kent and Al in adjoining beds in a ground-floor ward. They both beam at him.

"And how did you two goldbricks manage this?" Jake asks.

Kent beckons him closer. "Bribery, Bix. Downright, forthright, outright bribery. Said Al was my first cousin, and I promised our grandmother I'd look after him. And had a ten dollar bill in my hand as I said it."

"You two have really got it made!"

"Except for the constant humiliation and the loss of a fortune," Kent says with mock despair. "Do you know I bribed that orderly for the privilege of being shown up regularly, day after day, by this heartless Hawkeye? We play a game called 'Who Wrote That Tune?' With a small bet on each one. So far, I owe him $223! He claims to be a farmboy. I don't think he's ever done anything but read record labels!"

Jake has never seen Al grin so broadly.

"Bix, who would you say wrote 'Take The A Train'?"

"I'd say Billy Strayhorn. You didn't get fooled by that one?"

"Of course, I did! It's Duke Ellington's song!"

"I win more bets with that one!" Al can't stop smiling.

"$223!" says Kent. "I haven't taken such a thorough beating since hand-to-hand combat with Sgt. Cody!"

"You'll never have to take it again. Sgt. Cody got it," says Jake quietly.

"No!" says Al, his elation gone.

"Can't be," echoes Kent. "That man is indestructible."

"That's what I thought," says Jake. "It happened right after I left Al, just beyond the farmhouse. He had a whole hedgerow full of Krauts terrorized. I told Capt. Smith the story. He put Sgt. Cody in for a Silver Star." Jake realizes as he speaks that he never ever uses the name Cody without the "sergeant" in front of it.

On his way out, Jake sees a brawny red-headed corporal he recognizes from G Company, one of the stars of the 502nd football team. He remembers hearing that the corporal played at one of the big California universities—USC or UCLA—and was headed for professional football. No more. The man's right pajama leg is empty. Jake gives him a thumbs up. The corporal looks at him, smiles somberly, returns the gesture.

†

Early the next morning he and June start hitchhiking to the coastal village of Penzance in Cornwall. With the help of several army drivers, American and British, they arrive at 9 in the evening, but in the English summer there is still enough light to show that Penzance is as charming as June promised, a quaint village with whitewashed stone houses that go down to a tan, sandy beach, separated from it only by a narrow cobbled road.

The doctor's house stands on that road and fronts on Mount's Bay, on which Penzance sits. The first floor is occupied by a small living room, an even smaller dining room, and a kitchen. Up a steep narrow flight of stairs are two tiny back bedrooms and, in front, the master bedroom, which takes up the width of the house and half its depth and looks out on the bay.

As soon as they are settled in, they head off to the local pub, the Blue Dolphin, for a glass of stout and a shepherd's pie of indeterminate contents. For the first time since he arrived in England, Jake is wearing civilian clothes. At June's urging, he has borrowed them from the doctor, who, from the clothing, seems to be about Jake's height and a little thicker through the middle. He has on a pair of gray flannel trousers, an old striped shirt and a dark blue pullover.

"You could almost be English," she says to him as she looks him over.

"Pip pip!" he answers.

"Until you open your mouth," she adds, laughing.

"It feels great to be sitting here. Like . . . two civilians!" he says. "It's been so long, I've almost forgotten."

"How long?"

"I went in a week before Pearl Harbor. Great timing, huh? That makes it two and a half years."

"Will you remember what it's like to be a civilian again?"

Jake snaps his fingers, the crack so loud two old couples across the way turn to look, "Just try me. Go home, say to my folks, see, your son is safe and sound! Then go to Benny Goodman, and say Benny, I'm available! He'll probably fall on his knees and thank God. And then he'll fire me a week later!" Jake laughs at a joke she doesn't even understand. "So I'll become an arranger, organize my own band."

"And live happily ever after."

"Got to be an optimist."

"That's one of the things I admire about you," she tells him. "The way you promised me nothing would happen to you! You were so sure!"

"I was a fool," he says simply.

She searches his light blue eyes for the optimism. She can't find it.

The week is an idyll, lazy and sweet tempered, indulged by a lovely British summer with a full blessing of sun. Strolling on the beach. Walking up town lanes that become paths into the countryside, Jake shouting at the idling, ruminative cows, "Don't you know there's a war on?" Sitting in the pub, listening to swing bands on the radio. Lying in the double bed, from which they can see the sun rising over the bay in the morning. Existing in a world with no uniforms, no weapons.

Then the week is over and they make their way back to the rest of the world. Waiting for Jake when he returns to Chilton Foliat is a resumption of training as tough as any the regiment has ever been through. Al is back, his body pocked with scars but at full strength, a marvel of resilience. Kent is still in the hospital, his arm healing more slowly than was anticipated. On the next Sunday, Jake goes to see him.

"Still goldbricking, eh?"

"They're giving me a hard time, Jake. Talking about sending me back to the States. I keep telling them the arm is getting better every day."

"Is it?"

"Sure!"

"That's not what the doc said."

"Which doctor?"

"The one I asked out there just before I came in."

"*That* one! He's a podiatrist from Podunk! I've asked them to bring in a specialist from New York."

"You can't do it with one arm, Kent. Don't be a fool."

"I'll be back. Don't let yourself imagine anything else."

Leaving the hospital, Jake sees the doctor again. "When will he be able to rejoin the company?" The doctor just shrugs.

"Will he be able to, at all?"

The doctor hesitates, shrugs again.

There are new faces, replacements brought in to fill the ranks depleted by 3800 casualties. Much as Jake always hated the arrogance and snobbery of the veterans when he was a new man, he now finds himself showing those very traits, resenting the newcomers not for themselves but for the men whose places they fill. To replace Cody, a sergeant is brought in from battalion headquarters. Sgt. Emil Grunwald is from upstate New York, a stocky, dark-haired man in his late 20s, who is friendlier than Cody, yet very professional. But he cannot replace *the* sergeant; on that the men agree. Jake and Al talk about it one August night lying on their bunks after a 25-mile forced march.

"He's actually a nicer guy," Jake says.

"Maybe we'll get used to him," offers Al.

"Sure," Jake says. "But it won't be the same. I'm not sure why."

"Sgt. Cody knew everything there was to know about soldiering," Al says, in a rare bit of philosophizing. "He was never wrong. He was . . . there's a big word that fits in here, I don't know what it is. Kent would know."

"Infallible," Jake supplies, and adds, bitterly, "Then how come he jumped up out of that foxhole without seeing if he'd draw fire first?" As he speaks he can see one of the replacements watching and listening. The new man, a buck private, has been assigned to Amby Garner's old bed. He can't be more than 19, a big, rangy, blond kid, overawed by being thrown in with these combat vets.

Jake should invite the kid in; he knows it. But what part can he play? He didn't know Sgt. Cody. He didn't crawl along that causeway with bullets buzzing by like angry, deadly bees. He never jumped from a plane while tracer bullets made those beautiful, fatal arcs in the sky. What is the point of inviting him in? The eyes of the new kid, appealing, meet Jake's for just a moment, and Jake, rejecting him, looks away.

In the hospital, Kent is missing day after day of arduous training. It goes on through July and August. For the division, alerts come and turn into false alarms until the second week in September, when they are readied for an operation that will not be cancelled.

He says goodbye to June in her tiny room; they toast each other with scotch, a drink Jake likes very little better than warm beer.

"To your safe return," she says.

"I'll drink to that," he answers, and they both sip.

"Last time you promised me nothing would happen to you."

He laughs. "Wasn't I the cocky kid?"

"Aren't you going to promise . . . now?"

"Junebug, I'll do my damnedest."

Her dark eyes get wide and fierce, "No! Last time you promised. And you kept your promise!" She puts her arms around his waist and holds tight. "You're not leaving till you promise."

"The lieutenant is turning into a silly kid."

"I won't let go."

"All right. I promise." He tries to make it sound convincing. She releases him, smiles up at him.

He touches her cheek. "Look, Junebug. If for some reason, we don't see each other again . . ."

"No!"

"All I mean is, suppose they ship us somewhere else after this one. Or you go back and marry your supply officer and I don't even know your married name . . ."

"Miller."

"Or, I may not know where you'll be living."

"Garden City. He loves it there."

"OK! Let's say I send you a nasty letter, and you hate me and never want to have anything to do with me again. Just in case something happens! I want you to know I think you're . . . this is not my specialty. You and I, we never pretended that we . . . either of us, you know. But you really are . . . oh boy. You're a remarkable woman. Someone I like better each time I'm with her. You're grown up; you're smart; you don't play those . . . girl games. You're the first woman ever that I like being with as a . . . a person. All I can say is, this Lieutenant Miller is a lucky guy. I don't want to leave you without your knowing how great I think you are, Junebug."

She puts both her hands on his face. "Oh Jake, can I take you and hide you under my bed, so you never have to go? Isn't that stupid? I'm feeling very stupid, dear Jake, and slightly out of control."

She starts to cry, softly.

"I've got to go."

"Remember your promise."

"I will."

"Keep it!"

He nods.

"I love you, Jake."

"I . . . love you, too, Junebug."

For a moment they just look at each other, then, without their touching, Jake turns and quickly walks off.

Two days later the men are issued ammo and foreign currency. That night, they are in their barracks waiting for another D-Day. Right next to Jake is Kent's empty bunk. It has never been filled because Jake keeps telling Sgt. Grunwald and everyone else that Kent will be back any day, just as Kent keeps assuring Jake he will.

As if reading Jake's thoughts, Al says, "Won't be the same without Kent."

"Who should we feel bad for? Him or us? He's finished with all this. Gets to go home, wearing a Purple Heart. So his arm is banged up. It's not as if he's going to spend his life lifting furniture."

Then Jake looks up and Kent is there, looking drawn and pale, the left side of his face scarred, his left hand stuffed into the front of his fatigue shirt.

"Good evening," he says. "I heard there was a party coming up. Am I in time for the first dance?" He grins at Jake.

Jake does not grin back. "What's with your arm?"

"Never better."

"Then why are you . . . ?" Jake imitates Kent's pose.

"My Napoleon impersonation. Some of the guys outside were shouting, 'Vive l'Empereur!' so I imagine it's fairly good."

"Napoleon didn't need two good arms. He wasn't a paratrooper; he was a general."

"My arm is perfectly good, just a bit sore."

"Want to arm wrestle?"

"It will prove nothing; I never could beat you. Now I want you and Al to help me scrounge some gear."

It is not an isolated scene this night. Men throughout the division, being called fools, knowing they are fools, leave hospitals and infirmaries, bandaged, limping, partially healed, so they can rejoin their units for the privilege of risking their lives. Their reason is simple. It is not patriotism, not a desire to save democracy, not even any particular hatred of the Nazis. Certainly it is not heroism. They just want to be with their buddies.

By the next morning, as they are trucked to the airfields, Kent is fully outfitted and part of the platoon. The morning is socked in with fog, but as the meteorologists predict, by 9 a.m. it is lifting. In harness, the men wait to climb aboard the C-47s.

This time as they sit and wait, something is different. This time they know; the mystery is gone, so are the feelings of bravado and invulnerability. It is not detectable in their conversation; they laugh more this time, joke more, talk more about anything but the mission. But the truth is in their eyes, where innocence has been replaced by knowledge.

"Got the cornet?" Al asks.

"Yeah, in my musette bag. God knows why. Hell, it got me through the last time."

Grunwald barks at them to begin boarding. On Sept. 17, 1944, in broad daylight, the 101st Airborne takes off from its airfields in the southwest of England for Holland, to take part in Operation Market Garden. As the C-47 climbs, the coward inside takes just an instant to remind Jake he hasn't been left behind.

CHAPTER 25

Even through the tension of her busy workdays and the strangeness of her separation, Dede could not stop thinking of Amanda Turnbull, of her tears, her sudden exit from her own living room, all so uncharacteristic of this composed, self-contained woman. Yet she did not call; she was embarrassed to confront Amanda with that loss of composure. She could only wait and hope the older woman would call her. The call came a week later, with an invitation to come over for a simple dinner, though in the event, no dinner was eaten.

Amanda wore a simple sleeveless blouse of deep blue and white linen trousers. Her upper arms showed none of the flaccidity of an older woman's; her jawline was strong and defined. Once again Dede was struck by the strength of her face and body, and by what a week ago she would have called her serenity. Now it looked more like a quiet effort to maintain control.

As the two of them sipped at glasses of champagne in the living room, Amanda began by saying, "Forgive me for behaving the way I did."

"There is nothing to forgive. But I have spent the week wondering why."

"I promise you it was nothing like the week I've spent, half wanting to call you at every moment to say, come over, I must tell you . . . what I have to tell you . . . half deciding I should never tell you at all."

She refilled her glass; Dede, remembering the champagne last time, wondered if perhaps Amanda drank with some regularity. After another sip, Amanda went on.

"Obviously I have decided to tell you. It's a story I'd convinced myself was buried, forgotten, many years ago, yet really knew in my heart of hearts was never forgotten. It is a story of an Army nurse, sent over to England in 1943, sent home pregnant in 1944. You know that story of course. It's also the story of a love-struck girl, barely 19, who through incredible determination, luck, nerve, and her father's connections in Washington, managed to make her way to England in the summer of '44 on a Navy plane. She told herself it was to see her brother, who'd been wounded. And, really, it was. But it was more than that, too. It was to see the young man with whom she was so . . . stricken." Amanda paused, sipped at her glass. When Dede started to speak, she put up a hand to stop her.

"I must tell you the whole story, and you must not interrupt or question, or I may lose the courage to go on. Would you like some more champagne?" Dede shook her head no. "I've come to rely on a glass or two in the evening," Amanda said. "Rely on it perhaps a bit too much."

"The girl got to see her brother. And the man. She got to spend a little time with him, but then a little time was all she had; all any of them had. Her brother told the young woman—for heaven's sake, the girl—that's all she was—told the girl about the Army nurse he was not supposed to know about. But he knew, because he paid careful attention to his Army friend, because he felt very close to him in a way that . . ." Amanda stopped herself, "At any rate, the girl went back to New York just two days later, on the same special Navy plane that had brought her. Many months later, when she wanted to contact the Army nurse, she again used her father's government connections, and found the nurse back in civilian life and living not too far away on Long Island."

"But why," Dede asked, "would you . . . the girl . . . want to find . . . You haven't said why the young woman, the girl, would want to find . . ."

Amanda just put a finger in front of her lips to quiet Dede, "To share something with her. To get help from her. You see, what the two of them shared was more than just their feelings for the soldier. They were, also, both of them, pregnant. The girl did not discover it, or I suppose I should say, want to believe it, for several months after her return from England. Then, while agonizing over her own shame—those were old-fashioned days, when it was shameful—and trying to conceal her condition, which for months was easy—thank goodness she was a big girl rather than a petite one—and trying to decide what to do, she got the news that within days of each other, her brother and the other soldier had both been killed in action. With that came the girl's determination to have the child, as a living, what would you call it?—remembrance?—as a living continuum of her brother and the other soldier. But the romantic impulse is one thing, carrying it out is another. The concealment, under baggy sweaters and loose skirts, became more and more difficult. The prospect of raising such a child became impossible. So the girl went to the nurse for help, which the nurse was very generous about offering and, because of her occupation, in the perfect position to give. She would see to the delivery, arrange an adoption. Then a tragedy occurred, which in a sense, simplified the nurse's job."

Amanda paused. "Perhaps you should have a sip of champagne now."

Not understanding why, but like an obedient child, Dede sipped at her glass, barely tasting the fluid as it slipped down her throat. She did not *know*, but she was beginning to realize.

"First the girl's child was born. Within days, the nurse's child was born—with no chance to live beyond a day or two. The nurse who wanted the child of the dead soldier could not have it. The girl who had the soldier's child was in no position to keep it. And so the agreement was struck. It seemed right and simple at the moment. Perhaps if the girl had been older, had had more chance to think it out, she would have said, 'No, I do not want to know. Send the child to someone far away.' I do not want to lie awake nights—as the girl and then the woman did—knowing my child is so near, and knowing I must not see her or contact her in any way. Which was the hardest thing the girl, then the woman, ever had to do in her life. But something had to be done right then, and after all, who had a closer connection to the child's father than the nurse? And so . . ." Amanda stopped, as if not daring to say it.

"And so, you are telling me that you are my real mother." In answer the older woman just reached out a hand. The younger woman took and held it, in wonder. Asking herself, who am I now?

On a sticky August day in New York, George Whitman met with Roger Wheatley at the Gotham for a drink. Wheatley had called him up in Maine to ask for the meeting and he'd promised it on his next trip to the city, which was for a wedding in Oyster Bay.

The two men touched glasses. "And how is your father?" Whitman asked. Roger Wheatley's full name had a "IV" after it; III was now 75 and an old pal of Whitman's. He'd fought in the war, too, in the Pacific with the navy, and to Whitman that was a bond like no other. Mrs. Wheatley III he could do without.

"Fine, just fine. The usual drill. On their summer cruise—the fjords this year. Then back to Nantucket until Thanksgiving, and down to Hobe Sound. Both in fine health."

Whitman tasted his scotch. Watching the younger man sip his martini, he remembered how much Roger was like his mother

"Glad to hear it. Tell him it's been too long. Anytime he wants to come up to Boothbay Harbor, I've got a dandy little ketch I'd like to show off. As I remember, your mother doesn't like sailing."

Roger smiled. "I'll tell him. And I trust your family is in good health."

"All fine, thank you."

"Well," said Roger. He hesitated. If he was waiting for help from Whitman, he was to be disappointed. He pushed on. "I'd like to talk about Dede Miller."

"All right."

"I like Dede."

"I know. Some of your best friends are . . . women." Whitman was not going to make this easy for Roger.

"George, she seems to trust you in this thing. You'd be doing everyone a favor, if you went to her . . . warned her."

"Warned her? About what?" Whitman's first thought was to tell Roger to get lost. But he wanted to find out more.

"Look, some of the members are really angry. Serious harm could come to her." Roger was growing more uncomfortable, his thick fingers playing with the empty martini glass. What he wanted was to convey the menace without being specific.

Whitman let a little warning of his own come through. "If you're talking about physical harm . . ."

"Of course not!"

"Then what?" When Roger hesitated, Whitman went on. "Look. You want me to warn her. About what? What harm?" With the last two words, he rapped his knuckles on the table hard enough so that three men at the other end of the bar looked up. Roger cringed. Whitman could see that however big a jock Roger may have been, aggressive in football and lacrosse and whatever else he'd played, he was no good at this kind of confrontation. Now Whitman went from bad cop to good cop. He softened his voice. "What shall I warn her about, Roger?"

The younger man almost whispered. "A lot of her business comes through club members."

"And you think you could turn that off? Like a spigot? I'm not sure you could. Is that it?"

"There's a lot of talk about her running for the Senate . . ."

Whitman chuckled. "As a Democrat. The Goth is a gang of Republicans. What can they do? Vote against her?"

"Since the split with Tru, she's been seen out with some unsavory . . . If that came out . . ." Roger could barely manage the words. He was no good at this at all. Whitman liked him the better for it, but barely. Then, suddenly, the reason for this meeting hit him like a thunderbolt. The club vote! If it were going their way, why would Roger need a meeting?

"Roger, what is your sense of the membership vote?" The younger man's face told him he was exactly right.

"The deadline for returning ballots is not until Monday."

"I hear you've already gotten a heavy response."

"You've been out campaigning, writing letters . . ." Roger said.

Whitman smiled faintly. He knew Roger was trying to suggest disapproval without actually expressing it. "I'd call it staying in touch with the old crowd, the ones that don't use the place so much anymore. Ought to do it more often. All right, what's the tally so far?"

"I don't know that it would be proper, before it's completed."

Whitman tried to sound patient. "You want something, Roger. You're going to have be a little more giving yourself. You're the one who keeps saying it's an unofficial, non-binding vote."

"It's really indecisive . . ."

"What is the vote?"

"Very close."

"What is it?"

"709 to 688."

"709 for whom?"

"A slight edge in favor of . . . her."

"Well, well, well. A majority of this club votes to admit a woman! Who's half Jewish! Frankly, I am surprised. Delighted."

"A majority of those voting," Roger emphasized.

"Does Dede know this?"

"No one outside the executive committee knows it but you. And no one need know."

"Too late now."

"George! The vote is only for the purpose of advising the executive committee."

"Yet a majority—yes, of those voting—is in favor of her. So the big "No" vote, which you were counting on, hasn't happened. Which is why you and your group, whoever they may be, are now trying to head this thing off at the pass."

"We are under no obligation to release the vote."

"And I'm under no obligation not to. As a grandson of mine puts it, you can't get the toothpaste back in the tube."

"George!"

"What do you suppose this majority—yes, of those voting—is going to think when they hear of the campaign of sabotage and slander you're planning?" He saw Roger's eyes widen. "No, Roger, I'm under no obligation to keep that a secret either."

Now Whitman was the good cop again. He put a hand on Roger's burly forearm. "You want me to pass your . . . threat . . . along to Dede, to get her to back off. I'll pass it along. It won't work. At least I hope it won't, but that's up to her. I'll also give you some advice. You're no good at this sort of . . . intrigue . . . and it's to your credit. Whoever your ringleader is, tell him to do his own dirty work."

Roger looked miserable. Whitman had little doubt who the ringleader was. And he knew Tru was quite prepared to do his own dirty work.

Billy Vogel and Stan Hartsfield had been friendly adversaries so often they'd become friends, close enough that on an August Sunday, Stan, at his weekend house in Southampton, could call Billy at his weekend house in Easthampton, to suggest a very informal meeting to "wrap up the Martindale matter." Billy invited him over at once for a walk on the beach.

Hartsfield, still wearing the tennis whites and shoes in which he'd been playing at his club, pulled his Jeep up behind the Mercedes and the BMW in Vogel's garage, walked around the house and onto the brick patio, from which a path led across the dunes and onto the beach. Vogel, in a pink polo shirt and a baggy old pair of chino shorts, was sitting on a chaise, doing the *New York Times* crossword puzzle.

"In ink!" said Hartsfield. "I'm impressed."

"That's the whole idea," replied Vogel. "Of course the letters aren't right. They're just letters, any letters. But who's gonna know?"

As they headed for the beach, the two were a study in contrasts, Hartsfield tall, lanky, fair skinned, with blonde hair fast receding, although he was only 35; Vogel, 20 years older, a head shorter, 40 pounds heavier, his body hairy, his hair a thick mat of gray curls. When they got to the head of the dunes and were about to descend to the beach, Hartsfield turned and looked back at Vogel's beautiful old clapboard house, white with dark blue shutters and awnings, sprawling along its beachfront lot so that its two stories each offered a dozen windows to the ocean.

"I dream about owning a place like that," said the younger lawyer fervently.

"So, make me an offer," Vogel countered with a grin.

"Maybe in ten more years of slaving and scrimping."

"Poor fella, I'll wrap a CARE package for you."

They both enjoyed this bit of role playing: Vogel as one of the affluent stars of divorce law, Hartsfield as the struggling novice. In fact, Hartsfield was high-priced, brilliant, and hungry as only a boy brought up poor can be. Though he looked like a product of prep schools and the Ivy League, he was actually the son of English immigrants from the Midlands, who'd worked his way through a midwestern state university with two and three part-time jobs, a WASP who had most in common with the men who were usually his opponents—second generation Jews, Italians, and Irish who had grown up on the edge of shabbiness and were determined never to go back.

Vogel felt there was no harm in throwing the first punch. "He's got piles of dough. *He* left *her*. And she doesn't want a cent! You must feel guilty about taking the fee, Stan."

Hartsfield laughed. "Not till I can afford a house on the beach."

"Seriously. My client is nuts to be so . . . amenable. But she is. There shouldn't be a problem here, Stan." He looked to Hartsfield, who shrugged.

"So what is it?" asked Vogel. "The Southampton house?"

"The problem is, he's angry." Hartsfield stopped, stared down at the sand.

"Hell, he's the one who wants the divorce! You'd think he'd want to wrap it up ASAP!"

With the long pale big toe of his right foot, Hartsfield started tracing letters in the sand. First a G. Then O-T-H-A-M. "That's the problem."

Vogel looked down, had trouble making out the letters. Finally, he said, "Gotham? I don't get it."

"That's the hot button issue. She wants to get into his old-line club, that his great-grandfather or somebody founded. He is opposed to that . . . rabidly."

"Why?"

"It doesn't take women or Jews."

"So Diana has two strikes against her . . . one and a half, anyway."

They were at the point where Georgica pond reached almost to the Atlantic, separating Wainscott from East Hampton. Vogel stopped, looked around. The morning had clouded over and an ocean breeze was riling up the surf. Such days, not calm, sunny, blue-skied ones, were the times he really loved the beach, with its stark palette of bleached tans and grays.

"Beautiful place, isn't it?" Vogel said. "Makes you want to become a beachcomber, get rid of all the bullshit in your life and spend it right here."

"Speak for yourself," answered Hartsfield with a smile as they turned and started back.

"You'll be saying the same thing in 20 years, Stan. Maybe sooner."

"*After* I've got the beach house." They walked in silence for a while.

"Here's what I don't get, Stan. If he's so unhappy about the club thing, isn't that all the more reason he should want to get rid of her, finish off the divorce?"

"I don't have to tell you about angry spouses, Billy. Right now he's more interested in punishing her, making things messy, screwing up her life . . . and her chances to run for the Senate."

"So the answer is . . ."

"The club. Just tell her to forget the lousy club, and we can wrap things up real easy."

"Stan? Why is there never room for us at the inn?" Vogel's tone was only half joking.

"He wouldn't want a woman in the club even if she weren't half Jewish," Hartsfield replied.

"Oh. Now I feel a lot better."

When the phone rang Ken was sitting in his big old cracked-leather easy chair, his laptop on his knees, staring at the screen. Although the computer made his work much easier, every once in a while he wished he could pull a piece of paper out of it, crumple it and hurl it the length of the room to vent his frustration. Resenting the phone interruption, he took his time, letting it go to the fifth ring before picking it up.

"It was great running into you the other night."

That was just like Jane Reich. Before that "other night" they hadn't spoken for a year and a half, yet she began as if it had been five minutes.

A couple of years back, buffeted by a divorce, bored with women whose idea of writing was Danielle Steel, he thought when he met Jane that he'd found the perfect girl. She not only knew who Gabriel Garcia Marquez was, she'd actually read *One Hundred Years Of Solitude*. She was smart and funny. She went to the opera. She worked at a Madison Avenue gallery and knew art. She was very attractive—arresting if not beautiful—with long shiny brown hair, slender legs, and riveting dark eyes. She was sexy; she was Jewish.

She was also rich, used to having her way, and prepared to manipulate relentlessly to get it. Her way included dinner parties five nights a week, with her showing off her National Book Award nominee, suitably dressed in custom-made English suits paid for by her. He began to see himself as a trophy date.

He suggested it might be nice if they could stay home together a few nights a week, just reading or listening to music or making love. He insisted he did not want her to buy him expensive suits and shirts and ties and shoes. She countered that going out was for her both a business necessity and a choice of life style. She said they had a partnership in which he supplied certain things and she supplied certain things. He said he wouldn't mind at all if she were to find other partners for some of her outings; she took that as something he hadn't intended, a kiss-off. When he called a few days later to see if she wanted to go out for a movie and pizza, she said she was busy for the indefinite future.

A year and a half went by after that last phone call. Then one night, as he sat at the bar of the Madison Pub, having a turkey sandwich and a beer, half reading a magazine and half talking to George the bartender, she walked in.

"What a lovely surprise!" she said. "I was looking for someone and, well, here you are!"

She stayed to have a drink and then he walked her to the monumental building at Park and 92nd where she had an oversized apartment. The stroll reminded him of all the things he'd liked about her: the brains, the wit, the vitality, the eyes, the legs. She invited him up for a drink; he said no, but he'd thought about her since. She waited a week to phone.

"It was wonderful seeing you," he told her. "You looked sensational. As usual."

"Thank you, Kenny, if I'd known, I would have worn something better. It was such a marvelous surprise! To think I'd run into you in a place like that!"

He laughed into the phone. "Now that we're madly out of love with each other, let's talk straight. That simple little linen suit you wish you'd been wearing something better than, must have cost a thousand bucks. And

George told me you'd been in the place looking around two or three times a week for the past month."

"That's one of the things I treasure in you, Kenny, straight talk. Yes, let's talk straight. I've missed you. I have been dropping in there hoping to see you. And the suit cost 1400."

"Good for you, Jane."

"More straight talk. I'd like to have a drink and discuss the mistakes I've made. Would you be willing?"

"Would a drink be enough time? Just kidding. Why not a drink?"

Dede had developed the ability to focus on the task at hand with a kind of tunnel vision, excluding all else around her, and that stood her well now. Though she and Amanda spoke on the phone every day, she slogged through her busy days as if nothing had changed, although almost everything had. She dealt with her business, her political meetings, her family—now reduced to two, with one of them, Jimmy, away much of the time—and her social life, its surface now riled up by Denny Knight.

Determined to go on with a "normal" life, although she no longer had much idea of what that was supposed to be, she saw no reason to refuse Denny's invitation for a Saturday drive to his house in Southampton, spend a few hours on the beach, have lunch on his terrace, drive back in the early evening. She missed the beach. With Tru ensconced in their summer house, it was for the moment off-limits to her.

Driving out in Knight's second Rolls, this one a tan Corniche, with the top down, knowing she sounded like a prig, she asked, "When you drive a car like this, do you ever think of the starving people in the Sudan?"

"I prefer to think of the English auto workers who might starve if people like me didn't buy Rollses."

"Are you ever serious?"

"I told you," he said. "I gave it up when I turned 50. I give money to famine relief. I also drive a Rolls and love every minute of it!"

His house was six years old, an important design statement by a noted South Fork architect. Its assembly of boxes and turrets had decorated the pages of *The New York Times*, *House & Garden*, and *Architectural Record*. Looking at it from the beach in earlier summers, she'd considered it an eye-catching scar on the dunes. Now when he asked what she thought of it, she was diplomatic. "Interesting, but I'm an old bore. You know: white clapboard, shutters, brick chimneys, dormer windows."

On the beach, when she removed the long T-shirt over her modest one-piece black suit, she was uneasy. Her upper arms and shoulders were too pale, her body too soft to suit her, despite her relentless exercise. The problem, she said to herself, is that I am 45 and nobody with two eyes would mistake that for 25, or even 35. More than that, her uneasiness came from being thought of and thinking of herself as a "date." She hadn't been one for 20 years, never imagined she'd have to be one again.

She watched Denny setting up the chairs he'd brought from the house. Though he was powerful and thick-chested, as he bent over she could see he'd gone fleshy around the middle in a way that a naturally slender man like Tru hadn't. But his arms and thighs were big and muscled, twice the size of Tru's, and there was no softness there. When he straightened up she noticed the long scars on both knees, the result, she was sure, of football injuries. She smiled to herself at what story Ken Glass might invent about them. Lifting her eyes from Denny's knees, she saw him openly appraising her.

"You look great!" he said, with the enthusiasm of a boy. "Great body. You must really work out."

"Not as much as I should," she said, not knowing what else to say. "What happened to your knees?"

When he replied, "Football," she thought of Glass again. "A little pain a lot of the time," he said. "Still ski, though. And play tennis. Doctor told me to stick to doubles. I ignore him. Except when I sit down, then my knees remind me." His grin turned to a grimace as he settled himself on the chair.

Stretched out in the sun, she struggled to relax, make her mind a blank screen. But without a task to concentrate on, across that screen crawled the thoughts and images she'd been able to suppress all week: of her "real" mother and father, the husband divorcing her, the son hating the divorce, the club members riled up at her. And the two phone calls, both in the past week: Vogel telling her that if she gave up on the club, the divorce would be easy; Whitman with the surprising good news, the club vote was favorable, and the unsurprising bad news, Tru and his clique were out to hurt her. Finally, she got to her feet, ran down the beach, racing to stir up the endorphins, those natural tranquilizers she'd read about that made you forget your troubles for a while.

When she got back, Denny wasn't there, so she headed up to the house, where a Colombian housekeeper was setting the table for lunch *al fresco*. The woman smiled at her and pointed to the side of the house.

"Mr. Knight?"

"Si, Meester Knight." She smiled gratefully at Dede for understanding, and pointed again.

Dede smiled back at her and walked to the side of the house, saw a wooden door in a quadrangle of high privet hedges. She pushed the door open, looked in. Denny sat naked in a hot tub, eyes closed, smiling up at the sun. On the deck next to his arm stood a pitcher of orange juice and an open bottle of champagne in an ice bucket. Two glasses stood next to the bucket, one empty, one half empty, or, she thought, as Denny would say, half full.

She might have retreated, had not the squeaking of the door made him open his eyes.

"Hi!" he said. "Take off your suit, come in, have a mimosa."

She hesitated, trying so hard to look only at his face that she was sure the effort was showing. "I'd rather leave it on," she said, feeling very stuffy.

He handled it with his imperturbable smile. "All right. Come in; have a mimosa. Take the suit off when you feel like it."

She climbed into the tub, sitting alongside him rather than across, making it easier for her eyes to avoid his penis, which despite her best efforts, she could see was being wafted to and fro like a sleepy eel. He filled both glasses, handed her one.

"Cheers," he said.

"Cheers." They both sipped.

He looked into her eyes. "You're not relaxed," he said.

"No, I'm not."

"Because I have no suit on?"

"Yes."

Still smiling he shook his head. "Wrong. You were tense driving out here. You were tense lying on the beach. When you got up to jog, there was so much tension crackling out of you, I could almost see the sparks."

"Yes," she said. "I was. I am. Maybe the champagne will help." And indeed it did. With the help of the heat, the sun, the lack of lunch, two swallows had gone to her head.

"Do you know the danger of sitting naked in a hot tub, with a mimosa?"

"I think I have an idea," she said, trying to smile.

"Wrong again," he said. "The danger is that you will feel so relaxed, you'll fall asleep and slip under the water. But don't worry, it will wake you soon enough. It's happened to me when I've been in here with three women."

"You've been in this tub with *three* women?"

"We *all* fell asleep. But you won't."

"I know. I'm too tense." She held out her glass; he refilled it. She took another sip, waited for him to say something, when he didn't, she looked over, saw him with his head back, eyes closed, smiling, she did the same. The water, the sun, the alcohol, were putting her into a dream state. In that state, her swimsuit seemed so much a symbol of her tenseness, so irrelevant, its straps binding, its snugness keeping the warm water from caressing her body. With each sip of the mimosa, she became surer that he was right about the suit, whatever it was he said. Again she looked to him; his eyes closed, the smile on his face. He seemed so much a child, she had to giggle at the idea that this was the most dangerous "cocksman"—the word Mary Wheatley used in a warning phone call—in New York.

He looked so harmless, she reached with her right hand to her left shoulder strap, slid it down her arm, lifted her arm out of the strap, then repeated the movement on the other side. She pulled the suit down to her waist, intending to leave it there. But she thought that ridiculous. It somehow seemed lascivious to be sitting half naked, and besides, the water on her bare top half made her clothed bottom half feel so confined. This time she forced herself not to see if he was watching as she slipped her suit below her waist, below her hips, below her thighs, off her legs. She wrung it out, put it on the deck near her before she dared to look down.

Only then did she examine herself, gazing at her pale breasts, sagging a bit more than she'd like them to, but not bad—thank God for not having big breasts, they didn't age well—her pubic hair dark in the tub, her thighs fuller than she'd like them to be. This time when she looked over, he was staring at her.

"You should go around naked all the time."

"Shut up," she answered, shutting her eyes as if that could keep him from seeing.

"Now that we've both seen what we both look like naked, let's relax."

"Denny, you're not going to do . . . anything. Please do not do anything." She was mumbling the words.

"You mean you don't want me to stroke your breasts, play with the nipples, very gently."

"No!"

"And you don't want me to lean over, take your breasts in my mouth, suck the nipples?"

"Denny!"

"Just want to be clear about what it is you don't want." She was trying not to imagine how his hands and mouth would feel. His smile seemed to say he knew exactly what she was trying not to imagine. Now she could see what made him so dangerous.

"Don't want me to put my hand between your legs, stroke you? Or would you rather stroke yourself? Go ahead. If you don't know what that feels like in a hot tub, you don't know anything."

"Stop it, Denny!" She started when he moved his arm, but it was to refill their glasses, this time only with champagne. He handed her a glass; she put it down without drinking from it.

"And do you know what it would feel like if you just rolled over onto me, and I slipped into you, with the warm water stroking us and the sun shining down on us? Have you ever had a man slide into you in a hot tub, Dede, slide in and out, with the warm water bathing you, with his arms around you? Have you, Dede?"

"No! And I'm not going to this time, either!" With a great effort, she managed to get to her feet and climb out of the tub. As she stood above him, naked, dripping, she could see the sleepy eel was waking up. "You're an expert at this game, Denny, and I'm no good at it at all. I'm not going to play." She looked around, grabbed a beach towel, wrapped herself in it and went into the house to find her clothes.

In t-shirt, Bermuda shorts, and tennis shoes, she re-appeared on the terrace, feeling embarrassed and angry and uncomfortable. Denny, in a terrycloth robe, sat at the table set up for lunch, glass still in his hand. Smiling, he looked at her as if they'd never been in a hot tub together. Naked.

"How would an omelette and salad be?"

"Denny, I'm going back to the city."

"It's a sin to go back on a weekend like this; God only allots a certain number of them. We can have dinner at the G&T." The Golf and Tennis was Southampton's second oldest and most restricted club, its clubhouse and tennis courts a ten-minute walk along the beach from Denny's house.

"The G&T doesn't take Jews."

"You're my guest."

"You miss the point."

"We'll go somewhere else."

"I'm going back."

"I won't do that again."

"Of course you will, Denny! It's what you *do*! Sorry to have wasted a weekend for you. So many women and so few weekends."

The smile almost faded from Knight's face. "Dede, do you know what I think happened when I turned 50 and dropped all my seriousness? I think you saw it lying there and picked it up. Lighten up. Life is too short." His smile returned gently.

"How did they say it in the movie, what we've got here is a failure to communicate. You brought me out here to fuck me. I didn't come out here to be fucked. And like a fool, I find myself apologetic. I'm going to call a cab now so I can catch the next jitney back to the city."

"Let's have lunch and then I'll drive you back."

"Thanks, no. I'm not hungry and I don't want to sit in your car for two hours and go round and round on this."

She got back to her apartment a little after 4, on a hazy, steamy August day, a day on which no one she knew would be in the city. She longed for a friend to talk to, picked up the phone, realized that its 20-number memory had in it only one name that did not belong to family or business or service people. That name was Mary Wheatley's, and the Wheatleys were in Southampton. She put down the phone, found Ken Glass's number, punched it in, sure he would not be home. For four rings she was right, then he picked up. Elation washed over her as she heard his hello.

"You must have a big apartment."

"Who is this?" he asked. Only then did she realize she hadn't even identified herself.

"Oh. Sorry. It's . . ."

"Diana?"

"Yes, it took you so many rings."

"It's quite a small apartment, but I was in the middle of an important thought. No, not important. Clever."

"Sorry."

"Another one will come along, sooner or later. How are you?"

"All right. I've been better."

"Want me to come right out there and throw a life preserver into the hot tub?"

"How did you know?"

"Denny and I have few secrets from each other. He tells me about his love life. I lie to him about mine. Is he listening?"

"I'm in my apartment. I . . . I thought I'd like to go out and listen to some jazz tonight. I was hoping you might suggest a place."

"I know just the place."

"Good." Actually, not good. She wanted him to say, I'll take you.

"Here." Better.

"Your apartment?"

"Yup. Benny Goodman is here. Artie Shaw, Glenn Miller, Basie, Sinatra. Ellington. Crowded as hell, but oh the music!"

"I'll bring a bottle of wine. For the two of us. The musicians will have to do without."

"A jug of wine, Chinese takeout . . . and Sinatra beside us singing in the wilderness. Paradise enow."

She found the brownstone on 95th Street between Madison and Fifth, walked up four flights to an apartment with a large living room, modest bedroom, kitchenette, and a tiny terrace facing south. Almost all the wall space was taken up by bookshelves, on them thousands of books, magazines, records, tapes, CDs, sheaves of notes, parts of manuscripts. In one corner the floor was piled with more books. In another stood the cracked leather easy chair, against a wall a lumpy old convertible sofa covered in worn blue corduroy. On a big worktable sat a laptop, a printer, an old manual typewriter, a stack of books, another of magazines, a third of newspapers, a fourth of clippings, and a disordered arrangement of pages, manuscript and notes, typed and handwritten. Through the doorway to the bedroom she could see the unmade double bed, more bookshelves, more piles of books on the floor.

She handed him the wine. He took two glasses from the cupboard, went to work with a primitive corkscrew.

"I'd rather have a glass of water first," she said. "I've had a bit of champagne in Southampton."

"Want to tell me about it?"

"Taittinger. Vintage. Excellent."

"Champagne ages well. Venture capitalists don't."

She smiled at him. "You're fun to talk to."

"Have to be. I don't have a hot tub."

"Were you watching us on closed circuit TV?"

"Would I have liked it?"

"You would have been bored."

"Good."

"Now let's listen to music."

He found an audio cassette, put it into his player. Out came the sound of Glenn Miller.

He pointed to the lumpy sofa. "You sit there, left side. No busted springs there. I sit in my old leather chair."

When they were settled, he affected the tones of a classical DJ. "We begin with several selections by Glenn Miller and his orchestra. The first, 'Chattanooga Choo Choo,' is of particular historical interest because it was the number one selling record in the country on December 7th, 1941, when the Japanese attacked Pearl Harbor. The value of the Miller oeuvre as a whole is that more than any other band it evokes the feeling of dancing in the Swing Era. For cutting a rug, nothing would do but Miller tunes like this one or 'In The Mood,' or 'String Of Pearls.' My own parents could still be seen in the 80s lindying to 'Tuxedo Junction.' That last fact will not be on the exam."

"Are your parents good dancers?"

"My mother is . . ." He waved his hands in an equivocal gesture. "My father is really good."

"And you?"

He cast his eyes down in mock modesty. "I cannot tell a lie. I take after my father. And you?"

"Not bad, although it's been so long I've almost forgotten. I know I used to love it. Perhaps I take after my father. My real father. He was a jazz musician, a trumpet player. Quite a good one, I'm told. Have I told you that?"

"No! Remarkable! A Jew and a jazz musician: the perfect father. As would be required to produce a remarkable daughter."

"Kenneth, are you proud of being a Jew?"

"Sure. As proud as you should be of something that is nothing you've done, but rather an accident of birth."

"Do you ever go to a synagogue?"

"No. I'm an ethnic Jew, not a religious Jew."

"Explain."

"Let's take Tru Martindale. By ethnic origin he's Anglo-Saxon. By religion, Episcopalian. He could convert to, let's say Catholicism, but he could never convert from being Anglo-Saxon to, let's say, Italian. To be a Jew is to be a member of an ethnic group, and also, possibly, a religion. I could convert to Episcopalianism, but I would remain an ethnic Jew."

"It's wonderful to have such a sure sense of who you are."

"What's that supposed to mean?"

She told him about her mother. "So now my DNA—my genetic code—is 100 percent different from what I thought it was."

"Not to reflect on your original parents, it doesn't sound like you've done too badly, genetically speaking, with your new ones. A WASP aristocrat and a talented Jewish war hero."

"But it makes me someone entirely different!"

"Nonsense. When I first met you, you were a smart, stunning, sexy, desirable woman. Right now you're exactly the same woman, about whom, by the way, I am nuts."

"Kenneth . . . I'm not sure you should be saying that."

"I am. And I'm glad you're here, not in the hot tub."

"I'm glad to be here. And not in the hot tub."

"I have a confession to make," he said. "Denny and I made a bet. When he told me he was driving out there with you, I said something really childish, like, she's not like all the others."

"And he said I was."

"No. Not exactly. He's not a bad guy, really."

"Just thinks he can screw every woman he gets his hands on. Well, you won your bet."

"I'm glad. Not for the money." He laughed. "It was for all of five bucks."

"I feel so comfortable here with you," she said, "Relaxed. Safe."

"Gee, I was hoping to be thought just a little bit dangerous."

"Men are such boys. Phone for the Chinese food." The Miller band went into "Skylark." Ken got to his feet.

"Let's dance." He held out his arms in fox-trot position. She looked up at him. "Whoever you are." She wanted the comfort of his soft voice, the liveliness of his gentle humor. She wanted to be in his arms. She stood, walked to him, let the arms fold around her. As he moved into a simple two-step, he was surprisingly light and easy to follow. It had been so long since she danced with a man she'd forgotten how much she missed it. He kept the beat beautifully. The steps don't matter nearly as much as the rhythm does, just move to the music, her father used to tell her. Her old father. Forget that. Just relax in his arms, "I *am* crazy about you, Diana."

She looked up at him. "Dede," she said. "People close to me call me Dede."

"I want to get as close to you as I can. Dede." He leaned down to kiss her. As she tilted her head up, she felt the same surge of longing that had come over her, unannounced and unwanted, in the hot tub. Only this time it was not unwanted. Let it happen, she told herself; let it happen.

Later, after won ton soup, General Tso's chicken, and sweet and sour shrimp, he walked her downstairs to find a cab. As she was about to climb into it, he kissed her again. This time she put both arms around him and hugged him as hard as she could.

At her building, she gave Mac the doorman a cheery "Good evening," and was surprised when he responded with, "Do you have a minute, Mrs. Martindale?

"Sure."

He motioned her off to one side. John McCarthy was a retired cop, a handsome, broad-faced man who in his uniform always looked to Dede more like a general than a doorman.

"Mrs. Martindale, I don't want to alarm you or anything."

"What's the problem?"

"Do you know you're being followed?"

"No." At once she thought of Tru.

"I've seen 'em the past week or so. I was waiting to be sure. I'm sure."

She nodded. "Thanks, Mac."

Next morning, at what she thought was a reasonable hour for a Sunday, she phoned Billy Vogel in Easthampton; his wife had to fetch him from the beach.

"Sorry to bother you on a weekend, Billy."

Vogel chuckled. "You'll pay for it." She liked him because though he was one of the best divorce lawyers in the city, he was not one those take-no-prisoners guys called bombers. Dede could envision him standing, wet and sandy, in a bathing suit while she started to tell him about being followed. She was surprised at the abruptness of his answer.

"This is not something we should discuss now."

"It will only take a moment."

"Not now!" Vogel's voice was so peremptory it was almost harsh and she regretted having called him on the weekend. "Tell you what. I'll be coming back to the city this evening. Can you meet me at . . . 8:30?"

"Where?"

"My apartment all right? I live at 789 Park."

"Fine."

789 Park Avenue was a smallish building, its tiny lobby gleaming with marble and polished mahogany. Vogel's apartment was on the 12th floor; like every one in the building it was the only one on its floor. When the housekeeper let her in, she looked around with a professional eye. She'd seen a couple of the apartments in this building, but none that had been as thoroughly re-done as this one, all ultra modern, with glass brick and walls sculpted in grotesque organic shapes.

In a moment Vogel came padding in, barefoot, wearing blue jeans and a red-and-blue striped, short-sleeved knit shirt with a Ralph Lauren polo player on it. With his broad chest and thick hairy forearms he looked to Dede like someone who relished a fight, of any kind. In his stubby hand he carried an open bottle of beer.

"Traffic bad?" she asked, beginning the litany that all Long Island weekenders went through. A drive that took less than two hours in the best of times could take four on the worst of summer weekends.

"Took me about 40 minutes," he said.

"Forty minutes? What's your secret?"

"Helicopter," he replied. "I work like hell all week. When I take a weekend off, I want it to be fun. If I have to fight the Long Island Expressway, there goes the fun. The chopper's expensive, but what am I working for?" He shrugged.

"I didn't mean to break into your weekend . . ."

"Hey, don't worry about it for an instant. As I said, you'll pay for it!"

"I had the feeling I was imposing. I could almost see you on the phone, dripping wet. I wouldn't want to talk either."

Vogel got it. "Oh! That! The weekend had nothing to do with that. I'd just as soon matrimonial clients not tell me valuable information over the phone, especially not when they're calling from home. You never can tell . . ."

"You don't think my phone could be tapped?"

"Don't look so surprised. Let me tell you about divorce cases. At the beginning, so many clients are so protective of their spouses—oh, no, she wouldn't do this, he wouldn't do that. Then when things heat up and they begin to see what people can and will do when they're angry or vengeful, they usually end up believing there's nothing the other one wouldn't do. Which is a little closer to reality." He took another swig of his beer. "So my motto is, better safe."

"This is going to sound like you've written the script. I think I'm being followed."

Vogel's bright brown eyes widened. "What makes you think so? Spot somebody?"

She shook her head. "My doorman. He's an ex-cop. He says he's noticed them for about a week."

Vogel nodded. "First question: What have they seen? Been doing anything you shouldn't?"

She hesitated; Vogel caught it. "Listen to me, Diana. The double standard lives! The woman is much more vulnerable than the man. In divorce proceedings. And in running for the Senate."

She started to speak, but he put a hand up.

"A word to the wise," he said. "That's all. Next question: You wouldn't happen to know if your husband is fooling around, would you?" This time Vogel was looking for the hesitation. "Come on, Diana!"

"I would happen to know. Yes, he is."

"How do you know?"

"I . . . I know."

Vogel seemed delighted. "We've got it made," he said enthusiastically. "Opposing counsel is a pro. He will understand his client is playing a dangerous game. He'll call off the tail in a minute. Unless . . ." Vogel hesitated. "Unless you want to play their game. Go after him."

"No."

"I realize you've said that before. But as I've said before, sometimes when the case heats up, minds get changed."

"No!"

"Remember, he's having you followed! What do you suppose he wants to do with that information?"

"NO!"

"OK, OK. Next question: Why do you suppose, in a case where he's left you, and there seems to be no financial or property dispute, he'd want to get something on you?"

She started to say she didn't know, stopped herself abruptly. "There's only one reason. I'm trying to get into his club."

"... the Gotham, which admits no women or Jews. Bingo. You hit the jackpot. Now, again, I'm going to make a suggestion, which you are free to say no to. If the club is the sticking point, if it's the issue that will turn this divorce into a battle, a nasty, expensive, and very public battle, then why not drop it and make life easy for yourself?"

"No."

"What does this club have, a very good swimming pool or something?"

"It doesn't have a pool. Most of the people are bores. I'd probably never use it."

"Are you doing it to get him?"

She had to think for a moment. "No."

"Then what?"

"Do I have to explain that to another Jew?"

"*Another* Jew?" He looked surprised, then smiled gently. "You don't consider yourself a Jew, do you?"

She sighed. "What do you consider me?"

"Forgive me, it's hard to see you as anything but the prototypical WASP."

"Tell that to my husband. Tell it to Roger Wheatley. Do you see the problem, Billy? They don't think of me as one of them anymore. And you don't think of me as one of you. What does that make me?"

"Sometimes life is complicated. But I know a way to make yours easier."

"How?"

"Forget about the club."

"No."

He nodded, as if glad she'd rejected his advice. "You want to fight? We'll fight. Just be careful, *shayna maidel.*"

She looked puzzled.

"It means lovely girl. In Yiddish."

CHAPTER 26

September, 1944

The Marine First Division lands on Peleliu in the South Pacific, meets fierce resistance from Japanese troops holed up in the island's network of caves. The Soviets begin a massive offensive in the Baltic aimed at the cities of Riga and Tallinn. The Eighth Army, moving north in Italy, crosses the Rubicon.

President Roosevelt, campaigning for a fourth term, and his Republican opponent, Governor Thomas E. Dewey, both have star-studded campaign rallies, Roosevelt's at Madison Square Garden in New York, Dewey's at the Los Angeles Coliseum. Celebrities for Roosevelt include Bette Davis, Orson Welles, Katharine Hepburn, and Helen Keller; for Dewey, Ginger Rogers, Adolphe Menjou, Gene Tierney, and Walt Disney.

Hit records: "Swinging On A Star," Bing Crosby; "G.I. Jive," Louis Jordan and his Tympany Five; "You Always Hurt The One You Love," The Mills Brothers; "I'll Walk Alone," Dinah Shore.

Once again, the C-47s, weighed down by men and equipment, struggle to lift off the ground, then organize themselves into the formations in which they will fly to Holland. Staring down the two rows of men, every one but him smoking, Jake notices which of the 16 are new: Sgt. Grunwald, Tom the blond kid replacing Amby, and the replacement for Pete from Cincinnati, whose last name Jake could never get right and whose status has just been changed from missing to killed in action. Pete's replacement is a dark, muscular boy from Springfield, Mass.—Cindy's hometown, but Jake tries not to think about that. Kent, Al, Lt. Sobchak, and Cpl. Forgione were wounded but are back.

In daylight, the view is majestic. The English Channel is laid out beneath them, dotted with the rescue boats ready to help any plane that goes down over water. Then they reach the Belgian countryside, flying low enough to see people in front of their houses, vehicles on the roads, horses in the fields. It is a tranquil flight until they cross the border into Holland, about ten minutes from the drop zones.

Then the flak comes up at them in black and gray bursts, sporadic at first, then so thick it looks like you could walk across the sky on the puffs. The planes are bounced around like toys, but this time the pilots, veterans like the paratroopers, take no evasive action and hold their tight formations perfectly.

A plane to their left front gets hit and bursts into flames. One chute opens from it, a second, before it tumbles to earth and explodes. Even before their red light comes on, Lt. Sobchak orders them to stand up and hook up. He wants them to be ready to get out should their plane be hit. And just two minutes from the drop zone, they are rocked by an explosion, see half the right wing torn away. Smoke, then flames, begin shooting from it. From the cockpit the crew chief yells, "Everybody out! We'll try to ride this thing down!"

"Move up!" Sobchak shouts at them. "Get ready to go! Go!" The lieutenant is out the door, then Cpl. Forgione. In the third position, just ahead of Jake, is Tom, the new blond kid. He gets to the door, grabs the sides—and freezes. Jake, expecting him to go, runs up his back. But he doesn't move. The plane is losing altitude, in a couple of minutes it will be too low for jumping.

Behind Jake everyone is shouting. Jake himself, without knowing it, is yelling "Go, go, go!" to the kid, who remains frozen. Jake looks up to make sure the kid's static line is hooked up. Then he leans back on Kent for support, puts a foot in the small of the kid's back and shoves him out the door, following right behind him. Jake's chute pops out of its pack, he can hear the canopy rattling as it unfurls. It opens with a powerful jolt and he begins his float to earth. Ahead of him he can see the chutes of his stick blossom as the plane continues downward, held on course by a pilot who is sacrificing his own chances to make sure the troopers have time to get out. As he floats to earth, Jake's eyes follow the C-47 down. It crashes and explodes. He hopes that one of those chutes belonged to the pilot, but he doubts it.

Around Jake the air is filled with paratroopers. There is no ground fire and the jump is so consolidated it all seems like an exercise, its greatest danger the risk of getting tangled with another jumper. Despite their plane's being hit, Jake's stick is just where it should be, part of what turns out to be the most successful landing the division has ever achieved, in training or combat. In a half hour, 6700 men land in a concentrated area with a casualty rate of less than two percent.

The objective of Operation Market Garden is to send the British 30th Corps shooting north into Holland and across the lower Rhine. The big barrier of that river having been crossed, the Allies can continue north to the Zuider Zee, cutting off German forces to the west, and then sweep east into northern Germany.

The airborne role is to be played by three divisions, dropping behind enemy lines to seize 50 miles of road and open a north-south corridor for the British armor. That stretch of road will come to be known as Hell's Highway.

The British First Airborne, with a brigade of Polish paratroopers attached, is assigned the northern sector, around Arnhem with its bridge across the Rhine, which will become famous as "a bridge too far." Below them, the 82nd Airborne is to take the central stretch of the road around Nijmegen and Grave, with their bridges over the Waal and Maas rivers. The 101st is assigned the southernmost part of the corridor, 16 miles extending from Uden on the north to Eindhoven on the south. Its responsibility includes bridges over two large rivers and two canals. With the terrain as flat as a pancake, waterways are the principal barriers to the northward movement of armor, men, and supplies. And so capturing bridges becomes essential.

The 502nd is dropped in the midst of its objectives. The First Battalion, assigned to take the town of St. Oedenrode, has only a short trip to the northeast. The rest of the regiment, which will guard the drop zone and serve as division reserve, will hold where it lands.

From this prosaic plan unfolds a drama for Jake's H Company that turns out to be grueling and deadly and memorable: a drama that is part tragedy, part macabre farce, and part epic. Oddly enough, it is played out because of a mission that is not even part of the original battle plan, but rather an afterthought by the division commander, Gen. Maxwell Taylor.

The small town of Best is not on Hell's Highway; it lies six miles west of it. About a mile south of Best there is a bridge across one of the chief water barriers, the Wilhelmina Canal. General Taylor's afterthought is to send a small force to take Best and the nearby bridge, to offer an alternative route for the British, should the bridge on the main route be blown. It is a task at first thought so insignificant that only a platoon is assigned to it. But at the request of Third Battalion commander Lt. Col. Cole, regiment agrees to expand that force to a company and add to it a platoon of engineers and a machine gun section. H Company is chosen.

Under Capt. Smith's command, they start out and almost immediately go wrong. It is Smith's intention to head southwest from the drop zone so as to hit the road 1000 yards below Best and proceed south to the bridge. But making their way through a heavy forest, they lose their bearings, come out of the woods only 400 yards south of Best, a 600-yard error that at once puts them under heavy fire from unexpectedly strong German units in the town. The company takes casualties and becomes dispersed.

Capt. Smith radios back to battalion about the resistance, and is ordered to send his Second Platoon, with the engineers and machine gunners, down to the bridge at once. He dispatches them on their way under Lt. Sobchak, and moves the rest of his company back to the protection of the forest, where they dig in.

The Second Platoon moves through the forest, staying low, not sure where the main force of Germans is. On both flanks they are harassed by intermittent sniper fire that is too light to stop them but heavy enough to cause casualties.

"What's happening; where are we headed?" Kent asks the soldier's eternal question.

"Wait a minute," Jake says, "I'll call Ike." He mimes putting a phone to his ear. "Line is busy."

"Funny, Bix. We could die laughing. Where are we headed, Al?"

"Dunno."

"Now there's a proper answer."

As they move south through the forest, Lt. Sobchak finds himself with a group already reduced in size and soon to be reduced further. Sniper fire continues to be so troubling he sends out a patrol to suppress it. The patrol gets separated from the platoon and never rejoins it. As the platoon continues, taking more casualties, the machine gun section and one squad of the engineer platoon also get lost.

Finally they make their way through the woods and emerge into the open just above the Wilhelmina Canal, 500 yards to the east of the bridge which is their goal. Taking stock, Sobchak now sees his own platoon is down to 18 men and the engineers number only 26. With a badly depleted force and darkness falling on D-Day, he nonetheless goes ahead with his mission to take the bridge.

The men crawl to the dike, climb over it and down the far side to the bank of the canal. Then with Lt. Sobchak and the lead scout, Pfc. Joe Mann, out front, they cautiously make their way west toward the bridge. But as Sobchak and Mann reconnoiter in the dark trying to locate the bridge, they find they have gone too far and are within the route covered by a sentry. The German maintains regular voice contact with another sentry on the far side of the canal, so they can't jump him. They can only lie motionless, waiting for a chance to return to the rest of the men.

Meanwhile, with Lt. Sobchak absent, the men grow uneasy. The flat New England voice of the new man from Springfield, Massachusetts, sounds next to Jake, "What do we do now?"

"Sit tight, Springfield," Jake whispers. "Be patient."

"Where's the lieutenant?"

"Ike's line is busy. Should I call General Taylor?"

"What?"

"Nothing. The lieutenant is out casing the joint. Just relax. Save your strength. You never can tell when you might need it."

This is unnerving for a new man, Jake knows. German voices, but you don't know where or how many. Leader gone. Darkness, which makes everything worse. Jake can sympathize with him. But he can't be his nursemaid.

Then the sentries' voices stop. The silence is scary.

"It's quiet . . . too quiet. I don't like it." Kent repeats the melodramatic cliché he's heard in countless movies. "Play something, Bix."

Jake answers, "I don't perform without . . ." He never gets to finish. Up ahead of them someone shouts "Grenade!" followed in a split second by an explosion and a second and a third. German potato masher grenades are coming from across the canal, soon followed by rifle fire.

One man, then two, scramble to their feet, run to the top of the dike to get away. Others follow. As they get up there, machine guns and rifles open up on them from both sides of the canal. Now all the men race over the top of the dike to the reverse slope and cover. Sgt. Grunwald shouts, "Dig in!" but some just keep going, heading for the woods. Ahead of him, Jake sees the new man from Springfield running. He yells, "Here, Springfield! Hit the dirt! Dig in!"

Desperately wanting an order, any order, Springfield falls to the ground, keeps his head down, rifle and automatic fire still sounding but now safely overhead as they lie on the far slope. He and Jake start digging.

Meanwhile Sobchak and Mann have taken advantage of the firing and confusion to come racing back to the men. And so the remnants of the Second

Platoon spend their first night on Dutch soil, dug in, surrounded by Germans and short of their target, the bridge.

When the sun comes up on the morning of Monday, September 18th, Sobchak takes a head count. Paratroopers and engineers, they are now a total of 18, three of them wounded. Aside from their M-1s, they have one machine gun, one mortar, and one bazooka, with precious little ammo for any of them. Ahead of them lies an eventful day, one in which their problems will continue.

As the new day begins, Capt. Smith, whose own men are under heavy attack, sends out three separate patrols to search for his lost Second Platoon. Each is beaten back by enemy fire, reporting it has seen no sign of the platoon. Informed of the results, battalion commander Cole concludes that the Second Platoon has been wiped out.

Meanwhile, the overall battle for Best is escalating quickly. As luck—bad luck for the Americans—would have it, large groups of German soldiers are passing through the town just as the American attack begins. They are part of a German troop withdrawal, on their way east to Germany, but they are ordered to stand and defend Best. So what was once a mission for a platoon, and was raised to an augmented company, comes to involve the entire Second and Third Battalions of the 502nd.

But this larger force now confronting the enemy on the morning of the 18th is of no use to the beleaguered Second Platoon, because between it and the rest of the regiment is a strong German force. Yet though he is under attack from three sides, Lt. Sobchak does not consider retreat. That is not what the 101st is trained to do. He has been told to take the bridge and he is not about to stop trying.

From the forest, a skirmish line of Germans is moving toward them. The lieutenant orders the men to hold fire until they are 50 yards away. Then they open up, devastating the enemy line; 35 Germans fall, the rest retreat. One attack beaten off, the small force continues to come under fire both from the road and the far side of the canal.

In late morning, their mission becomes academic; the Germans blow the bridge in an immense cloud of concrete and metal. The men have to duck in their holes to avoid the rain of debris.

A few minutes later Joe Mann, carrying a bazooka, crawls up to the large foxhole in which sit Jake, Kent, Al, Springfield, and the new blond kid, Tom.

"Who wants to go on a little excursion?" No one answers.

"Where to?" Jake finally asks.

"German artillery dump," says Mann, pointing to the west along the canal.

No one volunteers. In the silence, Jake feels the coward inside stirring. Again, he must quiet him. "OK, you're on," he says. They crawl forward, find a protected spot, settle in. Mann aims the bazooka at the artillery dump and with two shots sets it off with a tremendous explosion.

"Want to get back right away?" Mann asks.

Jake stares at him. "No, let's go for a swim in the canal first."

"This is a good spot; let's stay here for a while."

They stay for an hour. Six times, Germans move toward them. Six times, they repulse them. Then they come under steady rifle fire. Mann is hit twice, once in each shoulder. He tells Jake to take the bazooka. Another 150 yards along the canal is a German 88.

"Try your luck," he tells Jake.

Luck it is, for Jake has fired a bazooka only in training, and has never been especially accurate with it. But this time luck is with him. With one round he hits the 88 and destroys it. The two scramble back to the relative safety of their foxholes.

Then comes a bit of good luck which will turn bad. By this time British armor has come north on Hell's Highway and finding the bridge over the Wilhelmina Canal on their main route blown, sends an armored car west toward the Best bridge, only to find it blown too. When the Second Platoon spots the armored car just across the canal from them, Lt. Sobchak yells to the others, "I think our troubles are over." He starts to move his men down to the bank so they can row across to the protection of the armored car. The Brits stop him. "Stay where you are," one of them shouts. "I'm sure help will get here soon. We'll cover you until it does."

Feeling better about things, Sobchack and his men hold tight in their foxholes. Under the watchful eye of the armored car, he transfers his most seriously wounded men, with an aid man, to a safer foxhole. As the sun sets on D-Day plus one, they hear the sounds of the regimental fight to the north of them, getting closer. They expect help will be arriving soon.

Then the night brings still another apparent bit of good luck that goes bad. A platoon from Company D of the Third Battalion somehow pushes its way south from the main body of the regiment until it makes contact with the lost Second Platoon and digs in on its left, or western, flank.

Sobchak's tired little group once again thinks the worst is over. With the protection of the D Company platoon to the west, many of the men fall asleep. What they do not know is that the British armored car across the canal, hearing the arrival of more Americans, assumes that deliverance has reached the lost platoon, and it leaves.

Now settled in, the platoon believes that morning will see the end of its troubles. But the night has still more trouble. A German force falls upon the Company D platoon, setting it in full retreat while—amazingly—the exhausted troopers of the Second Platoon do not even awaken. Their left flank now unprotected, they sleep until next morning, D-Day plus two, expecting relief from regiment soon. But what's waiting for them is not help; it's more Germans.

The morning of Tuesday, September 19th, begins under a cloak of mist. When the sun finally burns it away, what is revealed to the Second Platoon is a party of Germans less than ten yards off. Sgt. Grunwald, manning their only machine gun, spots them first, screams "Krauts," and begins firing. Al Breecher reaches into a pocket for his last grenade, pulls the pin and lobs it at the Germans. The Germans begin throwing grenades too. Someone in the big foxhole yells "Grenade!" Jake, firing his M-1 as fast as he can, looks up and sees a grenade arching through the air at them. Then sees Al catch it as he would a fly ball and throw it back at the Germans. Everyone in the foxhole is firing, everyone except scout Joe Mann who has been wounded in both shoulders, has his arms in slings, but has refused to be evacuated to the foxhole with the other wounded.

Sgt. Grunwald at the machine gun is hit, falls over backward, blood gushing from his jaw. Jake, next to the gun, gets behind it, starts firing and almost at once feels a stab of blinding agony. A rifle bullet has hit his helmet, but in going through it, is deflected enough so that it sears across his temple, causing more pain than he ever dreamed existed. He tries to keep firing, but blood is now streaming from the wound into his eyes. As he puts up a hand to wipe his eyes, he hears another shout of "Grenade!" Almost instantly he hears the grenade clunk on the machine gun and fall to earth. Blinded, he gropes for it, expecting it to blow up in his face. Miraculously, he finds it and throws it out of the hole, a second and a half before it explodes.

He reaches into a pocket for a handkerchief, wipes the blood out of his eyes and presses the handkerchief to his temple. He has seen so much gore, so many heads blown apart, that he is relieved to feel that his skull seems intact. But the blood keeps flowing.

Around him, the lieutenant, Kent, Al, Tom, Springfield, are firing relentlessly, Al with one arm because he has taken a bullet in the left shoulder.

Behind them, a medic has scrambled in from another foxhole and is treating Grunwald, who, miraculously, is alive and gesturing, though he cannot seem to speak. And at the other end of the foxhole, crouches Joe Mann, helpless.

Wiping more blood from his eyes, Jake is back behind the machine gun, firing what is left of the last magazine. No more than ten seconds go by before he hears Joe Mann shout.

"Grenade!"

This one has landed at the far end of the big foxhole, alongside Joe Mann and slightly behind him. But with both arms in slings and useless, he cannot pick it up. And no one else is close enough. For an instant everyone is frozen.

And then they hear Mann say, "I've got this one." He drops backward onto the grenade, taking the full force of its explosion with his body. As the aid man rushes to him, Mann says, "My back is gone." Within seconds he is dead.

Without him, the grenade would have killed or seriously wounded everyone in the hole. Even with his sacrifice, fragments have hit Jake in the stomach and hip, doubling him over and knocking him to the ground, and Springfield, wounding him in the legs and crotch.

Stretched out, blood sopping through his pants, his face distorted by pain, Springfield begs Sobchak, "Shoot me, lieutenant, please shoot me!"

"You're going to be all right," Sobchak answers.

"My balls are shot off," says Springfield.

Sobchak looks to the aid man, who is putting sulfa powder on the wounded man's crotch. The aid man looks. "They're both there," he says. "Everything's there." Springfield manages a smile through his agony.

The medic gives Springfield a shot of morphine, then goes on to treat Jake with the same steps: tries to stop the bleeding, puts sulfa and bandaging on the wounds, gives him a morphine shot.

Lt. Sobchak assesses their situation. No grenades are left. Ammo is virtually all gone. Only three of them remain unwounded. "OK," he says. "This is it."

He takes a handkerchief from his pocket, ties it to the end of his carbine and waves it in the air. The firing stops.

The men emerge from the two large foxholes, Kent half carrying Jake, others doing the same with the most seriously wounded. They are prisoners, their number now down to a half dozen. The Germans take them to a field hospital on the way to Best, where German medics treat them. As the reinforced American attack builds up, German casualties are pouring into the hospital, the staff is frantic and the small group of Americans is left pretty much alone.

Jake is lucky: The grenade fragment that hit his stomach has not penetrated deeply and his head wound is not as serious as it is bloody. The fragment in his hip is in deep and will have to be removed later by an operation. Morphine helps him bear the pain.

"What happens now?" Kent asks.

Jake, surprised and grateful to be alive, says, "Wait a minute, I'll call Hitler." He feigns putting a phone to his ear. "Line's busy. He must be talking to Ike."

"Jake, this is no joke," says Al, his left arm in a sling.

"Who's laughing?"

"I mean," Al continues earnestly, "the H on your dogtag. The Germans hate Jews . . ."

"I've got my rights, Geneva Convention and all that," answers Jake. He has not even thought of that, and despite his flippancy, it scares him.

"Bix, I've got an idea," Kent says. "Let's switch dogtags." He starts to remove his from around his neck.

"You must be kidding!"

"No. You need medical treatment, I don't."

"Kent, do you honestly believe anyone would ever take you for Jewish? They'll know in a minute! Without even checking for your circumcision!"

"I never thought of that." But Kent does not stop removing his dogtags. "I'll make up some reason they didn't do it." He holds out his dogtags on their chain.

Jake shakes his head no, but he is deeply touched. "Thanks, Kent. I'll be all right. Just get me some morphine when this wears off. I'm one of those cowards who can't stand pain."

As they sit in a large examination room and wait, the sounds of battle are growing closer, the German hospital staff looks more and more nervous. Finally, an orderly comes by, terror in his eyes.

"You speak English?" Jake asks.

"Yes. A little."

"It is terrible, isn't it?" Jake says.

"Yes. We do not know what we shall do."

This guy is ripe, Jake tells himself. He gives Lt. Sobchak what he hopes is a meaningful look.

"Now come the airplanes," Jake says. "And the cannon . . . the big guns. Boom. Boom. We will probably all be killed."

The German stares at Jake in fright. "This is hospital!" he pleads.

"Machts nichts," Jake answers in an approximation of German, pausing to let the effect sink in. "Boom. Boom." He waits. The man has gone from frightened to petrified. "But there is a way to save all our lives," Jake adds.

He sees a gleam of hope in the man's eyes. "You want to save your life?" he asks. The orderly nods. The lieutenant jumps in.

"Are there many guards?" Sobchak asks.

The German shakes his head no. "They are old."

The lieutenant looks straight into the German's eyes. "You go tell them, we want to talk with them. We will save your lives. Go get them."

The man smiles, nods, hurries away.

Sobchak is excited. "You'll make corporal for this, Ellinson!" He is one of the few who gets Jake's name right.

"Gee thanks, I always . . ." His crack is cut short by an acute stab of pain through his hip.

"Hang on," says the lieutenant. "If we can only get a couple of the weak sisters, we're in like Flynn!"

In five minutes the orderly is back with two elderly guards. In their 50s, they look thoroughly defeated and docile. Their rifles are slung over their shoulders, a clear sign, Jake thinks, that they have no hostile intent. The orderly knows how to pick his men.

"You tell them what I say," instructs the lieutenant. The orderly nods, and Sobchak, stopping frequently for translation, carefully explains that a big advance is coming, that there will be heavy bombardment from the air and from artillery. He says it would be a shame for them to die, with the war almost over. But there is a way out. If they surrender and turn over their weapons, they will be treated as prisoners of war, taken behind American lines to safety and good food.

The translator stops. Jake watches the two guards. They are close, but not there yet.

"Tell them they don't have much time," Jake adds. "American troops are right up the road. If they arrive and these men still have their weapons they will be shot on sight. They must act quickly!"

Jake watches them during the translation. One guard is uncertain; he looks at the other. The second doesn't return the look, just unslings his weapon and hands it to Sobchak. Saying nothing, the lieutenant holds it in front of him, left hand on the barrel in front of the rear sight, right hand on the small of the stock just behind the trigger, and looks straight at the other guard. The message is clear: I'm ready to fire; you're not. The guard takes his rifle off his shoulder and hands it to Sobchak, who immediately gives it to Kent, one of the few remaining unwounded.

The lieutenant looks at the translator. "Tell them they are now our prisoners. We will see that they are protected and treated according to the rules of warfare. No harm will come to them. Tell them." The translator speaks; they seem relieved, almost happy.

"Ellison, you know how to fire this thing?"

"Of course!"

"Let's go."

In ten minutes they return with three more guards and three more weapons, followed by a string of medical personnel.

The lieutenant turns to the translator and says, "Tell them the five guards come with us as our prisoners. All the medical people stay here and care for your wounded."

The translator protests, "But sir . . ."

Sobchack barks, "Tell them!"

The translator does, then turns back to the lieutenant, "You say I can go, too."

"You stay here. The wounded need you."

"But the airplanes. The cannons . . ."

"We're not going to bomb the hospital!" Sobchak says angrily. "We're not animals! Let's go. Hande hoch!" he tells the guards, using two German words most every American soldier knows. They lift their hands over their heads.

"But sir," Kent says, "We did tell him . . ."

"Tough shit, Ellison. War is hell. Let's go." But the lieutenant looks troubled.

With the morphine wearing off, Jake can barely get to his feet. Two of the other wounded cannot walk. It is clear they cannot go far without three stretchers. That takes six bearers, and there are only five guards. Sobchak has his escape.

"You!" he says to the dejected translator. "Are you strong?"

The man is now hopeful. "Yes! Strong!"

"We need three stretchers. You can help carry one."

"Yes sir!" shouts the translator. He leads the group down the hall, rifles now in the hands of the lieutenant, Kent, and Tom, the only men able to carry and use them. In a couple of minutes they have the stretchers and the group starts north, looking for Americans. A half hour later they walk into American lines. The lost patrol has been found. Sobchak will put Jake and Grunwald in for Silver Stars, Joe Mann for the Medal of Honor.

They learn to their sorrow that the day before, the other of the two 101st Airborne men who are to win Medals of Honor, their battalion commander, Lt. Col. Robert Cole, was killed by a sniper's bullet.

Although the ordeal of the lost patrol is over, for the 101st more than two months of hard fighting in Holland are still to come. For two weeks the division fights to keep its stretch of Hell's Highway open. Then, to its dismay, it is ordered north to replace British troops below the lower Rhine.

While Kent goes north with a Company H that is reduced almost to platoon size, Jake and Al find themselves in the division hospital in Son. Al, recuperating quickly, is healed in a couple of weeks and sent north to share the misery of the company.

The 101st will not be relieved until late November, after 72 days in action and 3300 casualties, nearly matching the 3800 in Normandy.

Though all three paratrooper divisions perform admirably, Operation Market Garden ends in failure. The British armor, starting late and moving slowly, passes through the 101st and the 82nd divisions on its way north. But it fails to reach the Arnhem bridge across the lower Rhine in time to relieve the First Airborne. Of the 10,000 British and Polish troopers dropped there, a little more than 2000 are eventually able to break free, many of them wounded. More than 6000 are captured, about a third of those wounded, and 1400 killed.

Jake seems to be recovering from his wounds until he develops an infection in his right hip, where a grenade fragment has been dug out. He is feverish for a week, critical for a few days of it. After he passes that crisis, he heals more slowly. It is seven weeks before he can leave the hospital. Promoted to corporal and awarded a Silver Star and a Purple Heart, he is ordered to a convalescent center for a couple of weeks, then given a week's leave and told to report to Mourmelon, in France, where the division will soon be headed.

"You take it easy," the doctor tells him. "You're not fit for duty, corporal."

Weak, gaunt, troubled by headaches from the head wound, Jake has forgotten he has been promoted. Secretly he thinks the doctor is mistaken about his condition, and he is getting away with something. But he doesn't argue.

The day before he is to get out of the hospital, he is lying on his bed in a convalescent ward. In the background is the big band music that is played constantly on the ward's loudspeaker system. Usually he is hardly aware of what's being played but this time something makes him listen. It is the Buddy Benson Big Band, playing "All The Things You Are," vocal by Cindy Laine, trumpet solo by Jake Ellinson. A year ago, he would have shouted exuberantly, "Hey, that's me!" Now he feels as if he is listening to ghosts. He looks around. In the other beds recovering GIs are writing, reading, dozing. None seems to notice the music. None notices Jake turn quickly and bury his head in his pillow. The tears well up so suddenly and strongly he barely makes it. He hopes the others can't see the heaving of his body as he sobs into the pillow.

Two days later, on his way out of the hospital, in uniform for the first time in nearly two months, he passes a full-length mirror and sees what the doctor saw. He says to his gaunt, ghostly reflection, "Your mother should see you now," then walks slowly out of the hospital.

CHAPTER 27

One afternoon when Herb was meeting with Joe Wiggins, Marian got into the station wagon and drove in from Malibu to Westwood Village. She parked in the lot next to a one-story building on which a tasteful but assertive sign said The Applied Computer School of Los Angeles, walked through the glass doors to the desk, where the receptionist looked up in surprise.

"Hi! Is it Saturday already?"

Marian smiled and shook her head no. "I'd like to see Douglas."

"Is he expecting . . ."

"No, it's important."

Douglas Barton looked up from a cluttered desk when Marian walked in. He was a tall, dignified man in his late 40s, his handsome leonine head topped by theatrically wavy hair, once dark brown, now shot through with gray. When people mistook him for an actor, which they did often, he would say modestly, "I only run a computer school." But he liked the mistake and would not hesitate to reveal that 25 years ago, just out of college, he had come to Los Angeles to "make it" as an actor. Good sense, as he put it, cured him of that in a few years and he got himself a degree in computer science on the road to forging a new and lucrative career.

He got up from his desk, said "Marian" in a deep, purring voice and walked to her.

"I've got something to tell you, Douglas."

He stopped short. The look on his face seemed more expectant than surprised.

"Where shall we sit for that?"

"You don't have to stage the scene."

"All right," he said in that magisterial way that had once so impressed her. She took the modern canvas and aluminum chair at a corner of his desk; he went back to the big leather chair behind the desk. He put his stubby fingers together in front of his chest and waited.

"No more, Douglas."

She was right; he wasn't surprised. When he said, "May I ask why?" she thought he was being polite, pretending to care more then he did.

"Because I feel like a rat."

"We agreed we had a right to our own happiness."

All at once she was repulsed, by the cliché and by the purring voice that had once seemed so intimate and sexy.

"Feeling like a rat doesn't make me happy."

"I really do admire your loyalty, Mar. One of the many things about you I care for. Is it because I wouldn't make any commitment?"

"God no! Did I ever ask for any? Want to know the truth? I really do care for my husband. I love him. I do. And I have felt lousy about doing this to him. For some time now."

"I have sensed it, Mar."

She didn't like that nickname, never had, but there was no point doing anything about it now.

"I really do love him. I never loved you, Douglas. I never led you to believe . . ."

"Of course, one needs a physical relationship, too."

"Did I ever say I didn't have one with him? Well, I may have implied it. But . . . it wasn't true, not entirely true."

"Are you going to tell him?"

"What would be the point? What he doesn't know, won't . . . although I think he suspects. Confessing would just be showing off; it can't undo anything, only make someone feel terrible. The only thing I can do for him is never do it again."

He stood, walked to her, leaned over, put his hands on her shoulders, looked into her eyes. "You know I care for you, I always will. And I wish you well. We had some lovely times."

She knew it all so well by now, the sincerity, the warm, intimate tone, the deep soulful looks, that so easily led to sex. A surge of resentment at all the *technique* came over her and she had to remind herself that it had not only been his con job, that she had been a willing participant. He let a mischievous glint come into his eye—so professional, so studied, she thought. "Should we . . . for old times sake?" He tossed it off lightly enough so she could take it as a joke if she wanted to.

"No, Douglas." She stood, brushing his hands away.

"So be it." He shrugged. Why hadn't she noticed before how much of what he did and said was a pose?

He headed for the door to see her out. He'd already written her off, had no more time for her. At the door, she stopped.

"One more thing, I do want the computer certificate. I've done all the work."

"Oh, you certainly have earned it."

She didn't like the way he said it, but maybe she was being too sensitive.

"It should be ready for you next week. Why don't you drop by for it? We could even have a drink . . . for old times' sake."

"Mail it please, Douglas."

Driving back, she felt as if someone had lifted a block of concrete from her shoulders.

When Roger drove up, Tru was hitting the ball with Jackie, who was a marketing rep for a popular brand of vodka and resented being called a blonde tennis beauty by the newspapers, although she was blonde, certainly beautiful, and a very good tennis player. It was a spectacular August weekend in Southampton, the sun bright, the sky blue and cloudless, the warm summer air stirred fitfully by a light ocean breeze, the houses on the beach off Meadow Lane sparkling.

Tru had to smile as he noticed Roger's silver BMW pull in. He's sniffing around, Tru told himself. He wants to get a look at her, and I don't blame him. Tru welcomed the respite. He was learning all too well that a man near 50 who drank the way he did could not keep up with a 27-year-old even if his strokes were better than hers. He found himself getting more and more tired these days, of tennis and of her.

"Jackie, my dear," he said to her as he walked to the net, "Would you drive to town, run a few errands?"

She put a finger to her tanned forehead and wiped away a single bead of sweat. "I don't have any errands to run."

"Would a case of Beefeaters be a suitable mission? Just sign for it."

She gave him an exasperated look. "I've got to shower first."

"In the pool house, you spectacular creature. Don't be difficult. Be gone." Finally, she understood.

"I thought you said everything was OK!"

"It is. But as my lawyer said, one can't be too careful. Now, please."

As she headed off for the shower, he walked to meet Roger, wiping his face with a small towel. Roger would be disappointed not to meet the blonde tennis beauty, but honestly Jackie was not the sort of girl you introduced to your friends, certainly not to their wives. And, her aspirations notwithstanding, not the kind of girl you married. Stick to your own class: that was his injunction to all his friends, and the very one he'd forgotten when he married Dede. At least Dede was smart, very smart. But then what would you expect of a half-Jew? To give them their due, no Jew could be as dumb as Jackie.

He met Roger on the porch. "What a pleasant surprise!"

"Hope I'm not interrupting," Roger said, looking around.

"Not at all," said Tru, pointing to a chair on the porch. "Just finished hitting the ball with . . . my tennis instructor."

"I hear she's good," Roger said, wanting to wink or at least give a knowing smile, not having the nerve to do either.

"She knows her stuff," Tru answered, teasing Roger with a totally straight face.

"Never too old to improve your game!" This time Roger, who was four years younger than Tru, felt free to smile.

"To be perfectly honest, tennis has become a way to sweat out yesterday's booze and make room for today's. Speaking of which . . . how does a tall gin and tonic, lots of ice, lots of tonic, lots of gin, sound?"

"Not just yet, thanks."

Tru disappeared inside, returned with two glasses. "I've brought an extra, in case you change your mind. If not . . . I'll find some use for it. Cheers." He picked up his drink and drained a third of it in one gulp.

"Jimmy out here with you?" Roger asked.

"Yes. Lifeguarding at the club. I didn't want him in New York, going to the synagogue. Don't think he'd look good in a skullcap."

"Come on, Tru!"

"I knew she was too pushy to be one of us." He washed the thought down with more of the gin and tonic.

"She is one of the most attractive women around, Tru. We all thought that, including you. Let's not rewrite history."

"I know you've always had a thing for her. That hot Semitic blood turn you on, eh?"

Roger had to laugh and shake his head. Tru polished off his drink, picked up the second glass. "If you're not having this, Roger . . ." He began drinking even as Roger motioned for him to go ahead.

"Gin and tonic is not exactly the way to quench your thirst after tennis, Tru."

"Of course it is," Tru answered. "The only way." He gulped from the second drink.

"Is it . . . final . . . between you and Dede?" Roger asked.

"Final. Finis. Finale. Kaput. Can you see me married to a Jew?"

"Now wait a minute . . ."

Tru got to his feet, picked up both glasses. "You need a refill Roger. But first I have one point to make. We worry about a dog's pedigree, why should we be any less concerned with a person's?"

As he headed inside with the glasses, Roger said, "Mineral water for me, please."

This is not going to be fun, Roger said to himself as he waited. Right before his eyes the man was getting drunk at fast-forward speed. In five minutes Tru was back, handed him a full glass, kept the other.

"Cheers," said Tru, taking a deep draft of his glass. When Roger drank from his, he was startled.

"What is this?"

"Mineral water instead of tonic."

"With gin. Half gin."

"You don't think I'd forget the gin!"

Roger couldn't decide if Tru was pulling his leg. "I didn't want gin." He looked at his watch. "It's only 11:45."

Tru sighed deeply. "Now we're both disappointed, aren't we?"

"What do you mean?"

"I wanted you to have a drink with me. You wanted to get a look at that little piece of ass, hoping she'd come out wrapped in a towel . . . or less . . . and say, 'Oh, excuse me, I didn't know there was anyone here.'"

"That's not why I'm here," Roger said stiffly. "I promised I'd tell you about the final vote on your . . ." He hesitated.

Even drunk, Tru was too quick for Roger. "Technically she still is my wife. Unless you'd rather refer to her as the Jewess."

"Really, Tru, there is no call . . ."

"You are so stuffy without a drink. But if you insist . . ." His own glass now emptied again, he picked up Roger's, drank from it. "Now, about the vote."

"Remember, it's only advisory."

"Don't like the sound of that. Damned vote should never have been taken!"

"Perhaps you're right. However . . ."

"What was it?"

"Quite close."

"I'm glad my great-grandfather is not around. What *was* it?"

"846 in favor, 791 opposed."

"Oh no! It's those damned yuppie wimps. They hear lawsuit and they run for cover. But you, Roger, can be a man. Do the right thing."

"And what is that?"

"The club has over 2000 members; 846 represents fewer than half of them."

"On the other hand, more favor it than oppose it. It is only advisory, of course."

"791 members do not want her in the club! It is unthinkable that someone be admitted who is not wanted by 791 members! In some clubs a single blackball will do it! Roger, your attitude is . . ."

"The problem is, we have asked the members to give us their view. To now ignore them . . ."

"Whose side are you on?"

"I do not want a woman in the club."

"A Jewish woman!"

"I don't want her in the club any more than you do, but now . . . I know some members who would make trouble."

"To hell with them! And have you read that . . . liberal garbage . . . George Whitman's been writing to the members? To hell with him, too! You asked for an advisory vote. It was inconclusive. Now it's up to the executive committee. Your hands are on the reins! Now, show us who's in charge! Don't let a few pussy-whipped radicals destroy the Goth!"

Face reddened by his tirade, he drained Roger's glass.

"Do you think you're over-reacting?"

"No, I think you're . . . wimping out! Know that expression, Roger? My son uses it. Just give me a list of the executive committee. I'll do some phoning . . ."

"That might be counter-productive." A lot of the committee think you're a fanatic and a drunk, Roger wanted to add, but didn't.

Tru spoke to his glass. "I blame myself. I should never have let a person like that near the Goth. Or near me."

"Hindsight, as they say, is 20-20. She seemed quite . . . acceptable."

"You're letting those legs warp your mind. Say, she might be available, Roger. When she's not screwing Denny Knight, that is. They say Jewish women are hot. You could give that secretary of yours a rest. Beg pardon, I think she's called special assistant. Is she special, Roger? I'll bet she's not as special as my tennis instructor."

"I've got to be going, Tru. My advice is don't fight the club thing. And go easy on the sauce." Roger stood.

"Roger, I will stop her, if I have to do it all by myself."

"You're beginning to sound a bit . . . quixotic."

"Oh, am I?" Tru jumped to his feet, listing to port for just a moment before he could right himself. "Well, I've got more than a lance, my friend! This is one Don Quixote armed with a lethal weapon. Know what it is, Roger?"

"No, Tru," Roger replied, wishing he were safely away from the place.

"Well, you'll know it when you see it!" Tru put his hands in front of his face as if holding something, squinted one eye shut and flicked his right index finger down. Then, triumphantly, he raised his glass and finished his fourth drink of the morning.

Wearily, Fred Rudolph grabbed the railing of the Stairmaster, shifted his feet to make them comfortable. Of course they never would be comfortable; a health club was no place for him, not at 6:30 in the morning or any other time. He'd always been a lousy athlete—"klutz" was the word Irene liked to use to describe his coordination—never liked the outdoors and hated exercise.

Luckily, he'd never had a tendency to gain weight. At 22, when he married Irene—three days after his graduation from NYU—he weighed 150 pounds. Now, 35 years later, he weighed 153. At his recent physical, however, the doctor had said a most definitive no to cigars, fat, and cholesterol, and yes to fish, salad, and exercise. So three mornings a week, instead of getting up at 6:00 and drinking three cups of coffee while he read four newspapers, he would have a glass of juice and go to the Sky-Hi Health Club for 40 minutes with a personal trainer and then 20 minutes on a Stairmaster.

He stared at his unimposing physique in the mirrored wall, the calves soft and the muscles in the front of his thighs—quads, his trainer kept calling them—quivering as he pumped up and down on the infernal machine. He closed his eyes to concentrate on the effort and spare himself the sight of his body. When he opened them again who was climbing onto the Stairmaster next to his but Robert Stinson, his colleague at the Democratic Issues Symposium.

Sizing up Stinson in the big mirror, Fred could see he did this kind of thing often. Though he was ten years older than Fred, he had muscle tone where Fred had quiver and he pumped easily and quickly. Now Stinson saw him.

"Why, Fred, I didn't know you worked out."

"Doctor wants me to change my lifestyle. I think maybe instead I'll change doctors."

"This is the best thing for you. I never miss a day."

"What a frightening prospect."

Stinson didn't smile at that. Fred knew he was the kind of guy who took things like workouts seriously. "You'll get used to it," Stinson said, barely breathing hard while Fred was puffing.

"Not if I live to be a hundred. And who'd want to if I have to spend it doing this?"

For a few minutes, Rudolph puffed while Stinson stepped in easy silence. When Stinson spoke it was with no shortage of breath. "Funny that I should run into you. I was going to call you today. About Diana Miller."

"What about her?"

"Now, Fred, you know I'm not a prude."

"But . . . ?"

"Does the name Dennison Knight mean anything to you?"

"I've seen it in the *Wall Street Journal*. Venture capitalist who dabbles in mergers. Put together a few deals that made him a ton of money."

"That's not what he's best known for. He's known as the most accomplished . . . swordsman, is what we called it when I was a young man . . . since Casanova."

"Yes, and what does that have to do . . ." Fred pretended he didn't know where this was leading.

"Do you know who his current . . . squeeze . . . is?"

"Squeeze?"

"A word my granddaughter uses. We used to say flame, heartthrob. By any name, the answer is . . . Diana Miller, the woman who would be senator."

"Where did you hear this?" Rudolph's anger made him pump faster.

Stinson shrugged. "I hear lots of things from lots of sources."

"So a separated woman goes out on a date. Big deal! Sounds like manure to me, and here you are spreading it around." The last part came out as a gasp. To hell with this stuff, Fred thought. He got off the machine, stood there trying to catch his breath while Stinson continued his easy stepping.

"There's more to it than a date, it's not just manure, and I'm not spreading it around. I'm telling you because you and I have the same interest; the right candidate."

"You've been against Diana from the start."

"I've been skeptical, only because I want the best person. One with no baggage. I don't want to have to spend half the campaign explaining what she was doing in a hot tub with . . ."

"What? Gossip? Peephole stuff?"

"Fred, listen. I don't like this anymore than you do. But it's more than gossip. There are pictures. I know that for a fact. Remember what the tabloids did with the topless shots of Fergie? Well, this is . . . believe me Fred, I know. I don't want to see any of us embarrassed."

As soon as Fred called Dede, which was as soon as he got back to the office, she got Billy Vogel on the phone and told him. He had the grace not to say, I warned you.

"The worm!" he snapped angrily. "The high-and-mighty WASP worm! Diana, this can hurt you. The divorce is the least of it. If I were you I would start thinking about withdrawing my name at the Gotham. That would solve everything."

"Absolutely not! If that . . ."

"Go on, say son of a bitch, it'll make you feel better. But think about what I said. And don't do anything hasty, Diana, I'm warning you!"

Only after she hung up did she say it softly to herself. "Son of a bitch." Feeling the kind of fury she'd felt confronting the two boys on the reservoir, she disregarded still another warning from Vogel and drove out to Southampton to confront Tru. She was sitting on the terrace when he walked back from the beach with Jackie, who wore a string bikini that was three tiny, wispy triangles of tan cotton.

"What are you doing here, Dede?" She'd rarely seen him so startled and shocked.

"I should have brought a camera."

"Dede, this is Jacqueline Connell. Jackie, my wife, Diana Miller." Tru never forgot his manners. "Jackie was just on her way."

"Nice to have met you," Dede said to encourage her in that direction.

"Likewise," Jackie answered and headed off for the pool house. Dede watched her go. "Quite a body," she said.

"She gives me tennis lessons."

"Uh huh. She the one you were oiling up in the dunes? Too bad I didn't have my camera then, too."

"Why do you keep talking about a camera?"

"You know damned well. You and your superior WASP standards . . . spying on me like a common . . . paparazzo!"

"Would you like a drink?"

"No, thank you."

"Well, I would." She had the distinct feeling that for once the drink was not the main thing. He was using the time to think. When he returned, glass in hand, he stretched himself out on a yellow and white striped chaise longue, sipped his drink.

"I warned you," he said. He expected her to reply. When she didn't, he seemed a little unsure. "Look . . . no one need ever see them. All you have to do is drop your attack on the Goth. You've never liked the place anyway."

"If I don't?"

"I don't want to say unpleasant things."

"To do them is fine. Just don't talk about them."

"All right. Photographs of you . . . and Knight . . . in a hot tub."

"Did the little worm you hired to peep through the hedges tell you that nothing happened?"

"You were in the hot tub with him. That's enough."

"How do you stand yourself?"

"You brought it on yourself. And you can undo it yourself. It need never get in the way of your run for the Senate, or anything else."

"And Jim?"

"Knows nothing. Of course if the tabloids get it . . ."

This she knew was her last chance to run for cover. She surprised herself with her quick decision not to take it. "No deal. Do whatever you want with whatever you have. The answer is no."

The next morning she phoned Fred Rudolph, told him she no longer wanted to be considered as a Senatorial candidate, asked him to pass that word along to Stinson and anyone else who needed to know. Two mornings later, the *Daily News* ran a short item saying that real estate queenpin Diana Penrose Miller, in the midst of a divorce battle, had abandoned thoughts of running for the Senate.

Since their last meeting Dede had talked on the phone with Amanda Turnbull every day. But on the morning the *Daily News* item appeared, Dede called her, told her all about the club and the situation with Tru.

"Dede, dear child," Amanda replied. "You will not fight this fight without my help. This fight or any fight."

The words were like a warm bath washing over Dede. "Amanda," she began and then, hesitantly, softly, for the first time: "Mother." It had been so long since she'd had someone to call mother, she began to cry.

On the other end Amanda waited patiently before going on. "My sons are members of the club. Nelson was a member. So was my father. So was Kent. I am not without some influence, and you may be sure it will all be used on your behalf."

"Perhaps you're against having women or Jews in the club," Dede said.

"On the contrary, I'm all in favor. I have been for a long time."

After they'd hung up, Dede tried the word again, aloud but softly. "Mother. Mother."

While the Madison Pub was a place where Jane Reich might search for Ken, it was not nearly the kind of place she'd choose for a drink with him. The bar at the Four Seasons, lofty, light and elegant, was more like it. During the summer, Friday evenings there had a tranquility that was dramatically different from the restless buzz on other days and at other seasons; the habitués were on their way to houses in Bedford or Litchfield or East Hampton or Nantucket or the Vineyard. Seen through the big windows, even Park Avenue seemed restful, the river of commuters flowing south toward Grand Central by this hour on a summer Friday slowed to a trickle.

Ken got there a couple of minutes early, sipped at a beer, waiting for her to make her entrance. She arrived in a black silk blouse and cream-colored skirt cut above the knee, daring onlookers to make their choice between those dark eyes and the slinky legs. Whichever the choice, all eyes were on her—which is where she wanted them. She strode right to him, kissed him on the cheek.

"I didn't recognize you at first. I just saw this devastatingly handsome man at the bar. A few more gray hairs and you'll be totally irresistible."

"Then irresistibility is just around the corner, kid."

She hitched up her skirt as she climbed on the adjoining stool, baring her legs to mid-thigh. He could see two men in business suits stop their conversation to stare.

"Let's see, what shall I have?" she said. "It's really exciting to be sitting here with you. I feel so festive! I know! A Bellini!"

"How come you're not gone for the weekend?"

"I stayed in town to have a drink with you! I know you picked Friday evening to test me. Have I passed?"

When the bartender brought her the glass of champagne and peach puree, she lifted it toward him. He sipped his beer.

"This is not a test," he said.

She was using those eyes on him. "I was hoping it was, so that I could get an A."

"Why didn't you just say let's do it another day?"

"Because I wanted to show you I am not the selfish girl I once was." She smiled the smile that was supposed to make you forgive her anything.

"Thirty-one is not really too old to be a girl," he said. "But it's getting there."

"All right, to show you the selfish girl is now an unselfish woman: You're mean. I won't be 31 till next month."

"Sorry, for being mean. And inaccurate."

"It's not like you. And yet . . ." She turned up the wattage in those eyes. "I'm encouraged by it. It means there may be just a few nerve endings that still twinge for Jane Reich."

God, he thought, this woman is a handful. "You want to do a victory dance around the dying embers of my pain."

"Ooh, that's good!"

"Tacky. Maudlin. False. Ashes, that's all."

"Not even one tiny little spark? Worth . . . blowing on?" She looked at him over the top of her glass. She had this way of tilting her chin down and peering up at you from the tops of her eyes. It was like a boxer throwing uppercuts, and landing. He smiled, knowing that when a boxer smiled to show he wasn't hurt, it meant he was.

"What do you want, Jane? Want to see if you've still got it? You have."

"The woman wants to see if she can correct the . . . mistakes made by the girl."

"Listen, Janey, we both made the same mistake. We hooked up with someone who was the wrong type. You're not wrong to want your kind of life. I'm not wrong to want mine. We were wrong to think they could mesh."

"Whatever happened to compromise?"

"One person wants to go out seven nights a week, the other wants to go out none. So they split it, which means that every night of the week one or the other is unhappy."

"Don't sound like an accountant! Is that all I meant to you?" She put a hand on his.

"Stop trying to seduce me. You do it too well."

"Oh, good!" She stroked his hand. He grabbed hers to stop her.

"In a month or two, we'd be back where we were," he said.

"People do change as they grow older," she answered heatedly.

"I used to think that too, Jane, because it was such a nice, hopeful thought. Now I think the opposite. As people get older they get more and more like themselves. They more and more want to do the same old things they've been doing. They become less and less flexible."

"That sounds dismal. Like there's no hope."

"The hope is, you find someone you're crazy about—the way we were about each other—with whom you don't have to compromise too often."

"Where do you find someone like that?" She stared at her glass. She sounded discouraged.

"I guess you just keep looking."

"And have you found her, Ken? Is that really what this is about?"

He looked at her. The seductiveness was gone from her eyes; replaced by apprehension.

"I didn't say that."

"You didn't say no either."

"No. I didn't."

"Are you crazy about her?"

"Jane. *Stop.*"

When Roger called to suggest a meeting with Tru, George Whitman's first reaction was to say no. Dede had told him about the photos; he'd been incensed.

"I expected more from someone with his background," Whitman had told her. "I know that sounds terribly snobbish, but it's true. If someone with his breeding behaves like a Mafia hood, what hope is there?"

But that very snobbish thought now gave Whitman an idea. "All right," he told Roger. "Have Tru bring all the photos and negatives with him."

By Whitman's wish, they met on the second floor of the Gotham, in a dark, high-ceilinged, venerable room dominated by a huge fireplace and a somber oil painting of the club's co-founder, Tru's great-grandfather, Adam Augustus Martindale.

"Why don't we sit down in the bar and have a drink, George?"

Whitman tried not to put too much irony into his voice when he answered. "Because I want to see if I can function without booze. I've gotten too damned dependent on it. No good for you. Besides, if we can work out a deal on this I want your great-grandfather smiling down on it, to give it his blessing. You've got the pictures with you . . ."

Tru nodded, patted his breast pocket.

"All of them?"

"Of course." Tru's eyebrows raised at the idea that Whitman would question his word.

"Tell me what you have in mind," Whitman began. The younger man hesitated. "First you must understand, that despite the membership vote, the executive committee is fully empowered to make whatever decision it wants in this case, and we have the votes . . ."

Whitman would have none of that. "Then why bother with this meeting? Because you know and I know you want to avoid a lawsuit and the publicity. You want to work something out. I'm listening." Then Whitman tried what during the war he would have called a reconnaissance in force. Probe a little, just to look around, ready to move back when you meet strong resistance. But if there's an opening, push through. He looked Tru in the eye as he spoke.

"I know this photo business can't be too pleasant for you."

Tru looked away, glanced, at least so Whitman thought, at the portrait of his great-grandfather. "It is not too pleasant for me." The opening was there; Whitman would attack when the moment was right.

"Well, then, tell me what you have in mind, Tru."

"It's quite simple. Dede ends her attempt to break into the club." Whitman noted Tru's choice of verb. "I turn over the photos, and within, let's say two years, the executive committee agrees to address the issue of women in the club."

"That's a non-offer. It promises nothing and gives you two years to pack the committee so it can stonewall."

Tru shook his head in disagreement. "It agrees to consider a possibility the committee has never considered before. I'd call that quite something."

"It is a figleaf for Dede, nothing more."

Tru paused before replying. "Then you make a proposal."

Now, thought Whitman, is the time. No consolidating your position, no calling for reinforcements, no asking battalion for permission, just break through and keep going.

"All right," he began, "but here's what bothers me. Suppose we work something out. How does Dede know you're turning over all the photos? Not holding some back for . . . who knows what?"

Tru's reaction could not have suited Whitman better if he had written it himself. First it showed in Tru's eyes, then he said, "Because you would have my *word* for it!"

Theatrically, Whitman let his eyes wander to the stern face of Adam Augustus Martindale peering down at them from the wall. About as subtle as a ton of bricks, he thought, but what the hell.

"I never knew your great-grandfather, but I certainly knew your grandfather and father. They were both men whose word you could count on. Both—I know this will sound old-fashioned, but I'm an old-fashioned guy—men of honor."

Whitman thought that maybe Tru was beginning to see where he was heading and didn't like it. "What's your proposal?" he asked sharply.

Now, Whitman told himself. Now. "I am going to offer you," he said slowly, "a way out of the spot you're in."

"The spot I'm in?" Tru was trying to look amused, Whitman thought, and not quite pulling it off.

"The very uncomfortable position of being a blackmailer. I know how repugnant that must be to you, because I know you want to regard yourself as a man of honor, someone whose life could bear the scrutiny of that man up there." Again, Whitman looked to the portrait. "Think for a moment, Tru. What's the worst case scenario here? Dede in the club? You know and I know she'll spend almost no time here, and in or out, the whole issue will be forgotten soon enough. What will not be forgotten, ever, by you and by those who know, is that like a Peeping Tom, a thief in the night, you took surreptitious photos. No, it was not you crawling through those hedges, but it might as well have been! And you used those photos to blackmail your wife, the mother of your son, the woman you swore before God to love and to honor."

"Consider what she's done!"

"What? Discovered that she's half Jewish? Applied for membership in the Goth? You may not like it, but it is hardly dishonorable. Compare that with what you've done. Even in war, Tru, there are rules! A . . . I have to use the expression, because there is no other . . . a moral code."

Tru looked increasingly uncomfortable. "What is your proposal?" he snapped.

"I propose that you turn over the photos—all the photos, negatives and prints—to me now."

Tru's eyes widened. "And what do I get in return?"

"In return, you get your honor back. And absolutely nothing else."

Tru just stared at him. Whitman went on.

"Your having done that, I will tell Dede you've turned them over expecting *nothing whatever in return*. I will then suggest to her the following: that the Gotham will accept her, and she will agree to resign as soon as another woman or a Jew becomes a member. This gives you the option, Tru, of keeping her out entirely, merely by taking another woman or a Jew in at once. When I make it clear that this is not a deal linked to the photos, I think she will go along with it."

Tru's stare never changed. For five full seconds, he sat there, long legs crossed, long fingers interlaced in his lap. Finally, with his left hand he reached inside his jacket, took out a business-size envelope, hefted it as if trying to decide how much postage to put on it and dropped it on the small lamp table that stood between his chair and Whitman's. Then, without a word, Tru got to his feet, turned and walked out of the room. As he left, he took one last look at his great-grandfather. Or maybe Whitman just imagined that.

On the Wednesday before Labor Day, the doorman and one of the building's handymen were helping Dede and Jim pack the station wagon for the drive up to Hanover, New Hampshire, for the start of Jim's freshman year at Dartmouth, when Tru appeared. He had had dinner with Jimmy the night before to say goodbye and so his arrival was a surprise.

"Chance for a final wave," he said soberly.

"Great, dad," said the boy. "Of course," Dede said almost simultaneously.

"Could you preside over the packing for a few minutes, Jim, so that I might have a few words with your mother?" He and Dede walked just a few strides down Fifth Avenue.

"Why didn't you tell me who your mother was? Your real mother."

"How did you find out, Tru?"

"She wrote to me in support of your admission to the club."

"Does it make any difference?"

"Why, Dede, the Ellisons are one of the finest families in New York!"

Pleased though she'd been by the outcome of Tru's meeting with George Whitman, she'd also been surprised by it. Now it made sense.

"You knew about my mother when you turned over the pictures to George Whitman!" It was almost, but not quite, a question. No denial came from Tru.

"I told you, Dede, Family does make a difference."

"Does it take the sting off my being half Jewish?"

"Why do you turn things in that nasty way? Don't you think family counts?"

"For too much. That's the problem, isn't it?"

"Look, Dede, let's not turn everything into an argument. Can't we just talk . . . reestablish some, sort of reasonable contact?"

You mean, now that I'm the daughter of an Ellison?, she wanted to say. All she did say was, "Jimmy would like that."

Up in Hanover she got teary as she put her arms around her son for the goodbyes; he was a little embarrassed at her tears, and, moreover, excited by his new surroundings. She wanted to comfort him at the parting; with the resilience of youth, he ended up comforting her. As she drove away, the station wagon empty of suitcases, stereo, computer, duffel bags, cartons—and son—she was glad to be headed not home, but to Boothbay Harbor, where she'd be the weekend guest of the Whitmans. She was given the discrete luxury of the guesthouse. In the cavernous main house were George, his wife, and a dozen children and grandchildren.

As soon as they could, she and Whitman had a private ceremony in front of the guesthouse fireplace. Whitman hefted the envelope of photos, just as Tru had done earlier at the Gotham, offered it to Dede.

She shook her head no. "You do it. I don't even want to touch them."

He hesitated for an instant, then tossed the envelope into the fire. The two watched the edges begin to brown, then flare as the film caught fire.

"George, did you know Nelson Turnbull?"

"Indeed, I did. Not a close friend mind you. But yes, at the Gotham. A straight arrow, a . . . what did we used to call them? A solid citizen. Big, tall, pleasant, never the leading man, more like the reliable sidekick, the hero's best friend in the movies."

"And his widow, Amanda Ellison Turnbull?"

"She was the leading lady. Quite the catch. We all wondered when Nelson was the one who caught her. But it turned out well, very well." He stared at her as if he wanted to say more.

"George, there's something I want to tell you about her."

"Dede, I know."

"How?"

"A letter from her, urging that you be admitted to the club."

"She's the one, really, who made Tru turn over the pictures."

Whitman stood watching the fire for a few moments before shaking his head no.

"I'd rather believe it was his great-grandfather. Tru is a snob and a bigot, but the reverse side of that snobbery is that family honor means a lot to him. That ancestral portrait, looking down at him, would not allow him to do what he was doing."

"So it's Adam Augustus Martindale who should be thanked."

"What he represents. We WASPs, from George Bush on down, have been taking quite a beating in recent years. Perhaps we deserve some of it. But I like to think there's more to us than Wall Street and martinis and places like the Goth. I like to think that along with the negatives, we have a certain code, a moral code—God, I hate sounding so sanctimonious!—that we pass on to our children, a code that could pull Tru back from the brink, despite his bigotry and his seething anger at you."

"And so now I can join the Gotham." She laughed, "What's the old saying? No good deed shall go unpunished. Will I have to call it the Goth?"

"Ah, but the deal offers you an out. If they take in another woman, or a Jew, they don't have to take you. Or, to put it another way, you don't have to join. Do you know who would be the perfect substitute? Amanda Turnbull, I could suggest it to Tru or Wheatley. Are you interested?"

"I'll have to talk with her . . . my mother."

CHAPTER 28

December, 1944

Soviet forces advance through Hungary, close in on Budapest. The Japanese counterattack fiercely on Leyte in the Philippines but are beaten off; American troops mop up and prepare to go after Luzon. In Western Europe, Hitler orders a last desperate offensive to save the dying Third Reich: the Battle of the Bulge begins.

At home, with defense industry money plentiful, Americans go on a Christmas shopping spree, buying toys that are long on materials like wood and paper and short on metal. The Sixth War Bond Drive exceeds its $14 billion quota by $1.5 billion.

Hit records: "You Always Hurt The One You Love," The Mills Brothers; "Into Each Life Some Rain Must Fall," and "I'm Making Believe," Ella Fitzgerald and the Ink Spots; "Don't Fence Me In," Bing Crosby and the Andrews Sisters.

When the troops of the 101st are trucked from Holland to Mourmelon le Grand, northeast of Paris and near Reims in champagne country, to rest, train, and take in supplies and replacements for their depleted ranks, Jake is waiting for them. Shipped there after his hospitalization and convalescent leave, he is just lazing around until the division arrives, then he works his way back into the army routine. The headaches caused by his head wound have mostly disappeared, his stomach has healed quickly, and though his hip is still stiff and sore, he is generally feeling pretty well repaired.

On the afternoon of December 16th, he is alone in the six-man tent he shares with Kent, Al, and three others. They have all gone to see some romantic movie he's decided to skip, and he is sitting on his bunk writing to Cindy. As far as he knows, she has not yet married Buddy Benson and he asks that she wait until he's home so he can talk her out of it. Her letters have the faint scent of longing, of hoping he can find a way to stop her. If that is an illusion, he will hold on to it. He seals the letter with hope, then starts one to June, who has written him with astounding news: she is pregnant and is being shipped back to the states. She will not have an abortion, in fact, she writes, she has conceived deliberately; she wants to have a baby with Jake.

He responds angrily. She tricked him, he writes. He does not want a child at this point, nor does he want a shotgun marriage. While he can't force her to have an abortion, he thinks it would be the wisest choice for her to make.

Then he starts writing to Amanda. He admires her for having dared to come to England, but their time together—well, it was a kind of wartime dream, that's all. He can't tell her that. Nor can he tell her about his fear that his luck has run out. He was bullet-proof in Normandy. Lucky in Holland. How long can his luck hold out? Sooner or later . . . He can hear the clock ticking. He can't tell her that either; after all, what is true for him is also true for her beloved brother Kent. He looks over the letter he has started, tears it up.

He walks to the mail drop to post the letters to Cindy and June, heads back to his tent. He is sitting there contemplating his prospective unwilling fatherhood, when Sgt. Grunwald runs in. Grunwald's recovery has been remarkable. His jaw was shattered in Holland; it now looks lopsided, and he has scars on his face and neck, but he seems back to full strength.

"We got a supply truck leaving for Paris in five minutes. Room for one more. There's a three-day pass goes with it. Wanna go?"

Five minutes later, Jake is on his way to Paris, cornet in his duffel. He checks into a small Left Bank hotel reserved for enlisted men. His room is tiny, but from the window, if he leans out and looks left, he can see Notre Dame. Across from the hotel there is a small park and to the right of it a church, its modesty a pleasing contrast to the bulk of the cathedral.

He walks down the three flights of worn stone steps from his room, says "bon jour" to the concierge, who smiles and promptly hands him a French-English phrase book put out by the U.S. Army. So much for my French, he says to himself. He smiles back and says "merci."

Phrase book in his pocket, Jake crosses the Quai de Montebello and walks onto the Pont au Double, the bridge that goes over the Seine to the Ile de la Cite at the foot of Notre Dame. He is reveling in the tranquility and the view when a voice startles him.

"'Allo soldier."

He turns and sees a skinny girl of about 19, dressed in a dark green skirt of shabby satin and a bulky jacket that seems to be burgundy in some places and dark brown in others. Though the December evening is cold, the jacket is open almost to her waist, and Jake can see she has nothing on under it. Her bosom, or as much of it as she is letting him see, is almost non-existent. She doesn't look like she's had many good meals recently and her attempt to look sexy he finds pathetic. But he thinks her astonishingly beautiful. Her pale brown hair is short and spiky, her skin startlingly white, with the only makeup a touch of lipstick. Her face is all big brown eyes, tiny nose and prominent cheekbones above the slash of lipstick.

"Hello," he answers.

"You want coucher avec moi, soldier?"

He has never been with a whore, not through any moral compunction, rather because he has always felt a real man should never have to pay for it. But this, this is different. This is Paris. This girl is so beautiful. And she is here; it's been three months since he was last with a woman.

"Yes," he answers at once.

"You buy me . . . to manger . . . diner."

"Diner? Dinner? Food?" He mimes putting a forkful of food into his mouth.

"Oui. Diner. Food."

"Yes," he says, wondering. Is she offering herself to him for the price of a meal? Those huge brown eyes stare at him. She stands frozen and for a moment or two Jake makes no move toward her. Then he reaches out and takes her hand. He leads her back across the bridge and to one of the cafes he noticed along the Quai de Montebello.

The place is crowded with a scattering of civilians and lots of GIs. The soldiers look up at the new arrivals, watch as the waiter leads them toward a table along the side wall. To reach it they have to go by a table of five enlisted men. Their uniforms are new; on them gleam the insignia of the Quartermaster Corps. Jake at once thinks of June's supply officer safe back in the states. He sees them looking him and the girl over, and he stares back. They are soft, a bunch of rear echelon heroes. Since September 16th, when he has been either in combat or in the hospital, Jake has seen few of these kinds of soldiers. In fact they make up the bulk of the U.S. Army, which, in what military scholars call the tooth-to-tail ratio, has the highest proportion of tail—non-combat soldiers—of any major army in the war.

To them Jake is one of those arrogant, pugnacious guys with the high boots, bloused pants and prominent badge of the paratrooper. But they are not aggressive men and when he stares back at them, they look away—except for one, a beefy, red-faced buck sergeant who is downing red wine as if it were beer. He not only leers at the girl, he thrusts his feet out into their path.

"Hey, corporal, you gonna fatten the pig before you lead her to slaughter?" he says to Jake.

Jake says only, "Get your feet out of the way," but he is infuriated at the insult to the girl, though she is a whore and, moreover, probably doesn't understand a word of what was said.

One of his friends plucks at the big sergeant's sleeve, but he shoves the hand away. "You're one of those jumpers. Just jump over them." He thrusts his feet out even farther, and Jake stares down, noticing for the first time that this desk jockey from the Quartermaster Corps is wearing the boots and bloused pants of a paratrooper.

Jake walks the girl around the feet to their table and sits her down. "Stay there," he tells her. Then he walks back to the sergeant, stands over him.

"Fatso, you're going to do three things for me. One, you're going to get your feet out of the way. Two, you're going to unblouse your pants. Three, you're going to apologize to the lady."

"Or else . . . what?" Now the sergeant looks straight at Jake. He sees a drawn, hollowed face sitting on a neck that is disproportionately thick and sinewy; the flush on the face makes the livid scar on the forehead and temple even paler. But it's the eyes that are most daunting. They are pale blue and so cold and angry they're eerie. The sergeant doesn't know soldiers like this. Uncertainty shows in his eyes.

"Or else you're going to find your nose coming out the back of your head."

"See these stripes?" The sergeant touches his sleeve.

"I don't give a fuck for those stripes." Jake balls up his fists. The sergeant looks to the others for support. They look down at their drinks. He thinks for a moment as the blue eyes bore into him, then pulls his feet under him, leans down and unblouses his trousers. He looks away from Jake, picks up his drink, winks at one of the others as if he's going along with a joke.

"It's 'pardonnez-moi, mademoiselle.'"

The sergeant pretends not to hear him. Jake opens the fist of his right hand and with his fingers stiff, jabs the man's shoulder—hard.

"Pardonnez-moi, mademoiselle."

"Pardonnez-moi, mademoiselle," says the sergeant, echoing Jake's mispronunciations and trying to turn the capitulation into mockery.

Jake goes to the table and sits down, "Pardonnez moi, mademoiselle," he says to her softly. For the first time, she smiles faintly.

He consults the phrase book. "Now . . . mangez. Mangez beaucoup."

The waiter arrives. She orders boeuf bourguignonne. Not knowing what it is, he asks for the same thing, plus a carafe of red wine. She barely tastes the wine, but she does order a second portion of the beef, then fruit and cheese, then mousse, then coffee, then mousse again. Before each order, she looks up at him and he nods, go ahead.

In the foyer of his hotel, he leads the girl to the stairs, not looking at the concierge, who nonetheless says jovially, "Bon soir monsieur, bon soir mademoiselle!"

With her clothes off, she is an emaciated thing, hips wider than he imagined they would be. When he gets on top of her, she helps him slide into her, then gives a few perfunctory thrusts; she has learned it doesn't take much to service these hungry GIs. When he is finished, she lets out one long sigh and pats him on the back a few times. She rises from the bed, gets a small cloth from her purse, which she wets in the room's tiny sink and uses to wash between her legs. She has not yet asked for money, but while she dresses, Jake pulls some bills from his pants. First, he takes 50 francs in hand, then says to himself, to hell with it, and makes it 100.

Dressed, she looks at him with those brown eyes which have not changed expression from the first moment he saw her, Jake hands her the 100.

"Ah, monsieur, s'il vous plait, deux cent!"

He doesn't understand. "It's all right," he says.

"Deux cent, monsieur," she repeats.

Still not understanding, he waves her off. "Keep it," he says, "It's OK."

She reaches into her purse for a pencil and a small, crumpled piece of paper. On it, she writes: 200.

He laughs. "OK." He fishes another 100 from his pants and hands it to her. "Au revoir," he says as she leaves, He gets no answer

Next day, after a morning of sight-seeing, he approaches the concierge, "Jazz," he says. "A cafe with jazz."

The concierge gives him the name of a place on the Boulevard St. Germain. Jake goes upstairs to get his cornet, then heads over there. It is small and though at this midday hour uncrowded, the few patrons have managed to fill the air with the acrid smoke of French cigarets. Peering through the haze, Jake can see an old upright piano in a corner, but no musicians. Nor can he hear any music. He walks up to the bar.

"Jazz?" he asks the bartender.

"Oui, jazz."

Jake checks the rudimentary dictionary at the back of his phrase book. "Jazz . . . ici?"

"Oui, monsieur! Ici."

Jake puts a hand to his ear, shrugs.

"Ah, monsieur." The man goes to an old record player, puts on a record. Between the nicks and scratches he hears Louis Armstrong's classic "Weatherbird." Jake grins, to thank the man and because he is so happy to hear the music.

"Vin," he says to the bartender. "Rouge . . . and . . . boeuf bourguignonne. And jazz . . . encore jazz." He gives the man 20 francs. "For jazz," he says, to make his wishes clear. Then he sits at a table.

Jake finds the red wine much easier to get used to than warm British beer, and he sits back, drinks and listens with pleasure to the records the bartender keeps putting on, although they are all at least as scratchy as the first. He finishes the beef and the first half-carafe of wine while listening to Armstrong, Sidney Bechet, Bessie Smith, Billie Holiday.

Halfway into his second carafe, he takes out his cornet and begins, softly, to play along. The few other patrons turn to him, listen raptly. After the first record, he looks at the bartender, points to the horn and asks, "OK?"

"C'est bon, monsieur!" the bartender replies, grinning. "C'est très bon!"

As soon as he resumes, the man disappears into the back for a few minutes. A half hour later, a man of about 30 hurries into the cafe, walks to the piano and sits down.

"Nous jouons ensemble," he says to Jake. "Oui, monsieur?" He mimes playing the piano. Jake gets it, points to himself, puts the horn to his lips. Then says, "Oui, oui."

He goes into "Stardust" and Jake joins him. The pianist sounds like he has listened to more Paul Whiteman than anything else. His playing is passé and his repertoire limited, but he is enough of a challenge for Jake, who is badly out of practice. With wine breaks, they play, easily, softly, together for an hour and a half, until Jake's lip is shot and he can play no more.

When Jake gets up to leave, he asks the pianist, "Demain?"

"Oui, monsieur. Certainement!"

Jake smiles, takes out a 50-franc note, extends it to the man.

"Ah non, monsieur," the pianist replies. "C'est mon plaisir! Et monsieur . . . demain. Aussi saxophone!" He mimes playing the saxophone.

Jake grins, gives him a thumbs-up sign.

The next day, as he reaches the cafe where he is to meet the pianist and the sax player, two passing MPs spot his shoulder patch and paratrooper badge.

"Corporal," says one of them, "you in the 101st, right?"

"Right," says Jake suspiciously. He likes MPs about as much as most GIs do.

"You're supposed to report back to your division, immediately!"

"What's up?" asks Jake.

"Not sure. Think it's a German breakthrough. They're shipping you guys somewhere."

"OK, gotta say goodbye." Jake enters the cafe, sees the pianist already there, along with a younger man with a shabby old alto sax. They both beam at him.

"I must go," says Jake. "I cannot stay to play with you. You understand?"

"Yes, I understand," says the sax player. He speaks French quickly to the pianist, whose face falls. "What has happening?" the sax player asks.

"I'm not sure. New fighting. I have to go."

Again, the sax player speaks rapid French to the pianist. Both men nod.

"It is pity," says the sax player. "But you will to return."

Jake grabs his phrase book. "Bientot."

"A bientot, monsieur!" says the pianist. "Et bonne chance! Good luck!"

"Merci beaucoup."

Clutching his cornet, Jake double-times back to the hotel, ignoring the pain in his hip as he runs. In his room, he packs his duffel bag. Then he stops short. All I have to do, he tells himself, is lie down on the bed, go to sleep. Pretend I didn't hear anything. He thinks of what he started to write to Kent's sister. How many times can you be lucky? It would be so easy. Let them do this one without me. Then he thinks of Kent and Al, Lt. Sobchak, Sgt. Grunwald. Remembers the coward inside, waiting to get out. He picks up his bag and heads out the door. MPs at the Boulevard St. Michel tell him where he can get a ride to Mourmelon. At a pickup point he climbs aboard a 2 and $\frac{1}{2}$ ton truck, joining a mixed bag of men from a dozen different units of the 101st.

†

In the early morning of December 16th, 1944, three weeks after the 101st has been moved to Mourmelon to bind its wounds and on the same day Jake gets his pass for Paris, the Battle of the Bulge begins. German forces massed in the Ardennes forest attack along a 70-mile front thinly held by only three American divisions, mostly men who are either exhausted by combat and resting, or else completely green, with no combat experience. In that bit of Europe where Belgium, Germany, and Luxembourg meet, the terrain is a nightmare: steep hills, ridges, ravines, heavy woods, narrow winding roads. That, plus surprise, German power and bad weather combine to make the initial assault highly effective.

Herbstnebel—Autumn Mist—is Hitler's last, frantic, offensive paroxysm as Allied armies press toward the Fatherland, from east, west, and south. From his stricken forces, he scrapes together 25 divisions which—according to his plan—will strike through the Ardennes, race across Belgium to the Meuse River, splitting the western Allied armies and forcing them to negotiate a peace rather than insisting on unconditional surrender.

The plan is foreordained to fail; the Germans have neither the men, the machines, nor, especially, the fuel to sustain it. But initially it sends the Americans reeling and it certainly ends Allied hopes—shared by men of the 101st at Mourmelon—that the war in Europe will be over by Christmas.

The day after the attack, SHAEF (Supreme Headquarters, Allied Expeditionary Force) decides to bring its reserve into the fight. At the moment, its reserve consists of the two airborne divisions, the 82nd and the 101st. When the decision is made, the commander of the 101st, Maj. Gen Maxwell Taylor, is in the U.S. and the assistant commander, Brig. Gen. Gerald Higgins, in England. This leaves the division artillery commander, Brig. Gen. Anthony McAuliffe, as the senior officer at Mourmelon. At 9 that evening he calls his staff together and speaks simply.

"All I know of the situation is that there has been a breakthrough and we have got to get up there."

Moving a division is not something done overnight—except in this case. Advance detachments leave the morning of the next day, the 18th; that night, without waiting for the return of men on leave or in hospitals or convalescing, the first trucks carrying the main body of the 101st start north toward the key Belgian road center of Bastogne.

Jake gets back to Mourmelon just as men are being loaded into 10-ton trucks for the ride north. Frantically he races to his tent, grabs his gear and finds H Company as their trucks are loading. Al shouts to him; he runs for the truck and the men in the rear haul him aboard.

"Why didn't you stay in Paris?" Kent asks.

"I would have, if I thought you two fuck-ups could manage without me."

"You fool." Kent says it with neither humor nor irony.

They ride through the dark of the night into the morning of Tuesday, December 19th, packed shoulder to shoulder in an open truck. There is no room for all of them to sit at the same time. There are no rest stops; if someone has to pee, he pees from the side of the truck. Luckily, the temperature is mild, around 40 that morning. It will be the last mild weather of the winter; in two days the snow will begin and nighttime temperatures will drop to zero and below.

It is still dark on the morning of the 19th when Gen. McAuliffe and his lead division, the 501st, reach the southwestern outskirts of Bastogne. He tells the commanding officer of the 501st to move his men east through the town and out the far side, to "make contact, attack and clear up the situation." The situation is as opaque as the gloomy, overcast morning, but luck is on the American side. The CO of the 501st is 29-year-old Lt. Col. Julian Ewell, who only a few weeks earlier, while on leave from Holland, spent a busman's holiday tramping around a place he had no reason to think would be a battleground again: Bastogne. So of all the 101st officers, Col. Ewell is probably the only one who knows the terrain. He asks no questions. With a "yes sir" and a salute, he leads his regiment out to bolster the beleaguered American defenders east of Bastogne. The 501st gets to, and through, Bastogne before the Germans can.

But it takes another bit of American luck for that to happen. Hours before Ewell and his men reach Bastogne from the west, the advance units of a German Panzer division under Gen. Fritz Bayerlein reach a point just three miles east of it. All they have to do is keep going and the town is theirs. But Bayerlein is nervous. In the dark of night he hears artillery and engines. He doesn't know that much of the artillery is German and most of the engine noise either his own or that of Americans fleeing.

Unsure of the situation, he interrogates a Belgian villager who has seen Americans nearby. Are their forces strong?, the general asks. Yes, the Belgian answers. Many tanks? Many, says the man. This is a gross exaggeration of American strength in the area. Is the villager, as a civilian, merely overawed by a few American men and tanks? Or is he deliberately lying to fool the Germans? That is not known. What is known is that, being a prudent officer, Bayerlein halts his advance and digs in, losing his chance to walk unchallenged into Bastogne. The Germans will never set foot in the town.

While the 501st is moving into position east of the town, the 502nd, lower down in the line of march, is still packed in its trucks, on its way to the sector it will defend, an arc of about 90 degrees on the north-northwest of the irregular circle around Bastogne. On its right flank will be the 506th paratroopers, on its left the glider infantrymen of the 327th Regiment.

When Jake's truck finally comes to a stop and the men, relieved and stiff-legged, jump down, Jake asks of no one in particular the soldier's standard question, "What's going on?" And Sgt. Grunwald, speaking to everyone in particular, comes up with the Army's standard answer: "Let's move out."

The terrain here to the west is gentler than the ravines and craggy hills of the Ardennes; Lt. Sobchak positions his platoon on hilly ground above the town of Longchamps. There is no action this day and as yet no snow, but the temperature drops sharply after sunset, and a night in a foxhole is not comfortable under any circumstances. Dinner that night is K rations.

The next morning Company H is ordered into action. The men are marched east, to cover the evacuation of the 506th from the town of Noville, where it's in danger of being outflanked. The Second Platoon moves along a dirt road in two columns, only two dozen of them now, and many of those new faces. For Al and Jake, seniority has brought with it a new danger. Al, who like Jake got his corporal's stripes in Holland, has been chosen lead scout for the platoon, and Jake is now the second scout.

They are out in front of the platoon. Al, with his dead aim, has the soul of a sharpshooter; he carries his trusty M-1. Jake has acquired a Tommy gun; he prefers volume of fire to marksmanship.

The road leads them to a small village, and as it comes into sight, Al spots a German armored car scoot around a corner and disappear behind a stone house. He signals the platoon to stop, and he and Jake drop into ditches on either side of the road. Lt. Sobchak comes running up, a radioman alongside, and they drop down next to Al. Jake races over from the other side of the road. The entire platoon has by now taken cover in the ditches, waiting.

"What's up?" asks the lieutenant, pulling a map from his pocket.

"Armored car in the village. May be tanks with it."

"Our orders are to make contact with the 506 and take the pressure off them. Let's circle south of the village and keep going."

Al looks at the map, points to the village of Recogne. "That the village we're at?"

"Looks like it."

Al then points to another village just beyond. It is Noville, from which the 506th is pulling back. "We're less than a mile from Noville. Bet those Krauts have their backs to us and they're hitting the 506 right now. Why don't we just go after them? That would sure as heck take the pressure off the 506."

Sobchak looks at Al, than at Jake, then at his radioman. He nods. "Let's do it. When I signal, start forward. We'll see what they've got. If we can roll through 'em, keep going. If we can't, let's dig in and give 'em something to think about."

Sobchak runs back with his radioman, to make contact with the company and tell them the plan. He then signals the platoon's two bazooka men out to the flanks, and moves the platoon into a skirmish line.

Al and Jake are keeping an eye on Sobchak as he signals the platoon to advance. For just an instant Jake watches as every man gets to his feet and starts forward at a run, a line of 24 soldiers strung out in the fields on both sides of the road. The sight sends chills of terror and excitement through him. He turns, wills himself forward, begins running.

Fifty yards from the nearest houses, it occurs to Jake they are completely unseen by the Germans and may make it to the houses without being spotted. He can hear firing, concludes that Al is right, that the enemy in this little village is firing in the other direction, at the 506th. Jake and Al make it to the side of a house and pause there, panting.

"Let's go right in!" Al says. Jake turns and sees, to his dismay, that some of the troopers are dropping to the ground. Frantically, he wheels his arm in a circle to keep them moving.

Then Al says, "Let's go! They'll follow us."

"Damn well hope so," mutters Jake.

He wheels around one side of the house, Al around the other. To their astonishment, they see the armored car and four German Tiger tanks, huge monsters that seem twice the size of the American Shermans and are actually three times the weight, sitting idly while three of their commanders stand and chat on the ground. Jake takes a step forward and opens fire with his Tommy gun, dropping all three men. Al races to the nearest tank, climbs onto it, drops a grenade into its open hatch, leaps to the ground, heads for the second tank, throws a grenade down its hatch. The two explosions are perhaps ten seconds apart. The fourth tank, whose commander has not been part of the conversation, rolls forward, trying to get away. As it does, its flank is exposed to the bazooka man who has moved up on the right. The first bazooka shell hits the tank's right tread, disabling it.

The third tank begins firing its machine guns at the line of Second Platoon men moving into the village, knocking two of them down. By now Al is climbing onto that third tank. Its hatch is closed; he tries it and to his surprise it opens. He tosses a grenade down it, slams the hatch cover shut and leaps away, seconds before the explosion finishes off the tank crew. Meanwhile the sole surviving vehicle, the armored car, has taken off.

This entire sequence of events takes but a minute, and by now the German infantrymen who have been firing in the other direction from foxholes in front of the village, turn and scramble for the shelter of village houses. They turn heavy fire on the men of the Second Platoon, who take cover and return the fire. It's clear from the volume of German fire that they are in company strength. The Americans are outnumbered and outgunned. The lieutenant races to Jake and Al, who have taken cover behind one of the immobile tanks.

"What a job!" he says.

Jake jerks his thumb in Al's direction. "There's the man."

"No . . ." Al begins.

"Shut up," Jake says. "Take a few bows. But keep your head down."

"Both of you, hell of a job," Lt. Sobchak says. "Lemaire wants us to keep 'em pinned down. The rest of the company is moving up alongside of us." Capt. Frenchy Lemaire has replaced Capt. Smith as company commander; Smith was badly wounded in Holland and shipped back to the states, his combat days over.

It turns into a firefight for the rest of the day. When night falls on the 20th, Capt. Lemaire gets word that the 506th has successfully withdrawn and the Germans are bringing up reinforcements, so under cover of darkness Company H pulls back from its exposed position to its original lines.

Things quiet down for the 502nd in the northwest, if not for the division. Though the Germans are stopped dead to the east of the town, they keep hammering at the Americans and continue flowing around Bastogne to the north and south. By the night of the 20th, the last corridor to the town is cut. Bastogne is surrounded. An officer compares the situation to a doughnut, with the 101st the hole.

"They got us surrounded . . . the poor bastards," is the response of one 101st soldier to their situation. The bravado notwithstanding, the situation is serious. The weather is frigid, they are low on everything: food, warm clothing, ammo, medical supplies—and for several days the skies will be too overcast for them to be re-supplied by air drops.

The Americans cannot get out. Nor can the Germans get in. On the morning of the 22nd the Germans try to take Bastogne the easy way, giving Gen. McAuliffe the chance to utter what becomes the most famous one-word statement in all of World War II. Under a white flag, two German officers, one English-speaking, approach American lines with a message, which is sent up to the American command. Typed in German and English, it points out that the Americans are encircled and the only alternative to annihilation is "honorable surrender."

When an aide tells Gen. McAuliffe what is in the note, he laughs and replies, "Aw nuts." Then he sits down to frame a formal reply of rejection. He asks aides what the wording should be. One of them answers that it would be hard to improve on what he's just said. So the official reply becomes: "Nuts." When the two Germans read the answer, the slang eludes them, so the American officer delivering it explains. "In plain English, it is the same as 'go to hell.' And I will tell you something else: if you continue to attack, we will kill every goddamn German that tries to break into this city."

Though the men of the 502nd welcome the comparative calm, they do not welcome the weather. It starts to snow and turns bitterly cold. Lt. Sobchak works out a rotation so that some of his platoon can get warmed up and decently fed in a farmhouse just behind their line, while the others are on guard in their foxholes.

On the night of the 23rd, German artillery bombardment picks up in the area defended by the 502nd's First Battalion around the town of Champs, and early the next morning Company H is moved to bolster that area.

"What's going on?" Jake asks when they get there.

"Dig in," is Grunwald's non-answer, as he points to a snowy hummock. The Second Platoon is to fill a gap where the left flank of the 502nd meets the right flank of the 327th glider infantry. Until then there have been no Americans in this spot. And that results in a deadly error.

No one has told the American fighter command that friendly troops are moving into the area, so when P-47s, taking advantage of the clear skies to attack German infantry, spot a group of men digging foxholes, they come in low and begin strafing.

Trying to gouge a foxhole out of snow-covered frozen ground is exhausting work, and the men have literally only scratched the surface when the planes appear. Recognizing the fighters as American, the platoon at first cheers them. When the machine guns begin spouting at them, that changes to screaming fury. There are the screams of the wounded, too; the men are especially vulnerable in dark uniforms against the white snow and with only the beginnings of holes to dive into. The planes make one pass and then wheel around to return.

"Who's got a panel?" someone yells. Orange recognition panels are used by the Americans to identify themselves in situations like this one.

"Ralston!" Sgt. Grunwald yells back, then shouts at the man himself. "Ralston! Ralston!" There is no answer; Ralston lies mortally wounded.

Kent is the nearest man to Ralston, about 30 yards away. "I'll get it!" Kent shouts. He has been digging his hole in the shadow of a boulder, a relatively safe spot. Now he moves from its safety across the open snow at a dead run—as the planes come back. He is crouched over the body of Ralston, searching through his pockets for a panel. Just as he finds one, he is hit in the back by a burst from a machine gun. He falls forward. When he tries to crawl into the hole alongside Ralston's body, his legs will not move. But he is able to spread the panel on the snow, then falls on it. A P-47 pilot spots it and within seconds the planes stop firing and pull up.

Jake sprints over, shouting, "Medic, medic!" Kent's eyes are open.

"Take it easy," Jake says. "You're going to be all right!" He can see the holes in Kent's field jacket; they look small and harmless. He has seen enough wounds not to be falsely cheered by that.

"Can't feel my legs, Bix."

"You're going to be all right. It doesn't look too bad," Jake tells him. He turns and shouts, "Stretcher!" with his trench knife he cuts the field jacket open, then the sweater under that, then the OD shirt, then the undershirt. The holes are not bleeding. From his first-aid kit Jake pulls bandages and sulfa powder, sprinkles the powder on the wounds, presses the bandages to them.

"Hold my hand, Bix. I'm cold."

Jake takes Kent's left hand in his and squeezes it. He kneels over Kent for ten minutes, talking to him, reassuring him, until two medical corpsmen scramble up to them, carrying a stretcher.

"He doesn't look too bad," Jake says to them. They take one look and one of them replies, "We got to turn him over." His look to Jake is grave.

"I can't feel my legs," Kent says.

"Take it easy, buddy," one medic says. "We're going to turn you over." When they do, his clothing is sopping with blood. Jake looks away as they open his clothing. They put more sulfa powder and pressure bandages on his wounds, give him a shot of morphine. As they start to lift the stretcher, Kent says, "Bix, hold on."

Clutching Kent's hand, Jake starts across the field with the two medics. He hears the sergeant shout, "Get back to your hole, Ellison!"

"Sorry, sarge," mutters Kent.

"He means me," says Jake. "That old confusion."

"Right to the end," Kent says.

"You're going to be OK."

"You hear me, Ellison?" yells Sgt. Grunwald, running toward Jake. "Get back to your position! Right now!"

"Fuck you, sergeant!"

Jake mutters it more to himself than to Grunwald, keeps walking with Kent, squeezing his hand. When Kent tries to squeeze back there is little strength to it. Jake accompanies him to the stable in the village of Hemroulle that is serving as the First Battalion aid station. A surgeon takes one look and orders the medics to send him back to the division hospital in Bastogne.

Jake questions the doctor with his eyes. The man shrugs, drops his eyes, turns away. One of the medics, trying to comfort Jake, says, "Sometimes these things look worse than they are," Jake nods. The medics load Kent on a jeep equipped to carry stretchers. Already on it are two other badly wounded men. Jake never lets go of Kent's hand until the jeep starts to pull away.

"You'll be back with the company before you know it."

Kent says, "Sure, Bix," but his eyes say no.

Jake watches the jeep go, then double-times back to the platoon, approaches Grunwald, who is still working on deepening his hole, scratching it out, inch by inch. The sergeant stares up at him.

"What do you want?" Grunwald asks.

"I'm back." He is offering himself for punishment; they both know that.

"Go dig your fucking hole!"

Jake stares at him, starts to turn away.

"How is he?" the sergeant asks.

"He can't move his legs."

"Is he gonna . . . ?"

Jake shrugs the way the doctor did, then says "Sometimes these things look worse than they are," the way the medic did.

"That panel saved our asses," the sergeant says. "I'm gonna put him in for a medal."

"I hope he lives to see it."

"This is a tough fucking business," says Grunwald.

Jake returns to his hole, finds Al working on it.

"What are you doing?"

"I finished mine," Al says, taking short, powerful, chopping strokes with his entrenching tool. "How is he?"

"Sometimes these things," Jake begins, then stops. "You're a praying man, Al. Start praying."

Jake begins digging alongside Al. After awhile Al says, "He's got to be all right. He owes me $223."

When they finish, Al returns to his hole. They spend the next hours on the hill, where all is quiet. At dusk, they are relieved by the First Platoon and return to the comparative warmth of a farmhouse.

"It's Christmas Eve," says Al suddenly as they sit there. "I almost forgot that, Etta told me she would say a special prayer for us on Christmas Eve. Her family and mine always go to the service together."

"Midnight service?"

"No. On a farm folks have to get up early for milking. You see, the cows don't know it's Christmas. My uncle Bob once said we should put up wreaths in the barn, so maybe they'd sleep late that morning. He's a card, uncle Bob. He ought to be dealt with." Al tries to smile, "I heard that from you a long time ago."

"A long, long time. Merry Christmas, Al."

"Same to you, Jake . . . I guess that's the wrong thing to say."

"Can't hurt," says Jake.

Their rest doesn't last long. Lt. Sobchak appears, orders Al to take another man and drive into Bastogne to pick up medical kits for the company. As soon as the lieutenant is out the door, Al asks Jake if he wants to go. "We could see Kent," he says.

In the town they find the seminary chapel that is serving as the division hospital. It is filled to overflowing with the seriously wounded, who lie on the floor, in the icy cold, packed row on row, with only a layer of hay and a blanket between them and the stone. While Al goes to pick up the supplies, Jake walks along the lines of wounded, searching for Kent. He finds him, lying still, as pale as death.

In the ad hoc triage system, Kent has been placed among the hopeless cases. Some are already gone, their faces covered by their blankets. Others, dying, have pieces of gauze over their faces as a sign they are beyond help.

On Kent's left lies the form of a man, blanket pulled over his face. Jake pushes him aside, knowing he will not mind, then wedges into the small space next to Kent, kneels.

"Hey, Ellison. Or is it Ellinson?"

Pain killed by morphine, Kent smiles, looking almost tranquil.

"You're going to come out of this."

Kent shakes his head no. "Hold my hand, Bix." Jake takes it. "Don't let go." Jake squeezes. There is no return squeeze. Kent's eyes are closed. Jake is afraid. Then the eyes open.

"It's almost Christmas, Kent. Hang in there."

Kent just looks at him.

"Al expects you to pay him the money you owe him."

Kent nods, his eyes fixed on Jake. "My sister will. Bix, did I ever tell you my sister's crazy about you?"

"Yeah, you told me, but it ain't necessarily so."

"Gershwin."

"Right."

"She is, Bix."

"OK."

"I am too."

"Sure. Everyone is. I'm irresistible."

"I love you, Bix."

"I love you, too, Kent."

"No . . . It's not . . . I'm . . . not like you. I'm . . ."

"Don't talk. Just rest."

"I'm going to rest. Long rest. You know what I am, Jake?"

"Yeah. You're a paratrooper. A member of the best squad in the best platoon in the best company in the best battalion in the best regiment in the best division in the whole goddamn war. You saved the platoon today, Kent. Grunwald's putting you in for a Silver Star." Grunwald hasn't quite said that, but Jake sees no harm in it.

"I'm a queer. A fairy. I've never said that out loud before. I'll never say it again. Huh." The last is more an expulsion of breath than a word. Kent closes his eyes, and again Jake is afraid.

He clasps Kent's hand with both of his.

Kent says, "Hold on."

Jake squeezes his hand and replies, "You hold on, too."

"I can't. Bix. I can't." His eyes close. Jake puts more pressure on Kent's hand as if to will his own warmth and life into the man who has been his buddy for the two years that have seemed like many lifetimes. He gets the weakest of return squeezes. A few moments later the hand goes limp. Jake does not let go. He keeps clutching the cold hand.

Al, having carried a load of medical supplies out to the jeep, returns but does not see either Jake or Kent. While he looks around an aid man asks him if he wants a Christmas drink. Division has found a cache of cognac and sent some of it over. Al, a teetotaller, does not say no. The aid man hands him the cognac in a canteen cup.

He stands there, sipping it, looking for his buddies, seeing the rows of wounded. He says a prayer for all the men, especially for Kent.

Everything is quiet; it is just a few minutes before midnight, and Christmas. Somebody tunes in the Armed Forces Network, turns it up loud. Through the frigid, silent hall resounds the voice of Bing Crosby, singing "White Christmas." The wounded lie there, listening.

The medical corpsman whispers to Al, "If they ever put this in a movie it would be too corny to believe."

Jake is just letting go of Kent's hand when he hears the sound of "White Christmas." After a few minutes he gets up and finds Al. Al starts to ask about Kent, looks at Jake's eyes, and stops.

As they drive back, Jake says, "I've got to write to his sister, I can't do it . . ."

"She'd want to hear from you."

"I know. She writes to me. She's the only one I don't answer."

"Why not?"

"I keep trying. What she writes to me is so beautiful, that my letters . . . I keep tearing them up. Her stuff is . . . poetry. In fact, she wrote me a poem. Unbelievable. If I get back . . ."

"We're going to get back, Jake."

"Yeah. Anyway, I thought I might try to put it to music. I carry it with me." Jake reaches into his breast pocket, pulls out a piece of V-mail. "Listen." He reads.

> *Sounds of heroes, young and proud,*
> *Ringing out their songs of war.*
> *Wings of eagles, stretching wide,*
> *Higher, faster, climb and soar.*
>
> *Oh, don't sound too proud, my heroes,*
> *Don't, my eagles, fly too high.*
> *Other voices have been silenced,*
> *Flyers fallen from the sky.*
>
> *Missing you, we only pray,*
> *When your ringing war songs cease,*
> *Come back home, back to our arms*
> *And sing a song of love and peace.*

Jake folds the letter and puts it back in his pocket. "God didn't answer her prayer, Al. Or yours. How do you explain that?"

"It's not given to man to explain God's ways."

"Sorry, not good enough."

"You have to have faith. You don't have faith."

"How can you have faith after things like this?"

"Faith would help you with them."

"I'll tell you what would help me right now, Al. It would help to kill a few Germans."

"They didn't kill Kent," Al says softly. "It was friendly fire."

For the first time, Jake feels anger welling up toward Al. "They're the reason we're here, those Nazi bastards! If it weren't for them, none of this would be going on! Don't tell me it isn't their fault!"

It takes him a while to cool down. "I never thought Kent would get it."

"He thought he would."

"Well, everyone knows he's smarter than I am. Was smarter. Shit."

They drive back to the village of Rolle, where the 502nd has set up regimental headquarters in a large chateau. The two bed down on a pile of straw in their cold farmhouse, considering themselves lucky not to be spending the night in a snowy foxhole. At 5 a.m. Sgt. Grunwald wakes them. "We need to relieve a First Battalion guy at an OP. Whose turn is it?"

"Mine," answers Al quickly. Jake was the last to take his turn at a forward observation post.

"It's Christmas, Al. This one's mine."

"Listen," interrupts the sergeant. "One of you get up there right away!" And he is out the door.

"You did that for me last Christmas, Jake."

"God, was there a last Christmas?" He remembers how Cindy hated his taking the name of the Lord in vain. "A hundred years ago. Well, hell, I'm still Jewish and you're still a Methodist."

"Presbyterian," says Al.

"OK, Presbyterian," Jake replies. "Anyway, last year you made up for it on Passover. Next Christmas, I'll go out to Iowa and work on Christmas day for you, then you come to New York and work for me."

"You going to milk cows for me, Jake?"

"Sure. And you're going to play 'All The Things You Are' for me. I'll start giving you lessons as soon as we get back to Mourmelon."

"Jake, you can't do this . . ."

"There's a service in a few hours, I saw it on a bulletin board. Go to it. And, hey . . ." He reaches into his musette bag, pulls out a letter. It is to June Hopkins, a softening of the anger in his last letter about her pregnancy. "On your way, drop this for me." Al takes the letter, puts it in his field pack. Jake says as he heads for the door, "Merry Christmas."

"Same to you, Jake."

"Kent didn't make it to Christmas."

"We have. Keep your head down out there."

"Any Nazi bastard shows his face around me, he's dead."

"You're there to warn us, Jake. Don't take them on all by yourself."

"Yeah."

Carrying Tommy gun and bazooka, Jake moves out onto hilly ground, where he relieves a man from Company A, who has been sitting and shivering in a forward foxhole.

"Man, it's fucking cold!" the soldier says. "Everything's quiet. Keep an eye on that road." He points to a narrow snow-covered road that comes around a hill and appears about 50 yards from them. Jake nods.

"And the fucking phone doesn't work. I don't know if the line's cut, or what."

"Great," says Jake.

"I'll report it to Battalion, they'll send a signal guy out."

"And if the Krauts get here first, what do I do, send smoke signals?"

The soldier manages to crease his frozen face into a smile. "No. You run like hell." Then he's gone, wasting no time in his search for warmth. Jake settles into the hole. He decides "fucking cold" is an understatement by at least 10 degrees. When the sun comes up it will get warmer, he tells himself, stamping his feet to keep the feeling in them.

He has hardly been there 20 minutes when he hears the ominous clanking of armor coming toward him. With no phone, he has a choice. He can run like hell to alert the company. Or he can hold his ground. He knows what the coward in there wants. He loads a shell into the bazooka and trains it on the road. Within a minute the first tank appears. It is a Panzer, faster but more lightly armored than the Tiger. He puts the bazooka on his shoulder, raises himself out of the hole.

He waits until the tank is completely broadside to him, aims and fires. The shell hits the tread, stops the tank dead. Jake ducks down into the foxhole, loads another shell into the bazooka. He knows the sound of his firing will alert his company and the First Battalion. He peeks over the hole, sees a second tank trying to push the first off the road. Defying the coward inside for the last time, again he stands, aims, gets ready to fire. This round will pierce the second tank's armor and kill its crew, stalling the column and giving the First Battalion time to call up tank destroyers which will rout the German armor.

Jake will never see his second shell hit. As he is about to fire, white-clad German infantrymen, fanned out behind the tanks, come over the hill alongside the road, the nearest no more than 30 yards from him. One of them puts his rifle to his shoulder and just as Jake fires the bazooka, squeezes off the round that has Jake's name on it.

JACOB ELLINSON NEW YORK
CPL 502ND PIR 101ST DIV
9/24/20 - 12/25/44

The day after Christmas, Gen. George Patton's Fourth Armored Division broke through the German ring around Bastogne. Though the siege was lifted, heavy fighting around the town continued for another three weeks before the Germans were pushed back.

Jake was posthumously awarded a second Silver Star, Kent a Bronze Star. Al won a Silver Star for destroying the tanks at Recogne.

On Jan. 18, 1945, the division was relieved at Bastogne and moved to Alsace.

On March 15, the 101st received a Distinguished Unit Citation, the first time in the history of the U.S. Army that an entire division was so honored.

On April 2, the division was shipped to the Ruhr Valley and then advanced across the Rhine and into southern Germany and Austria.

On May 5, while moving on Hitler's mountain retreat, Berchtesgaden, in southern Germany, the division suffered its last three combat deaths of the war.

On May 7, with the 101st in Berchtesgaden, the war in Europe ended.

Millie and Marty Ellinson got the news in late January, via a telegram from the War Department. In February, June Hopkins heard it in a letter from another nurse. In March, seven months pregnant, she married Lt. William Penrose Miller.

The Ellisons also got their telegram in January. Devastated, still hiding her pregnancy, Amanda kept hoping for a letter from Jake, telling her how Kent died. When she hadn't got one by late February, she phoned every Ellinson in the Bronx telephone book. Finally she got Marty Ellinson, who, whispering over the phone, told her.

Cindy Laine heard about Jake in April via a roundabout route. A trombone player in the 502nd band told a reeds man in an infantry division band which was being shipped back to the states. The reeds man told Johnny Black. Johnny called Cindy to tell her, and asked if there was anything he could do. Only sobs came over the phone.

By August, Al Breecher, with the help of the Silver Star, Bronze Star, and two Purple Hearts, had accumulated enough points to get out of the army. He was shipped back to the states and honorably discharged at Ft. Leavenworth, Kansas, on September 24, 1945, the 25th anniversary of Jake's birth.

Through 1945, Johnny Black occasionally called Cindy to see if she was all right, but it wasn't until the Christmas holidays of that year that she agreed to have dinner with him. As soon as she saw him she broke into tears.

CHAPTER 29

Mother and daughter sat side by side in the first class section of the Los Angeles flight, talking for a while about the problems of selecting clothing in the frigidity of a New York December that would be suitable for the warmth of Southern California. It was an idle conversation, yet Dede luxuriated in it. Growing up without a mother, living as an adult in a household with two males, by her choice deprived of idle time and the female friends to spend it with, she couldn't remember the last time she'd had a conversation like this one. She'd looked down on them as what she still believed them to be—frivolous. But, oh, what she had not known and now knew: the warmth, the comfort, the intimacy of those touches of frivolity!

In the few months since she and Amanda had found each other, they had gotten by the newness, the bursts of revelation as they tried to catch up with the events of lifetimes spent separately. At Thanksgiving Dede had met Amanda's other children, her two half-sisters and half-brother, all of them married, with children, and living far away, two in northern California, one on a ranch in Wyoming. Jim had met his new grandmother, his only living grandparent, and Amanda had set her eyes on and been astounded by the recapitulation of the young man she had known so briefly and so intensely so long ago.

Occasionally the intimacies cut close to the heart. "Just because you were conceived inadvertently doesn't mean you weren't wanted," Amanda told her daughter. "I could have had an abortion; that could have been arranged. When you have money and resources, anything can be arranged. I am pro-choice, mind you. I chose to have you. I spent years suffering for it, agonizing for it. But now I know I did the right thing."

"Who knew about me?"

"Only two people. And they were not my parents. June Hopkins Miller had to know, of course. And my brother Kent. I knew it would mean an awful lot to him. You see, we both loved Jake Ellinson. I knew he would want to share in Jake's child. I could carry you for both of us."

Dede didn't want to ask, but her eyes asked for her, and Amanda answered.

"You remember that I told you Kent was different. That was a euphemism for what back then we never spoke of, let alone named, but what we can now openly call gay. It was because of that he had to prove his manhood to our father by volunteering for the paratroopers."

"So Jacob Ellinson didn't know," Dede said. "Nor did Bill Miller. Neither of my . . . fathers."

"I don't think so. June Miller told me she would never tell her husband. That was her wish, not mine. As for Jake, well, I never told him. In those few months there were to tell him. Of course, Kent might have."

"The world is so full of surprises," Dede said.

"With more to come. Dede." Amanda hesitated. "Tru has approached me, about two things. First, the club. He wants to know if I would be interested in joining, and whether you would agree to have me join instead of you." She looked to Dede.

"What did you say?"

"My instinct was to say no. Then I decided it might be best to talk it over with you."

"Is there any reason not to say no?"

"Actually, a couple. The first is, you don't really want to be in the club. You would join as an adversary. Since I would not, I might more easily serve as the transition to a really co-ed club. Second, I don't believe in rubbing anyone's face in the dirt, just because one is in a position to do so. Who knows when the positions might be reversed, and a little goodwill rather than ill-will might be needed. There are things you will be negotiating with Tru, if you go ahead with the divorce: financial arrangements, domiciles, your son. A reservoir of good feeling might serve in good stead."

"Why do you say, *if* I go ahead?"

Gently, Amanda patted Dede's arm. "That brings me to Tru's other proposal. He very cautiously sounded me out on your relationship with Dennison Knight—my, but Denny used to be one wild boy!—and on the possibility of a rapprochement with you." The older woman stared at the younger. "By not saying no to his club proposal, I'd have a reason to go back to him on this other thing, if there was any reason to go back."

When Dede looked straight ahead, Amanda asked, softly, "Is there?"

"Do you know why he's interested again? Because of you, Amanda! Tru always resented my lack of 'good family.' When he heard that my father was a Jew, that was too much. That's what precipitated the club thing and the break-up. I now come of 'good stock.' Half-good, anyway. Does that sound like a basis on which to get together?"

"You may be right. On the other hand, he may actually have learned something from all this. Is there any reason you have to say no right now?"

Still staring straight ahead, Dede shook her head.

"Then don't. Unless . . . is there anything serious between you and Denny Knight?"

"Could there ever be anything serious between Denny and anyone? There is . . ." Dede hesitated, then thought, this is my mother, I can tell her anything. "There is someone I am very fond of." She smiled. "He is Jewish, by the way."

"Are you about to make a commitment to him?" Amanda asked.

"Oh no."

"Then try . . . here I am, giving advice as if I'd been your mother forever . . ."

"But you have been. Funny, isn't it? Go ahead, tell me."

"Like so many of us, you've gone from your father's house to your husband's house. Try life on your own for a while. Believe me, it has its charms. Let things play out. See what happens. There's no hurry. You know who you are as a business person. Find out who you are as a woman, not just as someone's daughter, wife, and mother. If you need advice or help, here I am. With my children—my other children—far away, no one's needed my advice in some time now. I'm so glad you came along." Again, she patted Dede's arm.

Dede took her hand and squeezed it. "You think things through so incisively! Why aren't you an executive? A lawyer? A diplomat?"

"If I'd been born in 1945 instead of 1925, who knows?" Amanda sat silently, looking off into the distance for a few moments, before saying, "The ceremony is going to be outdoors. I hope my black cashmere turtleneck is going to be warm enough!" The two women laughed.

Their first stop from the airport was Malibu and Herb's house, where they would stay while out there, and where Jim would join them when he arrived the next day on a flight from Boston. Dede and Amanda were standing on the deck, the sun beginning its descent into the Pacific, when they told Herb.

Amanda began by asking him, "Do you remember the song, 'Them There Eyes'? Then she reminded him about the night at the Unicorn on 52nd Street, back in 1943. But she let Dede tell the important part of the story.

When it was told, Herb asked Marian, "Don't we have a bottle of champagne put away somewhere?"

Marian smiled. "Gathering dust." She looked at the visitors. "There is little demand for alcohol in this household."

With their glasses raised, Herb said, "To our family. It's been a long time since I felt I had a family."

Joe Wiggins rapped his hand hard on the lectern, the mic picking up the sound and broadcasting it across the broad lawn. A cool breeze ruffled the flaps of the tailored blazer that was severely pinched in at the waist to show off his fitness. It was mid-December; the temperature was 60, the sun bright; standard Long Valley weather. In front of him were about 50 guests, most sitting on folding chairs set out on the lawn, a few standing off to the side, clustered, talking, holding the soft drinks they'd picked up from the long refreshment tables. Behind him sat 14 student musicians, three trumpets, three trombones, four reeds, piano, guitar, bass, and drums, the exact instrumentation of the Buddy Benson Big Band.

Wiggins looked around him proudly. The bandstand had been set up where the lawn started sloping up to the hill on which the building would stand, the amplification was loud and clear, the area where the first spadeful of dirt would be shoveled was ribboned off and the sod lifted, the ugly cafeteria tables covered with snowy cotton cloths. The Long Valley State events staff had done one hell of a job.

He daubed at his forehead with his handkerchief and looked over the crowd. In front and to the right sat Jake's daughter, Diana Miller, one of the most stunning women he'd ever seen. To her right was her son—Jake's grandson—who, well, if Joe hadn't seen it, he wouldn't have believed it. If that boy walked into the Etemore Cafeteria today, Joe would yell, "Hey, Jake!" Of course there was no more Etemore. And no more Jake.

To her left sat a tall, elegant woman in black turtleneck and gray skirt, a string of pearls around her neck, her silver hair pulled back and knotted into a chignon. Though Joe had been introduced to Amanda Ellison Turnbull only an hour or so ago, he knew who she was. A couple of months ago, he'd been surprised and delighted to get a letter from her, saying she was the sister of an army friend of Jake's and wanted to commission a bas relief likeness of Jake for the front of the new building. Joe sized her up as one of those classy Eastern women, a lot like Jake's daughter, both of them the Park Avenue types who used to come to 52nd Street before the war, looking like they never got dirty or wrinkled or had to go to the toilet. Next to Amanda, Wiggins spotted Herb and Marian. Joe had met Marian only a few times, but each time she looked better, fitter, like a woman who worked out; Joe appreciated that. With the Ellinsons was a short, square man who looked like he'd spent most of his life out of doors. He was a close army buddy of Jake's, who'd been through the big battles with him.

"Welcome all!" Joe began. "Honored guests, family and friends of Jacob Ellinson, veterans of the 101st Airborne Division, my fellow alumni of the Buddy Benson Big Band, students and faculty, members of the Long Valley State family, welcome to this magnificent occasion. I am Joe Wiggins, dean emeritus of the Long Valley State Jazz Studies Department. For the benefit of our visitors from New York, I tried to arrange some horrible weather, to make you feel at home. I'm afraid I failed. We'll have to settle for another one of those perfectly ordinary, ordinarily perfect California days!"

It got a few chuckles; he expected more, decided that it worked only with transplanted Easterners. Native-born Californians, of whom there were more and more all the time, took the weather for granted; visiting Easterners just refused to believe it was really like this every day. To Joe, who'd moved out from East Orange, New Jersey, 35 years ago, waking up to each gentle, balmy day was a continuing marvel—and the joke was still funny.

"This is a remarkable occasion," he went on, "a great day for our institution, and a chance to honor a remarkable man I was privileged to know and to make music with."

As he spoke he spotted the petite blonde woman and the saggy little old man with dyed brown hair. They had just come in, walked down alongside the rows of chairs and were about to take seats on the outside of the first row. She was clutching at his arm in one of those old folks' gestures that touched Joe because it was never clear who was supporting whom. He had to remind himself that these old folks were about his age. Of course, he was willing to bet neither of them worked out for an hour a day, as he did. It took him another few moments to realize they were Johnny Black and Cindy Laine. The recognition so shook him that he almost forgot what he was saying. Luckily, in his 12 years as dean he'd made it through lots of speeches while his mind was elsewhere.

"This occasion is more than just a ground-breaking ceremony," he went on, forcing his mind back to his speech.

Johnny Black felt his wife's hand tighten on his arm. "Are you all right?" he asked her. Their plane had been late landing and they'd just managed to get there in time.

"I was fine."

"Was?"

"Until I saw a ghost. Over there." She pointed to their left, to the second row.

"I warned you, didn't I? After I saw him in New York."

"You said he would look like him. You didn't warn me it would actually be him."

"We don't have to stay."

"Of course we have to stay." She patted her fine hair, which was ash blonde and set for this occasion. "I have to meet him. What am I going to say? Jake, how come I got so old and you stayed so young?"

"You look gorgeous," Johnny said. "Like a girl."

"That's what I like about hanging around with an old geezer. His eyes get so bad, I look good." She squeezed his arm tighter. "Imagine how miserable I'd be married to someone like Jake who hasn't gotten a day older in 50 years."

"That's not Jake, Cindy."

"I know, I know." She turned to him. "Are you sure?" Then she smiled so he wouldn't think she was nuts. And she forced herself not to stare at the reincarnation of Jake.

"There are so many people here I want to introduce," Wiggins went on, "people who shared parts of that short eventful life that ended so heroically, and tragically, on Christmas day 46 years ago. First, some of the people who back before the war played in the Buddy Benson Big Band that I am so proud to have been part of."

Joe had in front of him a list he'd made out so he wouldn't forget anyone. Once on an occasion a little like this one, he'd neglected to mention an L.A. club owner, and lost the school a cool $200,000. He never made that mistake again.

He glanced at the sheet of paper, looked over the crowd to spot his man. "First, the band's first trumpet, the man who played the sweetest horn this side of Harry James. I know for a fact that this man was a great influence on Jake and a major force in making him the fine trumpet player he became. I just learned a half hour ago, his real first name is Harald. We never called him anything but Swede, and I'm not going to change now. Swede Olsen, take a bow!"

Pushing down on the cane with one hand and grabbing the back of a chair with the other, Swede managed to heave himself up to a standing position. The hefty young man had, at 80, lost some of his heft, most of his muscle and almost all of his lank blond hair. He had acquired arthritis, cataracts and a touch of gout; he could barely see and had a lot of trouble getting around.

After quitting as a musician, Swede had moved down to Florida, but hated it and ended up in his native St. Paul, Minnesota, giving horn lessons and working in a music store. Since retirement he'd been living on social security, with some help from a son. When Herb heard of Swede's situation, he paid for his motel room, bought him a first-class ticket and arranged for cars to pick him up at both ends of the plane ride. He instructed Joe to tell Swede the school had a budget for such expenses.

Digging his cane into the turf, Swede managed to let go of the chair long enough to wave. He grinned and flopped back down onto his chair.

"And Swede," said Wiggins. "We've got the original Buddy Benson charts up here. We expect you to sit in, so warm up the chops."

Swede smiled and waved some more. Sure, he said to himself. Haven't touched a horn in 15 years and even if I had, couldn't make it onto the bandstand without a forklift.

"Seated right near Swede is another member of our brass family. Bones Riordan, who played a hell of a trombone and livened up life on the road with his sadistic practical jokes. Bones, take a bow, and that invitation to sit in is extended to you, too."

Riordan, his form stooped and softened by age, got to his feet, listened to the applause, smiled and bowed and sat down. After the war, when he saw the big band scene fading, he went home to Boston, where he started booking musical groups for weddings and parties. He prospered, and musicians anxious to be hired would listen patiently while he regaled them with the glories of the Big Band Era. For Bones, distance had softened the hardships of the road. He was now sure it had been the best time of his life.

"Down here in front," Wiggins continued, "and just arrived, the band's girl singer. She was—what can I say?—the best. We used to kid her, but we all loved her. She was a heartbreaker then, and I can see she still is . . . Cindy Laine!"

Wiggins wondered what he could say about her and Jake, then decided not to try. The ones who knew, knew, the others probably didn't care that much. Hell, that was 50 years ago. The students and the younger faculty people were probably already bored with all this nostalgia stuff. As if to confirm that, he heard the rustling of sheet music from the bandstand behind him.

Amanda looked over to the small blonde woman. Seeing her do it, Dede whispered, "Well?"

"Once, I was so jealous," Amanda whispered back. "Now I see an old woman. Which is what she would see if she looked this way."

"And with her," Wiggins was saying, "the band's very fine pianist, Johnny Black, who still tickles the 88s and is very much in demand in the New York area. They tell me he still has the magic touch that earned him the nickname 'the Fred Astaire of the piano.' No, no, he doesn't play with his feet!" A few laughs from the older guys. Kids today, Joe thought, have no sense of humor.

"I should add that Miss Laine has been Mrs. Black for . . . how many years now, Johnny?"

"44," Johnny said from the audience.

"43." Cindy corrected him in a whisper.

"That's great," said Wiggins enthusiastically. "Half of 88! We know you'll make it the other 44! And we certainly would love for you two to come up here and perform. We're going to be doing 'All The Things You Are' in a bit. Do you still remember it?" Joe started to hum the first few bars.

A few laughs, again from the older people. To Joe's generation of musicians, the Hammerstein/Kern song remained perhaps the greatest popular standard ever written; to the kids on the bandstand, it was an old song they had to learn.

Johnny smiled at Joe, then looked at Cindy. To his surprise she looked back at him expectantly. "Do you want to?" she whispered.

"Only to accompany you," he answered.

She nodded. Johnny looked at her again, to make sure. Then he turned and gave Joe a thumbs-up sign.

"Wonderful!" Wiggins said. "Cindy and Johnny will be up here. And maybe even old Joe Wiggins will try a few licks, too, if I can find a reed that doesn't hate me." He waited for the applause so he could quiet it. "No no no! But thanks, I'll try to fake it." He'd been practicing "All The Things You Are" all week.

"Finally, the man responsible for it all, the man who put the band together, gave it his name, and led it, and proved he was a great judge of talent by hiring

Jake Ellinson. The maestro himself, Buddy Benson!"

Benson was nearly 90, thin, frail, hearing failing, but still able to get around with the help of the grandson who sat next to him. Forty years ago, Buddy had started investing in Los Angeles real estate. Now he was rich enough to arrive in a limo, on which the license plate read BBBB. The grandson spoke into his ear, and he waved without getting up.

"When we start swinging, you'll have to come up and wield the baton, maestro!" Benson looked to the grandson, who spoke to him again. Then he just waved and shook his head no.

"Let's have a round of applause for these wonderful old-timers. Hey, who am I to talk?"

He waited for the smattering of applause to die down. Then kept waiting, dramatically, another beat or two.

"We also have with us some super guys who performed with Jake on his very last gig, under the baton of Uncle Sam. As you know, he gave a great performance—but then what would you expect of Jake Ellinson? First," he looked down to his list, "Jake's platoon leader in H Company, 502nd Parachute infantry Regiment, 101st Airborne Division, Lt. Peter Sobchak. Where are you, lieutenant? I figure you must be a general by now."

Sobchak got to his feet, waved and smiled. He wore an expensive gray pinstriped suit and looked as if the years since the war had treated him well, which they had. When he got out of the army, he went back for his final year at the University of Illinois, then on to law school. He spent several years in the Illinois state legislature before being elected to Congress, where he served four terms. He then become a senior partner in a Washington law firm, where he was now "of counsel" and in semi-retirement. He'd prepared a few words in praise of Jake, just in case he was asked. But Wiggins went on.

"Also here is Jake's old first sergeant, so all of you guys, just make sure your shoes are shined and your caps on straight." Wiggins checked his list again. "Sgt. Emil Grunwald! Where are you, sergeant?"

Grunwald got to his feet, looked around and waved. The left side of his jaw was still scarred and deformed from the wound at Best. He wore a brown checked polyester leisure suit with yellow polka dot shirt and white shoes. He'd put in 25 years in the army, retiring as a sergeant major, then moved down to the west coast of Florida, where he worked as a construction foreman until 15 years ago.

"How about it, sarge? Did Jake give you a lot of trouble?" Joe laughed, not expecting an answer. But he got one.

"He was the greatest!" Grunwald shouted back. He drew some applause, in which Wiggins joined. But Grunwald wasn't finished. He put up his hands, and everyone quieted.

"If it weren't for him, I wouldn't be here." Grunwald put a hand to his forehead, as if shading his eyes. Then, without looking up again, took his seat.

Joe stood motionless, silent, enough of a public speaker to know there was no point trying to compete with a moment like that. He waited for it to pass before he spoke.

"Thank you, sergeant. No one knows better than you what a great man Jake Ellinson was." He paused again, holding it, with a musician's timing, for three beats, looked down at the paper.

"Now, there are three people I would like to come up and say a few words. First is another of those brave men who served in the paratroops with Jake. He was Jake's closest army buddy, from basic training right through to the end. He's come all the way from Iowa to be with us. He is a man who won the Silver Star, the Bronze Star, and two Purple Hearts: Allen Breecher."

Al stood; Joe motioned for him to come up. At first Al shook his head no, then, slowly, in the rolling gait that was his accommodation to his old wounds, he walked up to the lectern. The slight young man had become a stocky older one, 40 pounds heavier than the paratrooper, yet looking as if not an ounce of it was soft. His hair was white and still clipped in a GI haircut, his face and neck creased and leathery. For a couple of moments he stood there, before clearing his throat with a sound that crackled over the amplification system.

"I have never made a speech in my life. It's kind of late to be starting now. But I want to say something. There were three of us. Jake, myself, and Kent Ellison. Kent's sister is here today." He pointed to Amanda, started applauding until others joined in. When he went on, he spoke slowly, pausing to think of what he wanted to say.

"I want her, and everyone, to know that her brother was a hero, too. Like Sgt. Grunwald, I owe my life to Kent and to Jake. They were two of the finest men I ever met. It was a privilege to know them, to be their friend, and to be a Screaming Eagle with them. They gave their lives . . . for their buddies, and their country. And if anyone here thinks that's corny and old-fashioned, I feel sorry for them. They might ask themselves where they, and this country, would be if it weren't for men like Jake and Kent."

Herb forced his expression to remain fixed. He squeezed Marian's hand so hard he was afraid he was hurting her. She put an arm around his waist.

"One more thing, I want to say to Jake's grandson. You look so much like your grandfather, none of us old timers can get over it. It's a shame you never got to know him. I can only hope you grow up to be half the man he was. I also hope you won't need a war to prove it. That's all I have to say."

Wiggins lifted his hands to applaud, then looked out at the others. Sitting or standing, they remained frozen, transfixed. He dropped his hands and waited. He waited a long while before applause started, then stopped, so he could resume speaking.

"Thank you Mr. Breecher. The Jacob Ellinson Jazz Studies Center will be a magnificent building. It will have classrooms, band rooms, individual practice rooms, as well as a large and a small concert hall and many other facilities. And everything will be sound-proof! A trumpet player can practice in the room next to a drummer, and they won't hear each other! When I was a kid back in Newark, New Jersey, my neighbors wished I had a room like that! It will be a class operation all the way. These kinds of things never come cheap, and at one point we found ourselves very low on funds. That's when a generous New Yorker named Diana Penrose Miller stepped in and wrote out a check . . . a large check . . . to put us over the top."

Wiggins allowed himself a dramatic pause. He looked at Dede; heads turned to look at her.

"Diana Miller, however," he continued, "is not just another generous New Yorker. Her connection to Jake is as basic as you can get. In one of those true wartime stories that's stranger than fiction, she is Jake Ellinson's daughter. Just as he will live on through the jazz studies center, he will also live on through his daughter and grandson. I'd like Diana Miller to come up and saw a few words."

Dede walked up to the lectern. "Thank you, Joe. Until earlier this year, I had no inkling Jacob Ellinson was my father. When Herb—his brother, my uncle—first told me about it, I wondered how I could be sure . . . until he showed me Jake's picture. All I had to do was compare it with the face of my son Jim. Then all doubt ceased.

"So I am here because of something that happened a long time ago. This day belongs to Jacob Ellinson and to those of you who shared so much with him. To my sorrow, I never knew him, and I never was able to share anything with him, except of course, the blood, the genes, that he passed on to me, and which have recapitulated themselves so astonishingly in my son, his grandson.

"Though I never met him, I have already learned a lot from him. Learned about what is important and what isn't. Learned to stop now and then, to take time to listen to the music.

"I'm proud to be his daughter, proud of both my parents. One of the ways I'll be spending my life from now on is in learning more about them. As I hope this jazz center can help young people learn more about the music my father devoted his life to, a life that was all too short. Thanks."

If Al's words were beyond applause, Dede's were perfect for it. All hands were clapping as she walked to her seat.

Joe approached the mic. "I guess class runs in the family," he said, continuing to clap. "And speaking of that, let's now bring up the man, without whom this building couldn't be happening. A fine tenor man, the founder of one of the giants of the business, Ellinson Production Services, the principal benefactor of the Jacob Ellinson Jazz Studies Center, and, last but not least—maybe most—Jake's brother. Herb Ellinson."

Marian hugged Herb as tight as she could before releasing the arm around his waist to let him walk to the lectern.

"Thanks. It was back in December of 1943, 47 years ago, almost to the day, that I last saw my brother Jacob Ellinson. I tried then to get him transferred out of the airborne and into a band. But it was not to be. Jake himself did not want it. And one year later, he was killed in action. Since then I have been haunted by the idea that I was unable to do that one thing that would have saved him. You see, I worshipped my older brother. All my boyhood was spent seeking his approval. And even as an adult, for all these years that he has been gone, I continued to be haunted by that same need. By the need to do something for him, something that would make him say, 'good work, Herbie.' Now, at last, I think I have succeeded. I know he would be proud of his daughter and grandson, and of the jazz studies center. That's why this day means so much to me, why I am so grateful to all of you who are playing a part in it, and who played such a part in my brother's life. I'm especially grateful to my wife, who has stayed by my side and tried to understand as I struggled for all these years with my brother's memory. So now I say to her and to all of you, thanks. And to my brother: Jake, this day is for you."

Marian watched as Herb tried to keep his composure. Joe watched the audience as it sat, silent and motionless, before beginning to applaud. He got to his feet, walked up to Herb, swiveled the microphone.

"I've asked Herb to unveil the artist's sketch of the building, and I would like to ask Mrs. Turnbull to do the honors for the sketch of the sculpture, since she is responsible for its being done."

Gracefully, surely, Amanda Turnbull strode up. Covering the event were a camera crew from a local TV station, a video cameraman hired by the college, and a still photographer and a reporter from the local weekly. They crowded around as first Herb lifted the cloth covering the sketch of the building, then Amanda uncovered the sketch of the bas relief.

The building, surprisingly light and airy for an institutional structure, was three stories high, with rows of windows that were floor-to-ceiling so young musicians could be invigorated by the California sunshine, and double-paned so the sounds would not leave the rooms.

The sketch of Jake, taken from the photo Herb kept in his den, was striking, missing only the piercing energy radiating from Jake's eyes. But that was supplied when the cameramen asked Jim to stand next to the sketch. It was uncanny, the old-timers agreed. When Cindy was asked to stand on the other side of the sketch, she first walked right to Jim, put her arms around him, and stretched up to kiss his cheek. Thank God he is a few inches taller than Jake, so I can see the difference, she told herself. Or else I couldn't stand it.

They walked to the roped area for the ground-breaking. Herb dug up the first shovelful of earth, Dede the second, Joe Wiggins the third. At the request of the cameramen, Jim dug the fourth. Then at Herb's insistence, Al Breecher took the shovel, and after him, Amanda Turnbull.

Joe strode back to the mic to announce, "Now let's have some music! From the authentic, original, one and only Buddy Benson charts!" He led Johnny to the piano, stood Cindy at the mic, put Bones in among the trombones and then he grabbed his tenor and ran to the sax section.

He turned, counted out the tempo, and they went into "All The Things You Are."

Standing there, waiting for her vocal, Cindy did what she'd done so many times on the bandstand, silently rehearsed the words: "You are the promised kiss of springtime that makes the lonely winter seem long"—the words Jake had spoken to her in a dance hall in Pittsburgh so many years ago. Don't cry, she told herself. And don't look at the boy.

As Herb listened, he tightened his grip on Marian's hand. He'd heard the arrangement so many times, but this was different: a live band, Joe, Bones, Johnny at the piano, Cindy snapping her fingers to the beat as she waited for her vocal on the second chorus.

A thin young man rose from the trumpet section. As he put his horn to his lips to play Jake's solo, the sun bounced off it and broke into splinters of light.

Herb squeezed Marian's hand harder, whispered, "Just like at the Paramount."

THE END

Made in the USA
Charleston, SC
28 February 2015